The Moon's C

Irene Black is a British writer with a multicultural background. At various times she has been a psychologist and a teacher and has lived in the USA, Australia and India. She has an MA in South Asian Art, specialising in South Indian temples. She has won a number of national and international prizes for short stories, poetry and articles, including the 2003 National Association of Writers' Groups Annual Short Story award. This is her first novel.

The Moon's Complexion ...

'A thoroughly unusual novel that will appeal to anyone who's interested in India or just enjoys a skilfully constructed page-turner.'

The London Student Newspaper

'Fantastic read. Couldn't put it down. Fantastic atmosphere. We get so close to the characters. Loved it!'

Gill James, writer and publisher

The Moon's Complexion

Irene Black

Goldenford Publishers Ltd
Guildford
www.goldenford.co.uk

First published in Great Britain in 2005 by
Goldenford Publishers Limited
The Old Post Office
130 Epsom Road Guildford
Surrey GU1 2PX
Tel: 01483 563307
Fax: 01483 829074
www.goldenford.co.uk

Cover design from a photograph by Antony Black

Printed and bound by CPI Antony Rowe, Eastbourne

ISBN-10 0-9531613-2-3
ISBN-13 978-0-9531613-2-4

ACKNOWLEDGEMENTS

I would like to thank the many people who have helped to bring this project to fruition. These include friends in India, who have vetted and advised on the Indian content, members of Guildford Writers' Circle, the editorial staff at Goldenford Publishers and, above all, my long-suffering family, especially my husband who, having read the manuscript, was moved to write the poem in Chapter 20.

All the characters are fictional. The following places are figments of my imagination:

The hotels and restaurants - the Krishna, the Pandava, the Chamundi, the Resident's Palace, the Seagull, the Madras Plaza Hotel, the Osman, Uma's, the Red Fox public house, Blue Heaven

The bookshop - Asian Books

The institutions - Queen Anne's Hospital, the Shanti Sagar Hospital, the East River Psychiatric Center, the Biotechnology University (South Indian University of Biotechnological Advancement), Ashley House School

The village - Burfold.

The Bandipur bungalows are real, but their numbers are not.

The civil unrest in Karnataka caused by the Cauvery River Water Dispute is an actual historical event that took place during December 1991.

CHAPTER 1

Ashok had come home to Bangalore to find a wife. Or to put it more precisely, Dr Ashok Rao, newly qualified consultant ophthalmologist at Queen Anne's Hospital, London, had been ordered by his mother back to Bangalore for purposes of matrimony.

It was December 1991 and exactly a month since his mother's letter had arrived at his Richmond flat.

Now that your sister's marriage is arranged, she had written, *time is for you also to settle down. Not wait for Priya being married. Your sister is strong-headed. She will not consent before she is graduating. You are already nearly thirty, and now you are a qualified consultant. You must come as soon as convenient.*

The rest of the letter was filled with news from Bangalore and immersed him in the sunshine of his native city. When he had finished reading, he had placed the letter in the rack on the kitchen table. Then he got ready to leave the house. As he turned up the collar of his overcoat and stepped out into the clawing November drizzle, he reflected that his mother was right. She had mirrored his thoughts, despite the cynicism of disbelieving friends, the perpetual students from his Oxford days, who still regarded themselves as carefree and without responsibility. Ashok had rocketed up the career ladder and had achieved the almost unheard of status of a consultancy before he was thirty, while his friends were still struggling young lawyers, scientists and doctors who couldn't even envisage 'settling down'. But over and above all that, it was hard for his English friends to stomach the idea of an arranged marriage. Ashok, though, could slip easily across the cultural divide. India, England - worlds apart, but nevertheless both part of Ashok's world, and combining to furnish him, perhaps, with broader insights than those of some of his acquaintances.

In any case his friends had missed the point. Once he had listened to his heart and not his head. He'd learnt his lesson. It had taken five years for the pain to cease, and left him steeped in remorse. Now he sought a surer, steadier road. It hadn't been a case of capitulating to his parents' wishes.

His parents' house in the Malleshwaram suburb of north Bangalore had weathered his absence without protest. Apart from the appearance of a few new appliances, nothing had changed. The jumbled papaya and banana plants were still locked in battle over the limited space in the small walled garden, where orange, pink and purple bougainvillea rambled in tousled abandon over the front wall into the lane. The old mango tree still hung on bravely to its corner at the back. His mother's collection of garden pots, with their assortment of mysterious plants grown from pips, stones and cuttings still gave the whole scene the sense of a gloriously chaotic jungle, in the middle of which two elderly coconut palms, heavy with fruit, stood sentry.

From outside, the house had a shoddy, crumbling appearance, which belied the comfortable interior. The excesses of the tropical climate saw to it that creeping mould and lichen quickly obscured the line between nature and the hand of man. The house was similar to the others in the lane, each like some eternal ammonite, set into the rich earth, which seemed to Ashok to have crept up into the once white walls, as if they were the ruins of an ancient forest hermitage. Every time he returned home, Ashok understood what it was that was absent from the clearly delineated, clinical, hygienic world that he had left behind in England.

In the West, nature was an enemy to be tamed and feared. Here, back in India there was no sharp, dividing line between man and the environment. Here he was part of nature, part of the earth, part of the gnarled old mango tree. He was kin to the butterfly that alighted on the arum lily, the ten-centimetre millipede plodding across the lane, the gecko lying in wait under the eaves. Despite the excitement of his family at his return, the many questions, the tales to tell, the serenity of the place enveloped him, obscuring the rigid urgency of English life. This time, more than ever before, he knew that England was a phase. His sojourn there was transitory. Today or tomorrow, this year or next, India would claim back her lost son.

*   *   *

It had all been fine until she saw the black-robed figure.

Newly arrived from England, Hannah Petersen had plunged with enthusiasm into the fevered atmosphere of the backstreets of Hyderabad. She was excited, and at last carefree, despite the sensation that she caused as she strode through the morning market crowds.

A head taller than most of the men, let alone the women, her feral halo of auburn hair blazed in the sunlight. She felt like the bobbing red balloon she had seen in an advert to promote some faceless English new town. It was fitting. The whole of England seemed faceless in the light of the colour and vitality here. She was doing her bit for the homeland. Promoting the old country by turning herself into an advertisement. The thought made her smile and her smile brought smiles in return. Hannah was charmed. The attention was friendly and curious. Not like... She shook the memory from her mind.

So many faces. Grizzled old men in turbans, large-eyed urchins, sinuous rickshaw peddlers, women with quicksilver eyes and flowers in their hair. A photographer's paradise. Theoretically this job should be easy, much easier than her usual form of journalism. But how could she hope to achieve any natural portraits? As soon as she got out the camera everything stopped. Market stallholders held up yard-long gourds or plump melons and stood to attention. People called to her from shed-like shop entrances. 'Photo, here please! Photo!'

No point in trying. Now was not the time. She was late enough as it was.

So where, in this pungent chutney of a city, was the damned taxi office?

Mr Reddy, the receptionist at the Krishna Hotel, had told her it was near the Charminar, an ancient Islamic arch that dominated the old town. Although she had never been to the East before, Hannah trusted her sense of direction. She had given herself what she hoped was plenty of time *en route* to explore the maze of alleyways.

She felt at ease for the first time in a year. Warmth stirred within her that was not entirely due to the weather, echoes of long ago, the Friday warmth of grandmother Rosen's kitchen after a tortured week at school. As if the pragmatism inherited from her Danish father had been punctured by the awakening of a more mystical heritage that surely still lingered in the genes passed down to her through her mother. Within her Petersen body, her Rosen ancestors were calling to her. Hyderabad felt somehow familiar. It held no threat. The city was vibrant, quivering like a wakeful stallion. Yet there reigned beneath the bustle of frenetic activity, and the clamour of competing motor horns, an undercurrent of self-assurance and control.

A group of children ran up to her. *English Pen? Your country coin?* A good opportunity to shed some of the loose change she had been dragging around since England. She might as well have been distributing the Crown Jewels. Each penny was received with cries of joy and scrutinised. She remembered the children she'd known in Belfast, innocence eroded by bombs and guns. Long may these Indian youngsters delight in pens and foreign coins.

After twenty minutes Hannah realised she was lost.

She stopped by a pair of giggling girls in bright saris, who sat on the pavement weaving garlands of jasmine and marigolds. 'Charminar?'

A flurry of gestures and shouts answered her. 'Charminar! Charminar!' Hannah nodded her thanks and turned down the bazaar-like side alley the girls had indicated. Too narrow even for a cycle-rickshaw, crammed with shops selling colourful *lac*-bangles, wares spilling out onto the streets. She threaded her way through

4

the handcarts and shoppers, plunging it seemed, into ever more chaos.

By now Willi would be waiting at the taxi office. Hannah felt bad about being late for the Dutch girl. She'd only met her yesterday. A lucky encounter. Just the sort of pick-me-up that Hannah needed in her jet-lagged state. It would be fun to drive to the fortress together. If she ever managed to find her way out of here.

'Charminar?' She confronted a *dhoti*-skirted lad, who had stopped to gape at her, a tray of deep-fried *pakoras* piled on his head.

'Char-min-ar,' he stammered, seemingly mesmerised by Hannah's eyes. *Like moss through a Polaroid filter,* Maighréad had once said. Vaguely the boy pointed and Hannah turned down an even narrower alleyway that seethed like a dark snake, the heat oppressive, unable to escape.

Something made her glance back. A black-robed figure sliced through the crowds like a cormorant through restless waves. The shrouded woman was enigmatic, and somehow splendid, but the sight threw Hannah. She felt a rush of disquiet as she contemplated the woman's fate. Dominated and discounted no doubt, like Maighréad had been. Funny that. It was some years since she'd let the thought of Maighréad trouble her and now she was pushing her way back into Hannah's mind for the third time in less than twelve hours.

Hannah clenched her fists as she fought the bitterness evoked by her reflections. And there was something else. Not panic, surely? She dismissed the idea, pushing away her momentary weakness. Yet suddenly images that minutes ago had seemed friendly and unthreatening, jumped out at her like monsters in a 3-D horror film. Women invisible behind the veil like prisoners. Men concealed behind beards and moustaches. As though they had something to hide.

Lighten up, she told herself, as she had done so often lately, you're tough, the very exemplification of solid, common sense. You have a reputation to live up to. Don't let yourself down with all this imaginative nonsense. Don't let last month colour your perceptions. It's over. You're free.

Besides, she told herself, glancing once more at the shrouded woman, you're not at home in Burfold now. You know nothing about that woman's life. Stop sitting in judgment.

A gaggle of men standing outside a chai-stall nudged each other and pointed as she passed. She stopped and turned to them, determined to shake off her distrust of their bristly, moustachioed faces.

'Charminar?' The men looked at each other and exploded simultaneously into instructions. Hannah couldn't understand a word, but she got the message. She was going the right way. She squeezed through the crowds, brushing against strangers, beating back an increasing sensation of claustrophobia. She bit her lip and cursed her thumping heart. One incident last November, that was all it had taken to defeat her. One incident against a lifetime of others that had left her undamaged, if not unchanged. In Belfast she had seen bombs explode around her, had watched good friends die, had been threatened herself on countless occasions. She had shed her tears and despaired, but she had coped. After her book *Crying Shame* had been published, the threats had increased for a while. She had managed her fear. Then New York: facing the abusive reaction of the East River hospital management when she openly confronted them with evidence of an insurance scam; she had wallowed in the excitement of it.

Why wouldn't it let her be, this demon?

At last she spotted the four turrets of the Charminar at the end of the alley and hurried forward. She found herself on a wide, if no less crowded street winding around the obstacle of the great Islamic archway that stood in the centre in a state of splendid decay. Through its open curves she saw a painted sign on the other side of the road: M Suresh, Taxi Hire. Dodging cars and carts, bicycles and buses, animals and autorickshaws Hannah manoeuvred her way across.

In front of the taxi office half a dozen assorted street vendors, selling tacky plaster copies of the Charminar had found a victim.

'Only look, Madam. Very cheap.'

'Real marble, lady, no fake.'

'Ten dollars only. No? How much? You say.'

In the middle of the mayhem a luminous yellow head bobbed up and down in apparent agitation, and a shrill Dutch accent pierced the air. 'Oh, go away. No! Please. I do not want. Leave me alone.'

As Hannah approached, the men immediately turned and started on her. 'Only look...'

Ignoring their entreaties she brushed them aside with a sweep of her hand. They wandered off muttering.

Willi stared at her. 'How did you do that?'

Hannah merely shrugged. It felt good though, a timely return of the trouble-shooting instinct that had so often saved her in the past.

You can be a right snooty bitch, Maighréad had told her. Hannah never meant to be snooty. It was a case of self-preservation. It had hurt at the time that Maighréad had been taken in.

She gave Willi a warm smile. The cloud that had threatened her mood earlier had disappeared. Once more she felt comfortable with her surroundings.

England was simply an unpleasant memory. She was in India now. Maighréad, hopeless dreamer that she was, would have said it was destiny.

Destiny. Was *he* part of her destiny too, that familiar stranger who yesterday had briefly touched her life? Perhaps they had been destined to meet. Perhaps they were destined to meet again.

*   *   *

Sitting barefoot on the long, low settee in the reception room, Ashok wiled away each morning, talking to his father. Srinivasa Rao's sharp brain had not suffered noticeably as a result of a recent stroke, but it had left his speech a little slurred and robbed him of some of the energy that had previously kept him going all day and for most of the evening. Srinivasa quizzed Ashok endlessly about developments and changes in British Law. Before his stroke had forced him into retirement, Srinivasa had been a clerk at the City

Law Courts, and still retained a keen interest in legal affairs. In collaboration with Mr Jagannath, a barrister in Mysore, he had recently begun to document the history of the legal system in India. It was a work to which he devoted every possible moment and all the energy that his physical limitations allowed.

Sometimes however, the talk became more personal as Srinivasa gently probed into more private matters.

'And did you never... how to put it... have you never become romantically attached to any one of the many ladies who have undoubtedly passed through your life?'

'There was one,' Ashok said, after a moment's pause. A face forced itself into his mind, but he pushed the image aside. He wasn't about to explain to his father why this affair had finally convinced him that a traditional match was the only way to avoid suffering.

'It was a long time ago.' He paused again before adding quietly, 'She died.'

Oh, Maighréad. If only it had been that simple.

*　*　*

'Some fortress.' Hannah gazed up at the hill on which the massive ruins of the Golconda citadel festered like an elaborate but crumbling sandcastle.

Willi Groot nodded, for once speechless. From the moment she had run into the Dutch girl, in the foyer of the Krishna Hotel shortly after she had booked in on the previous day, Hannah had warmed to her. How could she fail to get on with someone called Willi?

Hannah was always attracted to opposites. She put it down to her curiosity, the same curiosity that drove her career. Hannah Petersen: People's Investigator. But no, not career. Vocation.

Willi had taken Hannah to the local telecom office, from where she had rung Duncan, her publisher, and left a message on his answering machine to let him know where she was. Later, during a meal together at the Osman Restaurant opposite the hotel, Willi had suggested the excursion to Golconda.

It seemed that Willi, in her cropped, black mini-top and low-cut orange jeans had to work as hard to look conspicuous as Hannah did to look anonymous. Willi's ensemble framed her exposed belly button, which had been pierced with a ring, from which dangled a small green feather. And where in all India, wondered Hannah, did she manage to get hold of the colouring to touch up that extraordinary mop of punk-like, yellow hair? The expression on Willi's soft, round face was open and affable; an old-fashioned powder puff with a stubby little pushed-up nose, like a blob of Blutack. The edges of her ears bore at least half a dozen rings each - they reminded Hannah of a spiral bound book. She almost expected the ears to fly open and flap about. The effect was completed by another ring, this one through the left nostril.

In her beige cotton skirt and brown T-shirt Hannah needed no props to advertise her presence. She knew that her height and her hair did that for her. Her heavy tresses were hot against her neck: hair like a lion's mane, her mother used to say. During the last year she'd sometimes considered dyeing it, but thank goodness she'd resisted the temptation. What was the point? He knew where she lived. Now the very idea of danger in India was ludicrous.

Hannah bought a flimsy guidebook from a tout at the entrance. They made their way across the grassy base to the steps up to the citadel, past the first ruins and along the Grand Portico. From there they gazed up at the old granite walls, splendid and still powerful in their decaying glory. As if the hill upon which they stood had thrown them up in some cataclysmic collision of wills.

They climbed slowly up hundreds of steps that led to the top of the hill. They were alone, apart from one woman, who was also making the pilgrimage to the top, some distance behind them. Totally enveloped in a black *burkha*, her face was veiled and invisible. Hannah again pushed aside a frisson of discomfort. Don't be absurd, she told herself.

Halfway through their climb, they looked down at the countryside beyond the fortress perimeter walls. Dust clouded the air and clung to the low bushes and hovels scattered across the landscape. Animals meandered along the road - a cow with blue painted horns, yellow pariah dogs, a little flock of sheep and goats, heavy, grey buffalo. Out of nowhere women, bright as birds of paradise, appeared with silver pots upon their heads. Dominating the tableau like jet on a pebble beach stood the Qutab Shahi Tombs, each the domed mausoleum of some ancient Islamic noble.

'Wow!' Hannah breathed. 'Got to get a shot of that view.'

'Nice camera.'

Hannah nodded. 'Photography's my…' She was about to say hobby, but then remembered. 'My job. I'm really a portrait photographer.' She reminded herself that for the next few months she would indeed, quite legitimately, be a portrait photographer. That, after all, was the reason for her journey, the official reason at least. Duncan had put the idea into her head. He'd always admired the photographs that accompanied her investigations. 'Why don't you do a coffee table book?' he'd suggested. 'I'll publish it. You're a big enough name for this to be a success.' Poor Duncan. Little did he realise that his suggestion would give her the chance to escape from England and from him.

She muttered to herself. *'For standing on the Persians' grave, I could not deem myself a slave.'*

'What's that, Hannah?'

'Byron. Wrong country, of course. He was writing about Greece.' But it is the right sentiment, she thought to herself. Here I feel free again.

'Greece. Huh!' The Dutch girl sniffed at some memory.

'You don't like Greece?'

'Jan and I split up in Poros. Silly argument. You know how men are, always wanting things their way.' She shrugged. 'Relationships - better off without them.'

'Yes,' Hannah said. 'I do know how men are. Much better off without them.' As she spoke, she felt a pang of loneliness.

'How about you? You have a fellow? Or is it women you're into?'

Good God! How on earth did Willi know? Was it written in code across Hannah's forehead? Best not to get into that.

'I lived with someone for a while,' she replied, 'Duncan. Couple of years. We split up about a year ago, when I came to my senses.'

'Duncan. The guy you phoned yesterday? Still simmering on, eh?'

'Professional reasons. He's my publisher. I'm doing a book of India photos.'

As they climbed, they explored the citadel buildings and took photographs of their surroundings and of each other. They tried to build up a picture of what life had been like there in the sixteenth and seventeenth centuries, before the city of Hyderabad had become the capital and Golconda was finally abandoned.

At the summit they wandered into the twelve-arched Durbar Hall.

'Used for general assemblies,' explained Hannah, perusing the guidebook. 'If you clap your hands in the Grand Portico by the entrance to the fort, it can be heard in here. So the book says. Look, it's down there.' She pointed.

'Let's try it,' exclaimed Willi. 'Give me twenty minutes. I'll clap my hands when I get to it. You listen out for me.'

'I want to go down the other way - past the harem. You'll end up waiting ages for me.'

'No problem. I need to find a loo in any case - lingering touch of Delhi Belly. If you're still not back I'll just go on to the tombs. I'll tell the driver.'

A third figure had silently slipped into the Durbar Hall. The woman in the *burkha* studied the graffiti-covered walls intently, seemingly measuring each section in her mind before moving on to the next. Hannah wished she could strike up a conversation. Find out something about this woman's life. Were her presumptions justified? Or was there another dimension to life beneath the *burkha*? She smiled. But there was something chilling in the emptiness behind the black shroud from where the eyes, unseen, were watching. For one instant she thought she caught a whiff of something. Was the nightmare beginning again? No, she told herself. This time it really was her imagination.

Willi waved as she skipped off down the hill. Now Hannah was alone again. To her relief, the woman had also started the descent, some distance behind Willi.

Ten, twenty minutes passed, and Hannah started to get tired of waiting. In addition, a party of noisy school children had arrived, clad in crisp white and green uniforms, the little girls with their hair in identical bunches. They crowded around Hannah, who was clearly far more interesting than the ruins. Laughter convulsed them as they tried out their English on her.

'Hallo!' 'From where you are coming?' 'How do you do?' More laughter as Hannah snapped them with her camera. Such expressive eyes. Such innocent delight. Such intensity. All good material but it obliterated any chance of hearing Willi clapping.

Accompanied by choruses of 'bye-bye,' Hannah started off slowly down the hill, taking a different route so that she would pass by the harem palaces. Little was left to testify to their former magnificence except the huge façade that now provided perching places for small green parakeets. It was a beautiful setting and Hannah took her time.

No sign of Willi at the entrance to the fort and Hannah returned to the car.

'Madam has gone to tombs,' said the driver. 'Come, I will bring you.'

'Did she find a toilet?'

'Toilet? No, Madam. No toilet here. Toilet is in Hyderabad.'

Ah well, thought Hannah, knowing Willi, she probably found a convenient bush.

By now the sun was getting fierce. Hannah glanced at her watch. It was twelve o'clock. She sweltered in the heat. The driver offered her a bottle of Thums Up cola.

'Tums Up, Madam. Drink plenty.'

The tombs were moments away, and she left the driver in the small car park outside the gardens.

The whole place seemed deserted. Still no sign of Willi, and Hannah assumed that she was inside one of the massive mausoleum buildings that loomed over the dry, but once lovely vegetation.

She stood mesmerised. Unlike pictures she had seen of the pristine, white marble Taj Mahal, the blackened limestone domes of these colossal, square edifices testified to the passing of centuries, and despite the harmony of the architecture, they purveyed a sense of emptiness and desolation, which mirrored their purpose in a way that shocked.

Here Hannah lost all sense of time and forgot about Willi. She wandered along sandy paths under bougainvillaea-covered pergolas from one mausoleum to another, admiring the cold perfection of Islamic arches and elaborate stone balustrades. Inside they were empty except for a black basalt sarcophagus, or sometimes two, that formed the centrepiece of each mausoleum.

'Madam, that is not the real tomb.' A young man with an open face and honest eyes was smiling at her as she contemplated the sarcophagus of one of the rulers of Golconda. 'Real tomb is in room below. This is replica.'

'Why?'

'Ah. This is because in our religion ladies must not cast eye upon resting place of the dead. So they may see only the copy. If you wish you may go down. Steps are over there.'

'But I am a lady too.'

'You may look, Madam. For you is permitted.'

'Because I am not a Muslim lady?'

'That is so, Madam. Come, I will take you down. I am guide.'

Hannah looked at her watch. Two-thirty. She hadn't realised that more than two hours had elapsed since she had left the fortress. Willi must be back with the driver by now.

'Sorry. I hadn't realised the time. I must go back.'

As she walked to the car, she was plunged into thoughts of childhood that had been triggered off by the guide's comments. She saw herself once more in Manchester standing with the women at *Omi* Rosen's house door, watching her grandmother's coffin being loaded into the hearse, the male mourners leaving the house to follow it to the cemetery. She heard herself sobbing and screaming, trying to break loose from the grasp of a female neighbour. *Ladies don't go to funerals, dearie. It wouldn't do for us to see men cry.*

Omi Rosen, her mother's mother, who had survived Theresienstadt, her best friend and only confidante through the early years at boarding school. 'Never let life push you around, *Mädchen.* Always remember, you're the boss.' Friday evenings at *Omi's,* a weekend escape from Ashley House, enveloped in a featherbed of caring and the aroma of chicken soup. *Omi* never spoke of her past, memories not for sharing. She drove herself forward through life, and took pleasure in those she loved.

Funny, Hannah reflected. This place. So far from home, and yet perhaps not quite as far as mere physical distance would suggest.

She noticed that several other tourists were now scattered throughout the gardens; an Indian family with two children, a loud, elderly couple, evidently Australian, and a fat, blond man with a beard. She reached the car.

'One English fellow is telling that madam has gone back to Hyderabad,' announced the driver. 'Seems she is not feeling so good.'

'Was it her stomach?'

'I don't know, Madam.'

It sounded plausible. Willi was resourceful. 'You're never alone in India,' she'd told Hannah, describing some of the people she'd picked up on her travels. No doubt this Englishman had given her a lift. And after all, Hannah had kept her waiting for ages.

'In that case I'll just go and have another look.' she told the driver. 'Won't be more than ten minutes.'

She headed back to the tomb she had just left, stopping for a moment to watch a couple of workmen high up on a domed roof, as confident as crows, no safety devices to hold them in place. Hannah unscrewed her wide-angle lens and attached her massive telephoto. It was a heavy object and she regularly cursed it, but she knew it was essential. She took a couple of close-ups of the workers and continued on into the mausoleum. The young guide had disappeared. She was alone again.

No door marked the entrance to the vault, merely a black gash in the wall, like a gaping wound. Hannah stepped inside and felt her way down the stone stairway in the pitch darkness. After some ten or twelve steps she felt flat ground beneath her feet. She shivered in the clammy coldness and waited while her eyes got accustomed to the lack of light. Gradually she began to make out shapes: arches and thick stone pillars, behind them recesses like black holes. She stepped through an archway further into the room. Now she could see light shining in from the far side, a narrow exit directly to the outside. She remembered that she had had to climb up steps to get into the mausoleum in the first place, which explained why her descent into the vault had placed her back on the same level as the garden. The light illuminated a great sarcophagus draped in crimson silk that stood in the centre of the room. Hannah drew nearer to it. The walls receded further into blackness behind the arches. She walked around the tomb. Who was inside it? What kind of a life had he led - certainly the immense coffin belonged to a man, an ancient ruler of the Kingdom of Golconda.

A damp, musty smell pervaded the room, and something else; some abhorrent odour that invaded her like an unpleasant memory. As she circled the tomb a slight movement behind her startled her. She spun round. In the black void beyond the arches she could make out the outline of a *burkha*-clad figure. No eyes were visible behind the thin black strip of muslin set into the swathe of impenetrable black; only the all-seeing blankness that she had first encountered in the Durbar Hall. Lurking, watching...

... watching from behind the garden shed, lurking in the bushes, waiting...

Then Hannah knew. This was no Muslim woman. Behind the veil lurked the eyeless face that haunted her waking nightmares. Evil had followed her to India.

* * *

Duncan Forbes sat at the wood and metal 1980s desk in his garden room, watching December rain sliding down the window. His fingers tapped idly on his computer keyboard, as he considered the letter that his secretary had just faxed through to him. The question in his mind was should he, or should he not tell Hannah. Probably not. Certainly not while she was still obsessed with this mythical stalker. He'd had enough trouble as it was, getting any sense out of her during the past few months. In any case, there wasn't anything that Hannah could do. Especially from some remote town in India. Where did she say she was? Hyderabad?

His eyes strayed from the window to the photograph in a simple clip frame on top of a filing cabinet. He was standing by a river, his arm around Hannah. They were looking at one another, smiling. As he gazed at the picture, a flood of emotions overwhelmed him. She'd changed so much over the past year. All this stuff about being followed. He blamed it all on the American experience. What had they really done to her in New York? That psychoanalysis rubbish had addled her brain. Like his business partner, Piers Hamilton, Duncan now handled very few authors personally, an exception being Hannah. These days Duncan only trekked from Guildford up to his office in London a couple of times a week. Piers spent more time on the golf course than at his desk. Duncan hated golf. He got enough exercise at the squash club, and had no need to cultivate new business colleagues. His stolen days were spent on a more sedentary and, he hoped, fruitful pursuit. Information technology. That was the buzzword of the early nineties. Duncan knew that he had to be there, leading from the front. His colleagues, Piers included, might consider him eccentric, but Duncan knew he was right. The technological revolution was taking the world by storm, and soon the publishing business would be swept along with it. You either embraced the opportunities that were rapidly opening up or you sank without a trace.

Hannah was at the very heart of his professional success. She was his most prestigious author. All of her books had made it to the top of the non-fiction list. Hannah's subject matter was the kind of stuff the general public would normally ignore. But Hannah had a way of forcing attention onto injustice in society; a magic touch that could turn an insurance scam across the Pond, or the sad life of a battered teenager, into a *cause célèbre*. With Hannah, his reputation was assured. At least, that was the way it had always been. But now?

He turned his attention back to the faxed letter. Even the poor quality of the fax could not disguise the lavishness of the headed notepaper. J. Croxley Burnett. Attorney at Law. An address in lower Manhattan. So his fears had not been groundless. Elliot Bannerman, director of the East River Psychiatric Center was threatening him with a court injunction to stop the publication in the US of Hannah's new book, *Fair Game*.

Duncan picked up the phone and dialled his firm's US attorney, Hal Brodsky, in New York.

'Don't worry about Bannerman,' Hal told Duncan. 'Doesn't stand a chance. Hannah's dug up too much dirt on him. Croxley Burnett's a crook. He and Bannerman are in this together. He's just trying to spook you. Ignore it.'

'Easy for you to say, Hal.'

'Listen, Duncan. There's not a court in the land wouldn't throw that one out. Bannerman's well known. Hannah's only provided evidence for what we all suspected in the first place.'

'Is Bannerman going to let the matter rest, if this injunction fails?'

'Not if he can help it. There'll be litigation - he'll be out for blood, you can be sure of that.'

'Thanks, old man. That's just what I needed to hear right now.'

'Don't worry about it. Hannah's built up such a strong case against the guy that his number's up. Look at the evidence. There's the testimony of medics who used to work at ERPC. Then there's the evidence of the victims and their relatives. The insurance companies are desperate to get the matter cleared up. They're losing millions through these scams. As soon as *Fair Game* came out in the UK the American press got hold of it. It's opened up a floodgate of complaints from all over the country.'

'Empowering the people. Hannah'll be pleased. What kind of complaints?'

'Oh, everything Hannah mentioned really. You know the sort of thing - forceful detention and tranquillisation of patients; fraudulent insurance claims made on their behalf and so on and so on. The press are milking it for every cent's worth.'

'And presumably Bannerman's doing his usual slick cover-up job?'

'Funny you should say that. A friend of mine, Carole Waterman - works for the *New York Times* - has been trying to get an interview with Bannerman ever since this thing blew up. But no one, apart, I guess, from Croxley Burnett, seems to know where the hell he is.'

* * *

Hannah was convinced that she was about to die. She stared at the black-robed figure. A sense of outrage engulfed her disbelief.

'Who are you?' Her voice teetered on the edge of hysteria as she spat out the words. 'What the hell do you want with me?'

The figure seemed to shrink into the shadows before it rushed out of the gloom towards her. She caught the glint of steel in the exposed right hand thrust towards her. No time to think, she lashed out at the head with the only weapon at hand - her camera.

'Bastard,' she screamed, her fury overcoming her fear. 'Leave me alone!'

A cry of pain as the figure's hand shot up to the face. A man's voice. 'Fucking hell! I'll bloody well...'

Other voices permeated the mausoleum vault. Hastily the figure pushed Hannah aside and fled towards the light, just as a middle-aged couple emerged from the direction of the stairwell, accompanied by the young guide with a torch.

'Well! She was in a bit of a hurry. You reckon she seen a ghost, maybe?'

'Could be. Say, sweetheart, you OK?' The matronly Australian had discovered Hannah, slumped against the sarcophagus.

'Yes...yes thanks. That person pushed me - the one that just ran out.'

'Well, that just goes to show. Never trust these people,' pronounced the woman's male companion.

'No, no - I think something frightened her.'

'See, what'd I tell you, Martha. Seems there is a ghost.'

They both laughed.

'These folk are so superstitious. Now what you need,' the man turned to Hannah, 'is something for the shock. You come back with us, darling, and we'll soon get you sorted. Just name your poison - Martini, Scotch, even a drop of beer - we got the lot. Wouldn't go anywhere without it. Now come along.'

'Thanks, but I'm all right now. I'll just go back to my car.'

'Do you have anyone to take care of you?'

'My driver.'

'I wouldn't be too happy about that, m'dear. Come on, let's look after you.'

Hannah was sure that their timely arrival had saved her life. Now their outrageous comments probably saved her sanity, for her desire to escape from their clutches jolted her back once more into clear thinking.

'No need. I'm fine,' she said, mustering up the aura of self-confidence perfected over years of professional snooping, and hoping she sounded more convincing than she felt. 'Thanks, anyway.' She drew herself up and marched across the room and out into the daylight.

Taking a deep breath, she surveyed her surroundings, but the apparition had melted back into the landscape. She checked her camera. Undamaged. She'd caught him with the edge of the heavy, telephoto lens, still attached after photographing the workmen on the roof. She made her way carefully to the car, thinking about what had taken place. Now she had no doubt. The vibes from the *burkha* at the top of Golconda - it had not been her imagination. He was here. He had pursued her from England, like a malevolent shadow. Briefly, she wanted to tell the driver, and to ask him to take her to the police. How much faith could she have in the police here, where corruption was rife, she wondered, when she'd had no cause to have faith in them back home? Time after time she'd called them. Each time it happened. Week after week...

... Footsteps getting louder week after week, eh? And this always happens when you're walking home from the pub, does it? I see. Well, we'll look into it Miss Petersen, but you haven't given us much to go on...

No point in telling the driver. The police would only take her for an eccentric tourist, or worse. Who knows what demands they might make in return for agreeing to 'help' her? In any case without a clue to the man's identity she might only make matters worse by involving officialdom. Now that her pursuer had followed her abroad the situation had cranked up a notch. No longer simply a case of some demented stalker. With her propensity for meddling in high profile public affairs the CIA, the FBI or even MI5 might be implicated. She knew that she must keep silent.

The journey back to Hyderabad passed in a blur.

Still no sign of Willi at the hotel.

'Your friend is not returning, Miss Petersen?' asked Mr Reddy, the receptionist.

'No. She met someone. Gone for lunch, I suppose.'

Hannah went up to her room. She showered away the grime and sweat of the excursion, scrubbing at her skin as if cleansing her body would remove the stains of the morning from her mind. But it was no good; no soap and water could wash away the horror of the encounter at the tombs. She remembered the fear that had gripped her, and cursed herself for her weakness.

At Ashley House Hannah had learnt to be strong, like *Omi* Rosen. Her height had been her ally. She remembered her mother's relief, when she finally stopped growing. But Hannah bought shoes that made her look even taller. The starved look that was fashionable during her teenage years never appealed to her. She was proud of her body, a woman's body while her peers were still little girls. Too busy for regular exercise, she swam as often as she could, and walked long distances. She was strong, as strong as any man.

She remembered the times back in England when she had tried to intercept her pursuer, her terror subsumed under the rage that momentarily vanquished thoughts for her own safety. She had been indignant. Distraught too. How dare anyone infiltrate and dominate her life in this way? Of course she had been frightened. Terrified. She had managed to control it. Risen above it. Kept her fear from him, and from others. No one else had witnessed her goose pimples as she peered though her window at night, or heard her pounding heart. But the final encounter in England on that awful November night had planted seeds of self-doubt, now being nurtured in the strangeness of this land.

Had she made a terrible mistake in coming here, so far from all that was familiar to her? Well, the deed was done. But one thing she knew. She had to get away from Hyderabad.

*　*　*

'You are too thin, Ashok,' said Girija, Ashok's mother, setting out on the dining table a medley of spice-infused dishes that she had spent all morning preparing. *Dal, bringal, rasam, sambar, raita, aloo gobi, kofta, gulab jamon.* The variety was endless. Plus rice, *roti*, pickles, chutney and fruit. Sections of banana leaf served as plates, a festive tradition, to prolong the celebrations of Ashok's return.

'That English cooking,' she persisted, 'it is not agreeing with you. It is good that soon you will have a wife to make proper food.'

'*Amma*, I eat proper food. And once weekly I am invited to dine at the home of the Patels.'

'Then it is very wrong of you to neglect mother of Mrs Patel. You must take those parcels to her today afternoon.'

'Not today. I have other matters to attend to.'

In truth Ashok was putting off as long as possible the spectre of small talk with the mother of his eminent mentor. Dr Patel was the most senior surgeon in the Ophthalmology Department at Queen Anne's, whereas Ashok was a mere fledgling consultant. The Patels had taken him under their wing, and Mrs Patel was determined that his taste buds should not forget the flavours of his native land. Grateful as he was to them, his gratitude did not extend to Dr Patel's in-laws. In any case he was still marginally peeved at what he could only think of as Dr Patel's audacity in turning up on the doorstep the night before Ashok left England, a large brown package in both hands, an irreproachable smile on his face.

'Ah, my dear boy. I do hope you were not sleeping.' Without waiting for a reply or an invitation, Dr Patel had stepped into the flat.

'No. I'd just finished packing.'

'Packing. I see. Then I hope you will find room for this small gift for my wife's family. You will, of course, visit them when you are in Bangalore.'

'Yes. Yes, of course.' Ashok took the package, staggering under the weight. He tried not to look concerned.

'Medical books for my brother-in-law - including latest volume of my own book, you see. Not yet available in India. Oh, yes, and also some saris for my wife's mother.'

Ashok had resigned himself to getting another bag down from the loft. Why, he wondered, did so many people want books and saris from England, when Bangalore was bursting with the very best of both? Even his own mother had requested a sari, so he had spent a wasteful morning shopping in Southall. He wasn't even sure if she would like the end result of his endeavours. Perhaps the beige silk with its scarcely defined acanthus trellises reflected his taste rather than hers; at least the taste that seemed to have crept up on him as a result of years of exposure to British restraint.

'One more small package is in the car. I could not carry two.' Dr Patel smiled and looked expectantly at Ashok.

'Oh - do let me bring it for you.' Ashok had checked his rising irritation by forcing himself to remember Dr and Mrs Patel's generosity towards him over the last five years.

'Very kind of you. It is behind the front passenger seat.'

The second package was bigger than the first.

'A pressure cooker - British make,' explained Dr Patel. 'So many times they have asked. Of course you must tell me if you cannot manage to transport these small items.'

Ashok would stay silent on the matter. Even the excess baggage fee would remain his secret.

Now he said to his mother, 'I will take the packages tomorrow. Or the next day.' He turned his attention to the meal.

They ate with their fingers, which gave Ashok particular pleasure. It was such a basic, sensuous act that once again reinforced the oneness of man and nature. Sometimes, when he was alone in the flat in Richmond, he would eat in this way, but it was not the same. In Richmond he felt awkward, like an erring child, nervous in case a friend walked in on him, or the phone rang and he should forget and pick it up with a sticky hand.

After the midday meal, Ashok went downstairs to the lower floor of the house. It was here that his grandmother, Lakshmi Devi, kept her rooms, living amidst the security of her son's family, and yet, upon her own insistence, maintaining a degree of independence so that she could withdraw undisturbed into her memories.

'Come, Ashok,' Lakshmi Devi patted the space beside her on the settee. 'Come, sit and tell honestly. For so long you have been away from us. Are you not a little nervous about marriage plans *Amma* is making? You are a young man only, and I know how young men are - and now you are a young Englishman...'

'Oh, *Ajji*,' laughed Ashok, 'I am not so young. And anyway, how old were you when you married *Tata*?'

'Ah, yes,' the old lady said, her eyes bright with the memory. 'Eight years of age I was, as you well know, when I was married and brought from my father's home to stay in house of your grandfather.'

'And you fell in love when you were eight years old?'

'Perhaps. But what I am telling - by time we were of an age to live as man and wife, long since we had fallen in love.' The old woman's voice softened. 'Eighty years, Ashok. Eighty years we were married. Eighty years without one day apart.'

Ashok never tired of hearing his grandmother tell the story of her life, just as he had never tired, when he was a child, of hearing her recount for him tales from the epic Hindu poems *Ramayana* and *Mahabharata*. With her singsong voice and her infectious enthusiasm and devotion, she wove for him many a tale that broke

23

the boundaries of the imagination. If a monkey could move a mountain, if a chariot as big as a country rode the skies, if gods could be men, and men could be gods, if cities had walls as high as heaven, if fire could give birth to a princess, if demons could be good as well as evil, if a single arrow could destroy heaven and earth, if men could live for ten thousand years, then nothing was impossible. Nothing. Not even a small Indian boy's dream of an Oxford education and a brilliant career. Ashok always knew he could make it happen.

It was three years since his grandfather had died, during Ashok's last visit home. It was as if he had waited to see his grandson one more time, before he cheerfully, and without fuss, shed his present existence, a grand old man of ninety years. Characteristically, he had been helping his son Srinivasa investigate a mysterious rattle in the engine of their old Fiat, when he suddenly said he felt a little tired and would go and rest. He lay down for the last time, and slipped away with a smile on his face, and a sparkle in his eyes, which seemed to linger even after he had drawn his final breath.

Ashok considered his grandmother's words to him and smiled. She was wrong. He was not and would never be an Englishman. His love for his adopted country was boundless, but it would never absorb him.

* * *

When Willi left Hannah in the Durbar Hall at Golconda, she hurried down the hill by the same path that she had used for the ascent. She skipped down the steep steps, humming. Life was good. In spite of her aura of bravado, she'd sometimes felt isolated in her travels, and now she had found a pleasant companion. She reached the Grand Portico and waited until it was clear of people. Only the black-robed woman, who had followed her down the hill, still lingered.

Willi clapped her hands. She repeated this several times, but no reply came from the Durbar Hall.

Ah, well! Might as well give up and look for a loo.

Outside, she found the car driver draped across the front bench of the Ambassador dozing, his bare feet, brown and bony, poking out of the open passenger window. She rapped on the windscreen. 'Where is a toilet?' she demanded, before the startled man had time to gather his thoughts.

'Sorry, Madam. Not in this place.'

'Well, I will walk to the tombs. Perhaps I will find a toilet on the way. Please tell my friend I have gone on ahead.'

Instead of taking the road, Willi set off across scrubland, peppered with small, square, white dwellings, towards the towering onion-shaped domes beyond. Glancing back, she noticed that her *burkha*-clad shadow had the same idea.

The need to find a toilet was becoming urgent. She scoured the countryside in vain for a suitable bush or other obstacle, behind which she could relieve herself in comparative privacy. An embarrassing accident was becoming inevitable. Moreover her stomach cramps were now so acute that she felt faint. Her feet began to drag across the soft sand.

The woman in the *burkha* was gaining on her. Willi stopped and waited for her to catch up. Perhaps she lived in one of the little houses and would be able to help. If not, Willi would have to crouch down once the woman had gone by, and empty the contents of her bowel under the scrutiny of anyone who chanced to come past.

'Toilet!' she shrieked. 'Where?'

No glimmer of life was discernible behind the veil. However a strong, wiry hand emerged from the *burkha,* a pale hand, and grasping her elbow, steered her off to the right, weaving in and out of the little, whitewashed homes until they reached the edge of the settlement, and the outer wall of the tomb gardens. Leaning against this wall was a small wooden hut, possibly the property of workmen employed on restoration of the site.

'Toilet?' shouted Willi, by now too despairing to doubt that fate would have been so obliging as to plant deliverance in such an unlikely spot.

The black-robed figure continued to propel her towards the hut. The door was swinging open and Willi ran inside. A first glance revealed nothing that even approximated a toilet. In fact the hut was empty, apart from some rubbish swept into the corner.

That was the last thing she saw before she lost consciousness.

* * *

By the time Hannah had showered and made her way down to reception, darkness was setting in. Willi had still not returned. She began to feel uneasy.

'Any messages for me?' she asked Mr Reddy, hoping that maybe Willi had left word of her whereabouts.

'No, Madam, no messages.'

'By the way,' she continued, in as casual a voice as she could muster, 'Would you be able to book a plane ticket for me?'

'Plane ticket? Where you are wanting to go, Madam?'

'Bangalore. As soon as possible. Tonight if you can.'

'It is not usual. You must go to airline office. But I will see what is possible. My cousin is working in airline office. You go and eat now. Afterwards you can come.'

Best to be where there are lots of people, she thought, and nodded, although food had been the last thing on her mind.

Hannah went across to the Osman and picked at her meal. Then she went back to the hotel.

Mr Reddy called to her.

'Madam, ticket I have arranged.'

A sense of relief overwhelmed her. 'When do I leave?'

'Some problems we were having, Madam. All flights from Hyderabad to Bangalore full for whole of next week.'

Her heart sank.

'Never mind, Madam. I procured ticket to Chennai eight-thirty tomorrow morning, and from there flight to Bangalore morning after.'

'Chennai? Where's that?'

'Indian name for Madras, Madam. Tickets my cousin will bring. You will please pay him then. I have made for you reservation also

26

in Chennai at Hotel Pandava. Is good hotel, Madam, and price is OK.'

In her gratitude Hannah pressed a hundred rupee note into the astonished man's hand.

'Oh, thank you, Madam, thank you.' He seemed to feel that this generosity merited further effort on his part. 'Shall I reserve room at Chamundi Hotel in Bangalore also? Is international standard hotel, Madam. No worries.'

'Thanks. I'd be really grateful.'

Slipping back out of the hotel, Hannah headed off to the telecom office, picking her way through stinking puddles, mud and blotches of spittle, blood red from chewed lime and betel nut *paan*. She felt safe amid the turmoil on the streets. Her memory had served her well, and she found the office without difficulty. Duncan would be at work. She wouldn't have to talk to him.

'Tomorrow Madras, Hotel Pandava,' she told the answering machine. 'I'll be in touch.'

She returned to the hotel.

'Please let me know when the tickets are here, or if Miss Groot returns. I'll be in my room.'

'Of course, Madam, but why not sit in hotel lounge? English-language news broadcast is at eight o'clock on TV.'

She watched the eight o'clock news intently, almost expecting to learn that some dreadful accident had befallen a Dutch tourist. To her relief, there was nothing. She stayed in the lounge until ten, waiting in the vain hope that Willi would return. Then she went up to her room and tried to formulate some sort of plan while she packed her rucksack. Her nemesis had followed her. So what now? Once more, she agonised over her vulnerability. Whatever had happened to the feisty Hannah that used to inhabit this skin? How had she ended up alone and, yes, she had to admit it, scared, in a dingy hotel room in India?

A knock came at the door. Hannah leapt up.

'Who is it?'

'Message for you, Madam.' Unmistakably Mr Reddy's voice. She unlocked the door.

Mr Reddy handed her a rather dirty, scribbled note, written on the inside of a Charminar cigarette packet.

Hannah - Met a friend. Won't be back tonight. Willi.

'Who brought this?'

'Some small boy is delivering, Madam.'

'When?'

'Before ten minutes.'

Hannah frowned. Somehow the note did not altogether dispel her uneasiness. Too curt and unapologetic. But perhaps it was simply a manifestation of Willi's casual attitude. In any case Hannah could do nothing about it.

'Thanks, Mr Reddy.' She slipped him ten rupees.

Alone once more, she locked the door and leant against it with a sigh. She looked at her fingers. Trembling again. She cursed. Simply didn't make sense. Hadn't made sense for the past year.

She took a deep breath. Well, be that as it may. She had to get to the bottom of it. Whatever the game was, it was serious enough for someone to have followed her here. So OK, let him come. She needed to face him. But, she conceded to herself, she had to have backup.

Right - plan of campaign - first get to Bangalore.

She smiled. That uncharacteristic impulsiveness had won again when she had asked Mr Reddy to get her a ticket to Bangalore. Why hadn't she said Colombo? It would have made much more sense. But Hannah hadn't even decided whether she would bother to get in touch with her half-brother in Sri Lanka. They'd never met. There had been no contact between them. She didn't even know if he'd want to see her. In any case Sri Lanka was across the sea. She needed someone who knew India, someone who would not draw suspicion. If her unknown enemy knew so much about her, who's to say he hadn't found out about big brother George? So, Bangalore it was.

Checking through her documents, she pulled a scrap of card out of her wallet, and felt a flush of satisfaction. Still got what it takes, girl, she told herself. He didn't suspect a thing. Hard work though.

He didn't seem at all keen. It was now or never when the plane touched down in Delhi. But I got there in the end.

The piece of card in her hand had a Bangalore telephone number scribbled on it and underneath it a name.

Somehow I know I can trust him, she thought, even if he doesn't turn out after all to be the same Dr Ashok Rao.

CHAPTER 2

Hotel Pandava on the Poonemale Road in Madras, or Chennai as it was now called, was an almighty celebration of art deco eccentricity. Hannah's mood began to lift with the first glimpse of the coming night's sanctuary.

A central garden blazoned with flame trees and bougainvillaea. Around it was a colonnaded walkway and opening out onto it were the ground floor guest rooms. Perched over them, layered balconies, painted in a riot of yellow, lilac, red, cream and blue checks, curves and stripes. They reminded Hannah of Legoland.

She was shown to one of the ground floor rooms. It was simple but functional. Two small windows at the front, shaded by the walkway, gave little chance for the sun to burn a pathway into the dark, wood-clad interior. Far from being sombre, the room gave the feeling of a cool, cosy, log cabin. The bathroom was basic, but contained a jug and bucket for showering, and an antiquated flush toilet. A cheerful, embossed elephant motif smiled down from the rusty cast iron cistern on the wall.

Hannah ran a brush through her tangled mop of auburn hair, and tied it back at the nape of her neck. Duncan had always hated it like that. Said it made her look too stern. *Powerful women don't need to advertise the fact,* he'd said. *And powerful men,* she'd retorted, looking at him, *it's all right for them to look imposing, is it?* She knew she'd paid him a backhanded compliment. The older he got, the more distinguished he seemed to look, in line with his growing reputation.

She shook Duncan from her mind, irritated by his intrusion into her thoughts, and splashed her face with water, cooling her wrists with a spray of her favourite *Fleurs de Provence* cologne. Then she set off to explore. Secret stairways, snaking upward, connected the floors. Here and there the stairs opened out onto a roof garden from where the back streets behind the hotel were visible, with their strange mix of architecture: ramshackle little dwellings and tiny roadside stores snuggling unselfconsciously up to the great, wedding cake pink façade of a Raj-era girls' school.

Hannah was soon caught up in the joyful eccentricity of the place. Seduced by her surroundings and intoxicated by garden fragrances in the searing heat, reality became blurred. India was a strange psychedelic wonderland, whose dark forces were manifested in the Qutab Shahi Tombs. Now she was in Sugar Candy Land, where no harm could come to her.

She told herself that the atmosphere at the tombs had played tricks on her mind. There had been no attacker, merely a frightened Muslim woman, who bumped into her in her haste to get out of that forbidden, claustrophobic place. She hoped she hadn't hurt her when she lashed out with the camera. And the man's voice must have been the Australian coming down the stairs. Perhaps he'd tripped on the step. The flash of steel? A silver bracelet maybe, or a watchstrap. Nothing ominous about it. How silly of her to have thought otherwise.

Stepping out of the hotel, Hannah found herself engulfed in a different fantasy. The wide road was a pageant of colour and sound. A perpetual stream of strange vehicles filed past noisily in all directions. Autorickshaws spluttered and coughed as their two-stroke engines were pushed beyond reasonable limits. Lorries, as brightly painted and lavishly decorated as Romany caravans, roared and hooted, scattering autos and scooters, like foxes in a hencoop. Heavily laden with cricket bats, a cycle rickshaw plied its slow and steady course through the aggressive, mechanised competitors for road space. A solitary cow ambled obliviously, like a dropped stitch in a complex piece of knitting, through the centre of the traffic, while chaos reigned around it, secure in the knowledge that it was indestructible.

Hannah stopped at a fruit stall, a perfumed cornucopia of delights. Pyramids of limes, apples, oranges and grapes jostled with papayas, wood apples and pomegranates. Chillies, aubergines, tomatoes, cauliflowers and fat green gherkins glistened in the late afternoon sun. Enormous bunches of red, green and yellow bananas hung from the awning, together with large, juicy, bright golden pineapples and garlands of marigolds.

The vendor grinned at her, his bald pate glowing like one of his own polished aubergines, his face ripe and round. A marvellous face. Oh, yes. This one she had to have. But first the negotiations. She pointed to a bunch of tiny, yellow bananas.

'How much?'

'How many you want, lady?'

She held up five fingers.

'Fifty rupees.'

'Too much. Ten.'

'*Ten!* Oh no, Madam. Thirty.'

'Twenty. Twenty if you let me take your photograph.'

The vendor's head bobbed from side to side registering assent, and he wrapped the bananas in a newspaper bag. Then he laughingly let Hannah pose him next to a couple of fat, hanging aubergines and take his picture. The obedient clunk of the shutter in the late afternoon light was to Hannah like the pop of a cork on a good wine bottle. Knowing without tasting that the expense is justified.

Hannah was pleased with her picture and with her bananas, although she was quite sure that she had paid a 'foreigner' rather than a local price. But twenty rupees, when all was said and done, amounted to less than fifty pence.

A family with a bicycle had stopped to watch her, father pushing, older daughter on the saddle, baby straddling the cross bar, mother walking alongside.

'Photo?' The man gestured at his family.

Hannah happily obliged. India was proving to be a photographer's paradise. Before she had time to react, the fruit vendor took the camera from her, and amid much laughter, took a photograph of her with the bicycle family.

The father placed his hands together in thanks, and smiling broadly, the family cycled off into the mayhem, leaving Hannah to ponder the meaning of the act; leading her only to conclude that it was yet another of the many enigmas of this curious country.

The puffy, brown afternoon clouds began to recede in the wake of a crimson sunset. Already Venus shone in the sky. Laughing girls, in pink and scarlet gymslips, returned home from some sporting fixture. High in the trees, emerald parakeets gathered noisily to welcome the night. The high pavements were dotted with potholes and, fearing a fall in the fading light, Hannah decided to return to the hotel.

As soon as she opened her hotel room door, Hannah sensed that something was wrong. It wasn't simply that her bed had been made and her room had been tidied. It wasn't only the slightly rotten smell in the air. She looked around. Everything was in place, exactly as she had left it. Neat and tidy. That was it. Too neat and tidy. Someone had been through her things. They'd made a good job of covering-up, but it didn't fool Hannah. She'd seen it too many times before: in Belfast, in America, even in England. It went with the job. She felt herself starting to shake again. Stop being a fool, she chided herself. It's your imagination. Or it must have been the chambermaid having a nose around. She checked carefully through her rucksack. Nothing seemed to be missing. She relaxed.

At that moment a terrible cacophony erupted outside. She ran to investigate.

The quiet, unobtrusive hotel garden was unrecognisable.

A monster had landed on the grass; related, perhaps, to an old Hillman Imp, though this creature had been decapitated, so that instead of a passenger compartment, it carried a large platform on its carapace. The creature was brightly painted in red, yellow and blue. Two huge loudspeakers, like terrible all-seeing eyes, were suspended on poles at the front of the platform. A banner running along the side proclaimed that this apparition was the 'Gopal Band.'

Seated upon the platform, hammering on a variety of drums and a keyboard, were some of the band members. Others were standing in front of the monster, blowing in apparently uncoordinated abandon on strange clarinets and cornets.

Pristine uniforms. Black trousers with smart white side-stripes; cream shirt, covered with a riot of purple floral patterns; triangular epaulets with orange and gold fringes resting on the shoulders. The crowning glory: a shiny red ten-gallon hat, edged with blue ribbon.

Once Hannah had recovered from the shock, she noticed the festooned and garlanded white horse standing patiently outside one of the opposite rooms, totally ignoring the chaotic din around it.

'It is my brother's wedding.'

Words softly spoken, a gentle breeze in the flame tree.

Hannah turned. She found a young woman, perhaps twenty years old, smiling at her. The smile was radiant, delivered through sparkling white teeth, set in a generous mouth. Hannah caught her breath. Before her stood a goddess. From the iridescent glow of her burnished skin, to her dark, laughing eyes, from the flawless arch of her eyebrows to the thick, black plait of hair that reached to her waist, she was unadulterated perfection.

She wore a sari of richly embroidered burnt-orange shot silk, and beneath it a light golden blouse, whose long sleeves shimmered when she moved. Heavy gold jewellery adorned her ears, her throat, her wrists, her fingers and her ankles. Her hands were covered with intricate henna patterns, twists, curls, leaves and flowers, such as you might find on a Kashmir carpet. Hannah struggled not to betray the sensuality that the girl aroused in her.

'My name is Rasika.' The goddess placed her hands together in greeting. Hannah repeated the gesture, feeling slightly self-conscious at the unfamiliar expressiveness demanded of her own hands, as though the world were watching to make sure she got it right.

'And your good name?'

'Hannah. I'm Hannah.'

'You are coming from UK?'

Hannah nodded. The girl spoke English with just enough of an Indian lilt to accentuate the beauty of the voice, like a Welsh contralto.

'Your English is excellent.'

'I am taking English course at Chennai University. And you? You are coming to India for which purpose?'

'To take photographs,' Hannah said simply. 'Of people. For a book. I've only been here a couple of days. Already I'm hooked on your country.'

'Hooked?'

'Enchanted. Fascinated. Look,' Hannah continued, 'I hope you won't mind, but I'd like to take your portrait. May I get my camera?'

Rasika bobbed her head happily. Hannah slipped through the growing crowd, and returned with her camera a moment later. Rasika had assembled a retinue of womenfolk.

'Please meet my mother. And my auntie.' The two older women beamed at Hannah. Both wore lavish saris, one yellow, one pink, the ends of which they had draped over their heads. When they laughed, which they did frequently, the rolls of fat on their exposed, well-upholstered midriffs wobbled in unselfconscious delight.

'And this is my young sister.'

The girl, almost as tall as Rasika, was dressed in an elaborate dark green silk *shalwar kameez*. In a few years time, thought Hannah, she will rival her sister.

'Now,' said Rasika. 'You will please to take photo?'

Hannah took several close-up shots of Rasika, her mother, her aunt and her sister. Someone took Hannah's camera so that she could be included in a group picture.

Hannah returned to her room, intending to leave her camera and head off in search of a restaurant. On second thoughts she went across to the entrance lobby and asked the receptionist to lock the camera in the hotel safe. When she came back, Rasika was waiting for her.

'My mother is inviting you to my brother's wedding. You will please come.'

The invitation quickly dispelled a slight feeling of renewed unease. Hannah had discovered that something was, after all, missing from her room. The wretched chambermaid had removed from her bed a Krishna Hotel brochure, on which Mr Reddy had written the words *Chamundi Hotel, Bangalore.*

* * *

Ashok was stretched out in a garden hammock slung between the two coconut palms. It was early morning and the family was still sleeping, but he had been too restless to spend any longer in bed. Today he would start doing the rounds of prospective brides. He had brought out with him a set of neatly-typed papers that his mother had given him shortly after his arrival home, each bearing particulars of a young woman. His parents had certainly been busy in the past few weeks, compiling a shortlist of eligible brides for him to consider. He read through the details several times, and began to sort the candidates into some sort of order, according to his own mental list of required attributes for the ideal bride. As far as caste, education and family background were concerned, he had no need to worry. His parents had seen to all that. They had vetted the possible candidates and eliminated any that did not meet their exacting standards. Each one had had her *jataka* carefully checked to ensure that nothing was incompatible in the horoscopes of prospective bride and groom. The rest was up to him - and her of course. She had to like him too.

A slug of panic curled his stomach. Liking him wasn't enough. She would have to be adaptable to fit into his English life, a life that would be completely alien to her. And how would he feel, his bachelor pad forever ringing with the presence of another person? No longer his retreat, his place of solitude, to which he could return after a stressful day and flop thankfully into the armchair with only Bach and a cold beer to keep him company; *his* chair, stylish in maroon leather and superbly comfortable. Would it still be *his* chair when she moved in, he wondered. Could he explain to his new wife that he was the only person allowed to sit in it? Or would everything become 'ours' and the word 'mine' disappear from his vocabulary? What would she think of his flat, so subdued in its cool tones? He found himself imagining the decor, as seen through the eyes of a newly arrived Indian bride. It was all so understated. The rosewood coffee table held no more excitement than the grey Axminster or the two-seater sofa that matched his armchair. Expensive, yes, and classy. But what would she care about such neutered elegance? The fine mahogany desk in the corner of his room drew his mind's eye, reminding him that at least one item in the room would please her. Not the quality of the eighteenth century workmanship, superb though it was, but the brightly coloured poster-painting of Ganesh, the elephant-headed god, which hung above the desk - a small, joyous bastion of India shining forth in all its riotous glory through the facelessness of perceived good taste.

He tried to imagine his bride stepping out into a raw Richmond January morning, the cold air catching her lungs, trying to comprehend the bleakness of glazed shop fronts and fortress houses. Would she adapt, as he had, and shed her many-coloured coat? Or would she feel trapped, like a butterfly in a glasshouse?

Enough, he told himself, shrugging off his doubts and returning to his list of candidates. They all seem much of a muchness. Nothing here about their characters, or what they look like. Not even the attached photographs on some of them help much. Photographs can be so misleading.

What do I want her to look like? He closed his eyes and let his imagination run riot. Now let me see. She will be tiny, like a fragile, porcelain doll. She will have skin like golden turmeric. She will wear garlands of jasmine twined in her heavy black hair, which will flow down her back like rich palmyra syrup. Her eyes - large, widely set. Her lips - full and luscious. Wherever she is there will be the scent of sandalwood and roses.

Ashok sighed. He was a Maharaja with the pick of his kingdom to choose from.

He chided himself for such idle thoughts. What does it matter if her teeth stick out a little, and her body is, well, less than perfection, so long as her character suits?

He started to reflect on the personality of his imaginary bride.

She must have a sense of humour, and be open-minded. She must be very practical - it wouldn't do to have two dreamers in the family - that would not bode well for the children. She must not talk incessantly. I could not tolerate a chatterbox. Oh yes - and her voice must be smooth, like a slow tune on a tenor sax. I couldn't be doing with a woman who had a voice like... he struggled to find a suitable image and chuckled when he found one, like a band at an Indian wedding. She should be well read and it should be possible to discuss matters of the world with her.

Ashok started to doze. He let the papers fall from the hammock. But as he drifted into sleep, it was not an Eastern princess with turmeric skin that filled his dreams. It was the green-eyed girl with tumbling auburn locks, who had sat next to him on the aeroplane; the girl who had asked him for his telephone number.

Where on earth had her seen her before?

* * *

Hannah watched as the Gopal Band set off out of the hotel grounds, a riot of dissonant sounds echoing in its wake. After it on the horse rode the timid young bridegroom in his cream silk wedding suit and red turban, his youngest sister astride behind him, her hands firmly grasped around his waist. A hundred or more male wedding guests accompanied them.

'Now we go,' explained Rasika, and gently took Hannah's arm. Again Hannah fought off a thrill of sensuality. She reached back and tugged the band from her hair, feeling the silky strands caress her shoulders. Rasika steered her to join the back of the parade with the other women. They know their place, reflected Hannah.

The noisy cavalcade crossed the main road, halting the never-ending stream of assorted vehicles. Drivers of lorries and unlit buses hooted and waved. They turned into a side alley. Darkness. Then came a portable generator and light returned: porters with enormous electric lamps lighting the way. The Gopal Band's monster drew to a halt every fifty metres or so: an impromptu street dancing display by the men, which got wilder and louder as the procession neared its destination, fortified, no doubt by occasional swigs of something in a bottle that Hannah glimpsed being furtively handed around. The women, prohibited by dignity and tradition from joining in such cavorting, pointed and laughed at the antics of their menfolk.

Eventually, after many more twists and turns, several more dancing stops and a great deal of excitement, they reached the marriage hall.

Everyone, including the horse, piled into a starry corridor of white party lights, under the gaze of a video camera. It opened up into a meeting hall wildly decorated with streamers and multi-coloured lamps. The bride's guests were already assembled, some standing in groups talking, others seated on long rows of plastic chairs. Some rushed up to the arriving party to take photographs. Bridegroom, pillion passenger and horse posed patiently until the photographers were satisfied. Only then was the horse dismissed, and the bridegroom led onto the stage at the front to be joined by his tiny bride, enshrouded in red silk and weighed down with gold jewellery.

More photographs. Groups taking it in turn to pose alongside them besieged the young couple on the stage. A party of men, then women, the bride's sisters, the bridegroom's aunts. And so it went on. The only common link appeared to be Hannah, who despite protesting good-humouredly was dragged onto the stage again and again to be part of each picture. Without doubt she was receiving far more attention than the bride and bridegroom, who sat in silence, eyes downcast, looking thoroughly miserable. Hannah was angry with herself for leaving her own camera in the hotel safe. An opportunity missed.

She wondered about the pair. Perhaps they've only just met. Poor girl. Will they remember me in years to come, or will they look at their wedding photographs and puzzle about the identity of the white Amazon who appears in each one? They look so traumatised. Arranged marriage, she reflected, a strange, incomprehensible mystery. And yet... her grandmother's words came into her mind, briefly blotting out the uproar of the band. She'd been telling Hannah about her late husband, Grandfather Rosen. His parents had come to England from Romania at the turn of the century. *They met for the first time on their wedding day,* she had said. *It was the usual thing in those little East European shtetls. And even today, marriages are sometimes arranged among the very orthodox.* Once again the Rosen ancestors seemed to be telling her that India was not so remote. Hannah snapped out of her thoughts. The band's playing was wilder than ever now. Repetitive, atonal, uncoordinated, eardrum splitting. But it was also uninhibited, celebratory, exciting and mesmerising.

Time to eat. The guests rushed to the back of the hall where plates of food were distributed. Rasika came for Hannah.

'You will please come upstairs with my family.'

Upstairs peace and quiet hit like an anaesthetic.

Family members introduced themselves while Hannah tucked into the vegetarian feast of rice, *dal*, endless different vegetable dishes, sweet milk desserts, sticky cakes and fruit. Rasika told her that many of the guests who were staying at the Pandava had made the long journey from the groom's family home in Rajasthan. Nobody needed to tell her that these were people of considerable wealth, status and education.

Rasika introduced her to a young man with a large moustache.

'This is my cousin. A psychoanalyst.'

Hannah nodded a greeting. 'I'm surprised you need psychoanalysts here. You Indians seem so well balanced.'

He laughed. 'Well, in fact I'm working in US. I've only come over for the wedding.'

'America? Actually I did a short course in psychotherapy over there a while ago - nothing professional. Just wanted to get clued up because of some work I was doing at the time.'

'And what work might that be?'

'Oh, just studying faces in a rehab centre, that's all. I'm a photographer.' She wasn't about to divulge her insurance scam investigations.

'Interesting. And how d'you like Chennai?'

'I've only just arrived. Had a little walk near the hotel this afternoon, but that's all.'

'I know. I'm in the next room to yours. I was in the garden and saw you return. Did your friend catch up with you?'

'Friend?' Her heart began to pound.

'Slim guy in shades.'

Hannah stared at the man.

'Sorry, what did you say?'

'That guy who came out of your room.'

'I don't know anyone. I'm travelling alone.'

'Oh, that's odd. But sure he came out of your room. You didn't find anything missing?'

'No. Well...just a brochure. But I think that must have been the chambermaid.'

'Then he probably mistook your room for his own.'

'Yes. I'm sure that's what it was. So, where do you live in America?'

Hannah's outer calm belied the rapid contingency plans forming in her mind. *Must stay here as long as possible.*

'California.' said the psychoanalyst. 'Santa Monica. That's part of LA. You know it?'

Hannah nodded. 'Friend of mine lives in LA. Great place. D'you have any famous patients?' she asked, as she made silent decisions. *Don't be impulsive. Don't go back to the Pandava. He may be waiting. Stupid to try and tackle him alone. Let him find me in Bangalore. Everything I need is with me in the neck-pouch - money, credit cards, travellers' cheques, tickets, passport.*

'Sure. Can't divulge their names though, sorry!' He laughed.

'Course not. Wouldn't expect you to. Do you miss India?' *Forget clothes and rucksack. Buy new ones in Bangalore.*

'Well, to be honest with you, I have great life in US. My kids are totally American. It's my home now. But I do miss...'

Hannah tried hard to show interest, but her thoughts were elsewhere. *Go straight to the airport from here and spend what remains of the night there.*

The psychoanalyst was still talking. Should she ask this cousin of Rasika to help her? Could she trust him? The Bannerman experience made her recoil at the thought of confiding in anyone connected with a US Psychiatric Institution. Irrational, but she couldn't help her feelings. Once again, she was on her own. Years of exposure to sensitive situations had made her resourceful. For that she was grateful.

Then another thought struck her. How the blazes do I get to the airport? Celebrations will last till the early hours. Never be able to find a taxi then. Have to leave now. What time is it? Bloody hell! Already past one a.m.

Hannah spotted Rasika across the room.

'Excuse me,' she said to the psychoanalyst. 'I have to speak to someone.'

She sought out Rasika.

'I'm really sorry,' she told her, 'but I've got to go.'

'So soon? The festivities will continue until morning.'

'I know. But there's something I've got to take care of before I leave Chennai tomorrow.'

'I understand.'

'Could you call a taxi for me?'

'A taxi? Oh, that would be difficult. But perhaps we can rouse an auto. I will see what can be done.'

An autorickshaw. Unlikely to want to go all the way to the airport. Still, she reasoned, if I offer him enough...

It was a full half hour before a servant tapped her on the shoulder.

'Madam, car is here.'

So they did manage to find a taxi after all. Hannah looked for Rasika to say goodbye, but the girl was nowhere to be seen among the mass of people.

The car was parked outside the marriage hall in the dark, unlit street. A battered, rusting Ambassador. The front seat next to the driver was taken up by a pile of junk - boxes, papers and a mountain of old rags. The back benchseat was navigable, despite the stuffing that was shed over it. Hannah climbed into it. Next to her was a large box, from which a foul stink seemed to emanate. Hannah could make out a rounded, football-sized shape protruding from the top.

'Chennai Domestic airport, please,' The driver, whose tiny frame was so dwarfed by the tattered seat of the big car that only the top of his roughly-wrapped turban was visible over the seat-back, nodded silently, and set off.

For a while the taxi wound through the narrow alleyways. Sometimes it hardly had room to pass, and she thought it would hit the buildings either side. Finally they reached a wide road. The taxi followed this for several miles. It was still quite busy. Hannah looked out of the window and saw that they were driving along the coast. The sea, its infinite blackness punctuated here and there by the lights of a fishing craft, was to their left. The town centre receded, stores and offices giving way to sporadic outcrops of huts, ill defined against the dark, moonless sky.

Hannah felt uneasy. There had been no sea near the airport when she had arrived in the morning. She spoke to the driver.

'Excuse me. You're sure this is the way to the airport?'

The driver did not respond. Now he turned right, away from the sea, down another small, bumpy, unmade road, into total blackness. There were no habitations here to provide even a glimmer of candlelight.

Hannah screamed at the driver. 'Airport! Take me to the airport! This is not the way! Where are you taking me?'

No response. The car plunged on. What was going on? Was this her enemy from England? Or what if he wasn't working alone? Perhaps this man had been ordered to take her somewhere. She felt for the door. Better to risk broken limbs by leaping into the unknown than to face the terrors that awaited her at the end of this journey. The door handle was broken. She couldn't open it. The stinking box blocked the other door. She tried not to think about what might be inside it. But was it really coming from the box? This was the same, familiar rotten stench, wasn't it?

Her head spun. She struggled to get a hold of herself.

She screamed again. 'Who the hell are you? What d'you want with me?'

No response.

'You're a madman!' she shouted. 'Why have you followed me from England?'

No response.

She stopped thinking and instinct took over. Suddenly her hands were around the driver's scraggy neck, shaking and shaking until, no longer able to control the vehicle, he jammed his foot onto the brake. The car skidded for several seconds before it slammed into a bush and stopped. Only then did Hannah release her grip. The driver lurched forward against the windscreen moaning.

Hannah threw herself over onto the front passenger seat, kicking the driver's body as she did so. She tore open the car door and launched herself into the stifling, moon-deprived void. Sightlessly she staggered back down the road. Every few seconds she stumbled into potholes.

Footsteps behind her. Footsteps gaining on her. Hannah risked a glance back.

Damn it! The man had a torch. Nothing for it but to speed up, despite the hidden obstacles. She ran, faster and faster, but the light slowly crept up on her.

She fell. She lay spread-eagled on the gravel, aware only of the man's approaching footsteps and the need to disappear before she could be picked out by the torchlight. With a mighty effort, she rolled herself sideways off the road. She felt herself drop down into a muddy ditch, and lay still. The stink of her hiding-place filled her nostrils. A slimy, crawling thing slid across her legs. She dared not move, dared not breathe.

She heard her pursuer draw level. He stopped. She buried her face deeply in the mud, and silently cursed her auburn hair, which would betray her like a beacon when the torchlight found her. Even without seeing, she knew that the light was slowly moving across her body. The silence was absolute in the night-muffled air. Then, unbelievably, Hannah heard the footsteps carry on down the road.

Now what? Should she continue to play dead in case he returned? Not a good idea, she decided. Goodness knows what he might do to her if he found her. On the other hand, what if he heard her move? She remembered the car. What were the chances of starting it? Was it worth a try? Her filthy refuge was loathe to give her up, and sucked her down with a sickening plop when she tried to raise herself. After several more attempts, she staggered to her feet. She made her way back up the road as quickly as she dared, until she reached the vehicle. The headlights were still on and the key was in the ignition. Gingerly she climbed into the driver's seat and felt for the controls. She glanced out of the window and her heart nearly stopped. In the distance heading towards her was a tiny beam of light. He was returning.

Come on, baby! She said a silent prayer as she grabbed the gear lever on the steering wheel, and rammed it into neutral. She turned the key. The car sprang into action, only to shudder to a halt within seconds. Now she was sobbing. 'Please!' she begged, as she tried again. This time it took longer to start, but it held. Jamming her foot on the clutch, she forced the protesting vehicle into reverse and shot backwards across the road.

'Come on!' she shouted, pushing the lever into first, and somehow finding the strength to turn the steering wheel. The man was running and had nearly reached the car. Only two more steps and he would be able to grab the door handle and pull her out.

The car was back on the road. She had done it. 'Put your foot down!' she shouted to herself. With a leap, the car shot off. Hannah wept with relief as she negotiated the narrow road. Her joy was short-lived. A jolt as something jumped from the boot of the car onto the roof. A piece of cloth flapping across the windscreen, Part of the man's clothing? The turban? If only she knew how to turn on the windscreen wipers, perhaps the material would get caught up in them and drag him down. She fumbled with one hand on the dashboard as she fought to control the heavy vehicle with the other. She tried every switch. No good. Most of them were defunct.

The cloth disappeared, and the car swerved as if a load had shifted. A movement in the blackness outside the passenger side window: a hand. Putting her foot down hard on the accelerator, she saw in the headlights a large pothole and plunged the car into it. She hung on to the steering wheel to stop herself from crashing up into the roof. From overhead a loud bump and a wail. Surely that had done it? She glanced across.

To her horror the hand was still there, and something worse: a face, upside down and pressed into the windowpane, a face so distorted by the glass that it was impossible to make out the features. The disintegrating turban had wrapped itself around the upper part, obscuring the eyes, but Hannah could feel them boring through the cloth, cold as a mummy's curse. The car careered on. Hannah was aware that the body was gradually working its way down the side of the vehicle, one hand hanging on to the roof, the other groping for the door handle. Ahead a stone wall lined the roadside. Screaming, Hannah veered to the left. Without slowing down, she scraped the side of the car along it, but it seemed that the man was stuck to it like glue. Now his hand was on the door handle. A clunk as it opened. She stretched across and tugged at the inside handgrip with the full force of her body. But she couldn't control the car with one hand. It zigzagged across the road. She let go of the handgrip. The door opened wider. She slammed her foot on the brake. Still the man hung on. Once more she accelerated. Now the door was fully open and the man was trying to get a foothold inside the car. Ahead Hannah could make out some bushes protruding into the road. She steered at them. The strong, sharp branches squealed as they cut into the vehicle's side and pressed against the door, forcing it to close. A yelp of pain as it slammed onto the man's leg and the branches cut into the hand that was trying to resist it.

Then the thud of a body falling onto the ground.

She travelled on for another mile before slowing down to lean across and slam the passenger door shut.

CHAPTER 3

Although it was nearly lunchtime when Ashok and his parents boarded the Tipu Express from Mysore to Bangalore, none of them was hungry. Sweet and savoury offerings of every description had been pressed upon them all morning at the girl's house. Thus they waved away the vendors who plied their wares along the corridor of their compartment, manoeuvring their trays of carefully stacked lentil and rice-flour snacks - crispy, fried *vadas* and soft round white *idlis* - through the closely packed standing passengers. The usual crowds on the train had been boosted even more by a midday rush, and it had taken a while to argue and cajole themselves into seats that had originally been taken up by a contingent of bundles and battered brown boxes.

Neither did they give a moment's thought to any of the plastic scissors, yo-yos, balls, knives, sari lengths, pan scrubbers, wicks for oil lamps, ties, socks, hair slides, scarves, shawls and other objects on offer during the course of the journey. The old blind man who entertained the carriage with his sacred songs was favoured with a few paise. This aside, Srinivasa and Ashok were too engrossed in serious matters to take much notice of the enterprising cavalcade. Girija watched in silence, weighing up their conversation as if she were waiting for the right moment to intercede.

'I don't know, *Bapa*. I had so little chance to talk to her. She seemed nice enough, but so shy.'

'Well, what are you expecting? That girl does not know you. How else should a well-brought up daughter be behaving? Give time. This is, after all, first meeting only.'

'I know. And, yes, I agree, family is good. The girl has a good education...'

'A degree in Chemistry from Mysore University, no less. And she is working towards Masters.'

'I know. I suppose she is really quite pretty, not that I mind too much about such things...'

'A lovely girl. You will not find one more beautiful. I am thinking she is very much like your mother at her age.'

Girija waved her hand. 'Oh, what nonsense, such foolish talk.' But her eyes were smiling.

Ashok ignored her interjection and addressed his father.

'But to me looks are of minor importance. What are we having in common is what I am asking myself?'

'In common? That will come with time only. Once there are children. Believe me, I am telling only what is true.'

'I believe you, *Bapa*. But... somehow something is not right. She is a very serious girl. Nothing wrong with that, of course. Only I am wondering where is her sense of humour. There was no laughter in that house, I think.'

Srinivasa spluttered in disbelief.

'Sense of humour? Laughter? What is it you are wanting? A *funny* girl? A wife who is making you *laugh*? *A brazen hussy?* I think you are becoming too much an Englishman, Ashok. This is not Indian way. A wife should be modest...'

'That's not what I mean, *Bapa*. I should like a wife to be cheerful and smiling. This girl is looking miserable all the time. Perhaps it is thought of being married to me that makes her look like that.'

This was too much for Girija, who rounded on her son angrily.

'Now you are becoming ridiculous. My son, my handsome English doctor son is a great catch for any girl.'

Srinivasa added, 'Certainly the mother is very keen. That is plain for all to observe.'

'Perhaps I should forget the girl and set my sights on the mother. A good-looking woman, I thought.'

Srinivasa snorted. 'What are we to do with you? This is now third girl you have rejected since homecoming. Soon we will run out of suitable young ladies.'

'Now did I say that I am rejecting this one? I am saying only that I need more time, and she also. Certainly this one is a vast improvement on that first one, who was clearly a fortune hunter, and second also, who was very silly.'

Srinivasa shook his head and sighed.

'For sure you have picked up many strange ideas in England.'

Ashok sat back and closed his eyes. There was a hint of a smile on his lips. Keep the parents guessing for a bit longer, he told himself. After all, this isn't a decision that can be finalised after one meeting. But the truth was, he liked the girl. Janaki. He repeated the name in his mind. A nice name. A sweet, gentle young woman. True, she was shy. He'd hardly spoken to her. But perhaps that was his fault. He didn't want to be too forward at the first meeting. After all, this wasn't England. He'd been away from home for so long that he was no longer sure of the exact etiquette when it came to such matters, so he'd erred on the side of caution. Somehow though, despite this, and the gravity of her expression, he felt that there was depth to her character, and an individuality that he found appealing. Yes, he mused. One or two more meetings to be sure. But I think this is the one for me.

The train rattled out of Mysore. It passed the remains of the fifteenth century fortress, a tantalising reminder of a time when the great Vijayanagar dynasty ruled the land, followed by the rajas of Mysore, and the great Muslim leaders, Hyder Ali and his son Tipu Sultan, who were finally defeated by the British in the eighteenth century.

Then they were in open countryside, passing scenes which spoke of hard lives despite the veneer of rural tranquillity; men ankle-deep in water, ploughing the paddy fields with a couple of weary oxen; women in bright cotton saris pitilessly beating the laundry against a rock on the bank of a dirty lake; a painted truck backed into the lake for cleaning, a small girl washing and scrubbing her teeth in the same lake. They passed coconut plantations, mango groves and fields of mulberry bushes, grazing buffalo and herders tending their mixed flocks of sheep and goats, villages of mud-walled huts, nestling by the side of the line as though anxious to be within touching distance of this contact with the wider world. Sometimes they sped over level crossings where lorries, bullock-carts, cars and bicycles waited patiently for them to pass. Small boys waved at the train as it lumbered past them. At times the country became less cultivated, wide-open boulder-strewn spaces replacing the farmland. Ashok felt at peace. Yes, this was his land, the land to which he and Janaki belonged. They were both hewn from the same eternal granite. No need for prolonged introductions. They would understand each other.

At last, some two and a half hours after leaving Mysore, the train trundled into Bangalore, where it emptied its chaotic load of human cargo and assorted baggage onto the platform.

Ashok and his parents commandeered an autorickshaw and the three of them squeezed with some difficulty into the bench seat behind the driver. They passed out of the busy town centre and headed north towards the part of the city where green and leafy campuses of science institutions, hospitals and university departments flourish, untainted by the turmoil and poisonous effluence of the city. Life had a never-ending feel of normality here. Ashok felt as if he had never left. Superficially little had changed over the years. The corner cricket pitch was still continually in use by every aspiring Azharuddin - and that meant practically every boy around. A donkey family meandered along Margosa Road, shepherding tiny black gangly-legged foals with seeming nonchalance through the traffic, stopping only to munch the leaves spilled from a passing street vendor's cauliflower cart.

The autorickshaw stopped at last outside the family home. Ashok untangled himself from the vehicle and entered the house with his parents.

His sister came to meet them. Her face wore a puzzled expression.

'Somebody was ringing for you, Ashok. An English person. I think she said her name is Hannah...Rosen? She was telling that she is at Chamundi Hotel and please to ring there upon your return. I have written room number. Who is this person, Ashok? A friend from UK perhaps?'

Ashok had to think for a moment before he associated the name with the green-eyed girl.

'No, she is not a friend. I was sitting next to her on the plane. She seemed a little lost, so I gave our number. I did not expect her to turn up, however.'

His voice conveyed the awkwardness that he felt.

'No matter. She is most welcome. You must ask her to come here.'

Srinivasa's reaction surprised Ashok. Then he realised he had lost something during his years in England. A natural and unquestioning openness and hospitality. He had lost the generosity of innocence.

* * *

By mid-morning Hannah was installed in her room at the sprawling Chamundi Hotel just off Kumara Krupa, close to the centre of Bangalore. Remembering the missing brochure with her destination written on it, she had wondered whether to change her hotel. But what was the point? She wanted the man to find her, didn't she? So let him come. He'd lost the element of surprise. With help she would be able to deal with him.

She had been afraid that her dishevelled appearance and lack of baggage might bar her from entry. However her simple explanation that she had lost her luggage and was going to restock in Bangalore was accepted with a bored shrug. The hotel was comfortable enough, though without character and slightly shabby; a mediocre Indian chain establishment, with five star aspirations and two star accomplishment.

She had hesitated briefly before picking up the telephone and dialling Ashok's number. She had a feeling that her call would not be altogether welcome. This feeling was supported by the somewhat bemused tone of the voice of the woman who answered, presumably Ashok's mother, or a sister. She seemed wary and vague, but she agreed to pass on Hannah's number.

Hannah had stripped out of her filthy clothes, including the one dress that remained in her possession. Taking a chance that her garments would soon dry in the warmth of the morning, she washed the lot in the washbasin in her bathroom, scrubbing them with the anonymous bar of hotel soap that had been provided. She turned off the air conditioning and spread out her washing as near to the window as possible. Fingers crossed, she thought, wondering if her hasty laundering activity had been rather foolish. Yes, it was warm in Bangalore, but you couldn't exactly call it hot. Not compared to Chennai, where there seemed to be no escape from the suffocating blanket of sticky, steamy heat.

Chennai. Had that been only yesterday? During the flight to Bangalore she had been too exhausted, too numbed to reflect on what had happened. Now in the relative safety of her hotel room, she lay down on her bed, drew a blanket over herself and soon felt her eyes closing. In her half-sleep, memories of the previous night drifted into her mind. Despite the horror of it at the time, she could not avoid a tiny gloat of triumph. Drawing on her inner strength and ability to think quickly she had outwitted and outmanoeuvred her pursuer.

After she had appropriated the taxi, she had decided to drive on until she could abandon it in safety. Thankfully, dawn had begun to break into the night sky. Blackness gave way to grey. The road ahead seemed friendlier. After driving on for twenty minutes or so, a tarmac road crossed the track. To her right she could see signs of a village. She turned onto the road and headed towards it. She decided against waking the still slumbering inhabitants. How could she possibly have explained away the appearance in their village of a battered taxi driven by an English woman? It was doubtful in any case whether anyone would have spoken English. She drove on. The village extended much further than she had expected. It seemed to have no end. Soon she saw that people were beginning to get up and begin their morning ablutions. The dwellings became more numerous. There were stores and market stalls. The road was leading her back into Chennai.

She knew she would have to abandon the taxi fairly soon, while she could still do so without attracting attention. Suddenly she saw a neon sign ahead. 'Madras Plaza Hotel' - a grandiose name for a very modest establishment. It would do.

She left the car by the side of the road. As she gave it a last glance, she shuddered as she noticed the sunglasses lying on the dashboard. She was tempted to pull them out and sink them in the nearest puddle. But she left them. Escape was a more pressing concern.

Her dress stank. Hastily she tried to brush off some of the damp mud. She found her phial of *Fleurs de Provence* buried in the bottom of her neck-pouch, and hurriedly sprayed her wrists. Then she set off to the hotel and turned onto its forecourt. A gaggle of little autorickshaws was waiting there for emerging clients, gathered like flies on a cowpat, many of the drivers still sleeping on the seats. One of the autorickshaws pulled out from the throng and headed towards her. It circled round and hovered beside her. The driver did not speak. He merely looked at her hopefully.

'Airport?' she asked, doubtfully.

He hesitated, then wobbled his head from side to side. Ah, thought Hannah, remembering the fruit vendor who had sold her the bananas. This must mean yes.

As the auto roared off, Hannah thought about the Pandava and ludicrously, under the circumstances, was gripped with guilt because she was fleeing without paying her bill. Then she remembered that she had left her camera, which was worth a good deal more than a day's lodgings, in the hotel safe.

*   *   *

Hannah sat up and looked at her watch. Three hours had passed. She'd dropped off to sleep, hardly surprising, as she'd been up all night. Now she felt wide-awake, buoyed up by her escape, evidence that she still had some fight left in her. She smiled. You've not lost it, gal, she told herself, but a little help wouldn't go amiss.

She passed the time reading up on Bangalore in her guidebook. She discovered that the capital of the state of Karnataka was the fastest-growing city in India, a world centre for the computer software industry. The city was home to some of the greatest seats of education and learning in the whole of the sub-continent, its scientific institutions counting as among the best in the world. The language spoken was mainly the local Kannada, but Tamil was widely understood due to the presence of a large minority from the neighbouring state of Tamil Nadu. The geographical features of Karnataka ranged from thriving cities to mountainous wilderness, from ancient temples to tiger reserves, from the jungle to the sea.

By late afternoon, Hannah's clothes were dry enough to wear.

At half past four the telephone rang.

'Hannah? Oh, hallo, it's Ashok Rao here. Sorry I was out when you phoned.'

'Ashok! What a relief.' The words slipped out, before embarrassment caught up with them. 'I mean... well, sorry, hope I'm not being a nuisance...'

'Is something wrong?'

'Look, I'm in a spot of bother. Are you free?'

'Yes, of course. How about if I pick you up at the hotel at around seven, and we get something to eat.'

'Great, but you couldn't make it earlier, could you? On top of everything else, I've lost my luggage - tell you about it later. Is there somewhere I can do some clothes shopping?'

'Yes, sure. I'll be round in half hour and take you to Commercial Street.'

He arrived on the dot, and knocked gently at her door.

'Hallo, it's me, Ashok.' His voice sent an unexpected shiver of pleasure down Hannah's spine.

She opened the door. He looked down at her, for he was some four inches taller than she was, his dark eyes sincere, a lock of black hair straying across his forehead, a half-smile forming on his lips. Gosh, thought Hannah, as she felt her heartbeat quicken. Gosh.

'*Namaskara,*' he said, breaking a moment's awkwardness. 'Nice to see you again.'

'And you. Thanks for coming.'

'Here - I've brought you this. Evenings get a bit chilly.'

Hannah unfolded a huge, light woollen shawl. It was double-sided, green on one side and maroon on the reverse. The weaving was intricate and beautiful. She wrapped herself inside it. It covered her completely and she twirled around, laughing.

'It's enchanted. I feel as if I'm floating in gossamer.' Behave, she warned herself. Of course it's simply the shawl that's making me feel light-headed.

'It's Kashmiri,' said Ashok, adding, 'Suits you.'

'Thank you. It's very kind of you.'

'No problem.' After a moment's pause, he continued. 'You said something was wrong.'

'Yes.' On the flight to India Hannah had felt an inexplicable accord with this man. Now as they stood awkwardly in the doorway of her hotel room the feeling had already been rekindled. But she had learned to be cautious. She didn't feel inclined to pour out her heart. Not yet.

'Can I tell you about it later? Over a meal?'

Outside the hotel they commandeered one of the waiting autorickshaws. Hannah scrambled in awkwardly and slid across the seat to make room for Ashok, who, despite having to bend almost double, managed the manoeuvre with a grace that had eluded her.

'Not designed for well-fed foreigners like us!' he commented, 'Whoops… sorry… didn't mean to imply...'

'Don't worry. Been feeling like Dumbo's mother ever since I got off the plane.'

'Dumbo's mother? Dumbo, maybe, but his mother? That's taking things a bit far.'

'Gee, thanks a bunch. You've made me feel a lot better.'

'Well, you don't deserve to. Poking fun at elephants.'

'Sorry. Hope there weren't any listening, though I suspect that at least one was.'

Her eyes gestured to the little shrine, festooned with tinsel and wilted marigolds, sitting on the rickshaw's dashboard. Ashok smiled.

'Aha, you can be quite sure Ganesh is listening. But he's a god: son of Shiva, with head of elephant, not quite the same thing.'

'So how come you regard yourself as a foreigner? Thrown off the shackles of your native soil?'

'No, not at all. I suppose it's a trick being played on my mind. It seems as if, when I'm in England, the Indian part of me yearns to be set free, but back here the Englishman in me sometimes slips out.'

The rickshaw pulled up at the end of a narrow alleyway, crowded with shoppers.

'Come on. Down there is Commercial Street. Great place for clothes.'

Ashok steered her through the crowds on the bazaar-like alley, and out onto Commercial Street where she was plunged into a world of noise and colour and light. Shops and state emporia fell higgledy-piggledy over one another, bulging with advertisements and neon lights, crowded and cluttered with every kind of item imaginable on display; shops selling bags and suitcases, saris and *shalwar kameez*, cheap jewellery; heavily-fortified gold shops with entry-phones and guards; fruit sellers and food stalls exuding mouth-watering aromas, that drew Hannah's attention to the length of time since her last meal.

They made their way slowly up the street, their progress hampered by beggar children and half-dissolved lepers tugging at their clothing, and by the sheer volume of people flowing past them. A man tried to sell them an umbrella that you wore on your head.

'How about trying out some local fashions?' Ashok said, 'Much cheaper than trying to buy European clothes here. Better too.'

'Brilliant! I'd love to...' She was about to add "go native," and then stopped herself.

Two hours later, Hannah, clutching her purchases, found herself being ushered by Ashok up four flights of hotel stairs to a top floor restaurant.

'Power cut - no lift,' he said, 'but I think you'll find the climb worthwhile.'

Before they even reached the fourth floor, the aroma of freshly pounded spices wafted tantalisingly down from the restaurant to welcome them.

A table by the stairwell; *roti*-bakers at work across the room; the rhythmic slap, slap, slap of a score of hands beating out the dough into thin circles; the fires from many ovens playing on the bakers' faces and rekindling them into works of art.

'You should have brought your camera,' said Ashok, 'plenty of faces among that lot for your next book.'

Hannah remembered telling him on the plane. Professional photographer. Going to India to take photos for a coffee-table book. Now she'd even lost the camera. How could she ask this man to help her and yet keep half the truth from him? But how could she level with him until she was sure about him? And if he turned out to be *that* Ashok Rao, wouldn't it be harder, not simpler to come clean? Take it easy, she told herself. Get to know him. At least test the water before you throw yourself in.

The food arrived. Little measures of different vegetable mixtures and chutneys carefully ladled onto their banana-leaf plates. Freshly baked *rotis* and bowls of rice.

'Didn't realise how hungry I was.'

'Enjoy. We call this *baingan bharta*. It's from the north - a favourite of mine.'

Hannah scooped a little of the mixture onto a corner of her *roti* and tasted it. Her eyes opened wide. 'But this is incredible. This is exactly what my grandmother used to make. It was a favourite of mine too.'

'Your grandmother made *baingan bharta*?'

'Yes - well, she didn't call it that. I think she just called it mashed eggplant. But the ingredients must have been very similar...'

'...aubergines, tomatoes...'

'...chillis, onion -I think the onions were raw, but that's the only difference.'

'Amazing.'

'Yes, amazing. My grandfather came from Romania - he taught Grandma how to make it.'

'Perhaps not so amazing then. They say the Romanies came from India and some travelled west via Romania. Perhaps you have Romany blood.'

'Maybe I have Indian ancestors.'

By now any residual formality had been swept aside. Words tumbled between them like acrobats.

Hannah took more food from her banana-leaf plate, and transferred it to her mouth via the *roti*, using her fingers as deftly as if she had been eating this way all her life.

'That's pretty good.' replied Ashok. 'Yes, you must have been an Indian in another life. Incidentally - that *chudidar* looks great on you.' He nodded at her simple silver-grey outfit, long dress over loose, tapered leggings, gathered round the ankles, matching chiffon *dupatta* slung back across her shoulders. 'You wear it well. A true Maharani.'

'That's made my day.' Her smile faded. 'Perhaps it'll make me less conspicuous.'

'So...what's it all about?'

'It's a long story.'

'We're not in a hurry, are we?'

Hannah took a deep breath and tucked a stray strand of hair behind her ear. 'OK then.' She looked at him steadily for a moment before continuing. 'Someone's following me.'

'Following you? What - an Indian?'

'No. It started a long time before I came here.'

'When?'

'Just over a year ago. Someone began to follow me home from the Red Fox - my local pub. I ran the local photographic society. We met in a room above the pub on Saturday nights.'

Hannah kept the details brief; a will-o'-the-wisp in the hedge; a shadow that lurked beneath her window at night.

'So - who?'

'If I knew that I wouldn't be here. Tried everything; stayed awake, kept watch. Once I managed a glimpse of his back. He was in the garden one night. I went after him. But he was off like a shot. Seemed puny,' she laughed shortly, 'but still managed to outsmart me.'

Ashok was staring at her.

'What?' she said sharply.

'Whatever I say, you'll tell me I'm being sexist, so I'll keep quiet.'

'I knew it. You're just like the rest of them. Next you'll be blaming me for leading him on.'

'I didn't say that. It's just a little - unusual. But carry on telling.'

She threw him a dubious glance but his obvious concern dissipated her anger. 'First I didn't know if I was going mad, or whether it really was happening to me. The surer I became it wasn't just in my head, the less the police believed me.'

'So you decided to get away?'

'I'd been planning a photographic trip to India for years. So I came.'

'But whoever it is has followed you here?'

'Yes. Which is why I called you. So before you have any more digs at me, even I know when I'm out of my depth. After events in Hyderabad and Madras...'

'What events? What's happened?'

'The thing is, it will all sound so silly. Overactive imagination, hysteria even. But it's not. You'll have to take my word for it.'

'I'll believe you. Honestly. I can tell a sane person when I see one.'

For the first time since the whole business had begun, Hannah found she could talk freely. All inhibitions seemed to evaporate in the heat from the *roti* fires, and in the empathy that was written in Ashok's eyes. Something Maighréad had written in one of her crazy letters flashed into Hannah's mind.

I trust him to the end of the earth. He's the gentlest man I've ever known. But such inner strength. He has built a house of brick around my frailty. The next bit. *It's your house too, Hannah.* Yes, she thought. There is no doubt. It is him. How prophetic Maighréad's words had turned out to be.

She told him about the events in Hyderabad and Madras - the *burkha*-clad figure who had rushed at her with a knife in the Qutab Shahi Tombs; Willi's suspicious disappearance and subsequent unconvincing note; the intruder in her room at the Pandava in Madras; the ghoulish taxi ride in the dark, and her escape from the driver.

'What I don't understand,' Ashok commented, 'is why? Why is this person following you? Haven't you any idea?'

'Not really. For a long time I thought he was just trying to frighten me, God knows why. Began to think the police were right. It was all in my mind. The rest started to make sense then.'

'There's something you haven't told, isn't there?'

'How d'you know?'

'Just a feeling. How you looked when we first met on the plane. Haunted. A woman who goes out alone on a manhunt at night doesn't scare easily. There must have been something else to push you into packing up and getting out.'

'I wasn't pushed. I came to take photographs.'

'Ah, yes. Of course you did.' He inclined his head. 'So - do you want to tell me?'

Tell him? Doubts flooded back, jolting her mood of release like heavy raindrops. What the hell was she thinking of? Ashok was a stranger, after all. And a man. She was entrusting intimate details of her life to someone she scarcely knew. Turning herself into a victim. Making herself vulnerable. Dropping her guard.

'I don't know. Don't know anything any more.' she heard herself mutter.

Ashok's hand was on her arm, and she felt her uneasiness subside.

'Come on,' he said. 'Let's get out of here and find somewhere quiet.'

* * *

When Duncan came home, after his hastily arranged two-day trip to New York, the Guildford streetlamps were already lit at three in the afternoon. They diffused their sodium light, giving the smart, upmarket terrace of town houses a soft, almost Dickensian glow in the icy fog of December twilight. The scene hinted at warmth and of neat and ordered lives. Duncan, drained and exhausted despite Concorde, dragged his feet up the steps through the small, front courtyard to the door. He turned the key in the lock, and let himself in.

'Duncan!' Felicity almost ran as she came to the door to greet him.

She threw her arms around his neck. 'Why didn't you phone? Could have picked you up at the airport. You look exhausted. Here, let me take your bag. Sit yourself down. I'll get you a drink. Missed you so much.'

Duncan pushed her away impatiently. His mind was flooded with confused feelings. He had been looking forward to coming home. He'd had plenty of time to think things through on the flight from New York. Thinking about Felicity had taken his mind off Hannah, and the mystery of Bannerman's disappearance. At least he'd thought it was a mystery. As soon as Hal had told him, the obvious connection had leapt out at him. Bannerman... Hannah's stalker. Perhaps he'd misjudged her. At any rate, he had to go to New York to discuss the whole matter with Hal. Now it was time to spill the beans. Waste of time, as it turned out. Hal couldn't tell him anything new, and he scoffed at the idea that Bannerman had spent the past year stalking Hannah.

'Not his style,' Hal said. 'In any case, he hasn't been gone for more than a couple of months.'

'Well he could be paying someone. Or popping back to the States every now and then to allay suspicion.'

Hal simply looked at him and shook his head slowly in amused disbelief.

Duncan had returned to Guildford with his theory dented by Hal Brodsky, but not sufficiently for Duncan himself to discard it. He'd mulled it over for a while on the flight, and then turned his attention to Felicity. She'd been so different for the first few months after she'd moved in with him. It had all happened very quickly. He had finally had to accept that there was no hope of Hannah rekindling their affair. It had hit him hard. So he'd needed a woman. Felicity, a temp at the office, was sexy, fun and therapeutic. As the months went by their relationship seemed to undergo a subtle change. Duncan began to see beyond Felicity's undoubted accomplishments in the bedroom. He realised that he enjoyed having her around, and missed her when she went away to visit her sick brother Terry in Manchester every couple of weeks. At least, that's where she said she went. At first he'd had no earthly reason to doubt her. But after a while the sick brother excuse began to sound hollow. He tried to probe deeper and it led to bitter arguments. She wept, she threatened to leave, she berated him for his lack of trust. And as if to prove her integrity, she suddenly became over-solicitous to the point of driving him crazy. She'd have tied his shoelaces for him if he'd let her.

He mulled it over and over on the flight, and finally convinced himself that he was overreacting. Seeing problems where there weren't any. Things would be fine when he got home, he told himself.

But no, things weren't fine, were they? Here she was again, being over effusive, desperate to please. What other conclusion could there be? Felicity was having an affair.

*   *   *

They walked for some time in silence, down a straight, wide, tree-lined road in the warm Bangalore night. There was little let up in the traffic, but the pavements were wide, giving some illusion of space and solitude. A high granite wall ran alongside the uneven granite paving stones, and beyond were more trees. The lights from the traffic did not reach the footpath and only the merest suggestion of moonlight relieved the darkness. Ashok shone a small torch onto the path ahead, and held Hannah's elbow lightly.

He waited for her to continue her story, feeling inadequate because she still seemed reluctant to talk. He suddenly thought of Maighréad, one day soon after they had met, when she was still in the hospital. *You've done so much*, she'd said, *simply by listening to me. I feel I can tell you everything.*

Now he willed Hannah to feel as safe and free with him as Maighréad had felt.

'Do you want to go on with your story?'

Hesitantly, her voice spoke to him from the darkness.

'It's still not easy to talk about. Laughable really. I spend my life dealing with other people's traumas and I can't handle my own.'

'What do you mean? I thought you were a photographer only.'

'Oh. Yes. I am. I'm talking about friends.'

They were walking more slowly now. Just enough to keep moving, without seeming to go anywhere.

Hannah pointed ahead into the torchlight. 'Has the wall come down just ahead? Let's sit down on that rock for a while.'

Ashok focused the beam on the disintegrating section of wall. A huge slab of granite had dislodged itself from the top, and now masqueraded as a perfect bench.

For a moment they sat silently, side by side, their faces no more than silhouettes in the darkness, light from the torch playing absently at Ashok's feet.

Flatly, as if reporting something that had happened to someone else, Hannah articulated her fractured memories.

*   *   *

It was a particularly cold, rainy November. Even the cosseted gardens in the tiny Surrey village of Burfold were beginning to turn to mud. Only Hannah's cottage garden seemed impervious to the weather. It was a wilderness garden, at least that was how Hannah described it. Minimum interference, partly through lack of time, but mainly because she liked it that way. During the summer she kept the grass down with the old motor mower in the shed. Apart from that she allowed the bushes and trees to prosper unmolested.

That night she had gone to bed at ten o'clock, tired after a book-signing trip to Liverpool. Duncan had left a thick file labelled 'South Africa' and a note suggesting it as a subject for the photographic mission they'd discussed. He said he'd call in again later to see how the trip had gone. Not tonight, please, she willed. Duncan had a habit of turning up after midnight on some feeble pretext that involved an element of official business. Hannah knew the real reason. He was so transparent. Felicity. Another row, renewed doubts, exasperation, or simply the need to get away from her. And the need to run back to Hannah. Granted, Hannah was normally still awake, but tonight company was the last thing she wanted. So she'd locked up, switched off the downstairs lights and taken the file to her bedroom.

Propped up in bed she looked through the file for some twenty minutes. Duncan's proposal was undeniably interesting. A pictorial study of South Africa during the first two years after Mandela's release. But Hannah too had been thinking about ideas for the book. One place kept pushing itself to the front of her mind. India. For the last five years the idea of it had haunted her, and when Duncan had suggested the book it had all seemed to fall into place. She hadn't mentioned it to him yet. He would know exactly why she felt such compulsion to go there. She wasn't sure how he'd react. But she knew she couldn't let this opportunity pass her by. She needed closure.

Exhaustion defeated her attention span. She set aside the file and switched out the light. As she lay awake in the darkness her mind turned to the stalker. Dare she hope that the nightmare was over? She hadn't seen him for a couple of weeks. Maybe the cold had beaten him; maybe he'd grown tired of her resilience and gone to pester someone else. Or maybe, she hated to admit it, maybe he had been a figment of her imagination after all. Finally she fell into a fitful sleep.

Less than an hour later she was awake again. The wind was howling. The old apple tree scraped at her window. From the far side of the garden came a rhythmic banging. Hannah knew at once what had happened. The shed door had blown open. It would drive her mad all night if she left it. She cursed and scrambled out of bed. Pulling aside the curtain of her bedroom window she stared out into bitter blackness.

She only hesitated for an instant. The idea that someone might be lurking out there in the freezing night was absurd. She slipped on trainers and a coat, and grabbed a torch.

She let herself out of the front door, turning on the outside light. The cottage was more or less in the middle of her plot, slightly more garden at the front than at the rear, where it backed onto a paddock. The shed was at the far side of what would have been the front garden had there been a dividing line between front and back. Hannah's garden, however, simply encircled the house as one entity. She loved the feeling of space around her.

The porch illuminated part of the lawn to the side of the house, but the back part and the bushes beyond were in darkness. She slithered across the grass and scrambled through the shrubs to the shed. Her fingers were freezing and it took a few moments to secure the lock. She turned and started to make her way back to the house. She hadn't gone more than a metre or so when she heard something ahead of her in the shrubbery. A cough maybe? A suppressed sneeze? She shone her light at the sound but all she could make out was a close network of twigs and branches, white and luminescent in the torch beam. If anything was there it was well hidden.

The only way back to the house was through the bushes. Hannah held her breath for what seemed an eternity. It was still blowing a pretty fierce gale. Finally she convinced herself that the sound she had heard was only the wind scraping the trees against the house. She relaxed and started to push her way back.

She stepped out of the bushes onto the lawn. Later on she would remember very little of the next few minutes. He was simply there in front of her, outlined against the house light. A small, shadowy figure in a black mask. She felt herself slipping to the ground, slowly, as if through water. Her head crashed down hard on a sharp stone. The weight of a body on top of her; a stench, a horrible, rotting odour; bones sticking into her chest, her stomach, her shoulders.

She was too stunned to react. Her head was split open, though she didn't know it. She veered in and out of consciousness, her sight blurred. But the man's words cut through her delirium. They would stay with her forever. 'I'm gonna give it you, bitch,' he snarled. 'You see if I don't.'

She tried to fight. She felt herself hitting, pushing, biting, but somehow her limbs remained inert. Her mind was refusing to surrender but her body had been taken over. He was forcing her mouth open, invading her throat. His breath stank. Saliva ran down her face, slimy as a slavering bloodhound.

The sound of car wheels on gravel. Someone was driving up the lane.

Next minute Duncan was standing over her. The man had disappeared.

'Hey, girl,' he said. 'What the hell's happened to you?'

He helped her up. He must have taken her back to the cottage, though she couldn't recall this later on. One moment she was flat out on the grass, and he was staring down at her. Next she was lying on her living room couch, screaming at Duncan to call the police.

Duncan called an ambulance.

'I don't need an ambulance,' she murmured. 'Police - call the police.' Then she lost consciousness.

When she woke up she was in a hospital bed. Her head throbbed and she learnt from a nurse that it was morning. She had been concussed and had needed stitches but was otherwise unhurt. They were keeping her in for observation.

'I need a phone,' she told the nurse.

Some two hours after Hannah had called the police station, a constable arrived. Duncan had walked in ten minutes earlier, his arms full of flowers.

The policeman made sympathetic noises and took down the details. Then he wanted her to repeat it all again. Hannah had had enough. She felt her eyes closing. The constable turned to Duncan.

'Can you describe what happened, Sir?'

'I've no idea. I got out of the car and found her lying in the grass.'

'You didn't see anyone else?'

'No.'

'Wouldn't your headlights have picked out any intruder?'

'I would have imagined so, yes.'

They thought Hannah was asleep. In fact she heard every word. *No*, she wanted to scream, *the attack was at the back of the lawn, near the bushes. The headlights were on the drive. He couldn't have seen anything.* But Hannah's tongue felt as if it were made of lead. She couldn't even protest.

The policeman continued. 'Any chance that she could have dreamt it up? Or could she have been sleepwalking and slipped on the wet grass?'

'I'm sure that's the case. That's why I didn't ring you last night.'

'I've got to tell you, Sir, we've been called out to the cottage a number of times in the past few months because she thinks she's seen something or heard something. Never a shred of evidence. You couldn't throw any light on it, could you?'

Duncan was quiet for a moment.

'Well,' he said finally, 'she did have psychotherapy in America, last year. It surprised me. And yes, she seems more vulnerable lately. Something about her has changed.'

Hannah knew at that moment what loneliness felt like.

*　　*　　*

Ashok was appalled but at the same time mesmerised by Hannah's story. For a few moments they sat in silence in the darkness.

Hannah's courage was indisputable but her action that night was completely incomprehensible to Ashok. He simply could not understand what would drive a young woman out into an isolated garden in the middle of the night, knowing that there might be something unpleasant out there. He wanted to ask her but he held back suspecting that the question would not be well received.

Hannah broke the silence. 'So there you have it. Poor, sad Hannah, dotty as an overripe banana - well, that's what most people think anyway. I suppose you agree with them, now you've heard it.'

'You should have more faith in me. I told you from start I believed you.' He hated himself for the lie. Half-lie. Part of him did believe her. The intuitive part. The cognitive part was filled with doubts.

'Sure,' she said and gave a sharp little laugh. 'Sure.'

Ashok ignored the sarcasm. 'No idea who the fellow might be?'

'None. When I'd seen the man that time before in the garden, remember, I'd only seen the back view - he wouldn't face me - he didn't want me to be able to identify him.'

'Or recognise him,' Ashok said in as impassive a voice as he could muster, 'if it was someone you knew.'

'Well, yes, that's also a possibility. Anyway, this time he'd clearly planned the shed door thing to get me out of the house and into the bushes. He'd been hatching this scheme over the year. Watching me and testing me, to see how I reacted; but always making sure I didn't see him until the police had written me off, and until he was pretty sure I'd come out to close the shed door.'

'Where on earth did Duncan get that psychotherapy story from?'

'It was true in a manner of speaking. I spent a year in America and did a course. Part of the course involved undergoing the therapy myself.'

'That's quite standard procedure.'

'Try telling a copper that. I did, next day. He came back and asked me why I'd been to see a shrink. Just patronised me - little smiles, yes dear and all that.'

Hell, thought Ashok, digesting this latest information. What if she really is a basket case? Perhaps her friend Duncan was right and she has made the whole thing up? After all, I hardly know her. How do I know what she's like?

'Can I ask you something?' he said.

'Of course.'

'Why did you go out alone again in the middle of the night?'

'It wasn't that late. The moon was shining. Wouldn't you have done the same?'

'I wouldn't have gone out the first time, if you want the truth. Not after what you told me. And I'm a...'

'A man, you were going to say. What difference should that make? I'm as tough as you are.'

'I don't doubt that for one moment. But there are times when self-preservation has to come before principles.'

'OK. So it was stupid of me. But no way was I going to be made a prisoner in my own home. Can you understand that?'

'Yes, of course.' No, of course not, he thought.

Hannah reached out and placed a hand on Ashok's. 'It's just so great to have someone to talk to. Being here, tonight, being with you, I mean, it's like for the first time in a year, someone believes me.'

An echo from the past. 'That's what I'm here for,' he said.

Hannah stiffened and drew back her hand, as if reining in her reprieve.

'He's out there somewhere,' she said, 'I know he is. No point in me lapsing into a false sense of security.'

'Not false, Hannah. As long as you're a guest in my city, I won't let you come to any harm.'

Her voice hardened. 'I'm going to get him, you know. But I'll need your help.'

'I'm right beside you.'

Ashok was grateful for the darkness that kept his face hidden. At that moment he knew that it was he, not Hannah, who wore the haunted look. Hannah had unwittingly drawn him into her nightmare, and trapped him there. He was with her in the cottage garden, watching helplessly, unable to move, unable to change the course of events. Once more he thought about Maighréad. It hadn't been enough to be a good listener. She'd seen his silence as strength, but in the end he'd failed to protect her, he'd failed to put things right. He couldn't let that happen again.

Now he made a silent vow. Regardless of whether Hannah's story was real or imagined, he would help her; not only listen to her, but also help her to bring this matter to a close. Then finally, the ghost of Maighréad could be laid to rest.

CHAPTER 4

During the autorickshaw drive back to the Chamundi Ashok seemed brooding, deep in thought.

He accompanied Hannah into the foyer.

'Will you be all right now?'

She hesitated. Go on girl, go for it, she said to herself, and looked him in the eye. 'Fancy coming up for a nightcap?'

'A nice idea. But I'm afraid I've got to get back. Would you like me to go with you as far as your door?'

'No, no,' she said, trying to hide her embarrassment. 'I'll be fine now. And thanks for all you've done. You've been a very patient listener. Sorry to have taken so much of your time away from your family.'

'Hold on there. Are you giving me the old heave-ho? I haven't been that boring, have I?'

Hannah's laugh reflected the relief that she felt. So he did like her, even if he thought she was a crazy, scarlet woman, who propositioned guys on their first date. How insensitive she'd become. She'd forgotten that decent, altruistic men still existed.

'Oh no. Just thought you'd have had enough of this mad cow.'

'Remember, cows are sacred here.' He handed her the bag. 'Don't forget your clothes. I'll phone you first thing tomorrow morning to make sure you're all right. Then we'll decide what to do next. OK?'

'OK.' Their eyes met. He leant towards her, and brushed her cheek briefly with his lips.

'You've got my number. If you have slightest worry, phone. Anytime. Understood?'

'Understood. Good night, my knight in shining armour.'

'Good night, my damsel in distress.'

She watched him disappear through the revolving doors, which seemed to parallel her feelings, as they continued to spin after Ashok had vanished into the night. She struggled for a rational explanation for the effect he had on her. She couldn't have fallen for this guy after a couple of meetings. Such things didn't happen to Hannah. No, it was obvious. She was experiencing something like a psychotherapeutic transference - intense feelings towards the therapist that sometimes developed during a course of therapy.

Thus reassured, she went over to the reception desk to collect her room key. The receptionist handed her a small, square box. 'Someone left this for you.'

'For me? Are you sure?'

'The gentleman was quite definitely asking for it to be given to Miss Hannah Petersen.'

'Did you see who it was?'

'An Englishman I think. Small, thin...'

Clutching the box, Hannah raced outside. It was too late. Ashok had gone. Calm down, she told herself. No point in panicking. This might be perfectly innocent. She went back to the reception desk and picked up the bag of clothes that she had dropped in her rush to chase after Ashok. She spoke to the receptionist again.

'The man who left this for me. Is he staying here?'

The receptionist shrugged. 'I don't know, Madam. Many English guests are here. Yesterday I did not see that man. Maybe he is arriving today morning, before my shift.'

Hannah took the lift to her room and locked herself in. She sat on the bed and looked at the box for a moment before carefully picking it up and turning it over in her hands. It fitted comfortably into her palm, was exquisitely worked, with curvy Islamic flourishes engraved over every inch of its shiny silver surface. Probably real silver, she mused. She debated for a moment before opening it. Her curiosity outweighed her fear, but she decided to hold it at arm's length to be on the safe side, and to get ready to run if necessary.

A slip of printed paper lay on top of the contents. It was headed R.I. Poonamchand and Sons, Pearls Merchant, and briefly exalted the virtues of freshwater pearls, and the particular virtues of those selected by R.I. Poonamchand and Sons. Hannah removed the paper carefully. Underneath, nestling on a bed of crimson velvet, lay a string of perfect black pearls that glinted purple, green and blue as she turned the box slowly under the lamplight.

Hannah was totally mystified. If this was her stalker, he'd changed tack. He'd never given her anything before. It didn't fit the pattern. So maybe it wasn't the stalker. Perhaps there was some misguided young man in the hotel who had bought it for his girlfriend and changed his mind. Perhaps they'd had a row. It might even have been the hotel receptionist, pretending it was someone else. Perhaps - heaven forbid - someone had recognised her. After all, it wasn't unusual for her readers to show their appreciation, particularly someone who had benefited from her investigations: in Belfast a child's drawing or a poem, in New York flowers or simply tears and a hug. Yes, there were all sorts of feasible explanations. Except... also printed on the slip of paper was the address of R.I. Poonamchand and Sons. The pearls had been bought in Hyderabad.

* * *

'So - you have come back to us. You have passed enjoyable day with your friend from aeroplane?'

Since his stroke, Srinivasa Rao had taken to bedding down on his mother's living room sofa. Ashok's attempt to tiptoe up the stairs and enter their own quarters quietly was futile. Srinivasa was a light sleeper, and had in any case had one ear open for his son's return.

Ashok had even instructed the rickshaw driver to stop at the end of the lane, so that his father wouldn't hear it drive up. In vain. His father was like a faithful hound that could detect from afar the return of those he loved. Ashok gave a resigned sigh and sat down on the edge of the sofa. What would his patients think if they could see him now? Their respected surgeon: all meek and mild, a child again.

'Yes, *Bapa*. She is a remarkable person. It has been a most interesting evening.'

'And have you given any more consideration to that young lady in Mysore? Or is it that you have been too busy with other matters?'

Had he ever been anything but a child? Even in England, had he ever actually needed to make a choice, to take a stand, to swim against the tide? Only once before had that prospect loomed before him, but in the end he never had the chance to put it to the test. And what had he felt when it ended? Grief mingled with relief, he remembered. His family had always been everything. He as an individual counted for little. Families travelled together through life, as one entity, even if it meant personal sacrifices. But today his equilibrium had been knocked sideways. Somehow he would have to try and steer a peaceful passage through the churning seas of his emotions.

'Truth to tell, I haven't had time to give much attention to her.'

'Haven't had time? Or haven't had interest?'

'I don't know.' It was no good trying to fool the old man. Ashok knew his father had read his mood accurately. He had tried to marshal his thoughts on the drive home from the Chamundi. What was happening to him? He had fought to remain calm when Hannah had told her story, to maintain a dispassionate, but sympathetic bedside manner, to be simply a good listener. He knew though that he had not altogether succeeded in this. The vibes that had surfaced between them were too insistent, despite his attempts to reason them out of his head. At this point in his life, the last thing he could afford was to get involved with her. As the autorickshaw had approached Malleshwaram, he had made an effort to pull his thoughts back to the purpose of his homecoming. In any case, what did he know about Hannah? Nothing. Was her story true? Had these terrible things really happened to her? It didn't bear thinking about. Or was she, as everyone else seemed to think, merely a disturbed young woman with a persecution complex? But why did he feel as if he'd known her for much longer than two days? Why did he still feel that they'd met before sometime? He'd asked her on the aeroplane. 'No,' she'd said. 'We've definitely never met.'

There, you see, he'd told himself as he drew up at the end of his lane, she's in my head again. I can't get her out.

'This woman, Hannah,' he now said to his father. 'She is troubled. She believes she is in grave danger. But I don't know. Maybe what she is telling is true. On the other hand...'

'And you are becoming very fond of her, I think.'

'Is it so obvious? Something about her fascinates. A crazy enchantress.'

'And knowing my son, she will be very pretty too.'

'More striking than pretty I think. No typical English face at all. Such expressive eyes - green, they are, and wonderful hair. It is a very intelligent face, a strong face.'

'My son, my son. Beware of strange ladies with strong faces. Take care that you are not too deeply involving yourself in a hopeless cause. At any rate I can see that you are currently in no fit state of mind to make any decision about that girl in Mysore. We must pray this enchantress breaks her spell on you in due course. But how to explain your present distraction to your mother? It is going to be no easy task, I think.'

Ashok squeezed his father's arm. 'I know you'll find a way. Now I must turn in. I am very tired. Goodnight, *Bapa*. And... thanks.'

'Huh! For what?' Srinivasa shook his head in the darkness and muttered to himself. 'What to do? You give the boy an English education, and so how can you complain when he behaves like an Englishman?'

* * *

At eight o'clock the following morning a knock came at Hannah's door.

'It's me. Ashok.'

Hannah had been dressed for some time. Confused feelings resulting from the evening with Ashok, mingled with doubts about the box of pearls, had nagged away enough to prevent a good night's sleep. When she woke up, she suddenly thought, for the first time since Hyderabad, about the impending US publication of *Fair Game*. Hal had warned them that Bannerman would go down fighting. Had he made his move yet? Damn. It would be the middle of the night in England. Can't really wake Duncan. Have to leave a message on his bloody answer-phone again. And this time I do want to talk to him. She dialled the number of his private phone, the one he kept locked in his garden room. She left the usual message. *Thursday - Chamundi Hotel, Bangalore. How's Bannerman? I'll ring again. Cheers.*

When Ashok arrived, she was sitting by the window looking at the hotel garden, and waiting for his telephone call. She unlocked the door and let him in.

'Sorry I didn't call first. For some reason I felt uneasy and thought I'd better come straight here.'

'You must have a sixth sense,' she said, and showed him the pearls.

Ashok tipped them out onto the table.

'No doubt about quality. These are excellent. Not cheap. At least fifty of them here. And that clasp - gold. Looks to me as if you've got an admirer. I'd like to be able to say I sent them, but I can't.'

Hannah suppressed a tingle of pleasure. He was probably simply being polite.

'It's the fact that they're from Hyderabad that troubles me most,' she said.

'That's not surprising. Hyderabad's a centre for pearls. Anyone wanting to buy pearls would be likely to end up with a Hyderabadi label. You realise that if it is him, it means you can't have done him much damage when you tipped him from the top of the taxi.'

'I know. But why send me an expensive gift?'

'He's obsessed with you, one way or other.'

Hannah shook her head. 'Obsessed with hatred. I'm sure of that. It just doesn't fit somehow.'

'Look - someone's written something on back of that velvet.'

Together they scrutinised the scrap of writing.

'RIP. Oh my God! Rest in peace. I told you. He means to kill me'

'Calm down. It probably doesn't mean that at all. How about 'rip', as in 'tear'?'

'That's a bit far-fetched, isn't it?'

'No more than your suggestion. Perhaps there's something stuffed inside. Let's see.'

He tore the backing off the velvet and examined it carefully.

'Just bits of foam rubber.'

Hannah suddenly gave a short laugh. 'Look! R.I.Poonamchand. It's just his initials. Someone wrote them on the back of the velvet. When it was delivered from the makers, presumably. So that it would end up at the right dealer.'

'What?' He gave a moan. 'Well, I'll be... Shows how easy it is to jump to conclusions.'

'Maybe, but it doesn't alter the fact that he must have sent them. What the hell's his game? If only there was some way of pre-empting him. I'm sick of being a victim. I want to go out and get him.'

'You know, I was thinking the same.' said Ashok. 'We've got to turn the tables on this fellow, go on the offensive - smoke him out and come up with some evidence so we can get him arrested. I had a thought about your photography. Presumably you took some pictures at Golconda. Any chance that you snapped our *burkha* woman without realising? Don't know what it would tell us anyway, but maybe a clue is there. Or you may have caught that man on another picture. Anyway, it's worth getting your pictures developed.'

Hannah groaned. 'I did take some photos at Golconda. In fact I took some everywhere. Only thing is - I left the camera at the Pandava, and the film's still in it.' She shrugged. 'Expect they've sold it by now - especially since I didn't pay my bill.'

'I wouldn't be so sure. Anyway it's worth giving them a ring. Got the number?' He went to pick up the receiver.

Hannah stopped him. 'Ashok, there's something you should know. Sit down.' She ran her fingers through her hair. 'Oh, my God. How the hell am I going to break this to you?'

Ashok, clearly baffled, sat down on the chair by the window. Hannah stood, looking out at the waving palm trees, not daring to catch his eye.

'I haven't been exactly honest with you. For a start, my name isn't Rosen. That's my mother's maiden name. I didn't want you to know my real name. You've called my bluff now - I couldn't let you ring them and ask for Hannah Rosen's belongings.'

'So you lied about your name. Is that such a big deal?'

'There's another reason why I didn't want you to know my name.'

'Go on.' The tension in his voice made Hannah's confession all the more difficult.

'I'm not a professional photographer, not really. Except for the current assignment. Normally it's just my hobby. I'm a writer.'

Ashok stared rigidly down at his feet.

'It wasn't a coincidence that I sat next to you on the plane. I heard the check-in clerk call you by name. I wondered if…. So I asked for that seat. I'm Hannah Petersen.'

The silence was unbearable. Ashok finally broke it.

'All along I think I knew.'

'Oh?'

'As soon as I saw you, something nagged at me. Perhaps it was your name. I shoved my suspicions to the back of my mind. Too much of a coincidence. Told myself there are hundreds of Hannahs. But I was sure I'd seen you before, just couldn't, or perhaps didn't want to remember where. Now of course, I realise it must have been the picture on the back cover of your book.'

She nodded, grimly. '*A Small Life*. I guessed you'd have read it.'

'Then you guessed wrong.' There was a sharp edge to his voice. 'I've picked it up countless times, but couldn't bring myself to open.'

Another silence, charged with unspoken questions. This time Hannah broke it, in an attempt to lighten the atmosphere.

'I'm surprised the picture even rang a bell. I look so much older now. Not much wiser though, it seems.'

He got up and stood next to her. Together they stared, unseeing, at the garden, lost in individual memories of the person who had, unwittingly, drawn them together.

'No point in trying to avoid the issue.' There was a catch in Ashok's voice as he said the name. 'Maighréad.'

'Yes, Maighréad.'

Now she turned and looked at him. 'She really loved you, you know.'

He shook his head. 'I couldn't compete with you. It was you who saved her from that dreadful marriage, brought her to England, looked after her...'

'How much did she tell you? About me?' She had intended to stop there, but now she felt compelled to drive the confession to its bitter conclusion. 'About... about us I mean.' She spoke quietly, and averted her eyes from his face.

'Everything. She couldn't let go of you. She had some crazy idea that she could hang on to both of us, that I'd understand. For a while I went along with it. But when it came to making a commitment, I just couldn't accept that she was... that she was...'

'Go on, say it! Or does it disgust you too much?' Hannah's words cut like broken glass on bare feet. 'Say it! Bisexual. That's the word you can't say. Well, if she was bisexual, then so was I.'

'Was?'

'Am, was, I don't know. What's the difference? I'm a pervert, aren't I? In your eyes anyway. You just made that very clear.' Hannah's face was taut, her expression grim.

Ashok stood, drawn and silent, in shock.

'You'd better go.' Hannah turned her back on him and stood staring ahead at nothing.

Ashok made no move. She wheeled round again to face him.

'Go, go! Leave me alone. Just go!'

He turned and walked out of the room, shutting the door quietly behind him.

* * *

The day he got back from New York, Duncan was jetlagged but determined to stay awake. He shook off Felicity's attentions and went to the garden room, carefully undoing the three locks on the door that kept it secure. He couldn't clear his head. Hannah-Felicity-Felicity-Hannah. They were both driving him mad. He sat down at his desk and shot a wistful glance at the picture on the wall of Hannah's green eyes smiling up into his own. God, he'd adored her. Still did, if he was honest with himself. And, there was no getting away from it, the similarity between Hannah and Felicity was striking, but whereas Hannah had been created tenderly and naturally by a loving god, Felicity had been pieced together hurriedly by a robot, like a Barbie doll copy of the original. Dammit! Why, oh why had he blown it with Hannah? Why couldn't it have lasted? It was his own fault, he knew. It was only after she'd left him and gone back to the cottage in Burfold that he forced himself to face the truth about the way he had treated her. He'd wanted to run her life personally as well as professionally. What a fool he'd been. Nobody ran Hannah.

But it had, until recently, worked out quite well with Felicity, hadn't it? They had their difficulties, it was true. And then there was this fixation of hers with Hannah. Duncan would never quite understand that, but it wasn't a problem, quite the contrary. So what had gone wrong? Why couldn't he get it out of his head that Felicity was seeing someone else?

Angrily he pushed the button labelled 'Play' on the answering machine. *'You have three old and one new message'* it told him. *'New message: Oh, hallo. It's James here. Just phoning to say I've got something that might interest you. Can you give me a call? Friday the twentieth of December. Twelve-fifteen p.m. End of message.'*

James was a literary agent and a good friend of Duncan's. Manuscripts that he recommended were usually worthy of consideration. Duncan glanced at the clock on the computer monitor. Four o'clock on a Friday. Would James still be at work? Worth a try. He picked up the telephone to call him back. Then he replaced it slowly onto the base unit. Something was troubling him. Something about the message was not right. What did it mean -

three old and one new message? He was sure he had cleared the machine after dealing with the last messages. Except for the two from Hannah - one to say she was in Hyderabad and one about going on to Madras. He left these on purpose. It was a good way to store them. He pressed 'Play' again. This time it said 'You have four messages'. It repeated the two saved messages from Hannah. But before repeating the message from James, it said: '*Message three: Thursday - Chamundi Hotel, Bangalore. How's Bannerman? I'll ring again. Cheers. Thursday the nineteenth of December. Two-fifteen a.m. End of message.*'

Duncan sat back and rubbed his chin thoughtfully. He hadn't heard the last message from Hannah before. The truth was forcing its way unpleasantly into his mind. Someone else had listened to Hannah's message. There was no other explanation.

Duncan got up slowly, unlocked the door and left the garden room, locking the door again carefully.

* * *

When Ashok walked out, Hannah knew it was her own fault.

'Damn,' she said, as the door closed behind him, 'damn, damn, damn!' Why had she made such a fool of herself, turned it into a drama, made it so obvious that she'd hoped for more than friendship from him? If she'd played it cool, he'd still be here. Now she'd scared him off. She hated herself for the weakness of her reaction, unable to accept that any man could affect her in this way, and yet she was unaccountably devastated at losing him.

Moments later the door opened.

'Hannah.' He sounded chastened but still shocked.

'Forgive me,' he said.

Hannah had her back to the door. She stiffened, then remained rigid for a moment before wheeling round to confront him, her face still feeling flushed with confusion and anger.

'I'm so sorry,' he said.

Then they were in each other's arms, doubts swept away by a greater truth than the sum of splintered fragments of reason.

Afterwards they lay for a while, holding one another lightly in sated stillness. Hannah turned her head towards her lover. She smiled. 'Let's just stay here, for ever.'

Ashok pressed her hand lightly. 'Hide away, you mean? Opt out? Not you, Hannah. That's not your way.'

'My way? Until yesterday, I was sure I'd lost my way. Now, suddenly, here with you, I seem to have come home.'

Ashok didn't reply. For a moment she felt that he was slipping beyond her grasp. His eyes spoke of distant things about which she knew nothing.

She regretted her sally into romantic fantasy and tried to extricate herself. 'You're miles away. What is it?'

'Mm? Oh, just thinking about yesterday morning.'

'Oh?'

'Nothing, don't worry.'

'For some reason I get the impression that I'm not the only one with secrets.'

Ashok kissed her gently on the forehead. 'Nothing for you to be worrying about.'

'Hey. Stop patronising me.'

'Do you know? I forgot you're a celebrity. Presumably I should be overcome with awe.'

'Of course you should. I thought you already were.'

'How did you guess? I'm trying not to show it.'

'Idiot!' She punched him on the arm. 'I'm not that sort of celebrity. People have heard of me, but no one recognises me on the street - not unless they happen to watch BBC Two or Channel Four in the early hours.'

'I'm usually either at hospital or asleep at that time. If I am up late, I'll be listening to music or watching a film.'

'Can't say I blame you. I wouldn't watch me either. Still, you have to do these things if you want to sell your stuff. The critics watch, even if no-one else does.'

'Suppose I'll have to start reading your books now. Though personally, I don't hold with the idea of career women.'

Hannah's jaw dropped. She stared at him.

'No,' he continued. 'In my opinion women are superior by nature to men, therefore it's totally unfair for them to compete in the job market. So they should stick to the kitchen.'

Had she heard him correctly? Surely he didn't mean it? She raised herself up onto one arm. Her hair fell across her face. 'You're joking, of course?'

'Not at all. This is Indian logic.'

'But it's outrageous. An educated man like you. How can you possibly believe such utter tr…?'

He was laughing at her. Trying to restrain himself, but his eyes said it all. Got you! 'Relax. Don't take everything so seriously. I'm surprised you're so gullible.'

'I'm not gullible. Can't afford to be. You did sound pretty convincing.'

'Sorry. Can't help teasing people when they lay themselves open to it.'

'Well, you certainly know how to go for the jugular.'

'Didn't take a fantastic IQ to figure out that'd get you going.'

She changed the subject. 'So you're not going to tell me?'

'What?'

'Your secret.'

He smiled awkwardly, but said nothing.

Hannah looked at him steadily. 'Oh what a tangled web we weave.'

'When first we practise…' He stopped abruptly.

'To deceive?'

He sat up. 'Don't be silly.' But he avoided her eyes as he said it.

That's right, Hannah told herself. Don't be silly. What's it got to do with me anyway? Ridiculous to be possessive about a man I've only just met. Making a fool of myself again. Pull yourself together, girl! She forced a cheerful grin. 'You showering first, or am I?'

He looked at her, smiling easily now. The hint of a raised eyebrow was the only answer needed. He got up and reached for her hand.

Later she dried the glistening drops of water off his back and felt intoxicated. She had stepped out of the dry world of journalism into realms that she had, until now, taken to belong in the rich imagination of poets and storytellers. She sighed. Ashok turned and stroked her cheek with the back of his hand.

'Now who's miles away?'

'Just thinking about this crazy never-never land. A mythical land of a million gods, where dreams come true. Even ones you haven't dreamt yet.'

She snuggled against his body, and felt him comb his fingers through her hair, which, left to its own devices, was drying into an unruly mop of auburn curls.

'I never imagined you'd have red hair,' he said, 'from that dreadful black and white photograph on the book cover.'

'It's an awful photo. I'm glad you didn't recognize me from it.' She traced her finger down the curve of his spine. 'And I never imagined dark skin could drive me crazy.'

He shook his head. 'You're an enigma. Most English women I've known have simply avoided the subject of skin colour. As though it's taboo. You come right out with it.'

'They're scared, that's why. That they might let their guard down.'

'That's a bit harsh.'

'Prejudice is deep-rooted. I know that.'

'Knowing isn't quite the same as experiencing.'

'Which you have done?'

'Oh, yes. There have been times - both at university and later, when I've been made to feel distinctly second class.'

'I hope you told them what you thought.'

He shook his head. 'Sometimes it's best to hold your tongue.'

'Never. You should always speak your mind.'

'Easy for you to say.'

'You think it hasn't happened to me?'

'Has it? When?'

Where, she wondered, do I begin? She remembered the confines of Ashley House Boarding School, where at the age of eight, she'd refused to be cowed by her fellow inmates, the bullying minions, who constantly attempted to victimise her. But no, it was no good avoiding the real issue.

'Well, the last time was a couple of hours ago. Here. In this room.'

She waited for his reply. He looked uncomfortable.

'That's not quite the same thing, is it? I mean, we were talking about racial prejudice here, not... not...'

'Not sexuality? For a doctor you're a prude. It's a good thing you're not a gynaecologist.' Hannah decided not to push the matter any further at that point. Eventually, if their relationship were to last, they would have to face the awkwardness of their intertwining past together. They dressed in silence.

'I'll make that phone-call now. Do you have the number?'

Hannah retrieved a crumpled slip of paper from the depths of her document pouch and Ashok dialled. She couldn't understand his conversation with the clerk at the Pandava. She assumed it was in Tamil. Occasionally an English word slipped in, and once or twice she heard her name.

'We're in luck,' said Ashok, as he put the receiver down. 'They have your rucksack, and he's just checked that the camera's still in the hotel safe. I told him we'd pay the bill when we pick up the things tonight.'

'Tonight? We can get there by then?'

'Certainly. I'll go and book the seats. With a bit of luck we'll get the afternoon train.'

CHAPTER 5

Bangalore City railway station bubbled and boiled with travellers and their fantastic array of bags and bundles, boxes and cases. The platforms were awash with colour. It seemed to Hannah as if a rainbow had melted and showered them with a multitude of droplets or that they were the canvas of some celestial Van Gogh. The women in their saris, *chudidars* or *shalwar kameez* were dazzling butterflies. Many of the little girls wore elaborate frocks, which Hannah reckoned were more suitable for a party than a train ride. The men were more soberly dressed, mainly in Western clothes. Wiry little red-shirted porters with impossible loads on their heads wove through the crowds.

The anticipation of a journey permeated the air, a sort of controlled excitement, an ominous self-discipline, waiting to explode at the arrival of the next train. When the 1430 Brindavan Express for Chennai drew into the station, the storm broke. Hitherto patient passengers hurled themselves at the carriages, in futile attempts to jostle and push their way to the front of the maelstrom that was by now jamming the train doors, elbowing and shoving out of the way any who were too weak or chicken to plunge wholeheartedly into the fray.

'Hannah!' shouted Ashok from somewhere in the midst of chaos. 'Don't lose me.'

'You must be joking,' she shouted back. Eventually, by a combination of brute force and good luck, she managed to manoeuvre herself to within hand-grasping reach of Ashok, who grabbed her and somehow managed to pull her free of the crowd and down the platform to the second class air-conditioned carriage, where Ashok had reserved seats. Their compartment was the first one in the carriage. Miraculously, they found themselves alone.

'Sorry about that. I sort of got caught up in the flow before I remembered that we're travelling second a.c.'

'I'd have thought you'd travel first.' said Hannah, lowering herself thankfully onto the hard, somewhat shabby seat.

'Not all trains have first. Anyway sometimes second a.c. is better than first. Depends whether first is a.c. or not.'

'I'd have been quite happy travelling in the cattle-truck back there. Looked like fun.'

'Don't know about that. As you saw, things can get a little frantic. And hot. I thought we could do with some peace and quiet.'

Hannah nodded. 'But, don't make a habit of it. I'm quite prepared to take my chances in the rough and tumble.'

'You might not be so sure after five hours of travelling.'

'Five hours of just each other's company.' She nudged him. 'D'you think we'll still be talking at the end of it?'

'Well, if not, it will be as well to have found out sooner rather than later.'

'Oh yes? Meaning?'

But Ashok had clammed up.

'Now you're giving me one of your *Noli me tangere* looks.'

'My what?'

'It's Latin - you should know. I thought all doctors understood Latin. It means "hands off" - loosely translated, that is.'

Ashok gave a short, quiet laugh, and looked out of the window at the railway station. The window was sealed, on account of the air conditioning, and splattered with dust and mud.

'Look! We're moving.' He took her hand in his and gently kissed her fingers. He looked uncomfortable and distracted. 'Give me time, Hannah. Things at home are a bit confused at this moment, that's all.'

She peered at him through narrowed eyes.

'You're married?'

'No, of course not. What do you take me for? Here marriage still counts for something, you know. Don't brand me with your

Western attitudes.' His face was momentarily shaded by a suggestion of annoyance.

She deserved the rebuke. 'Sorry. Thoughtless of me. I guess I'm still too new in this country.'

'Let it drop, please. Once I've sorted it out in my own mind, I'll tell you, I promise.' The shadow passed and his voice became tender and concerned. 'Hannah, at this moment I can't say what the future is holding. All I know is that no one - and yes, that does include Maighréad - has ever made me feel like this. I don't know what it is. Love? How can it be? Let's face it, we hardly know each other. But there's this bond between us, isn't it?'

She stared at him, and fought back the telltale signs of unaccustomed, openly displayed emotion. 'Weird,' she said. 'And yet...' She looked down.

'And yet?'

'Look, I know you don't want to hear this, but... I have to talk about my relationship with Maighréad. I think my feelings towards her were based on a power thing somehow. And I can't get it out of my mind that the same might be true of what you're feeling for me.'

'What do you mean? I don't have power over you.'

'But that's just it. You do. I'm vulnerable because of this... thing, this stalker. Maighréad was weak and vulnerable when I rescued her from that brute she was married to in Ireland.'

'So? I don't know what you're getting at.'

'I wonder if perhaps the fact that I was protecting her may have been why I found her so attractive, and thought I was in love with her.'

'If you think I'm just getting a kick out of being protective, we might as well call a halt now. I've never heard such rubbish.'

'Methinks he doth protest too much.'

'Give over, Hannah. You know it's nothing to do with power. We just seem to gel, that's all. We both felt it on the plane, while you were still feeding me a pack of lies. You felt it too, don't try and deny it.'

Hannah smiled and pensively ran the back of her finger down his cheek. 'Yes, you're right. I suppose I've become very touchy as a result of what's happened.'

A few moments of silent contemplation; then Ashok spoke, forcing reluctant thoughts into words.

'Maighréad wasn't always dependent on you. You can't use that as an excuse. By the time she was rehoused in that Oxford shelter, she didn't need you for anything.' He paused before adding grimly, 'she just wanted you.'

'That's true I suppose. But she was still bound to me by a debt of gratitude, and she never let me forget that. After all, once I'd brought her to England, she lived with me for the first six months. Did you know that? It wasn't just a casual thing. We *lived* as partners, you know. Sorry if that shocks you.'

'Yes, I did know. It did shock me when she told me. And yes, it still shocks me now.' He paused searching for words. 'It hurts me to think about it. I know you can't understand this. If I'm honest, knowing Maighréad slept with women was part of the attraction - it fascinated me somehow as well as repelling me. At that time it was trendy to have a kinky girlfriend.'

'Kinky. I see.'

'But with you it's different. I really can't bear to think of it. You'll have to help me to get over this. Perhaps I will, with time.'

Once again he stopped himself.

'Do you think we have time, Ashok?'

Tension bristled between them as they ached with the longing to embrace, to drown their differences and fears in life-affirming contact. Both of them held back, restrained by the unspoken knowledge that such a public display of affection was taboo here, even in the comparative privacy of their compartment.

'I don't know. But I hope so.'

'You know, it's odd.' said Hannah, 'How long have we known each other? A couple of days? And yet I feel as if I've known you far longer. As if I know everything about you.'

'Well, let's face it. If Maighréad told you half as much about me as she told me about you, we probably do know all about each other.'

Hannah's laugh was sharp, ironic. 'I guess we've got a lot to thank her for. It must have driven you mad, to hear all about me.'

'Not at first. She had to get it off her chest. Part of healing - or so I thought. But it got to me after a while, as I told you.'

Hannah said carefully. 'Did you break it off, Ashok? Is that why she went back to Belfast?'

'I told her she had to choose between us. I gave her an ultimatum. Yes, that's why she left. And yes, before you ask, I expect that's why she jumped.'

'So we were both guilty. She knew it was over between us. Even before she met you. She still wrote to me though. Long, detailed letters - later mainly about you.'

'She never told me that. I thought she was still seeing you sometimes.'

Hannah shook her head. 'What a waste of life. And we have to live with the guilt of it.'

'A waste of life, yes,' said Ashok. 'But we shouldn't have to bear the burden of guilt, Hannah. We couldn't, after all, be expected to live our lives to suit her hang-ups. She was the one with problems, not us.' They sat quietly for a moment before he continued. 'Perhaps we were misguided, thinking we could sort her out somehow. If we'd been older and more experienced, we'd have realised we were playing with fire, no? But with us or without us, I think she was destined for tragedy.'

'You would say that, I suppose. Karma and so on. I don't believe in destiny. If I did, I'd have chosen a different career. We're not pre-programmed to act in a particular way. If we were, what would be the point in trying to change anything? Anyway, what's past is past.'

'Do you think any of your books have really changed the course of events?'

'Yes, I think they have. Take Belfast, for instance. No-one before me had made a serious study of what was happening to the kids;

no-one that is, in lay terms, that the average reader could understand.'

'And how d'you know it's done any good?'

'You should see the correspondence I get. It's opened their eyes. Made them more sensitive to their children's psychological needs.'

'Then obviously, it's your destiny to be a great guru,' Ashok teased.

'And what's your destiny?'

'Ah…' He looked thoughtful. 'Well, I hope it's also my destiny to leave something positive behind me.'

'You must be doing that already in your work.'

'No, I mean something more. It's all been too easy. Things have always slotted into place for me. I've never had to make any real decisions.'

'You want a challenge, you mean?'

'Well, want may not be the right word. I feel I need one though. I'll never be a complete person until I reach some crossroad and have to decide which way to go.'

'Didn't you have to do that with Maighréad?'

'In a manner of speaking. But she took the final decision out of my hands. If I'm honest, I don't know whether I'd have gone through with it, even if she'd agreed to give you up.'

As they left the city behind, the heat intensified and the air grew heavy and soporific. Air-conditioning appeared to be an overbloated term for what sounded like a weak fan whirring away in some hidden corner of the compartment.

Hannah yawned. 'I'm shattered. Too much unaccustomed morning activity.'

'Rest on me, and go to sleep.'

'Is that done here? Or will we risk eviction?'

Ashok's reply was muffled in the rhythm of the train wheels. Within minutes she had dozed off, aware only of the gentle motion of the train, and the comforting beat of her lover's heart as she rested her head on him.

In her sleep she seemed to become part of him, her body, her mind fused with his. She felt that she was slowly slipping into him.

Soon they would be one entity; the fulfilment of a long-forgotten prophecy, the last arc in an eternal circle. He was the rock that held her firmly, but also the earth to which she was finally returning. He was her birthplace, her temple, her burial-ground. For the first time in many months the spectre of that other face did not haunt her sleep with its eyeless stare. The long, slender fingers of a healing surgeon soothed away all traces of the sallow, skeletal spurs that had gripped her that night in the cottage garden. He had smoothed the pillows of her turbulent dreams.

*   *   *

After just a few minutes, or so it seemed, Hannah woke with a start. The lights in the compartment were on. The train was chugging gently through inky, unseen night.

'What time is it?'

'Ten past six. You've been asleep for more than two hours.'

'Really? Did you sleep too?'

'Yes. On and off. I could murder a cup of tea.'

They immediately became aware of a strange tapping noise outside the train window. When Hannah turned to look, her face registered horror. There, as if bidden by Ashok's wish, was the *chai-wallah* hanging from the side of the speeding train clutching his hot urn, his plastic cups dangling from his side. Ashok calmly got up and opened the carriage door, which was next to their compartment, to let the *chai-wallah* in. They spoke in Kannada. The man calmly poured them two cups of tea, smiled brightly and went off down the corridor.

Hannah's face was fixed in an expression of complete disbelief.

'He couldn't open the door between our carriage and next. They sometimes lock them to keep the riff-raff out of second a.c.' explained Ashok, as if the tea-vendor's unconventional entry were nothing extraordinary, 'so he climbed along outside of the train instead. Drink your tea, before it gets cold.'

Hannah smiled; a private, contented smile.

'What's the joke?' asked Ashok.

'No joke. Happy. In spite of everything. I love this country. I feel as if I've strayed into someone's bizarre imagination. It's like being a child again. Perhaps I've fallen down the rabbit hole, or wandered through the magic wardrobe.'

'I think if you lived here for longer you might adopt a less sentimental viewpoint.'

'You think so? Perhaps I'll try that.'

'Ah. The romantic Englishwoman.'

'I'm not really English. Not by ancestry. My father's lot were probably Vikings, and my mother's walked with Moses to the Promised Land - at least that's what I like to tell myself. So I have one foot in the East already.' And my half-brother's Sri Lankan, she almost added, but thought better of it. George, after all, played no part in her life.

'Remind me to take you to see the Jews of Kerala one day.'

'I'd like that,' said Hannah. Having any sort of cultural identity seemed so much more significant here. It certainly never meant much to her mother. She presented an image of an English rose despite years of scrabbling about in the muck of bygone civilisations, in dodgy parts of the world. Paradoxically Hannah's rumoured Jewishness was seen in the eyes of her bullying classmates at Ashley House to be a flaw in her father, not her mother. Hannah didn't disillusion them. It didn't matter.

'What did Maighréad tell you about me?'

Ashok grinned. 'She said you were a tough nut and pigheaded. She also said you're a pussycat beneath that granite exterior. That do for starters?'

'Pigheaded, am I? Yes, she's probably right. I must say, you've got a good memory.'

'Maybe I was more impressed than I realised at the time.'

'But of course! Who wouldn't be?'

Ashok was gazing at her, studying her face. 'You have such beautiful eyes.'

'Ah! A professional opinion. It must be true then. Tell me, why did you decide to study medicine?'

'Because I didn't want to study law.'

'What sort of an answer's that? Did it have to be law or medicine? Why not science? Or politics?'

'Politics? You are joking. I've no time for such shenanigans. Let others make mischief, not me.'

'You can't pass the buck. We're all part of the political system.'

'Correct. I have my own opinions and I use my vote whenever I can. But politicians are all crooks. It's a question of damage limitation.'

'You're a cynic. Not that I disagree with you entirely. But if people like you leave the field open for the crooks, you can't complain.'

'And you, Hannah? Are you so different?'

'I think so. I'm not a politician, but I've taken on a few crooks in my time.'

'So you have. But I cannot afford to take such risks.'

'Why not?'

He glanced away. 'Perhaps I have obligations that you do not have. It is hard for you to understand.'

'Try me.'

He half smiled and looked at her again. 'My father wanted me to study law. But my interest lay in science. However, there is very less security in research these days. So I opted for medicine.'

'Is security so important for you?'

'It is paramount. My parents are not so young. Also there is my grandmother. In India, you see, we do not have social security as in UK. Our children are our security.' He paused. 'I told you it is not easy for you to understand this.'

'Don't underestimate me, Ashok. Of course I understand. And in a way I envy you. I've only myself to think about. This is the way of the West. Our parents give us life and at some stage release us into the wide world. They relinquish their obligations to us, and hand us over to the state. We owe them nothing. If we're lucky, or likely to inherit anything, the ties of our childhood endure and we go through life holding on to those tenuous links of love and concern. If the links are too tenuous, the ties are broken.'

'Now who's being cynical? Have you broken all ties?'

'Not all. But I was always taught to be independent. Right from when I was pushed into boarding school at the age of seven. My parents knew they couldn't always be there for me, or I for them. Their work as archeaologists took them away. I had to learn to cope.'

'And it has made you tough.'

'Tougher than most maybe.'

'Tough but not hard.'

'Are you sure? Perhaps you don't know me as well as you think.'

'Aren't you the voice of battle-scarred children and vulnerable women? If it is only fame and fortune you are wanting, there are easier ways of achieving it.'

'You're right. Fame and fortune are nothing compared with the feel-good factor. When things go right. It must be the same for you.'

'Certainly. To see the face of an old lady blind with cataracts for years, when you take off the bandages; still it always gets me right here.'

'Well, there you are. We're not so different.'

'You're tougher than I am, Hannah.'

'That's where you're wrong. I manage to look tough, but you've seen me crumple. You're tough on the inside.'

'I hope your faith in me is not misplaced.'

'It isn't. One thing my job's taught me is to be a good judge of character. I knew I could trust you the first time I set eyes on you.'

'A dangerous assumption, young lady. One day your instinct will let you down.'

'Never has done yet.' Her eyes were steady on his face. 'Tell me about your family.'

Ashok stood up and stretched.

'Later. I need to go for a wander. Stay put. Won't be long.'

Hannah felt a surge of frustration, but she kept silent. Alone in the compartment she tried to paste together in her mind some of the fragments that she still recalled from Maighréad's letters. She smiled sadly as she remembered.

'...*often think how fine it must be to have a proper family, like Ashok....*'

'...*seems very proud of them, but keeps them to himself.*'

'...*did once show me a picture of his parents and his little sister outside their house - all in traditional Indian clothes, it looked like a film set...*'

'...*hasn't talked of taking me to India, but I hope he will, one day...*'

Hannah was not sure how long Ashok had been gone, but it seemed like ages. She began to get worried. She stood up and wandered along the corridor, peering into the other compartments. No sign of him among the dozing passengers. The train chugged steadily on. Hannah went over to the toilets, which were at the end of the carriage, opposite the exit door next to their compartment. Gingerly she tried the door to the first toilet cubicle. It swung open. Apart from the pungent stink of ripening urine, it yielded nothing. The second toilet was also vacant. She returned to her seat, by now feeling distinctly uneasy. Minutes passed, and still no sign of Ashok.

Gradually she realised that someone was tapping on the outside window. Horror-struck she forced herself to look. There in the darkness was Ashok, clinging on for dear life. Hannah rushed out to open the door and hauled him in.

'Christ Almighty! Have you gone mad?' she gasped.

'Calm down,' he said, straightening his clothes and tidying his hair. 'Used to do this a lot when I was a kid. Not quite at this speed, mind you. But I decided that if the *chai-wallah* could do it, so could I.'

It was a few minutes before Hannah regained her composure. Ashok, it seemed, had never lost his.

'What the hell are you playing at?' Hannah finally blurted out.

'Well, something was nagging at me ever since we got on the train. You know how it is. It's not quite in your head and not quite out of it.'

'Go on.'

'When I got jumbled up in all that scrum on the platform - before you caught up - I had this strange feeling of *déja vu.* Almost immediately in all that confusion it passed, but while you were asleep I started thinking. And then I realised what it was. Someone pushed me aside to get onto the train.'

'Someone? What someone?'

'A man, a European. I knew I'd seen him before but I couldn't for the life of me remember where. I thought it might have been at a restaurant or in a shop. I assumed he was just a tourist. Then suddenly it came to me. He'd been on the flight from London - I met him coming out of the loo. He was looking like death in dark glasses. He'd pushed me aside that time also.'

By now Hannah was sitting bolt upright, her face tense, her hands flat either side of her on the seat.

'Are you sure?'

'No. That's why I went to double check. It was his eyes - or rather his lack of them that make me think it was same man. Those reflective glasses are quite distinctive. Also I thought on the plane how very sickly-looking he was - for a youngish man, and the man on the platform gave a similar impression from the fleeting glance I had of him.'

'You went to double check,' said Hannah slowly, 'without telling me?'

'No point in worrying you unnecessarily. I remembered the *chai-wallah* telling that the door between the carriages was locked.'

'So you resorted to aerial acrobatics...'

'Well yes, it was the only way to the next carriage, and besides it gave me a chance to get a good look at him in secret.'

'And did you find out anything after all that? Was it worth your dice with death?'

'Yes, as a matter of fact. Luckily he was in the first carriage. Presumably wanted to be as near us as possible. I flattened myself against the side and edged under the window - it was non-a.c., barred, open. Not like this one. The bars were useful to hang onto. I managed to pull myself up and peek in without him seeing me. The carriage was so crammed with people that nobody noticed me.'

'So - describe him to me then.'

'Average height, emaciated, very pale. Does it sound like your stalker?'

'Sorry, never got a real look at him - except in the dark with a mask, or from behind. And in the taxi in Madras I only got a back view of the top half. But on all three occasions I got the impression of a stick insect. Could be a coincidence, of course.'

'He'd taken the glasses off. That was the worst thing about him - those eyes, like lightly poached eggs. There was something creepy about him.'

'Creepy.' Hannah shivered as she said the word. 'Yes. So are you convinced it was the man on the plane?'

'Convinced, no. But ninety-nine point nine percent sure.'

'If you're right, and he's the stalker, he's been hot on my trail since before I left England.' Hannah stared at Ashok. 'How the hell did he know which flight I'd be on? I told no one.'

'No one? Are you quite sure? Think.'

'I'm positive. Except...' Her face froze, 'except Duncan. But Duncan wouldn't...'

'Wouldn't he, Hannah? You are sure? Spurned lover and all that?'

'How did you know?'

'I didn't. I guessed.'

'Whatever made you... oh, never mind. But I told you. You can put that right out of your head. He wouldn't do that to me. He wouldn't lower himself.'

Ashok shrugged. 'If you say so. But you'll have to come up with a convincing alternative.'

'I can't. Not yet. But I will.'

Ashok said nothing but his expression said everything.

When the train finally rolled into Chennai, they waited at the carriage door and watched the passengers from the neighbouring carriage spill out onto the platform, searching among the sea of faces for a thin man with poached egg eyes or reflecting sunglasses. In vain. Their quarry had evaded them.

* * *

At the Pandava the receptionist, who recognised Hannah, and seemed completely unruffled by her disappearance two nights earlier and sudden reappearance now, greeted them cheerfully. They retrieved Hannah's rucksack and the camera from the hotel safe, then booked in for the night. Ashok booked two rooms, Hannah's previous room and the one next door to it.

'Wouldn't do to have one room only,' he explained on their way across the courtyard. 'I'll just dump most of my things in my room to make it look used. Don't open your door to anyone but me.'

Ashok closed the door of his room behind him and put down his bag. Alone in the sudden stillness, he sat down on the bed, feeling unaccountably weary. What the hell was he doing here? Whatever had possessed him to undertake this journey with a woman he hardly knew? The tentacles of reality gripped him. Had he been out of his mind to suspect the fellow on the train of some unspeakable act, merely because he'd seen him before? And the photographs? Did they really justify a chase across half the country? Come on, he said to himself, admit it. There's another reason for all this. It's an excuse, isn't it? An excuse to make time alone with this crazy, charismatic echo from the past, away from the frenetic marriage market atmosphere at home, and his father's gentle, but nevertheless sharp-edged probing.

The telephone rang.

He picked up the receiver. 'Hallo? Who is this?'

On the other end of the phone was silence, but it was an ominous silence. Ashok sensed a powerful presence intruding into his solitude.

'Who is this?'

Still no reply, only a few more seconds' silence before the phone was slammed down.

CHAPTER 6

'Listen,' said Ashok, as they rested on Hannah's bed at the Pandava, letting the fan cool their bodies, spent and soaking after making love in the night heat. 'Something odd happened in my room earlier, just after we arrived. It's probably nothing, but I think you should know.' He told Hannah about the telephone call, making as light of it as possible.

Hannah listened, tight-lipped.

'Great. Now I've put you in danger.'

'I'm not in any danger. He's just trying to spook me.'

'How can you say that? After what he did to me.'

'I didn't say he wasn't a danger to you.'

'You can count on it. His plan to get me that night in the garden failed. Now he's out to finish what he began. Whatever that may be.'

Ashok reached up from the bed to the fan control switch on the wall. He turned the dial a little, until the steady whirring slowed and broke into a rhythmic, whooshing beat.

'Perhaps.'

'At any rate, if you had any doubts about the fellow's existence before, at least today proves it's not my imagination.'

'Hannah - I always believed you - I told you that.'

'Don't take me for a fool. I'm not even sure I believed myself. I do now. The guy's made his first mistake. If part of his strategy was to undermine my sense of sanity, he's shot himself in the foot.'

'If it was him.'

'Of course it was.'

'Well, whatever. Perhaps we'll know more when we get that film developed.'

'We've got to get back to Bangalore first. That's another day gone. A couple of days at least till we get the film back...'

'Hold on, hold on. I've been talking to your friend in reception. He was telling that he can get our film developed in one day. His brother has a studio.'

Hannah raised her eyebrows. 'Resourceful chaps, these receptionists,' she said. 'They all seem to have a brother, or a cousin or some useful relative when you need one.'

'I've been thinking that if we drop it off tomorrow morning we could take a car down to Mamallapuram for the day.'

From outside the window came the indignant cawing of a crow, disturbed perhaps by an intruding squirrel as it roosted in the flame tree.

'Mama... what?'

'Ma-ma-lla-puram,' repeated Ashok. 'Birthplace of temple architecture in the far south. There is a shore temple. Also other remarkable stone carvings and rock temples. I'd like to show them to you. Be nice to spend some time in a peaceful place, don't you think so?'

'Fine by me. I'm in your hands.' She held him close. 'However,' she added, 'that phone call - I can't help worrying, even though you said you don't think he's dangerous. I'm sure you're wrong.'

Ashok sat up and looked at his watch. 'Look, it's only eleven o'clock. Your friend will still be in reception. I'll go and drop off the film and order a car for tomorrow. I can ask if anyone of our man's description has booked in. I fancy a cold drink. How about you?'

'Bring me one back, will you? I couldn't go out again.'

When he had gone, Hannah closed her eyes and tried to separate the conflicting emotions that were playing in her mind. How could she be so happy under the circumstances? It didn't make sense. There was something else too. Something about Ashok that she didn't understand. Had Maighréad felt it too? She forced herself to cast back her mind five years. Slowly disjointed pieces of another letter started to slot together like a well-used but now neglected jigsaw puzzle.

My darling Hannah,

... your letter came... could hardly tear open the envelope fast enough... still weak... pathetic creature... can't stand for more than a few moments... difficult to feed myself... Ashok has found this Amstrad for me... I can write a little more fully... easier than trying to hold a pen.

Can you believe it's three months... brought me here, to the John Radcliffe... How my life has changed.

... Joy at receiving your letter... consternation when I read it. Darkness in your words... certain you did not intend.

... Wonderful Indian doctor who has become my friend - and more... when I am strong again.

... Rarely talks about his life in India... keeps it hidden... too strange and distant for me to understand. The little he does say sounds... romantic. Not at all like... but I don't want to think about that.

I want you to know Ashok as I know him... as much part of you as of me. You and I... indivisible. You think you're 'doing the right thing'... staying away... act of supreme self-sacrifice... so misguided... three of us... meant to be.

... police taking renewed interest in me... interviewed me several times over the last few days - seem to want to convince themselves of my statement... additional facts... can't seem to get it into their heads... details crystal clear. Hannah. Please come... talk about you all the time... what you mean to me. He listens quietly... feels your absence as I do, though he says nothing.

Please come.

Your loving and faithful friend

M

Poor Maighréad wrapped up in her self-delusion. Hannah's absence from her sick bed had been nothing to do with self-sacrifice. It was a sense of the passing of things. It had been time to move on. For both of them. Hannah wanted to see Mark Salers' trial through and finish *A Small Life*. Then her final link with Maighréad would be severed. She thought about the letter again, and Ashok. Was that it? Did he think it impossible for a Western woman to truly understand him? She shook her head. Maighréad, yes. That made sense. Maighréad was young and traumatised. She was also, Hannah admitted painfully to herself, quite unworldly.

But did Ashok really believe that Hannah dwelt in an incompatible mindscape? No. Utterly impossible. Quite the opposite in fact. The empathy between them was uncanny. There was another reason for him to be holding back. Something he was keeping from her.

* * *

Ashok described the man on the train to the receptionist, telling him that they were expecting a friend, and not forgetting to mention the glasses.

'No, sir. During time I am here, no gentleman of that description is arriving today evening. But there are plenty other hotels nearby. Maybe your friend is staying in one of those.'

'Have you been here all evening?'

'Short break I took, sir, after signing you in.'

'And the person who relieved you. When does he come back on?'

'Tomorrow night only, sir. He is helping out sometimes.'

'Please look to see if anyone arrived while you were taking your break.'

'One moment, sir. What is name of your friend?'

Sod it, thought Ashok. Blown it! He had no option but to bluff it out.

'Well actually we just met him on train from Bangalore. He told he'd be staying here and would meet us for a coffee. He gave me his name, but I'm afraid I've forgotten it.'

The receptionist waggled his head and browsed through the hotel register.

'Mr P. Fenton and Mr R. Thomas both from UK were signing in at nine-fifteen,' he read, 'and Mr and Mrs M. Heffer at nine-thirty, from UK also.'

'Mr Fenton - do you know what he looks like?'

'Yes, sir. He was here just now. But he is not your friend.'

'How do you know that?'

'Oh, sir,' the receptionist laughed, 'Mr Fenton is one very big man. I mean, not slim at all, like your friend. And he has beard.'

'And Mr Thomas?'

'I have not seen him, sir.'

'Please tell me Mr Thomas's room number.'

'No need.' An elderly Indian gentleman had just walked up to the reception desk. He held out his hand. 'I am Mr Thomas. How can I help you?'

Mr Thomas was an affable old man, who accepted Ashok's muttered excuse of 'mistaken identity' with good humour.

Before he went back to Hannah, Ashok ordered two glasses of *musambi* juice. While he waited for them, he sat down in the foyer to glance at the latest copy of *The Hindu*. An article, submerged in the local news section, caught his eye and galvanised him. It was headed *Cab Hijack in Chennai*. He read on apprehensively.

Chennai cab driver, Mr R. W. Ramsingh survived with cuts and bruises when his cab was hijacked by a mysterious foreigner on Tuesday night. The foreigner, a woman, appears to have panicked when Mr Ramsingh doubled back along the coast road to avoid a traffic snarl up, instead of taking the direct route from the city to the airport. After forcing Mr Ramsingh to stop, and luring him from the cab, she absconded in it, travelling several miles before finally abandoning it. The driver, in a reckless attempt to prevent the hijack, clung to the roof of the vehicle for some minutes before falling off. Fortunately neither driver nor cab nor a consignment of gobi, which was lodged on the back seat, sustained serious injuries. Mr Ramsingh describes the woman as being blonde, in her forties, and wearing a blue dress. She may have had a German accent.

Ashok closed his eyes. *Gobi*, he said to himself. Bloody cauliflowers. He fell into a fit of laughter as he pictured the unfortunate man evicted from his own vehicle, and Hannah hurtling with the malodorous vegetables down the back streets of Madras in a hijacked Hindustan Ambassador. The arrival of the sweet-lime juice forced him to pull himself together. He wiped the tears from his eyes, carefully tore the article out of the paper and slid it into his pocket. Then he silently thanked God for providing such an unobservant cab driver.

So that settled it. The whole stalker thing was, after all, a figment of Hannah's imagination. The man in the train was innocent, so was the donor of the pearls. His phone-call? Only someone dialling the wrong room. Yes, that was probably it. How easily one could be taken in. His relief was suddenly clouded by foreboding. Hannah needed help, certainly, but it was a different type of help she needed. It would be a hard task, and he risked losing her trust. Gently does it, he told himself. Tomorrow at Mamallapuram. He'd tell her then.

'That was a close shave,' said Hannah, when Ashok told her about his encounter with Mr Thomas. 'I didn't know you were such a convincing liar.'

'You've taught me well.'

'Ouch! Anyway - what now? Since Mr Thomas is innocent, and Mr Heffer is with a Mrs, we've reached stalemate again.'

'Well,' said Ashok, 'there's absolutely no point in worrying. As there's not much we can do about it, let's hope we give him the slip tomorrow and can forget him for once.'

CHAPTER 7

The sea air was warm, despite the violence of pounding waves, as Ashok and Hannah strolled along the beach at Mamallapuram in the morning sunshine. Ahead the twin spires of the Shore Temple kept watch over the Bay of Bengal, as they had done since the eighth century. To Hannah they resembled golden pyramid cakes sandwiched with butter-cream, where layers of sandstone carvings had been eroded by centuries of salt wind.

A group of women and children, rainbow saris and long skirts pulled up to reveal glimpses of slender, rust-brown ankles, were playing chicken with the tide, running to the water's edge and retreating with excited shrieks as the dying waves rushed in and splashed their feet. The odour of rotting seaweed and salt-fish hung dankly in the air, reminding Hannah of a field trip to Morecambe Bay with Ashley House. She smiled at the memory, one of the few happy ones of her schooldays, but the graceful temple spires rising out of the sand like silent metronomes seemed disapproving, as if her mind had committed sacrilege.

'This temple is dedicated to two of our greatest gods,' Ashok said, 'Vishnu and Shiva.'

'So many gods,' said Hannah, 'and such harmony.'

'India has a million and more gods or one God, depending on how you look at it. *Bhagavad-Gita* teaches that all gods lead to God, as all rivers lead to the sea.' He smiled at her. 'Anyway, they're not always in harmony - take the story of Ganesh for example. His father Shiva lost his temper and chopped off his head. He then repented and sent out his servant to bring back first head he saw - which happened to be an elephant.'

They reached the temple compound and let its tranquillity wash over them. The outer walls, where long lines of huge, stone bulls looked out to sea, had fared little better than the temple buildings themselves, time-ravaged but still recognisable.

Hannah said 'There is so much written in those stones.'

'Yes,' said Ashok, 'but few take the trouble to read them. So what do you read in them?'

'Continuity, and at the same time they remind me of the transient nature of existence.'

'You've read the stones well. You have understood something fundamental about our religion. The gods would applaud your interpretation.'

Hannah walked across to the wall of bull figures. 'Why the bulls?'

'Nandi the bull was the *vahana*, the vehicle of Shiva. Most of our gods have *vahanas*.'

'Even Ganesh?'

'Sure. Ganesha's *vahana* is a mouse.'

'A mouse. Of course. I should have guessed.'

Now, he thought. Now I'll tell her. 'Talking about vehicles, Hannah. You know that incident...'

Just then a family came up to them - elderly parents and two adult sons with wives and a bunch of children. One of the young men pointed shyly at the camera slung around Hannah's neck.

'Photo?' The family were already arranging themselves against the backcloth of the temple. Hannah obliged. 'Ask them for their address so that I can send them a copy,' she said to Ashok, but the family, pressing their hands together in delighted thanks were already laughingly on their way.

Hannah shook her head. 'I don't suppose I'll ever really understand,' she said.

'Most foreigners don't,' replied Ashok, 'although they like to think they do. But you - you think you don't, but you have natural understanding. You don't let preconceptions cloud your judgement - well, not much, anyway.' Perhaps that's it, he thought. Too receptive, too open-minded for her own good. Ideas take root too easily, imagination runs riot. He would tell her about the taxi. Today. Now he'd have to wait again. For the right moment.

'Come on,' he said, taking her by the arm. 'There's a lot more to see.'

For three hours they discovered Mamallapuram's ancient sites, treading barefoot on the sacred soil. By now the sandy earth had become a frying pan for feet unaccustomed to the ferocity of India's midday sun. Even Ashok, his soles grown delicate over the English years, hugged the narrow strips of remaining shade.

'The five *rathas*,' Ashok explained as they came to an area dotted with rock cut temples and life-sized, granite animals.

'*Rathas*?'

'Chariots - used in processions to carry the gods out of the temple. But these *rathas*, they're misnamed. They're actually little temples cut out of a ridge of solid granite. Things aren't always what they seem, Hannah. Which reminds me...'

'Oh, look at that stone elephant. It's simply amazing.'

Damn. Was she doing this intentionally?

'That *ratha* is dedicated to the rain god, Indra, and the elephant is his vehicle. Hannah, I'm trying to tell you something...'

She placed a hand on his arm and looked into his eyes, her brow slightly furrowed. 'Leave it, Ashok. I don't want to think about it. Not now.'

'How do you know...?'

'I just do. But please, here I want to be free of all that.'

For once, thought Ashok, she looks at peace. He nodded. 'OK. It's good to see you so relaxed.'

'I feel as if I'm drowning in the impossible spirituality of this land.'

'India does that to people.'

Hannah stared at him. 'Something's happening to me, Ashok.'

'Happening? In what sense?'

'I don't know. Somehow...I can't explain.'

'You're losing your anger.'

'Not my anger exactly. Injustice still exists. There's still a sharp dividing line between rich and poor - even more here than at home.

But all the things I've fought for and shouted about; I wonder what would have happened if I'd come here first.'

'You might have tackled things differently, you mean?'

'Maybe. This place turns everything inside out.'

They explored the site, unable to linger at each shrine for more than a minute, and then only by hopping constantly from foot to foot, until overwhelmed by the forces of nature and man, one ferocious, the other sublime, their animated spirits could barely prop up their exhausted limbs.

They came out onto the village road and hurried into the shade of a roadside workshop, where a stone carver crouched on the ground putting the finishing touches to a fist-sized, blue-grey soapstone Ganesh. Around him stood the fruits of his previous labours, gods and goddesses of every shape and size, some scarcely bigger than a thumbnail; others huge enough to stand alone upon a temple floor or grace the household shrine of a wealthy family.

'Stone-cutting is speciality of this region,' said Ashok. Hannah picked up the newly completed Ganesh. Her eyes travelled over the reclining figure's curved lines.

'He's perfect. He should be the god of happiness.' She ran her finger over the smooth surface of the stone.

'He who is attired in a white garment,' said Ashok, taking the figure gently from Hannah, and smiling at her with his eyes, *'and has the complexion of the moon; on him we meditate for the removal of obstacles.'*

Hannah's eyes smiled back at him; unfathomable pools of longing and wonder.

'It is part of a prayer to Lord Ganesha,' Ashok said. Would she still look at him like that after he confronted her with proof of her delusion? He tore himself from her gaze. He hated himself for what he had to do. For Hannah, even being pursued by a stalker would be preferable to having her rationality questioned. Ashok knew that. There were things he'd always known, although he had not admitted to Hannah quite how much Maighréad had told him about her family. He knew that Hannah's was a tough inheritance; her ancestors lost in concentration camps across Europe; her own mother, arriving in England in a *Kindertransport*, taken in by an English family until Theresienstadt was liberated; her grandmother, one of only a handful of survivors, later joining her daughter in England. Then there was her father, who as a young teenager enrolled in the Danish Resistance, lying about his age. Hannah wasn't one to stand aside and watch destructive elements tear away at the foundations of a stable and just society. To fight for what she believed in came as naturally as breathing. And to do this she had to believe in herself. Ashok had worked this out from Maighréad's ramblings. Strange. He should have been jealous, but he was fascinated. Perhaps he'd fallen in love with Hannah, even then, through the dream of her that Maighréad was weaving. Perhaps that was the real reason why he couldn't commit to Maighréad.

Ashok spoke to the stone carver and, after a few moments of good-natured haggling, handed the Ganesh to Hannah.

'It's yours. So that you'll remember Mamallapuram.'

'I'll treasure it. But do you really think I could forget today?'

Their eyes met again and made love in the unsuspecting crowd that had gathered around the carver's workshop.

The *Mandapas*, ancient rock temple halls carved into a boulder-strewn hill, provided a refuge from the overbearing heat, and comfort to their sore feet. Here they could study the carvings at leisure.

'*Yalis*,' explained Ashok, pointing to mythical leonine creatures at the base of a row of heavy entrance pillars. 'They guard the temple. This *mandapa* is dedicated to Lord Krishna. He saved the people from the torrential wrath of Indra, by holding up a mountain to shield them from the flood. Look - it's all carved on the wall.'

'You sound as if you believe it. Do you?'

'I don't know. Perhaps I do. My grandmother taught me to believe that anything is possible if we want to make it happen.'

Her gaze was searching. Ashok turned back to the wall carving.

'And under the mountain life goes on as usual,' he said. 'Milking the cow, carrying water, depicted for eternity.'

'Nothing is for eternity.'

'So you don't believe in afterlife? I thought that was fundamental to Western religion.'

'Western? Remember that Judaism and Christianity like Islam sprang from the deserts of Arabia.'

'What do you believe in, Hannah?'

'Humanity.'

'You're an atheist then.'

'I didn't say that. What you said before, about all gods leading to God - sounds good to me.'

'Nothing is for eternity.' Ashok repeated Hannah's words. 'You dispute the existence of heaven?'

'I don't know. I meant nothing earthly is for eternity. Even evil passes,' she added, a momentary vision appearing to cloud her pleasure.

Was this the moment to try again? After all, Ashok mused, she'd reintroduced the subject herself.

'Talking of which,' he said, trying to sound calm and casual, 'you know that incident in...'

But Hannah had stiffened and was staring out of the cave temple into the sunlight beyond.

'Hannah, what is it?'

'That smell, that rotten, stinking smell.'

'It's just sewage in the wind, that's all. Locals use the northern beach as their toilet, I'm afraid.'

'No! Listen to me. There was another smell - just for a moment. It was the same smell as in my garden that night. The same as in the tomb. The same as in my hotel room at the Pandava. He's here, I know it.'

She took hold of Ashok's arm and pulled him out into the light. For a few seconds they were blinded.

'There.' Hannah pointed to the top of the hill. Ashok just managed to catch a glimpse of a disappearing figure. It told him nothing, probably only a tourist, but Hannah needed convincing.

'Wait by that *yali*. I'll check him out.' He pointed to a pillar at the temple entrance and, before Hannah had time to argue, he began to stride along the footpath up the boulder-strewn hillside.

Hannah rushed after him, but he was well ahead of her. Sensing that she was following, he stopped and turned. 'Get back,' he called.

It was over in a flash. One moment he was on the path. The next, a small figure hurled itself at him from behind a boulder, knocking him off his feet, and out of the way of the football-sized rock that came hurtling down the hill and crashed down on the spot where seconds earlier he had been standing.

* * *

'What's up with you?' Felicity, relaxing on the living room sofa, looked up from her magazine.

Before she had time to catch her breath, Duncan caught her by the shoulders, hauled her up and rammed her so hard against the wall that her head slammed against it with an excruciating crack. She shrieked. 'What the hell are you doing? Have you gone mad?'

'Now,' he said, breathing rapidly, 'you're going to tell me exactly what you're playing at. I want to know everything - how you got into the garden room, why you've been tampering with the phone there, what you've been doing with the information - everything, d'you hear?'

Felicity's face registered a look of terror, but she said quietly, 'I don't know what the hell you're on about.'

'Oh yes you do. It may be the last thing you do, but you'll tell me.' He slammed her hard against the wall again, making her head spin with pain and confusion.

Felicity's expression was spectral. 'For God's sake, Duncan. Let me sit down.'

Duncan thought she was about to pass out. Panic seized him. He'd lost control. He'd meant to scare her but he didn't know his own strength. He let go of her shoulders.

She slumped onto the sofa.

'Now talk. Everything. Talk. I want to know exactly what you were doing, tampering with my phone.'

'It wasn't me, Duncan, honest it wasn't. How could I have got into the garden room?'

'I don't know. You tell me.'

Felicity began to cry. Duncan watched her, coldly.

'Oh, Duncan,' she said at length, 'I've been such a fool.'

Her tears appeared almost as if they were tears of relief that she had been found out.

'Promise you won't hate me?'

'Hate you?' For a moment, looking at her vulnerability, Duncan almost hated himself. Had he over-reacted? After all, she'd only listened to his phone messages. Was that such a big deal? But he knew it was. His garden room line was sacrosanct, Felicity was perfectly aware of that. It was his hot line to the office; the desk upon which it sat was often the repository of confidential documents. Apart from that, there was the promise he had made to Hannah, that despite his conviction of the absurdity of her stalking claims, he would keep her whereabouts secret.

'No,' he sighed, 'I won't hate you.'

She took a deep breath. 'Well, you're right. Someone's been listening to your messages.'

'Obviously. Get on with it.'

'I set you up. Right from the start.'

Duncan frowned. 'What d'you mean, set me up?'

'I was pushed into it. By Terry.'

'*Terry? Your brother?* What the hell are you talking about?'

'How can I possibly hope you'll understand? He needed me. He's been through so much...' She stopped herself and bit her lip.

Was this a bad dream? 'Just get on with it. Tell me the worst.'

'It was all part of the set up - me getting the job at your place. Chatting you up. Terry decided that I look a bit like Hannah and he wanted me to play on that - only sexier, if you get what I mean. So he got me to dye my hair.'

Duncan could hardly take in her words. It couldn't be true. *She used him in order to to help her brother?* Too ridiculous.

'The first part was a synch. It was easy to take you in. What a plonker.'

'Keep to the bloody point!'

'That is the point really. I suppose all men are easy prey if they're sex-starved, lonely and their latest bird's just legged it.'

Duncan gritted his teeth. *Don't let her get to you.* 'What the hell's all this about? Why did this brother of yours want you to stitch me up? Who are you working for?'

'I don't know, Duncan, and that's the truth. It's all very hush-hush. All I know is that Terry's involved in something big. Government maybe.'

'Don't be so ridiculous. No government would be in the least bit interested in me.'

'Not you. We were supposed to get the low-down on Hannah Petersen.'

'What?'

'OK, OK, keep your hair on. Whoever it is is interested in her activities. Makes sense doesn't it? She does ask for trouble.'

Duncan had to admit to himself that it was indeed a possibility. Any of a number of organisations might be interested in Hannah - the CIA, the FBI, the IRA - even the British Government. And of course there was Elliot Bannerman.

Felicity managed a half-hearted grin. 'It was no trouble getting *you* to spill the beans about Hannah.'

Duncan wanted to crawl into a corner and die, as he remembered their months of creative cavorting. *Favours in return for information.* Why didn't he see it at the time? 'I want to know all about her, sweetie,' she'd said, 'I want to be Hannah.' How could he have flipped so completely as to be taken in by her? Had he lost his marbles? Had he had a breakdown?

He cringed as he recalled how easily she had manipulated him. He wouldn't deny her the route to sublime satisfaction, surely? And if he had to be honest about it, he got just as much out of fantasising that Felicity was Hannah as Felicity did. Or said she did. What a fool he'd been. Why hadn't he seen that there was a more sinister reason for her questioning than a craving for sexual fantasy?

'What about the phone-tapping scam?'

'Yeah... well. For a computer nerd you're a right wally when it comes to other things. I'd noticed that with the video. You never get it right. And the microwave. Food's always half raw or burnt when you do it.'

She glanced at him. Her eyes flashed. Duncan was tight-lipped.

'You don't know the ins and outs of your own answering machine.'

'Go on.'

'A couple of months ago Terry said he'd been ordered to listen in to the answer-phone in your den. He told me to get hold of the instructions. I knew you kept all your instruction booklets in the sideboard drawer. I found out that you can access the answer-phone from anywhere if you know the code. That was easy too. All I had to do was follow the instructions in the booklet and press the right buttons on the phone for it to tell me the code. I managed to slip in one evening when you left the door unlocked to go to the loo. It only took a minute. I passed the code on to Terry. It should have been foolproof.' She frowned. 'How did you find out?'

'You can tell if a message is new or not,' he replied shortly.

'I managed to wheedle out of you that Hannah was going to India.'

It had all seemed so harmless. Duncan had been convinced that all Hannah's problems were in her mind. He had never associated Felicity's interrogations with Hannah's stalking claims.

'I realised that you'd be the only one she'd contact, and that the phone she'd be using was locked in your garden room.'

'So Terry taps my phone messages.' Duncan was thinking out loud. 'Then what?'

Felicity didn't reply. Duncan took hold of her shoulders and shook her roughly. 'Then what?'

'OK, OK. Just leave me alone, will you. Then Terry passes it to... whoever.'

Duncan nodded impatiently. 'Let's cut the crap, shall we? It's Bannerman, isn't it?'

A split second's silence. Then she looked at him impassively. 'Bannerman?'

'Yes, Bannerman. Don't play the innocent.'

'It's like I said. I've no idea who it is.'

'OK, we'll play it your way. So tell me how? How does Terry pass it on?'

'I don't know. I never asked.'

'Well, at least they won't have got anything useful. Just hotel names. It's hardly likely Bannerman would send him after her to India.' He scrutinised her face. 'Or would he?' His eyes grew menacing, as he remembered that Felicity had told him that Terry had "gone away." He grabbed hold of Felicity's arms and slowly tightened his grip until she squealed with pain.

'OK,' she shrieked. 'He's in India. Satisfied now?'

*   *   *

Hannah raced up the hill. Ashok was back on his feet and was helping up the person who had saved him from being hit by the rock. A few yards before she reached them, Hannah pulled up short. Ashok's saviour waved at her cheerily. 'Hannah! We meet again!'

Willi stood there looking exactly as Hannah had first encountered her at the reception desk of the Krishna Hotel.

Hannah looked from one to the other in bewilderment.

'There I am, enjoying the view, when I see this gentleman is about to get in the way of a falling rock.' Willi said, 'so I do my Good Samaritan act. Are you all right, sir?'

'I'm fine.' Ashok went over to Hannah and gave her a brief hug. 'I'm fine, Hannah, honestly.' He held out his hand. 'You must be Willi. I can't thank you enough for what you did.'

Now it was Willi's turn to be confused. 'You know each other?'

It was all too much for Hannah.

'For goodness sake, you two,' she burst out, 'Let's get away from here before he strikes again.'

'Who strikes?'

'Willi's right, Hannah. It was probably just a piece of loose rock. But let's get down anyway.'

Once they were back on the street, shock and relief caught up with Hannah. She turned to Ashok, shaking her head. 'Falling rock! You know you don't believe that any more than I do.'

Ashok said nothing.

Willi's curiosity was palpable.

'Ashok is my guardian angel,' Hannah said, hoping to allay any further probing into how they had met.

Willi flashed her eyes at him in unabashed lust.

'Perhaps you will now be my guardian angel also?'

'It seems that you are mine,' Ashok said.

'Hands off, Willi. He belongs to me.' Hannah slipped her arm through Ashok's.

'I see,' Willi grinned. 'A great deal seems to have happened.'

'Yes. But what about you? I've been worrying since I left Hyderabad.'

'I guess you wondered where I'd disappeared to, eh? It's a very odd story.'

'We need to talk.'

Willi nodded. 'But first I have to go and sort out a room for tonight before they are all booked up. This place is a Mecca for travellers.'

The sun was low in the sky. Ashok spoke.

'Willi. I don't know about you, but we haven't eaten yet. Look,' He pointed to a sign on a low building, 'Blue Heaven. That should be good for something decent. Suppose we meet up there in half an hour - say at six o'clock?'

After Willi had gone, Ashok and Hannah wandered in silence across to a massive, sandstone rock face rising almost three hundred feet out of the barren earth.

'It's known as The Penance,' said Ashok.

Carved upon the rock face a cavalcade of men, deities and animals converged on a cleft in the centre that represented the Ganges River. The pageant on the rock was in perfect harmony.

Not so Ashok and Hannah. Their unsung melody had slid almost imperceptibly into a minor key.

'Ashok, I know you don't believe me, but that rock fall was no accident.'

Ashok shrugged. He looked preoccupied, Hannah thought. What on earth had happened?

'Did something happen up there that you're not telling me? Or is it Willi?'

He flinched, but said nothing.

Hannah shook his arm. 'Please don't clam up on me.'

'It's nothing.'

'No lies, Ashok. Don't you think we've had enough of those?'

Ashok relaxed.

'You're right.' A moment's pause followed before he continued. 'About that boulder. I'll reserve judgement for now. As for Willi, I guess I'm frightened that you feel something for her.'

Silence. Hannah struggled to hide her indignation.

'You're right. I do feel something for her. Relief because she's turned up safely. And until a minute ago immense gratitude because she saved your life. Though I may have second thoughts about that.' She fixed him with reproachful eyes. 'For goodness sake, stop being an idiot.'

At last the bubble of tension burst as Ashok looked sheepish, and muttered 'I'm sorry. That's what love does to you.' The words slipped out. Hannah fought a desire to respond. No. Let him sweat. She'd stay cool.

'Let's forget it, shall we?' She touched his hand briefly, rekindling the spark between them.

Over *puris* and *thali* at the Blue Heaven Restaurant, they listened, aghast, to Willi's story.

* * *

Willi had awoken, as if from an operation. Her body was clammy and hot. She blinked in the darkness. Her neck felt as if an overzealous osteopath had grappled it. Movement eluded her. Her nostrils were filled with the stink of rotting sewage. What was this hellhole? She had stayed at some pretty rough places since her arrival in India, but she couldn't remember booking into this one. Had she dined out on ganja last night? She didn't think so, but it was the only possible explanation.

Gradually, accompanied by waves of rasping pain in her head, she manoeuvred herself into a sitting position and leant back against the wall. She shuffled along it until she felt the door, and heaved herself up by the latch. Her legs felt like bread crusts. Why had she been asleep in her jeans, she wondered, and why were her jeans so stiff? She ran her hands down her legs and recoiled.

'Oh shit!' she muttered, aptly. So that's what the smell was. She recalled that the need for a loo had dominated her last waking thought, before she had passed out.

Now it was imperative to find the bathroom of this doss house. She had no idea what time it was, or how long she had been asleep.

She pushed against the door, but it refused to open. It was at this point that the fog in her mind suddenly cleared. Scenes passed through her head like a fast forwarding video-tape - the trip to Golconda with Hannah; the walk to the tombs; the search for a loo; the *burkha*-clad woman; the hut; oblivion.

She must be in the hut still. Had she fainted or had she been knocked out? In view of the locked door and her sore head, the latter seemed more likely, but why? The whole thing was incomprehensible, but she knew that she had to get out as quickly as possible, before her gaoler returned. She mustered the little strength left to her and threw herself against the door. It held fast. However, she managed to loosen a piece of the rotting wood. She wrenched it free and peered through the resulting hole. She could make out bushes dotted around like low grey clouds in the first glimmers of dawn.

OK, Willi, she told herself. Keep calm. You've been in worse fixes than this. She didn't delve too deeply into that thought. In reality, she was kidding herself. True, there was the incident that nearly cost her life when her bus turned over on the Grand Trunk Road in Uttar Pradesh, and the blood poisoning that put her into a

Bombay hospital. But these were accidents. She simply happened to get caught up in them.

Now though, she was in a different situation. Someone had targeted her. She had walked into something malevolent, but had no idea how to handle it, because she had no idea what it was.

Working with her hands, she tried to enlarge the hole by pulling away bits of the wood. Blisters formed on her fingers, and her legs felt as if they would give way. It was useless but she had to keep trying. Every few moments she stopped and called, 'hallo - can anyone hear me?'

Then she felt someone rattle the door from outside. She peered through the hole. A swathe of black cloth filled her vision. Her heart started to race. Her kidnapper had returned. She shrank into the corner to await her fate.

Now someone was pounding the lock with what sounded like an iron bar. Suddenly the door sprang open. A figure in a black *burkha* filled the entrance. Willi cowered in the corner waiting to be hit with the steel rod that the figure was wielding.

But a hand emerged from beneath the black cloth and calmly unfastened the all-concealing veil, revealing the face of a young woman.

'Don't be afraid,' said the woman in perfect English. 'I will not hurt you.' She moved slowly across to Willi. 'What has happened?'

'Who are you?' was all that Willi could bring herself to mutter.

'An ornithologist,' said the young woman. 'I came to watch birds and I heard you call.'

'You didn't lock me in here last night?'

'Some person locked you up? But why?'

'I don't know.'

'You have a description?'

'The person wore a *burkha* - just like yours ...'

'Why would a Muslim woman want to kidnap you? This makes no sense.'

'That's what I thought. In fact,' she remembered the pale, wiry hand that had grabbed her, 'I think it may have been a man. Possibly a foreigner.'

'Who left his clothes behind.' The woman pointed to a pile of black cloth in the corner of the hut. On closer inspection Willi realised that it was a *burkha*.

'Come,' said the young woman, holding out her hand.

Willi struggled to her feet but dizziness overcame her and she sank back down.

'You are ill,' said her rescuer. 'I will bring help.'

'It's just exhaustion. Really, I only need an autorickshaw to get me back to my hotel.'

'Come then,' said the woman, readjusting her veil before she stepped out of the hut. Slowly she helped Willi across the scrubland to the main road.

A car was parked on the sandy verge, the driver busily cleaning the headlights. 'This is my vehicle. I will take you to your hotel.'

Willi collapsed thankfully on the back seat. Her companion slipped in beside her and ordered the driver to move off. After it was all over Willi would regret bitterly that she was too confused and worn out to thank the young woman properly, or even to find out her name.

She stumbled out of the car when it drew up outside the Krishna, assured her rescuer that she was fine, muttered words of thanks that seemed hopelessly inadequate and wondered how on earth she could get past Mr Reddy, the receptionist, without being seen.

Peering cautiously through the glass door, she saw a fat, bearded, fair-haired man with a suitcase standing at the counter paying his bill. Willi slipped noiselessly into the hotel while Mr Reddy was preoccupied, and ducked up the stairs, silently thanking her unknown saviour.

Only when she reached her room, did Willi check the contents of her little haversack. Address book, travellers' cheques, passport, Visa card, open return ticket to Amsterdam, toilet roll, and purse containing two hundred rupees. Nothing had been taken. Incredible! Relief turned to bewilderment. So robbery had not been the motive. If not, then what was?

After a hot shower and a change of clothing, she felt reborn. She sauntered nonchalantly into the dining room in time for breakfast.

CHAPTER 8

Willi's story was greeted with stunned silence. At length Hannah burst out, 'I'm so sorry, Willi, I don't know what to say.'

'It's all over now. Quite exciting looking back on it. One thing I don't understand - the receptionist - Mr Reddy - said you told him I'd gone off with a friend. Why?'

'That's a long story, Willi, and I owe you an explanation.'

'But unfortunately,' Ashok interrupted, 'our driver will be getting impatient. We have a long journey back to Chennai.'

'Yes, and I still have to find somewhere to stay.'

'What?' Hannah said, 'You mean you haven't anywhere?'

'All the rooms I tried were full. I expect I'll end up kipping on the beach.'

Ashok and Hannah exchanged a quick glance.

'Look,' Ashok said, 'we have two rooms in Chennai, and we're only using one. You could have the other. Management won't mind. We're paying for two doubles. They don't have singles.'

'One thing though,' Hannah cut in. 'It could be dangerous for you to be seen with us. We'll fill you in on the journey and you can decide.'

Willi looked intrigued, but laughed.

'Ever been on an Indian bus? That's dangerous. I thrive on danger. Lead me to your lair!'

By the end of the high-speed, teeth-rattling ride through the Tamil-Nadu night, Willi knew all about the stalker. No point in keeping anything from her. Hannah felt that she owed it to her. Willi greeted each new development with the reaction of an Indian child to the gift of an English coin. It was clear that she meant to stay.

'I'll just get my bag out of the room,' said Ashok when they reached the Pandava. 'And since it's past midnight and I for one am tired, I think we should say goodnight.'

'Bolt your door,' added Hannah. 'Any problems bang on the wall. We'll be there in seconds.'

'Hannah,' said Ashok as he closed the door behind Willi, 'I've got something to show you.' He reached into his breast pocket for the newspaper article. Hannah wasn't listening. She was staring at Ashok's travel bag, which he had placed on the floor next to the bed. Now she put her hand on his arm, in a gesture that meant 'be still.'

She said. 'Don't open it. There's something in it.'

'What? How do you know? Did it move? Did you hear something?'

She shook her head. 'I don't know. I think so, yes.'

'Oh, come on. Mamallapuram's gone to your head. You're seeing spirits.'

'Shut up, Ashok. There's something in that bag.'

'Not a lot though. I took most of it out yesterday. Just a shirt and some boxer shorts, if I remember right. Not much of a threat, I think. Not the shirt, anyway.'

'Stop fooling.' Hannah was still staring, transfixed, at the bag.

'Look.' Ashok made a move towards it. 'I'm going to open, just to show you it's OK. Stand back if you like.'

Hannah launched herself at Ashok with such a loud scream that Willi rushed out of her room, and hammered on their door.

'What's up? Open the door!'

'Hannah thinks there's some ghost in my case,' said Ashok, letting her in. 'She won't let me open.'

'We women are intuitive,' said Willi. 'If Hannah says something's wrong, then it is.'

'Well, how are we going to find out without opening?'

'OK,' said Hannah, 'but not in here. Outside, on the lawn. Get your torch.'

She took a reel of white cotton from her rucksack, handed the loose end of the thread to Willi, unravelled it and broke off some

123

ten metres. Gingerly, but without hesitating, she went up to Ashok's bag and pulled the thread through the zip toggle, doubling it up and tying a knot at the end.

'Good,' said Willi. 'Now let's get the bugger out!' Hannah noticed that Willi, for all her brave words, kept well back from the bag, and did not offer to help.

Ashok stood, arms folded, leaning against the door looking at the two women with an amused expression on his face. Ignoring him, Hannah picked up the bag and trooped out into the humid night with Ashok and Willi trailing behind her. She placed the bag on the lawn.

'Shine your torch, Ashok.'

Hannah located the thread and holding onto the end, backed off several metres until it was taut.

Slowly, she started to pull the zip open.

*　*　*

Terry in India? Felicity's confession whirled around Duncan's head. The room had suddenly become a prison; air so stale that Duncan could not breathe. The sofa with Felicity upon it was an instrument of torture.

A voice, not his, spoke calmly to Felicity from somewhere inside Duncan's body.

'If he's gone, why are you still here?'

She sighed and glanced up at him.

'Oh, Duncan, you're so thick at times. Isn't it obvious?'

'Not to me.'

'Do you really think I could have kept up living with you for months if I didn't really care for you? OK, so Terry pushed me into the whole business in the first place, but then you asked me to move in and, well, I wouldn't have done that if I hadn't wanted to be with you. In the end I was torn between the two of you.'

'Bullshit. No one in their right mind would let their brother push them around like you say you did.'

She shrugged. 'I guess I wasn't in my right mind.'

'So tell me this. If your brother was really just investigating Hannah, he'd have made sure she didn't see him. How d'you explain that?'

For a moment he thought he'd called her bluff. But then she answered him calmly. 'OK, so he messed up a couple of times and she got a few glimpses of him. Her imagination ran riot. You know what she's like. You saw it for yourself. The last thing he'd want would be to draw attention to himself.'

Remorse and fear for Hannah gripped Duncan's stomach and twisted it. It all made sense, dammit. He looked at Felicity, slumped in the corner of the sofa. There was no way round it. It would devastate his reputation, but he had to act.

'Come on, we're going to the police. You're going to spill the beans.'

'I don't think that's very clever.'

'What d'you mean?'

'Has it occurred to you that the police might be involved? It certainly occurred to me. Too risky to put their own men onto her, so get Terry to do their dirty work instead. Think about it. They weren't too keen to believe her stalking story, were they?'

There was a certain logic in what she was saying, even though Duncan was fairly sure that Elliot Bannerman, and not some government agency, was at the root of the whole affair. He was guiltily relieved at having an excuse to keep Felicity's story from becoming public property just yet. There had to be another way. First of all, he had to decide about Felicity. Should he throw her out onto the street, or let her stay? He decided that the latter course was the more expedient. He'd be able to keep tabs on her, and in any case something about her vulnerability still touched him, despite his anger and humiliation. Had they both been victims?

He sat down next to her on the sofa. 'I've been a right idiot, haven't I?' he said, putting on what he hoped was a sheepish expression. 'Can't say I blame you for taking advantage.'

She looked down at her hands that were playing restlessly in her lap. 'It's... I mean, I did take advantage of you, of course, but after I'd got to know you, I hated what I was doing. We knew what they'd do to us if we tried to pull out. But... well, I really like you, Dunc.'

She glanced up at him and he could see that she meant it. Or did she? She'd taken him for a ride once. Was she doing it again? Play it cool.

'Look,' he said, 'we've got to sort this - our lives could all be in danger - you, me and Hannah. Yes, and Terry too. Let's say you're right and it's not Bannerman. We don't know who these people are or what they want. We've got to carry on normally at the moment. Just give me time to think. Meanwhile promise me you won't do anything silly.'

'Don't worry, Dunc. I'm staying right here.'

He went back into the garden room. Five o'clock. Just time to phone a local travel agent before they close and ask for the telephone number of the Chamundi.

Then he dialled the number. Yes, Hannah Petersen was staying there, but there was no answer from her room. Blast. Have to leave a message. This he did with considerable misgiving.

* * *

On the lawn of the Pandava, two night porters had turned up, intrigued by the strange, foreign ritual. Ashok ushered them to what he judged Hannah would consider to be a safe distance from the bag.

As Hannah pulled the zip open with her cotton thread, the torch picked out a faint movement inside it.

The torchlight quivered, as Ashok's hand started shaking, and Willi stepped hastily back even further, but Hannah showed no surprise.

'Get away from it, Hannah. Let me do it.' Ashok said.

'Shh!' She gestured him impatiently out of the way. 'Keep that damned torch still, can't you?'

Now the bag was fully open. Hannah dropped the thread. They waited. Moments passed. The silence was broken by one of the porters, who questioned Ashok in Tamil. To save the awkwardness of trying to explain the inexplicable, Ashok put his finger to his lips.

Hannah took the torch from Ashok and shone it briefly around the garden. She spotted a long thin branch that had broken off the flame tree. Handing the torch back to Ashok, she picked up the branch.

'Keep that torch steady on the bag.'

Carefully, as if in a slow motion film, Hannah used the branch to tip the bag gently onto its side, the open top pointing away from the onlookers.

For several seconds even the air stopped breathing. Then as imperceptibly as the minute hand of a clock, the bag's occupant emerged.

The five-foot cobra raised its head towards its audience, with the slow, powerful elegance of a Tai Ch'i expert. Transfixed in the torchlight, they could see quite clearly the black and white markings on its golden-yellow hood.

No one stirred. Like pawns on a chessboard, the watchers waited to be taken. Ashok's trembling hand froze; no ripple now in the torchlight. Impasse. Time hung suspended, meaningless.

It was over. The snake sank slowly back onto the grass, and slithered away from them into the night.

Like a concert audience waiting for the last note to fade there was a fragment of silence, before the porters burst out in excited Tamil, pressing their hands together, as if in greeting.

Ashok spoke to them briefly before picking up his bag, and walking silently back to the room.

The two women found him sitting on the edge of the bed, staring at the wooden panels on the wall.

Hannah put her arm around his shoulder and hugged him. He turned slowly to look at her, and shook his head.

'I can't believe what you just did. You saved my life. And I stood by, like a wimp and let you endanger yourself.'

'Let's get this into proportion,' Hannah said. 'I was never in any more danger than anyone else. I just thought on my feet. I suppose I've had to do a lot of that in my life.'

'And I've had to do very little, is what you're implying.'

'For goodness sake, I didn't say that at all. How on earth should I know that?'

'As Willi said, women are intuitive. And you're right, of course. Life's been a bit too kind to me, so far. I haven't had to tough it out, like you.'

'I used to be pretty tough, yes. I lost it when the stalker thing happened, but now I seem to have regained some of my confidence.' She kissed him on the cheek.

'Time for me to go.' Willi was still standing by the door.

'No, Willi.' Hannah patted the bed. 'Come and sit down. We need to talk about what happened.'

Willi came across to them, but pulled up the one chair in the room, carefully moving Hannah's clothes onto the bed.

She said, 'This snake - it must have come while you were out today.'

'No. It didn't just come. It was put into Ashok's bag on purpose.'

'We don't know that, Hannah,' said Ashok.

'It opened the zip and closed it again I suppose?'

He shrugged. 'Maybe it got in during yesterday night. I left it open when I fetched some of my things out of it. Must have been open for a good hour before I went back and fetched the rest of my things. That's when I closed it.'

'You don't really believe that, do you?' Hannah said. 'I don't, any more than I believe in your loose rock theory.'

'Well, maybe not. But we can't dismiss completely.'

'No. But let's assume it was put into the bag sometime today. And let's assume someone lobbed that rock at you. Also you had that weird phone call yesterday, let's not forget.'

'I know. OK, what have we got then? Willi gets stuck in a hut in Hyderabad, and I have a couple of near misses in Madras. There could be other explanations for all these incidents.'

'No. Face it, Ashok. Our stalker intends to wipe out anyone who gets friendly with me.'

'He's obsessed with you,' said Willi.

Hannah shook her head. 'Won't wash, I'm afraid. I've been attacked too, don't forget. Once in England, then at the tombs and again in the taxi.'

'Well in fact, from the way you described it, you weren't actually attacked in that taxi.' No way, thought Ashok, am I going to humiliate her by showing her the article in front of Willi.

Hannah snorted contemptuously. 'How naive you are sometimes, Ashok! Of course he would have attacked me, probably killed me if I hadn't got away.'

'You don't know that. Not for sure.'

'So what about the incident in England?'

'Perhaps he's become even more obsessed with you, and can't bear to harm you,' Ashok said, desperate to water down Hannah's fears, which he still felt were unfounded. Probably. The day's events had dislodged his absolute certainty.

'Perhaps he's saving something extra special for me,' Hannah said. 'You still haven't accounted for the tombs. I saw the steel glinting in the hand that came at me.'

'I have an idea.' Willi, who had been listening intently, now joined in the debate. 'Someone later sent you pearls in a silver box. Could it be that in the tomb what you were seeing was not steel but silver? Could the person have been trying to give you the pearls?'

They looked at Willi as if they were seeing her for the first time.

'That's it!' said Ashok. 'What d'you think, Hannah?'

Hannah looked thoughtful. She shook her head slowly. 'At the time I was so sure. Now... I don't know. What I do know though is that he's after anyone who has anything to do with me. And he's out to get me too, sooner or later.' She paused. When she continued, each word was carefully weighed. 'So... the fact is that I can't go on expecting others to take risks for me. Willi, tomorrow we'll have to part company. I've had you on my conscience once already. I don't want it to happen again.'

'What, miss all the excitement? No way! And if anything happens to me I've only got myself to blame, Hannah. So stop being a martyr. Now I leave you two alone and go to bed.'

'We'll talk about it again tomorrow. Goodnight, Willi.'

Willi left. Hannah took Ashok's hands in hers. 'What I said to Willi goes for you too. Leave me, Ashok. Take me back to Bangalore and then get on with your life. You... I... you mean so much to me. If anything happened to you, it wouldn't just be my conscience that suffered.'

Ashok grasped her firmly by the shoulders. 'You can put that right out of your mind. No more talk of it. Right?'

'But...'

'But nothing. Do you think I could walk out on you now? You say I mean a lot to you. Don't you think you mean just as much to me? Heavens, I felt bad enough tonight when I stood by like a gibbering idiot while you dealt with my cobra.'

At that, Hannah burst into relieved laughter. She locked him in her arms. 'OK, my gibbering idiot. I guess I'm stuck with you. For the time being anyway.' As an afterthought she added, 'so it's your cobra now, is it? Those two porters seemed pretty pleased to see it as well.'

'The cobra is one of our gods. It was an honour that he paid us a visit. They will probably build a small shrine to him in the garden.'

'You're kidding. Aren't they afraid of what it might do to their guests?'

'He is unlikely to attack unless provoked. But you're right. He is a bit of a liability here. By tomorrow he may well have been bagged and taken to somewhere less populated.'

'But they won't kill it?'

'Of course not. It's what I'm telling you. He's a god. He's favoured us with a good omen. Again your stalker has shot himself in the foot. So be happy, my Hannah. There's no need to fear.'

She held him close and felt the rapid beating of his heart. She kissed his eyes, his mouth, his neck. A sigh of capitulation escaped from his lips, as he thought about the article from the *Hindu*, still concealed in his shirt pocket. He leaned across and turned out the bedside light.

*   *   *

Ashok waited until Hannah was asleep. He slipped silently out of bed, into his clothes and out of the door.

'Can I help, sir?'

'Were you here yesterday evening, when your colleague had his break?'

'Yes, sir, indeed.'

'Can you remember if an Englishman checked in? A thin man, possibly wearing dark glasses.'

The receptionist looked blank. Ashok placed twenty rupees on the counter.

'There was such a man. But no dark glasses.'

'Did you notice his eyes?'

The desk clerk shrugged. 'Sorry, sir, I am not good at noticing such things.'

Ashok put down fifty rupees.

'Well, can you tell me anything about him? His name?'

'One moment, sir.' The man scrabbled under the counter and re-emerged with the box of registration forms. He leafed through them several times, then frowned.

'Very odd, sir. This person's details are missing.'

'Perhaps he's left.'

'But form should still be here. They are removed to archives at end of each week only.'

'Can't you remember his name?'

'No sir. I am not good at remembering names. It was not a well-known English name.'

'His room number then.'

The man gave an inane little smile. 'So sorry. I am not good...'

'Yes, yes. OK. Can you remember anything else at all?' Fifty more rupees joined the pile on the counter.

'Well... there was one thing.'

'Yes?' Ashok struggled to hide his impatience.

'He was making a phone call.'

'Phone call? Who did he call? Did you connect him?'

'Yes, sir. It was to one of our guests...'

'Which guest? Try to remember, please.' Another twenty rupees.

'So sorry, sir. I am...'

'... not good at remembering names. Of course.'

'But he was asking to look at registration forms. He was looking for his friend's room number.'

'Did he find it?'

'Yes sir. I dialled that number for him.'

'What was the number?'

'Oh, sorry, sir. I am not good at remembering numbers.'

'Did he speak to his friend?'

'No sir. He was listening for several moments, then he was telling that his friend is not there.'

*   *   *

Next morning, Ashok dressed early and slipped away to reception to pick up the photographs. He'd lain awake for what seemed like hours, wondering about the phone call. Was the man described by the desk clerk really Hannah's stalker? Or was he some innocent chap trying to get through to a friend? There was no proof, after all, that the phone call made at the desk was the one to Ashok's room. He thought about the desk clerk. Was the fellow really an imbecile? *So sorry, no good at remembering...* Or had someone got at him? The more Ashok turned things over in his mind, the more confused he became. Hard evidence. That's what he lacked. He needed hard evidence to convince him that there really was a stalker.

'*Namaskar*. Are the photos ready?'

The night clerk had gone. Once again the regular receptionist was manning his post. He smiled. 'Your friend was picking them up not half hour ago.'

'Miss Groot? I didn't know she was up yet.'

The man frowned. 'Not she, sir. He. Your friend you were asking after when you first arrived, I think. Small, very slim, sunglasses.'

Ashok stared at the man. What the hell is going on here? He walked slowly back to the room, wrestling to come to terms with his discovery. Is this it? Hard evidence at last? So Hannah must be right. It's not her confounded imagination. But hang on - what about the taxi incident? It seems that the line between imagination and reality has become very blurred. Is that so surprising under the circumstances? I'm confused too. However, we have proof now that the man does exist. Somehow we've got to keep clear heads. At the same time we can't afford to ignore anything. He remembered the snake and shivered. Planted after all? And the rock?

In view of this latest development he decided not to tell Hannah about the article in the *Hindu*. Maybe he would tell her at a later date. For now it was his secret.

*   *   *

Hannah still lay in bed, trying to drown the disturbing memories of the previous day in the early morning symphony of parakeets and pariah dogs, servants and sweeper women, and the rustling of a slight breeze in the bougainvilleas.

'No photos?' she said in a resigned voice, registering Ashok's fraught expression.

Briefly, Ashok relayed the news.

'Well,' said Hannah flatly, 'if you needed any proof...'

'I didn't,' Ashok lied. 'I've never doubted your story. But you have to be prepared to consider all alternatives. That's what I was doing only.'

'Why would he want my photos anyway?'

'Same reason we wanted them, no doubt. Perhaps he thinks he might be on one.'

'But how does he manage to keep tabs on me?'

'Yes, I'm asking myself the same question. Money talks. That's part of your answer anyway, but I don't think that's all of it. How he knows exactly where you're going? At the very least he needs some knowledge of the country and the languages.'

'Well if money talks, I'm not short of cash. Let's do some investigating when we get back to the Chamundi. Someone there may have tipped him off.'

They caught the lunchtime Express back to Bangalore. Hannah insisted that they travelled second class, non-a.c. remembering that this was how the stalker had travelled to Chennai. The hot, crowded compartment with passengers tumbling out of every niche was certainly more entertaining than the air-conditioned calm of second a.c. but the crowds made observation difficult. People, baggage and vendors cluttering the corridors prevented Ashok from straying further afield to scour the rest of the train. For this Hannah gave silent thanks, remembering the previous journey.

They had been unable to deter Willi from her resolve to travel with them.

'I want to see Bangalore,' she said. 'Three or four days, then I will be on my way. I intend to spend Christmas in Kerala before I return to the Netherlands.'

By the time they reached the Chamundi, it was nine o'clock.

They stopped off at reception for Hannah to collect her key and to inform them that Willi would be sharing her room for a night or two.

'One moment, Madam - message for you.' The receptionist handed Hannah a note that had been hastily scrawled on a Chamundi Hotel memo sheet.

Urgent message for Hannah Petersen, she read. *Phone Duncan as soon as possible. Do not leave a message.*

'It's Duncan. Wonder what he wants? Hope it's not another hiccup with *Fair Game.*'

'Well, surely it can't be that urgent,' Ashok said.

'It is. Some people are giving us grief with the US publication.'

'Can't it wait till tomorrow?'

'No, it can't. I'll phone him now. From my room.' She looked at her watch.

'Won't be long,' she said. 'Wait for me in the bar.'

She returned ten minutes later, frowning.

Ashok said, 'Well?'

She continued to frown in silence while she collected her thoughts.

'What is it?'

'Not sure at the moment. Duncan knows something - about the stalker. Wouldn't say over the phone. He sounded worried - didn't like leaving a message with reception. He doesn't want to risk doing it again. Wants to email me tomorrow if I can get hold of an email address by then. Is that possible?'

Ashok thought for a moment.

'Yes. I have a friend at BTU. I'm sure they've got email up there. Give me Duncan's email address. I'll go there now and set it up. There's always someone around in the lab - at this time of night also. I'll tell Duncan to mail the information to Salman's address and we'll check it out first thing tomorrow morning.'

'Thanks. By the way - BTU?'

'Biotechnology University. We Indians have even more of a passion than you for abbreviating names. Right - I'm on my way. Meanwhile, you two go up to the room and lock the door. I'll see you in the morning.'

*   *   *

At the Biotechnology University, Ashok managed to locate his friend Salman, an assistant professor in the Biochemistry Department, who was still busy at the bench.

Salman abandoned his Petrie dish and wiped his hands. 'Bash! I was wondering when you would show up. I heard you were in town.'

Ashok smiled at hearing his teenage nickname. He embraced his old school chum warmly. Salman looked older than his thirty-two years. His hair was thinning and already he was showing the telltale paunch of middle-class affluence and undisciplined eating.

'Hallo, Slam. Still dabbling in alchemy, I see.'

Salman roared with laughter. 'Bash and Slam, dazzling duo of under-eighteen cricket team! Those were the days, no?'

'Those were the days. You still playing?'

'But of course! Each Sunday afternoon I am coaching youngsters. It's keeping me fit.'

'Fit! What's this then?' Ashok patted his friend's ample belly.

'For that you must blame my wife's wonderful cooking.'

Ashok hid his surprise. Three years ago Salman had still been openly bitter about the marriage that his parents had foisted on him at the age of twenty-four. Two children had arrived in quick succession, and he had considered his family to be a millstone around his academic neck. Ashok proceeded cautiously.

'They are all well at home?'

'Yes, they are well. Both boys top of class in their school. Shaziah is a good mother, Bash. And excellent wife.'

Ashok raised his eyebrows.

'Ah, you are wondering, I see. Three years ago I was telling differently, no?'

'Very differently. I'm glad to see things seem to have sorted themselves out.'

'A matter of time only. Getting to know each other. Getting used to each other's ways. Now all is well.'

Time? Five years of misery before the healing hand of familiarity had blotted out the anguish of his lost youth? Ashok hadn't forgotten even if Salman had, and he had promised himself that he would never make Salman's mistake. He would never be drawn into a marriage to anyone who did not measure up to the ideal he had conjured up in daydreams. Ashok had been lucky. Salman had had no siblings for his parents to consider. He had been the sole focus of their attention, and his life, including his marriage, had been mapped out from an early age.

'Now at last is your turn,' Salman said. 'Time to leave field open for younger fellows, eh?' He nudged Ashok. 'Still one for the ladies, Bash?'

'What do you mean? I was never a ladies' man.'

'Oh no? You think you got your nickname for the way you wielded cricket bat only?'

'Yes, what else?'

'Bash - bashful. Joke. Remember how you eyed up girls from Ladies College?'

'I only looked at them, Slam. Same as everyone else.'

'Ah yes, but only you it was caught the eye of the pretty ones. We could all see you had great future in that department.'

'Well, I'm sorry to disappoint you. My life's been very unexciting in that respect.' Ashok remembered his student days at

Oxford and chuckled inwardly. But it was time to change the subject.

'Salman, I have a favour to ask you.'

'You want me to find you a wife?'

'I want to borrow your email address.'

'Oh, that is all? That's easy.'

'It's not for me. It's for a friend. She's having some trouble and needs to contact UK.'

Salman looked amused but, with typical discretion, knew to refrain from comment.

There had been no problem in sending off an email to Duncan. Ashok had simply written

Anxiously awaiting your information.
Please reply to this address,
Hannah

CHAPTER 9

Duncan had waited in the garden room for Hannah to return the call he had made to the Chamundi. It was a full hour before she did so. She sounded tired. No wonder. It must have been midnight there. What had she been doing until then? She'd mentioned that she would ask some Indian friend to set up an email address. He felt uneasy. Who'd she palled up with? Had she been taken in, as he had by Felicity?

Ah yes. Felicity. Reluctantly he went back to the house to check on her. She was in bed. She looked pale and tiny, curled up in the corner of the big bed, hugging the duvet close to her body. For a while he stood staring down at her with a mixture of pain and pity. After all she'd done to him, she still had the power to evoke some sort of emotion in him. Funny. He'd believed her when she said she cared for him. It was the only thing she'd said that day that he did believe. And what did he feel? Horrified, humiliated. And very frightened for Hannah. Above all, he had to get Hannah out of this mess, which was partly of his making. For once in his life, he felt like praying. Please don't let anything happen to Hannah. She means the world to me.

When he had satisfied himself that Felicity really was sleeping, he returned to the garden room, where, after hours of agonising self-analysis, he finally fell asleep at his desk. When he awoke in the night he checked his email and found that Hannah had made contact. He mailed her back.

*   *   *

When Ashok returned home from the Biotechnology University, Srinivasa and Girija were still up, despite the late hour.

'You had enjoyable visit to Chennai with your friend?' enquired Srinivasa casually.

'Friends,' corrected Ashok, in a vain attempt to dilute his father's interest in Hannah. 'There were three of us. We were joined by a Dutch girl.'

'Ah - always one for ladies. Talking of which...'

Ashok knew what was coming.

'Yes, *Bapa*. The girl in Mysore. I know.'

'We can't keep that family hanging around, Ashok. We must tell them something.'

Ashok looked at his feet and said nothing.

Girija, who had been standing in the doorway, now stepped forward. She placed her hand gently on Ashok's arm.

'You are troubled, my son. I know.' She turned to her husband. 'Perhaps Ashok would like to visit once more before he will make up his mind.'

Ashok shook his head slowly. 'I have made up my mind, *Amma*. I cannot marry her. I cannot marry anyone.'

'Because of your English temptress?' said his mother.

Ashok shrugged.

'My son, how long have you known her? Three days? A week?'

'Longer than I have known the one in Mysore.'

'That is different matter entirely. You know nothing about this English woman.'

Ashok wanted to shout out, yes, I do, I know everything I need to know about her, but he bit his lip and kept silent.

'At least,' said his father, 'Let us go and see the girl again one time. Perhaps you need longer.'

'It's no good, *Bapa*. I've made up my mind.'

'Do this one thing for us only, Ashok,' Srinivasa said. 'If after that you decide against, we will not be putting pressure. Tomorrow I have business with Mr Jagannath in Mysore. Come with me.'

Ashok knew he could not escape.

'All right. But tomorrow, no. I will come next day.'

'I will wait there for you.'

*　*　*

By the time Ashok arrived at the Chamundi at eight the following morning, Willi had gone.

'Off to explore Bangalore,' announced Hannah. 'She was up at the crack of dawn, and out before breakfast. She said she wanted to *breathe in the air of the city before it became unbreathable*. Personally I think she was just being discreet. She said she'd be back tonight.'

'Good,' said Ashok. He chuckled and raised his eyebrows. 'Discreet, eh? I didn't think she had it in her. Anyway, listen. Something's been nagging away at me.'

'Again?'

'Listen. Ever since I saw those pearls you were sent. Only I couldn't put my finger on it. Then suddenly, in the night it came to me.'

'You've got a theory?'

'Yes. But you're not going to like it.'

'So try me.'

'It's quite simple really. You criticised my Latin. Fair enough. I always preferred Greek.'

'This is too obscure for me.'

He took a pen and a sheet of paper from the dressing table.

'Look. This is Greek for pearl.'

On the paper he wrote :μαργαριταρι

'Mar-ga-rit-ari.' Hannah read out. 'Yes? So?'

'She never told you that Maighréad comes from the Greek? Margaritari.'

A puzzled frown. 'Pearl? Are you saying that her name means pearl?'

Ashok raised an eyebrow in assent.

'And you're suggesting a connection between Maighréad and the stalker?'

'It's a thought, isn't it? Also remember R.I.P. in the pearl box? At the time I thought you were overreacting, but now I think maybe you have been right.'

'R.I.P: Rest in peace,' muttered Hannah. For a moment she sat, deep in thought. Then she shook her head slowly. 'Doesn't fit, somehow. Why, after taking so much care not to show himself, would he suddenly leave a clue?'

'Well, I'm thinking partly it was because he wants you to know, and partly because he wants to leave his mark. Warped compulsion. He's enjoying the chance to be much more up front here than he was in UK. He believes no one will bother to trace him here.'

'But why does he suddenly want me to work out who he is?'

Ashok frowned. 'I can't answer that. Maybe he doesn't think you'll work it out. He's getting the satisfaction of leaving his calling card and at the same time tormenting you. Or maybe he's building up to something. Removing wrappings layer by layer, so to speak.'

'OK,' said Hannah. 'Maybe you have hit on something. But who? The only one who'd have a grudge, as far as I know, is Maighréad's husband, that despicable Mark Salers. But he was put away for fifteen years with a recommendation for no early release, and he's not served five yet. Anyway, Duncan checked him out.'

'Well he's my number one suspect also. Better ask your Duncan chap to look into it again.'

'Did you manage to set up the email?'

'Come. I'll show you.'

They took an autorickshaw northwards, leaving the city behind them. Wherever she cast her eye, Hannah found something that fascinated her on the noisy, riotous journey. Here was a street vendor pulling a barrowload of bananas along the road, and another with a pyramid of tomatoes. There, on the dusty pavement, a man sat under a tree repairing bicycles.

'Now I can see where the city got its nickname,' Hannah called over the din of the two-stroke engine.

'Yes - Garden City is still very apt out here. Most of the buildings that you can see through the trees are science institutes, university departments, you know, that kind of thing.'

Hannah read the names as they passed by: Raman Research Institute, Forestry Research Laboratory, Indian Institute of Science.

'They all seem to have vast grounds.'

'So does the Biotechnology University, as you will see.'

'And these grey stone walls, they seem to go on forever. It's granite isn't it?'

'Yes. The paving slabs are made of the same material - though many, as you see, are in need of repair. Ah,' Ashok pointed. 'BTU grounds.'

The driver circled round and pulled in at the imposing entrance gate to the complex.

'We'll walk rest of the way.'

Ashok led Hannah through the gate and they made their way up the straight, tarmac roadway beyond.

'Some people who live on campus rarely venture beyond the gate,' Ashok said.

'Don't blame them. It's like an arboretum.'

'It is South Indian University of Biotechnological Advancement. We also sometimes call it SIBA. If you were a scientist you would have heard of it.'

'What does your friend do here?'

'Salman? He's assistant professor. Biochemistry. Here, we've arrived.'

The building was cool and dark. A staircase faced them as they entered. They made their way up it to the first floor. A wide gallery opened on the left onto a central garden with a lawn and several coconut palms. Hannah could have leant over and touched them. The laboratories, behind tall, dark wooden doors, led off at intervals from the right. Ashok pushed open the end door and entered. Hannah squeezed into the narrow space behind him. There seemed hardly room to move. Most of the floor space was taken up with heavy wooden benches seemingly cluttered with scientific equipment of all types. Fumes from chemicals pervaded Hannah's nostrils. Three or four people were engrossed in whatever experiment they were cooking up on their patch of bench. Among them were two young women, one in a sari, the other in a *shalwar kameez* and a long matching *dupatta*. This, and the loose

142

pallu end of the sari, trailed dangerously close to the equipment they were using. Hannah winced.

'Salman - meet Hannah.'

A portly young man greeted them, grinning broadly.

'I have not checked mail,' he said. 'That I have left for you.'

He took them to his office at the far end of the laboratory, where there were two computers, and switched one on.

Within minutes he had printed out Duncan's email.

Have verified existence of person stalking you. Think he has followed you to India, tracking you via my answer-phone so do not leave any more messages on it. Contact me through email only.
The man's name is Terry Bull. Does this mean anything to you?
Bannerman's taking out an injunction. Any connection, do you think?
Sorry to have doubted you. Be careful.
Duncan

Hannah mailed him back.

Name means nothing to me. Please go to the police and tell them what you know. Perhaps it is an alias. A connection with Bannerman? Your guess is as good as mine.
Also check again with police whether Mark Salers has been released. I will check mail again later today.
Hannah.
P.S. How did you find out about Terry Bull?

'Come on, we'll go for a walk,' said Ashok.

They ambled through the campus grounds, mulling over the contents of Duncan's email.

'Let's consider all possible alternatives,' said Ashok. 'Supposing the Mark Salers lead is a dead end. Then what?'

'I'm totally stumped,' said Hannah. 'It's got to be a false name. I've never heard of anyone or any agency called Bull.'

'But you've made plenty of enemies through your books. Who's this Bannerman?'

'I exposed him in my latest book, *Fair Game*. It's a long story. It did cross my mind at the start of all this that he might be involved, but then I decided it was too absurd.'

'Why?'

'Bannerman's far too sophisticated to stoop to this sort of thing.'

'I wouldn't be so sure. He's a crafty blighter, whoever he is.'

'So what now?'

'We should check out all possible individuals or organisations that crop up in your books. Starting with *Fair Game* and *A Small Life*.'

'I can't possibly remember them all. We'll have to get hold of the books.'

'There are plenty of good bookshops in town. We'll try Asian Books. Now, tell me about *Fair Game*.'

At the campus gate they turned out onto the main road, mechanically sidestepping the potholes in the uneven paving-slabs, ignoring the speeding traffic and the exhaust fumes, engrossed in their deliberations.

'I've had another thought,' said Hannah. 'You got a good look at the man on the train without his glasses, didn't you?'

'I did.'

'And you remarked on his eyes.'

'Poached eggs.'

'Well, now I know why it rang a bell. Salers had pale, watery, evil eyes. I remember the way he stared at me at the trial.' She grimaced.

'If it is Salers that explains why he didn't want you to get hold of the photos. If you have snapped him accidentally you might have recognised him.'

'Yes, and that explains what he was doing in my room at the Pandava - looking for my camera. But I had it with me at the time. Though he did outwit us in the end. However,' she grinned. 'We might still have the last laugh.'

'Meaning?'

'There are photos of Mark Salers in *A Small Life*. If we can get hold of it at the bookshop you might be able to get a positive ID.'

'Brilliant. Let's go.'

Ashok hailed a passing autorickshaw that was cruising the road in search of clients. He pulled Hannah in beside him.

Asian Books, on Mahatma Gandhi Road, seemed to harbour everything and anything that had ever been written. It had three floors of books, cards, calendars and posters.

'This is the Garden of Eden,' said Hannah as they browsed through the general book section on the second floor. 'I could quite happily lose myself to temptation in all these shelves of literature.'

'Yes, well don't forget the purpose of our visit. What's your publisher called?'

'Hamilton and Forbes. Duncan is Duncan Forbes. But surely they won't have my books here?'

She was wrong. They managed to find copies of *Fair Game* and *Crying Shame*.

'They haven't got *A Small Life* though,' Hannah said.

The young shop assistant heard her comment.

'One copy only we have left, Madam. I myself saw it earlier today.' She walked over to the bookshelf where Hannah's other books were displayed. 'Oh. Sorry, Madam, it appears to have gone.'

*   *   *

After his night in the garden room Duncan returned to the house in the hope that the previous day's events had been a hoax by a malevolent sandman. However the sight of Felicity in the kitchen, brewing up coffee, dumped him straight back into the land of reality. She looked shattered and ill. There were dark rings under her eyes. Her hair was dishevelled. She winced each time she moved.

'I missed you!' she said, 'Why didn't you come to bed?'

'Had to do some thinking,' he said quietly.

'Any conclusions?'

He shook his head. He certainly wasn't going to tell Felicity about the email link with Hannah.

They drank coffee in silence.

'What are you going to do?' Felicity said.

'Nothing - yet.'

'Do you still want me to stay?' She seemed ill at ease. Was there something else that she wasn't telling him? 'I'll go if you like.'

'No,' Duncan said pushing his doubts to the back of his mind. 'Stay. We're in this together now.'

He went back to the garden room. An email from Hannah. His heart sank when he read her request.

Please go to the police and tell them what you know.
Also check again with police whether Mark Salers has been released.

Mark Salers? Why on earth does she suspect him? Utter twaddle. He was put away for fifteen years. Anyway Hannah had already checked out Salers right at the start, when the so-called stalking had first happened.

Or had she? Now it all came back to him. They'd discussed it, but he'd said he'd do it, and later he assured her that he had, although he'd not in fact followed it up. He had been so sure that no stalker existed.

Now what? They'd know if he'd escaped. Still, better do as she asks and make sure. As for telling the police what he knew - how on earth could he explain Felicity? What a bloody mess. Still, he had to do something. At least he could pursue the Salers lead without revealing the source of his sudden interest in the matter. With a heavy heart, and without letting Felicity know that he'd gone, Duncan took himself off to the local police station.

The constable on duty recognised him.

'Hallo, sir. How's Miss Petersen? Been a bit quiet lately. Sorted out her problems, has she?'

'Not altogether,' he said,' In fact, I'm beginning to wonder if there's something in what she says.'

'Oh yes? And what makes you say that, sir?'

'I'm not sure. I've been thinking about some of the people who'd have a grudge against her. There are a couple of shady characters who might just resort to this kind of thing.'

'I wish you'd mentioned this earlier, sir.'

'Neither of them seemed likely candidates at the time. One of them, Mark Salers, assaulted his wife some five years back. Miss Petersen wrote a book about the case. He went down for fifteen years, so I still think it's a bit of a non-starter, but Miss Petersen asked me to chase it up. Can you check it out?'

The constable frowned and looked sceptical.

Nevertheless he disappeared into the back office. When he returned some five minutes later, he had a puzzled expression.

'Well, sir, it seems your man was released on parole about a year ago. We didn't connect him with the stalker at the time because he was so ill - TB - caught it in the nick and didn't seem to respond to treatment. Now it seems he's done a runner. We don't know where he is.'

So Salers was on the loose as well as Bannerman. Somehow Duncan couldn't dismiss the idea that Bannerman was involved.

'We'll investigate the matter, of course, sir,' said the constable. 'You said there were a couple of likely suspects?'

'Yes, the other's an American psychiatrist, name of Elliott Bannerman. I discounted him at first because my firm's American lawyer thought it was ridiculous. But now Bannerman's trying to stop the US publication of Miss Petersen's latest book. He seems to have disappeared too.'

Duncan filled the constable in on the insurance scam. The constable made notes.

'Could you ask Miss Petersen to call in at the station, sir? We really need to get her version of all this.'

'Can't do that. She's in…' he began, but stopped himself. No, he wouldn't tell the police where she was. Not yet. What if Felicity was right? What if the police were involved? But then they'd know where she was in any case, wouldn't they? Nevertheless, this needs thinking through. Better not to say anything I might regret. 'She's away at the moment. Not sure when she'll be back. She'll let me know.'

'Oh, I see. Well, when she does get back be sure to tell her, won't you, sir.'

'Of course.'

'Right you are, sir. Meanwhile we'll work on what you've given us. Thanks for your help.'

With a heavy heart Duncan made his way back home, wondering if his visit to the police had done anything to help Hannah. He'd kept back vital information. Hannah was in India. So was Terry Bull, according to Felicity. At least Hannah was aware of that now. But was he right to mistrust the police? Had he placed Hannah in greater danger?

*　　*　　*

'One other email has come,' said Salman, when Hannah and Ashok staggered back into the laboratory. He handed them a printed sheet. 'Is OK. I have not looked.'

Hannah read:

Have been to the police. Very helpful for once! Mark Salers released early on compassionate grounds - contracted TB in prison. Could be Terry Bull. Will make further inquiries.
I'll mail again later if I get more info.
For God's sake take care.
Duncan

Hannah handed the printout to Ashok.

'I don't follow this at all,' she muttered, shaking her head. 'Duncan said he checked on Salers months back.'

Ashok folded the sheet and slipped it into his shirt pocket. With a brief wave of thanks to Salman, he took Hannah's arm and led her out of the laboratory.

He took her to a garden, set deep within the green arboretum of the campus. It had once been beautiful, but now its shrubbery had acquired a neglected air, an old master, lurking unsuspected in a museum storeroom.

Neither of them had spoken since they left the laboratory with Duncan's email tucked in Ashok's pocket.

They found a bench and brushed it clear of fallen hibiscus blossoms from an overhanging shrub.

Ashok broke the silence again. 'Well. Where do we begin?'

'Let's have another look at the email.'

They pored over it for some minutes before Ashok spoke.

'Either your friend Duncan didn't check that time when he said he had, or the police messed up. No point in losing sleep over it.'

'What on earth made Duncan suddenly decide to believe me? I asked him, but he hasn't said.'

'Never mind that now. Let's concentrate on what to do next.'

She nodded. 'Well, now I know why I didn't suspect Salers - if that's who it is. If he's got TB it's not surprising he's changed so much. He was built like an ox in those days. And no wonder he kept his eyes hidden. Those I'd have recognised. I could never forget the way he stared at me across the courtroom - so much malice.' She turned to face Ashok. 'You realise that he must know who you are too.'

Ashok shook his head. 'No. I never saw him then. By the time I met Maighréad he was locked up, don't forget. Unless... you didn't mention me in the book, did you?'

'Give me some credit. I'm not a tabloid journalist.'

'Sorry.'

'It's all beginning to make sense to me now,' Hannah said.

'What is?'

'We've been wondering how the stalker managed to keep such close tabs on me.'

'Yes?'

'Well, he had a bit of head-start, didn't he?'

'How?'

'Because he was born and brought up here.'

'What? I didn't know that!'

'Not here. In Pondicherry. He's from an old French colonial family on his father's side. He was christened *Marc Salers*. Mother's family came from England and settled in Madras. Mark's family stayed on after independence. When Mark was fourteen his father deserted them for an Indian woman - a doctor.'

'Maighréad never told me that he had an Indian connection.'

'She didn't want you to know. You may have jumped to conclusions.'

'What are you saying?'

'Mark never forgave his father. His mother took him and his younger sister to live in England.'

'And where do I fit into this?'

'I think this is what attracted her to you in the first place. For Maighréad you represented an unconscious way of getting at Mark.'

'I don't believe you. That's horrible!'

'I did say to start with. After a while it was obvious that her feelings for you went much deeper.' Her hand found his. She squeezed it. He did not respond. 'Maighréad would have died in that hospital if there had been any other doctor looking after her. She didn't want to go on. You gave her the will to fight.'

'She died anyway.'

'But she had those wonderful months with you before...'

'I wonder if there's anything she didn't tell you.'

'Like I said on the train, Ashok. I hardly saw her once you'd come on the scene. As far as I was concerned it was over. I was happy for her. I didn't know she'd die, none of us did. I wanted to let her get on with her life. And I wanted to get on with writing up her story. But as you know, she wouldn't let go. So she wrote to me. A lot. I have all her letters at home. Maybe you'll read them one day. She dreamt of going to India with you, you know. She thought that she'd find something here, some kind of fulfilment perhaps.'

'Is that why you decided to come to India too? When you were running away? Perhaps you thought you would find fulfilment here also. Just as Maighréad did.'

'I've told you. I wasn't running away. I had an assignment.'

'Sorry. Didn't mean it like that.'

'You did. You still think I ran away.'

'Hannah, being afraid is nothing to be ashamed of. Stop being so defensive. This is me you're talking to, not your public who expect you to be superwoman.'

His hand tightened on hers. She stiffened. 'I didn't run away. And as for being defensive, you'd better take a good look at yourself, before you start accusing me.'

Ashok laughed, in a small, tired way. 'Don't, Hannah. I can't take this at the moment.'

She drew away, isolated once more in her nightmare. Ashok covered his eyes with his hands and started muttering to himself, to her. 'Hannah, Maighréad, Salers, Duncan Forbes... me. Where does it all begin? How does it fit together? What is it all about?'

*　　*　　*

When he returned home from the police station, Duncan found Felicity back in bed, her face as grey as the sky outside.

'What on earth's the matter?'

She was incoherent. He caught the occasional word. 'Pain... my head.'

'Felicity,' Duncan cupped her face in his hands and tried to make her look at him. Her eyes wouldn't focus.

'Have you taken anything?'

'Distalgesics... four.' By now her voice was a whisper and her eyes were closing.

'*Four Distalgesics?*' Bloody hell, he thought. He picked up the phone and dialled the local medical centre. 'Just keep an eye on her,' said the anonymous voice, 'Let her sleep it off. If you suspect any deterioration get her round to casualty at once.'

Duncan put down the phone, feeling uneasy. He would have expected an immediate home visit. What the hell was wrong with doctors these days? This one sounded Indian. Perhaps he hadn't understood. Not that he had anything against Indians, of course, and the man seemed confident in his advice. Duncan shrugged off his doubts.

He went back to the garden room and emailed Hannah.

A couple of hours later he shook Felicity awake. He carried her to the bathroom and turned the cold shower onto her. Then he wrapped her in a bathrobe, took her downstairs and made her a cup of black coffee.

'How's your head?' he said.

'Better,' she replied, 'but not good. It's where you banged it on the wall yesterday.'

Duncan froze. Oh, my God. What if I'd killed her?

'Why didn't you leave me to sleep?'

'I want to go over it all again,' he said. 'I don't believe you've told me everything.'

'I don't know what else to tell you.'

'Mark Salers,' Duncan said. 'Is he Terry Bull?'

Felicity flinched so violently that Duncan knew he had hit the spot. It took a few seconds for her voice to struggle into sound.

'How did you know?'

'It doesn't matter. This time I want the truth.'

Her shoulders sagged. Her expression was one of futility. 'You're right, Dunc, I'm sorry,' she said flatly. 'Mark Salers is my brother. Terry doesn't exist. Everything else I said was true. Almost everything.'

'I'm waiting.'

'It is true that I set you up to find out about Hannah.' She struggled to sit up straight. 'But there's no one else involved. Just Mark and me.'

She told Duncan that Mark Salers had written a book about Hannah, in order to prove his innocence. 'That's why he asked me to spy on you.'

'A book? What sort of a book?'

'When Mark was released I couldn't believe what prison had done to him. And it was all down to her, Hannah. He blamed her for everything. She took away Maighréad from him. She got him arrested and put away. She wrote all those lies about him. He wanted to set the record straight. I did what I did to help him.'

'Lies? There were no lies. He would have killed Maighréad if Hannah hadn't taken her to England. As for his arrest and imprisonment - he got what he deserved.'

'Oh God, Dunc,' Felicity said, looking at the floor. 'If only you knew the half of it.'

Duncan looked at her with loathing. Any lingering sympathy towards her had dissipated with her latest disclosure.

'I'm not interested in any more of your half-cocked stories. Mark Salers is a crazy bastard who got what he deserved. The only thing that interests me now is getting the Indian police to pick him up. With a bit of luck they'll finish him off in the process.'

He chose not to see the tears welling up in Felicity's eyes, or the broken look on her bleached face. Mark Salers was as guilty as hell, and dangerous. Duncan had been there. He had seen Hannah's book through, stage by stage, following with her every step of the tragedy as it unfolded. He knew beyond a doubt that Hannah's sensational exposé of Mark Salers, his arrest, his trial, his conviction, his imprisonment were irrefutable facts. They had to be. He had published them. Nothing that Felicity could say could change anything.

'In any case, if the book's finished, why is he still after Hannah? Tell me that.'

Felicity shook her head nervously. 'I don't know. Mark seemed to suss out that...' she glanced up at Duncan, 'that I hated what I was doing to you. He got angry and stopped confiding in me. He's so ill. I don't really think he knows what he's doing or saying anymore.'

'That bastard knows exactly what he's up to. Always has.'

Felicity ignored the comment. 'When he left for India, I thought that was that. I thought I was free. I wanted to make it up to you.'

So that's why she'd been so over-the-top recently, Duncan realised. And I thought she was having an affair. Pity I was so wrong.

He tried to email Hannah.

Have confirmed that Salers is Terry Bull - but I guess you'd already worked that one out, he wrote.

Damn it! Email's down. Must have blown due to pre-Christmas rush. Will have to keep trying.

* * *

When Room Service delivered the packet, Hannah decided that there was no point in phoning Ashok before she set about inspecting it. He was due any minute and would probably be on his way already. He had dropped her off after they had left the campus garden. The morning's discussion had left them both uptight and in need of time alone. She said she wanted a shower, and he wanted to try another bookshop for *A Small Life*. He said he'd pick her up at midday for lunch.

She turned the packet over. Thin, the size of an A5 envelope. No hint of its origins but Hannah knew. Only one person could have sent it. Carefully she slit it open with scissors and removed the content. A paper wallet containing photographs. She looked at the first one. A view of the Qutab Shahi tombs taken from halfway up Golconda. Hannah remembered taking it. They were her photographs. She looked at the next few, all images of Golconda. On one of them, a shot looking back down the hill, she could make out, in the distance, a woman in a *burkha*. So what? She said to herself. It told her nothing.

She heard a knock on the door. 'Ashok.'

She let him in and showed him the wallet of photographs.

'I really can't understand why he should go to the trouble to return them to me.'

'Have you looked at them all yet?'

'No.'

'Then shouldn't you?'

Hannah pulled out the next one. 'Oh, God.'

'That was you, wasn't it, Hannah? Before the face was scratched out.'

She nodded. 'Willi took it in front of the Durbhar Hall. How ghastly.'

'Yes. Let's check the rest.'

They tipped the photographs onto the bed.

'Look. That was me, with a family on a cycle. A fruit vendor took it.'

'Here's another. This looks like that wedding you went to.'

Hannah nodded, regarding her scratched out image with revulsion. 'It was taken at the Pandava. Before I had the camera locked in the safe.'

'All other pictures are intact. Even ones of Willi.'

'He went to some trouble, didn't he?'

'You mean the precision with which he did it? Yes. Odd, isn't it? Look how carefully he's removed every trace of colour from exactly where your face was. Except for your eyes. Just left eyes in a white mask.'

'Like a ghost.' She shuddered. 'So he's saying that he's going to wipe me out.'

'Or simply that he hates you.'

'Glad you think that's all.'

'I'm not saying that. One way or another the man's a menace. Time for positive action I think. We're going to get him.'

'You bet we are.' Her expression softened. 'Sorry I got into such a strop earlier. You're right. I'm not superwoman. Maybe I did use the photography project as an excuse to get away. There, I've admitted it. I was scared.'

'You were brilliant. I'd have fallen apart long ago.'

She brushed the comment aside. 'So - what's our next move?'

'First compile our list of suspects.'

'Any luck with *Small Life*?'

'Afraid not. Out of stock. Come on, let's talk about it over lunch.'

Uma's restaurant was crowded with lunchtime shoppers and barristers from the nearby law courts. Scruffy-looking travellers from Australia and Europe ordered blindly and affected a posture of blasé confidence that cried out 'foreigner' more clearly than their blue eyes and lank blond hair.

Ashok and Hannah pushed through the noisy scrum in the huge, canteen-like interior on the first floor and managed to secure a table on the terrace overlooking the road, where traffic fumes from the street below did not penetrate the air.

Ashok ordered a *masala dosa* for each of them.

'Mmm,' she murmured. 'I'm beginning to feel human again.'

155

Ashok furrowed his eyebrows. 'How can you be so damned cheerful with that cretin after you? I don't understand you. You're up and down like a yoyo.'

'Listen,' she said, her mouth full of *dosa*. 'I'm back on form now we're going after him. Pity I didn't have your support back home. Might have put an end to it much sooner.'

'Sorry I couldn't oblige,' Ashok said.

'Listen to me. I'm beginning to lose my independent streak.'

'Never!' He smiled, but his eyes were serious. 'Say, Hannah. I've got to tell you... tomorrow... it's going to be difficult...'

She jumped in quickly. 'It's OK. I understand. You can't always be with me. You've got other obligations.'

'Will you let me finish? I have to go to Mysore to see my father. Some business he wants me to help him with.'

'I'll be fine. Honestly. I'll explore the city with Willi...'

'No! Listen to this and tell me what you think. To nail this man, we've got to isolate him somehow, right?'

'Right.'

'So how about if I arrange a bungalow for the three of us in Bandipur National Park for tomorrow night. Mysore's on the way. We'll go to Mysore together by bus and you and Willi can wait for me there. I'll only be an hour or so. We'll take a taxi up to the park from there. It's about forty-five miles south of Mysore. If Salers, Bull or whoever follows us we'll nab him. There's no place for him to hide up there. The park only has a few bungalows and a small lodge. Rest is wilderness - tiger and elephant country. And if he doesn't follow us - well, it's a great place for a safari.'

'Why don't Willi and I go on ahead to the park? Better than hanging around the bus station in Mysore waiting for you. You can join us later.'

'No, really, that's a bad idea. Anyway, you won't be hanging around the bus station. You can go and visit Maharaja's Palace.'

'Tempting. Even I've heard of that. Someone told me they made the iron pillars in Glasgow. Is that true?'

'I believe so, yes. Anyway, agreed?'

Hannah sighed. 'Very well then. The Maharaja's Palace it is.'

Ashok was thinking out loud. 'Let's assume for a moment that it is Salers. We know he has sound knowledge of the country, knows how to get information from locals and can probably make himself understood - at least in Tamil which will be of some help here.'

'So what do we do?'

'We don't know if he's dangerous - but we must act on the assumption that he is.'

'Of course we know he's dangerous. Have you forgotten what he did to Maighréad?'

Ashok realised with a jolt, that so wrapped up was he in Hannah's dilemma, that he had suppressed his own past indirect entanglement with Salers.

'No, of course not.' he said, brusquely. 'We must lure him out somehow - hopefully we can do that at Bandipur.'

'Any ideas?'

'Yes, I have as a matter of fact. But...' he hesitated, 'I don't know whether it's right to put you through it.'

'Put me through what, for heaven's sake? I've told you, I want to put an end to this. So what's the plan?'

'Well. First we've got to make sure he takes the bait and does come up to the park. You must tell hotel reception exactly where you're going.'

'Do I mention you and Willi?'

'No, I don't think so. Let him think you're travelling alone, as long as possible. That way he'll be more inclined to make the trip. I think he'll want to be there before you, to plan. He won't know till you arrive that we're coming with.'

'How will he know what time I'm arriving?'

'Tell the people on reception you're taking the nine a.m. bus to Mysore and a taxi from there up to the park.'

'I could leave another message on Duncan's answerphone.'

'Brilliant - yes! And how about leaving a note pinned to your hotel-room door for some fictitious friend?'

Hannah looked dubious. 'Think you're getting a bit carried away there. Let's not overdo it.'

'Maybe you're right. After all, he hasn't needed much help in tracing you so far.'

'OK, so what's the rest of the plan?'

'Well. I know Bandipur very well. Used to love going up there as a child. At night it gets very dark - only moon and stars, and a few lights from the bungalows and the lodge. Only way to get around outside is with a torch. And even then it's a gamble. Animals tend to come out of the deep jungle at night. Who knows what you might run into? Probably the dangers are minimal, but it feels real enough.'

'A true adrenaline-rush.'

'It is for me. Anyway, there's a small hillock with a bench on the edge of the compound. My father and I used to sit up there at sunset and watch chital herds and monkeys gathering near the boundary. They feel safer there at night.'

'Sounds magical.'

'My idea is that you'll come out of the bungalow and climb the hillock, to wait alone for sunset. Only I'll be hidden in bushes nearby.'

'I see. I'm the bait.'

'I knew you'd hate the idea. Sorry I suggested it. Thoughtless of me.'

'Don't be so silly! Of course I've got to be the bait. And I'll be perfectly safe with you nearby. I know I've got to give him a chance to get at me alone. Otherwise he'll be sidetracked into seeing off you and Willi again. I'll do it.'

'I'll be right there with you. You'll have nothing to fear. We'll get him.'

'Then what?'

'Turn him over to police. The rest's up to them.'

'Hopefully they'll deport him.'

'Then you'll only have to face the problem again when you get back to UK.'

Hannah stood up and gazed over the terrace wall, down at MG Road. The ordered turmoil of life seemed encompassed in a panoramic time capsule. She watched a street vendor cutting guavas. His knife seemed to glide effortlessly through the green fruit. She could taste its honey-mellowed sweetness, and sense the heavy, organic fragrance. Her eyes wandered lazily across the busy thoroughfare, in and out of the ant-like armies of autorickshaws to a wall of thick bamboo scaffolding. For some moments she watched a billboard painter at work, balanced on his bamboo perch, painstakingly creating a work of art to advertise the latest Bollywood blockbuster.

She turned to look at Ashok, so calm, so tender. He had something noble about him; an intangible nobility.

'UK? Who says I'm going back?'

*   *   *

On Monday, Duncan called Piers and told him he wasn't coming in. He said he'd been sick all weekend. It wasn't altogether a lie. He was sick, sick with worry and self-loathing. He should have gone to the police twenty-four hours ago, as soon as Felicity had come clean. But he'd held back. He'd needed time to get to grips with Felicity's story, to make sure she wasn't lying again. Perhaps she'd fabricated the Salers story when he put the idea into her head. He'd spent Sunday fitting the facts together. By Monday morning it was clear to him that Felicity's story made sense. She'd finally told him the truth.

After Felicity had confessed that Terry Bull was Mark Salers, Duncan's first instinct had been to sling her out of his house, no matter what the consequences. It had taken a supreme effort to admit to himself that she would be more use to him if she stayed where he could keep an eye on her, and an even greater effort to sweet talk her into doing so. To his relief, she insisted on moving into the spare room.

'We both need some space to work this through,' she said.

Now he agonised over what to do next. He ought to shop Felicity to the police. If the story got out, he'd be a laughing-stock. It would be professional suicide. He remembered that hadn't told the police where Hannah was. But now it was imperative to tell the cops that she was in India, and that she was still being followed. He could do this without implicating Felicity, but he was overcome by guilt and worry. Not only had he let Hannah down badly in the past, but even now he intended to keep the full truth from the cops to save his own neck. Was he endangering Hannah further by keeping back that he knew the stalker in India was Salers? He thought not. They'd soon work that out for themselves, but, dammit, he was worried sick about Hannah. How could he help her? What if the police started asking questions? The whole thing was a goddam mess and there was no way out. Unless… He was rocked by a sudden inspiration. If Felicity was Salers' sister… He went into the house and sought her out. She was lying on the sofa, still nursing her sore head.

'Tell me,' he said. 'Where were you born? The truth, mind.'

'India.' she replied. 'My mother brought us to England when Mark was fourteen and I was twelve. I don't remember too much about India though.'

'Do you speak the language?'

'The language? There are dozens of languages. I still remember some Tamil.'

'Where is Tamil spoken?'

'In the south. Mainly Tamil Nadu, but it's widely understood in places like Bangalore, where there are a lot of Tamils.'

Bingo, Duncan said to himself. He knew what he had to do. A drastic decision but he still felt an inexplicable unease on top of his worries about Hannah's safety. He would go to India and persuade her to come home. Salers would follow her. The British police would be watching the airports by then. They'd catch him. Duncan needed someone to get him around India. Who better than Felicity? And if Salers made trouble in India, Felicity might come in useful. Afterwards he could dump her there and forget about her. She'd never rat on him. She was in too much trouble - spying, phone-tapping, aiding and abetting a criminal - they'd throw the book at her. Hannah would have to know, but she'd have no reason to tell anyone else. Despite his aversion to places that harboured heat, disease and poverty, this, right now, seemed the only way forward. Yes, he would go to India.

He didn't tell Felicity about his plans. Better to book the seats first and spring it on her. He went into the garden room and dialled the number of the travel agent. No problem, the travel agent gushed, first class seats can always be found though it may take a while. An hour later he had secured two tickets for the same evening - giving him just enough time to nip up to the High Commission in London for visas.

He emailed Hannah.

Sit tight, I'm on my way. Arriving Bangalore Christmas Eve. Try not to worry.
Duncan
P.S. Don't go out at night. And keep your hotel room door locked.

Shit! Email's still down. Better grasp the proverbial bull and phone the Chamundi.

'Sorry sir. Miss Petersen is not available.'

Daren't leave another message. Too dangerous. Just keep trying the email.

CHAPTER 10

The bus for Mysore left from Bangalore Bus Station at nine in the morning. It glorified under the official designation of *Non-stop Luxury Bus*. Ashok, Hannah and Willi had to sit separately, as it was so crowded. Willi found herself squashed next to a woman with a small boy, who needed no entertainment during the long journey, as his fascination with the strange yellow-topped alien next to him was tantamount to a blow on the head. Open-mouthed and rigid, he stared at her unrelentingly for three hours. She tried to alleviate the stifling nature of his assault by grinning, pulling faces, showing off her knowledge of Kannada (*namaskara*), but all to no avail. The luminescent mop had him transfixed. His mother slept, blissfully.

Ashok, three seats in front of Hannah, was equally uncomfortable. His neighbour, an old woman in widow-white, made it perfectly plain by her disdainful look, when he sat down next to her, that she considered this invasion of her seat by a *man* to be a direct challenge to her feminine sanctity. She hastily and with maximum fuss squeezed herself as far as she could into the corner.

The young man seated at the window next to Hannah was clearly nervous, since he wrung his hands together and fidgeted continually while they were still at the bus station, waiting to set off. However he seemed too distracted to concern himself with her and was thin, so she had plenty of room on the seat. Suddenly, just as the driver climbed aboard, Hannah's neighbour gave an exclamation of what sounded like terror, jumped up, banging his head on the luggage rack above him, leapt over Hannah and rushed off the bus. Hannah, taking advantage of this, slid across to the window. She was just about to call Ashok to join her, when an immense woman struggled onto the bus and, seeing the empty seat, bore down on her. Breathing heavily, the woman, who had apparently not noticed that half the seat was already occupied, heaved herself onto it, her buttock landing on Hannah with a resounding slap. Try as she might, Hannah was unable to extricate herself, so, by the time the first part of the one hundred and forty kilometer journey was over, half her body was rigid.

Hannah concentrated on minimising her physical discomfort by trying to forget it. She had a lot to take in as the bus leapfrogged its way across Karnataka. They sped past tiny palm-thatched dwellings, basic and impoverished; women washing children or collecting water at a village pump; prostrate bullocks with fettered feet, waiting at a blacksmith's forge; a woman, painstakingly sweeping the dust away from the front of her little hovel; a man, tending his stall of carefully piled and polished aubergines; a boy wheeling a cart of oranges along the road. Everywhere dogs, buffalo and cows sauntered unchecked among the villagers. White bullocks tilled fields of sunflower and millet, sugar cane and paddy. The glossy leaves of a million mulberry trees awaited their fate as silk-worm fodder. Bright, sari-clad women sifted rice by the roadside. Frequently the bus drew to a halt, when impediments on the road demanded - an overturned lorry, a level crossing, a sleeping cow.

An hour and a half into the journey the bus made its one scheduled halt. The passengers tumbled out, and headed for the little café or the coconut vendor. Hannah limped across to the other two. Ashok had already ordered coconuts, but Hannah and Willi had more pressing needs.

They were directed to what appeared to be a cave behind the café.

The stench stopped Hannah in her tracks. Nausea overcame her. She forced herself to crouch down in the goo, holding her breath, like the rest of the women.

By the time they returned to Ashok, he was wrestling with three large coconuts, prepared for drinking.

Willi said. 'If we don't catch anything from that little detour, we must be tough old birds.'

Hannah added, 'I guess there's all sorts of nasty germs flying around. TB, dysentery, typhoid... plague, even. What's wrong?'

Ashok was staring at her. 'Oh... nothing. Just thinking.'

'Salers?' said Hannah.

'Yes... when you mentioned TB.'

'I know. There was something else reminded me as well. The stink. There's been that foul stench whenever I've had an encounter.'

'If he's in the terminal stages of TB that would account for it,' said Ashok.

Later Ashok was thankful that he hadn't worried Hannah with the unpleasant notion brought on by the conversation at the bus halt. What was it her attacker had said to her that night in the garden? 'I'm gonna give it you.' Of course. He was trying to infect her. That explains why he... Ashok shuddered as he recalled Hannah's graphic description of what had taken place. And the photographs. Yes. That was it. Hannah's face: nothing but eyes in a white mask. The old name for TB: plague, *white* plague. Better get her checked out when we get back to Bangalore.

*　*　*

Ashok couldn't be sure how it had happened. Certainly it was unpremeditated.

He had delivered Willi and Hannah safely to a taxi office in Mysore, and ordered a car to take them to the palace, wait for them there and drive them back to the taxi office where he would meet them in two hours' time. The journey to Mysore had exhausted him. Not being able to sit next to Hannah, he had hankered after her, missing their easy companionship, the scent of her *Fleurs de Provence* perfume, the candour in her green eyes. He missed her ideas, her zeal, yes, even her defensive feminism. He missed the vulnerability that she tried so hard to disguise. He missed her indomitable spirit. As the bus bounced along, his fears for her multiplied. He worried about what lay in store for her in Bandipur.

Wasn't he asking too much of her, after all that she'd been through? Then there was the matter of the TB. He slipped into imagining life without her, an emptiness too horrible to contemplate. The purpose of his trip to Mysore tormented him. He felt like a dishonest rat, and yet the thought of confessing the truth to Hannah terrified him. How could he ever expect her to understand? And the girl in Mysore - he'd liked her more than he'd let on to his parents, and had almost decided to give the match a chance. But that was before Hannah had appeared on the scene. Now Hannah dominated his every thought. He recognised the irrationality of it, but was trapped by his feelings. By the time the taxi turned up, he ached as if he were being torn apart.

As they were about to get into the taxi, Willi spotted two women with trays of oranges balanced on their heads and rushed off to buy some to sustain them through the afternoon. The resulting moment alone with Hannah seemed to trigger some demonic impulse in Ashok's brain. Hannah was already half in the car, when he grabbed her in his arms and said, to his own amazement, 'Marry me!' to which she found herself answering unhesitatingly 'Yes.'

Before any further communication was possible, Willi returned triumphantly bearing bargain oranges, the car revved up and, hooting bombastically, disappeared in a cloud of Mysore dust.

Ashok was left standing in the road, his mind, as well as his clothes, enveloped in the dust storm. As the dust settled, reality dawned. To his surprise, he felt elated, as though he had been set free from some unsuspected encumbrance. With a spring in his step, he set out to meet his father. He would go through the ordeal of speaking to his shy suitor once more, but now there would be no conflict, no dithering, no possibility of compromise for the sake of his parents. His decision had been made, and the contract sealed. In two hours he would be on his way to join his... he smiled... his fiancée. As he walked he began to daydream again. Everything seemed to slot into place. Hannah was the princess of his childhood fantasies. He would be Rama to her Sita; but unlike Rama, who, in the end, banished innocent Sita from his kingdom, he would always be by Hannah's side.

The girl's mother plied Ashok and Srinivasa with cakes, samosas, Thums Up, bananas. Her father plied them with questions, politely, formally, diplomatically. He wanted to know about England, London, the weather, the public transport, schools, communication systems, cricket. The girl hovered in the background, eyes lowered, passing dishes to her mother. Srinivasa's side-glances at Ashok told him that his father was getting impatient. Ashok was making no attempt to talk to the girl.

'Perhaps, Ashok, you would find Janaki's university course of interest,' Srinivasa suggested in obvious desperation.

'Of course,' Ashok replied politely. 'Please tell me about it.'

'Come, I will show you my books.'

Ashok followed her downstairs into the reception room.

'I was wondering when you were going to pluck up courage to speak to me,' she said, straightening her head and looking him in the eye. 'I'm sure you are not really shy.'

Her bluntness disarmed him. He saw her properly for the first time. He looked down into her steady gaze and saw beneath the stage make-up and costume jewellery that had been pressed upon her for his visit. She was young, but her poise was unnerving.

'I'm not shy,' he said gently.

'You just don't want to marry me,' Janaki said.

Ashok was overwhelmed by confusion and unaccountable sadness. He wanted to comfort her, to stroke her cheek, to take her in his arms. He fought to keep his hands from touching her.

'Janaki,' he began, not knowing how to look at her. He wanted to tell her that she was lovely, she shone like the morning star, that if he'd had a chance to speak to her alone three days ago, that it was too late, that Hannah was now a part of him, the part that his gentle nature had hitherto never known and thus had never missed, but now knowing, could never relinquish. She was the spirit that breathed life into him. She was the kingfisher to his quiet brook.

Janaki's soft hand touched his arm. 'I know,' she said, 'please don't feel bad.'

'You are very young,' he said to her helplessly, 'it would be hard for you in England.'

'Yes,' she agreed, 'it would be very hard. And yes, I am young. I have been telling my father so, and that I wish to continue my studies also, to pass examination for BTU so that I can pursue career in science. That would be very hard for a married woman, no? For me, it will be better to marry when I have secured my PhD only.'

'Janaki,' Ashok began again, 'please don't think that I don't like you. I like you very much. Very much. It is only that... only that...'

'... that now is wrong time. For you as well as for me.'

'Yes.' he said. 'Yes. That's all.'

He could have been content with her, he thought, if only Hannah had not happened. They would have grown together, he and Janaki, at first side by side like two forest palms, later intertwining, yielding sweet, flawless fruit. But Hannah was the wind that ruffled the palm fronds and set them dancing. Without her now, the stillness would stifle him.

'Perhaps we could write?'

Mechanically he nodded. It was a graceful, if temporary, way out of the dilemma.

*   *   *

Ashok's preposterous proposal and Hannah's equally preposterous response to it left her feeling decidedly light-headed. Before she had time to digest what had happened, the tattered Morris Oxford look-alike roared off through the streets of Mysore like a crazed canine released into the garden after a bath. The road was fairly narrow and bumpy, with just enough room for two vehicles to pass. The driver's hand was more or less permanently left on the horn.

'The convention in India,' shouted Willi through the din, 'is to sound the horn whenever you approach a vehicle either from the front or the rear, which is just as well, as wing mirrors are something of a rarity.'

Hannah pointed at a sign on the back of a van. 'Sound horn - OK! Seems a somewhat superfluous instruction under the circumstances.'

As they neared the palace, it was clear that the crowds were becoming unusually dense, even for Indian standards. The driver, Hannah noticed, was getting agitated. Angry men were gradually hemming in the car on all sides; anger not directed at them, but nevertheless threatening and claustrophobic. Suddenly the driver pulled across the road, almost pushing the nearest people out of the way with the car. Without stopping, he executed a U-turn and made his way back to the taxi office.

'Could be problems,' he explained, 'better to go back.'

The taxi chief greeted them with a worried expression. 'I think it is not safe for you to stay in Mysore,' he told them. 'You should go now to Bandipur. When he returns I will explain to your friend. Other taxi we will be keeping for him.'

Hannah and Willi were more than happy to agree to the man's suggestion. Mysore suddenly looked ugly.

Horn blaring, their taxi driver set off again, scattering bicycles, tongas drawn by delicate-looking ponies, cows and rickshaws, as he headed out of the town and into the open countryside. He tore noisily past cars, buses and lorries.

'We seem to have swapped one danger for another,' muttered Hannah, noting that at least they seemed to have left the threatening crowds behind.

Willi wasn't listening. 'Oh, God!' she exclaimed grasping Hannah's arm and staring at the road in front. Some way ahead, travelling in the same direction as they were, was a large, wooden-wheeled cart, laden to the height of a small house with hay, and pulled by a pair of oxen. Coming from the other direction was another one exactly the same. It was clear that if the taxi maintained its present speed it would be at the point of overtaking at the precise moment that the carts would pass each other. Hannah and Willi were transfixed. Disbelievingly they watched as the driver pulled out at full speed between them. There couldn't have been more than an inch to spare either side of the taxi.

'One can only admire his driving,' whispered Hannah.

'I'm wondering about the bulls,' said Willi, 'look at them, plodding on their way, totally unconcerned. Are they brave, stupid or blind?'

Hannah laughed. 'I guess it's such a routine occurrence that they're simply inured to it. Anyway, they're bullocks, not bulls.'

'I know that, Hannah. Bulls, bullocks, oxen - what does it matter?'

The landscape became hilly as they wound their way upward onto the undulating plain between the Western Ghats and the Nilgiri Hills, leaving the last villages behind them.

They spoke very little after the bullock cart incident, which had driven all other preoccupations, including Ashok, the stalker and the unpleasantness in Mysore out of Hannah's head. She felt compelled to concentrate on the driving, as if she had some divine ability to guide the car safely to its destination as long as she willed the driver into making the right moves. Willi was also uncharacteristically quiet, as though the incident had triggered a chain of thoughts.

'Cattle!' Willi burst out suddenly, 'that's it! They're cattle. I knew something was bugging me.'

Hannah stared out of the window in confusion. For once no cattle whatsoever were to be seen, only a burnt-out lorry partly obstructing the road. The driver whizzed round it in his customary manner, without slowing down.

'That can't have been there long,' commented Hannah. 'It's still smoking. I don't see any cattle.'

'No! You don't understand. Terry *Bull*. Mark *Salers*. They're all to do with cattle.'

'Salers?' Hannah raised her eyebrows.

'It's a breed of French cattle. I know these things, Hannah. My father's a farmer.'

Hannah frowned. 'Well,' she said. 'I know what you're saying, but it's a bit of a long shot.'

Willi was jumping up and down on her seat. 'No! Listen! What did you say the name of the English couple at the Pandava was? The ones you didn't check out?'

Hannah tried to remember. 'Oliphant... no... Heller... *Heffer*! That was it. Heffer.'

Willi clapped her hands. 'Heffer - like the word for young cow. There - I told you.'

Hannah came to her senses. Salers would know about the meaning of his name; he was, after all, half French. Nothing mattered now except Willi's startling discovery. She and Ashok had worked deep into the night, compiling their list of possible suspects, but the finger was pointing more and more at Salers.

'Only one thing,' continued Willi, 'what about showing his passport at hotels?'

'Salers used to be a journalist,' said Hannah. 'He knows a trick or two. It wouldn't be too difficult for him to get a few forgeries made up. Probably got some contacts while he was in prison too. He'd have needed a forged one anyway to get out of England - he's supposed to be on parole, remember? Also, let's not underestimate him - he's a clever sod. Always did have the gift of the gab. I'm sure he could think of a number of good reasons why he's misplaced his passport.'

Between them they dredged up every word they could remember that had a bovine connection, and that would double as a name. Willi wrote them down in a hand that mimicked the taxi's jolts and judders as closely as an electrocardiogram echoed a heartbeat.

'Bullock, Hurd, Lowe, White, Dexter...'

'As soon as we've settled in we'll check the guest list,' said Hannah. 'Hopefully we'll have something concrete to tell Ashok when he arrives later.'

*   *   *

After he had left Janaki, Ashok said goodbye to his father, who was returning by bus to Bangalore. Neither of them mentioned Janaki after they had left her house. It seemed that Srinivasa had seen into his son's heart, and felt his confusion. The subject of Ashok's impending trip to Bandipur with Hannah and Willi was tactfully avoided. Srinivasa said simply, 'Let us see how you feel tomorrow.'

Ashok walked back to the taxi office. Something was different about the crowds on the streets now. People were milling around. There was a lot of shouting. Ashok felt uneasy somehow. Several times he heard the word *bandh*. A strike. He wondered where.

At the taxi office, the proprietor was nowhere to be seen, neither were Willi or Hannah. Ashok was greeted by a new face behind the counter. A nervous face. Preoccupied perhaps by the chaos outside.

'Where's the owner? I ordered a taxi to Bandipur with friends.'

'Called away, sir. You are Dr Rao? I have message for you.'

'What message?' Ashok felt a surge of alarm.

'Our driver was experiencing some trouble getting through to Palace with those two ladies,' the man said, a somewhat obsequious smile forming to reveal stained gums and a solitary tooth. 'So many crowds. There is talk of *bandh*. Water dispute. People are getting angry. And you know, sir, angry crowd and Western ladies... So our driver was turning car round and coming back here.'

Ashok nodded. 'So where are they?'

'Well, sir. You are able see for yourself that situation here is not good. Boss was thinking if it is getting worse, it could be very bad for those ladies. Therefore he was sending them back in car to Bangalore city.'

CHAPTER 11

Two hours after leaving Mysore, the taxi deposited Hannah and Willi at the reception centre at the park lodge in Bandipur. The terrain was rough, grassy, dotted with deciduous trees. The air was clean and fresh despite the stifling heat. Apart from the lodge and half a dozen grey wooden bungalows, which were scattered nearby among the scrub, the place was isolated.

They were allocated one of the bungalows, and also a wizened old attendant called Siraj to cook for them. He showed them the accommodation. It was simple but adequate. The two bedrooms each had two beds, and basic bathroom facilities - a toilet and the usual jug and bucket showering system.

It also had a living room and a small kitchen where the crockery and cleaning materials were kept. The meals themselves were not prepared there, but brought over from a communal kitchen.

Hannah opened the net mesh across the window of the bedroom that she and Ashok would share.

'No, no!' said Siraj. 'Monkeys will come.'

She closed the mesh again hastily. 'No thanks. I'd rather not share a bed with a monkey, or have my luggage carried off into the jungle.'

The ranger at the park reception let Hannah see the list of people who had signed the visitors' book.

'Not all have arrived yet,' he explained. 'Some trouble on road to Ooty.'

There were not many visitors. Four names were in the book besides their own. Willi read them out.

'Mr and Mrs J.V. Chandrasekaran from Mysore, Dr Kumar from Delhi, Ms Gower from London, Mr P.S. Nandi from London also. No oxen, bullocks or lowing herds.'

'No?' said Hannah, 'There's a Mr Nandi in bungalow three. You know who Nandi is, don't you?'

'Of course. Shiva's bull.' Willi was ecstatic. 'Let's get him.'

'Hold your horses, Willi. I promised I'd do nothing till Ashok gets here.' She turned to the ranger. 'Mr Nandi - is he English?'

The ranger looked puzzled. 'He lives in UK, Madam. He was telling he was born in Tamil Nadu.'

'Is he a small man?'

'I think so, yes, Madam.'

'Did he speak to you in Tamil?'

By now the ranger was totally perplexed. 'Yes, Madam, but if you wish to meet him you should come on afternoon safari. He is sure to come also.'

From the terrace of their bungalow, they had a good view of the door to bungalow three, a view that Willi enhanced with the aid of binoculars.

'Let me know if he materialises, Willi.'

'What then?'

'If it is him, we'll just watch him, and keep out of his way till Ashok gets here and can hand him over to the Law.'

Hannah was suddenly tired and more apprehensive about Salers than she cared to admit to Willi. She closed her eyes and focused her thoughts on Ashok and marriage. *Marriage!* Did he ask me to marry him? Did I say I would? How bizarre. She suddenly thought of Maighréad and her ill-fated marriage to Mark Salers. Poor Maighréad, she didn't really stand a chance, did she? Not even Ashok could wipe out all those years with that monster. I wonder what she'd think of all this. What to do? Well I said yes, didn't I? Crazy, the pair of us. OK, I'm in love with him. Is that enough? No, it isn't. But there's much more to it than that, isn't there? We just *understand* each other. It doesn't require analysis. All right, so we've both been evasive. I wish I knew what his secret is.

Soon she was fast asleep. She dreamt of their wedding day. She was in a Marriage Hall in Mysore. Ashok had arrived splendidly arrayed, on a white horse. She had an argument with the vicar, who would not allow the horse to give her away, but they compromised so that it was allowed to stamp on the wineglass. Four clarinettists from the Gopal Band held up the chuppah, and played off-key, very loudly throughout the ceremony. Since neither she nor Ashok could hear what the vicar was saying to them, they answered yes to everything. Consequently she found that she had married the Rajasthani psychoanalyst and Ashok had married the horse. She woke in a panic.

'Where's Ashok? Is he here yet? What's been happening?'

'Nothing happening in bungalow three, I'm afraid. Maybe Ashok's at the reception centre. It's time to go anyway, if we want to do the safari.'

* * *

Ashok had chased back to Bangalore after Hannah and Willi, continually urging his driver to go faster. But even along the Mysore-Bangalore section of the road, travel was becoming precarious by now. Groups of angry men, clustered on the roadside, seemed menacing, and the taxi frequently skirted stones and boulders strewn on the tarmac. On two occasions the car was forced to pull up at impromptu road blocks, and only allowed to continue on its way when the self-styled guards manning the blocks had ascertained that neither Ashok nor the driver were Tamils. Two thoughts preoccupied Ashok. Had his father got home safely, and where were Hannah and Willi?

The taxi dropped him at the Chamundi and headed off. The driver was clearly nervous about getting back to Mysore and glad to be on his way. Ashok went straight up to Hannah's room at the hotel. He received no reply to his knock on the door. Back down in reception, the clerk was nonplussed.

'Miss Petersen, sir? No, she hasn't returned, sir. She has signed out for two nights. Look sir, you can see for yourself. Oh, I do hope

174

she decided not to go up to Bandipur after all, sir. Things very bad on that road, sir, very bad.'

Frustrated, Ashok took an autorickshaw to his parents' house. He tried to suppress his worries. After all, he told himself, the two women had left Mysore well before he had, and should have had little difficulty in getting back to Bangalore. Perhaps they'd gone into the city to do some sightseeing.

Srinivasa and Girija greeted him with relief, matched by his own relief that his father had also made it home safely.

'Radio news broadcast is telling that situation is bad,' Girija said. 'It is good that you did not attempt to get through to Bandipur. Your two friends have returned with you?'

Ashok described briefly what had happened.

'We must hope and pray that they are not experiencing difficulties.'

How like his parents, he reflected, to behave with such impeccable decency, despite their obvious dismay over his involvement with Hannah.

'They have probably gone into the city,' Ashok said. 'I am not too worried.'

He was bluffing. By now he was very worried. As he had been talking to his parents, he'd suddenly remembered discussing the stalker situation with Hannah in Chennai. Money talks, he had said. Now he started wondering, uneasily, whether money had talked to the shifty man in the taxi office. Had he been bribed, or even threatened into telling Ashok that the girls had gone back to Bangalore? If not, where were they? Surely they wouldn't really have gone off sightseeing, knowing that he would come back to find them? Had they been sent to Bandipur perhaps, or... It didn't bear thinking about. Well, easy enough to find out if they were in Bandipur.

He dialled the number of the Park Reception Centre.

'Oh yes, sir. The ladies arrived some hours back. They are taking safari tour at this time. You will please call back in half hour to speak to them.'

Ashok could hardly believe what he was hearing. Terror overwhelmed him. The main thing now was to get up to the park as quickly as possible. He picked up the phone again and dialled his father's regular taxi firm.

'Can you get me a taxi?'

'Where you are wanting to go, sir?'

'Bandipur.'

'Sorry, sir. No taxi possible. Road is now closed. Situation is much too dangerous. No bus, no taxi, nothing.'

'How long is this likely to last?'

'Who can tell? Maybe one day, maybe more. They are burning lorries on road.'

* * *

A group of a dozen or so people, mainly local, but some from as far away as Delhi and some 'foreigners' gathered outside the park reception centre for the late afternoon safari.

Ashok was not there, and Hannah, whilst not unduly worried about him, realised that they had no contingency plans. She did not expect Salers to materialise at this point. He was sure to keep himself well hidden until nightfall.

Willi interrupted her thoughts. 'Say, Hannah. What if this Nandi shows up? Do we jump him? Or what?'

'No, we don't jump him. Even if we could restrain him, what then? I already told you. We need Ashok to deal with Indian officialdom. How d'you think the police would react to two foreign women kidnapping someone who hasn't committed an obvious crime?'

'Yes, I see what you mean.'

'In any case, he won't show himself until he thinks he can get me alone.'

The ranger called them. 'We're ready to leave.'

They scrambled into the battered off-road mini-bus. As Hannah had predicted, Mark Salers was not among the passengers. But Mr Nandi was. He turned out to be a small non-resident Indian, originally from Chennai.

'A wasted afternoon, spying on the poor chap,' muttered Willi, through clenched teeth.

'At least we've eliminated him,' said Hannah, as they set off. 'But we're back to square one.'

The vehicle was noisy, as it heaved its way along the potholed track. A forest ranger accompanied them to point out the wildlife, but soon everybody joined in, shouting to the driver to stop whenever they spotted anything interesting.

They saw abundant herds of chital, the graceful white spotted deer, which obligingly congregated in the open spaces on either side of the track, instead of hiding in the denser forest like many of the shyer animals. The land on either side of the track had been cleared for some thirty metres or so to allow for better game watching and to create a firebreak. Beyond this, dindalu and kakke trees, flame of the forest and bamboo covered the ground fairly densely in some areas, less so in others, where single trees were scattered among the long, yellowing grass. Here they had splendid views of the distant Nilgiri range, silhouetted against the skyline.

A sambar deer stag stood in a clearing, head erect, every muscle in its taut, grey body alert to the possibility of danger.

'Majestic,' breathed Hannah. Once again, as so often in the past few days, her fears had been washed away and she was bathed in a kind of magical amnesia.

Further along the track, two peahens moved jerkily through the long grass. Nearby their mate strutted out, his feathers raining iridescence into the surrounding air. Hannah giggled. 'Duncan,' she said to herself.

In the trees, langur monkeys danced among the branches or sat chewing leaves, staring down curiously. Thick, grey fur framed their black faces, giving them an air of aristocracy.

'Over there,' whispered the sharp-eyed ranger, pointing to the right. 'Gaur. Largest of wild Indian cattle. Today we are lucky.'

There were four or five adult females and a number of calves standing some thirty metres away, at the edge of the thicker forest, their white stockinged legs half hidden in the long grass. The beasts were an impressive sight, not only because of their massive size.

The extraordinary splendour of their coats glowing liver-chestnut in the evening sun reminded Hannah of huge polished bronze carvings.

The safari ended as the last rays evaporated the outlines of the distant hills and turned the trees to brooding shadows.

Back at the reception centre there was no sign of Ashok.

'Has Dr Rao arrived yet?' Hannah asked the duty ranger.

'No, Madam. But he has telephoned. He is experiencing some difficulty. There is *bandh*. No vehicles are getting through at present. Dr Rao will be telephoning again in twenty minutes' time. You will please wait here for call.'

The two women stared at one another, aghast.

'A *bandh*? What's that?' said Hannah.

'It's a strike,' Willi said in a resigned voice. She turned to the ranger, and accosted him angrily, as though the whole situation were somehow his fault. 'What is it this time, this *bandh*? Why is the road closed?'

The ranger looked befuddled.

'Sorry, Madam. No more detail is there at present.'

The telephone rang.

'For you, Madam.' The ranger handed the receiver to Hannah. The line was fuzzy and they spoke for only two minutes before they were cut off. Hannah replaced the receiver slowly, her face failing to hide her disappointment and worry.

'He's in Bangalore. Someone in the taxi office told him we'd gone back there. There's trouble on the road. Riots apparently. Something to do with water. He thinks it'll all be over by tomorrow. He's still trying to get here. If he doesn't make it, he said we should get a bus back to Mysore tomorrow morning. From there we can get a bus or a car back to Bangalore.' She refrained from adding that Ashok had insisted that in the event of any hint of further trouble on the roads, they should remain in Bandipur.

'Well, at least I could tell Ashok that Salers isn't here. Obviously he couldn't get through either,' she added.

'Hm,' said Willi, looking distracted. 'Maybe.'

'Maybe? You're about to dazzle me with another inspiration,' Hannah said. 'I thought you were hatching some new theory on the way back.'

Willi smiled enigmatically and spoke to the duty ranger. 'Can I have another look at the guest list, please?'

She studied it carefully.

'Aha! Thought as much. Look.' She was pointing to a name on the list.

'Ms Gower,' said Hannah. 'Bungalow five. She was here earlier. Remember?'

'Only it isn't Ms Gower. It's M.S. Gower.'

'Yes? And?'

'Gower - you know - like those big cow things we just saw.'

'Gaur. Of course! Mark Salers Gower.' Hannah turned to the ranger. 'What does M.S. Gower in bungalow five look like?'

'He is English, Madam. Very thin. I think maybe he had been unwell. He is always wearing dark glasses.'

* * *

After Ashok had spoken to Hannah in the Reception Centre at the Game Park, he felt less than reassured. He didn't have time to reveal to her the full extent of what was taking place on the Mysore-Ootacamund road, as the line was poor, and the connection brief. At least he'd had the chance to tell her that someone had deliberately diverted him back to Bangalore. So, in spite of her certainty that Salers was not at Bandipur, she would be extra vigilant until he got there. How on earth was this to be achieved? The road was impassable, so they said. But was it really? Well one thing was clear. No taxi driver would be willing to chance it. He'd have to drive himself. The fact that he'd never driven in India was irrelevant. Ashok spoke to his father.

'*Bapa*, can I borrow the Fiat?'

His father shook his head. 'Fiat is in repair-shop still, Ashok.'

Damn. He'd forgotten that his father had told him yesterday that the steering had gone, and that it would be taken in for repair while they were in Mysore.

'When will it be ready?'

'Not before tomorrow morning. I hope you are not thinking of driving to Bandipur.'

'Well I was, yes. Now I'll have to take train to Mysore and try to get a car to take me from there.'

'Ashok, don't be foolish. There are riots. No one will be willing to take you.'

'I have to try.'

At the railway station he found pandemonium. All trains to Mysore were cancelled. Tracks and signalling equipment had been damaged in the riots, and there was no knowing when the repairs would be completed. Dejected, he went back to the house. First thing tomorrow, he decided, pick up the Fiat, then get through somehow.

'Some boy was delivering a parcel for you,' Girija said. 'It is in your room.'

'Boy? What sort of boy?'

'He was telling he had come from Chamundi Hotel. An Englishman is giving to him early today and asking him to bring to this house.'

*   *   *

Siraj, the bungalow attendant, brought Hannah and Willi a simple supper of vegetables and rice, which they ate in silence.

'I've been thinking,' said Hannah, while Siraj cleared away. 'Salers is obviously ill. I reckon we're a match for him. Let's finish what we set out to do here.'

'You mean you're going to sit on that hill and wait for him to get you?'

'No need. We know where he is. I'll just get the warden to call the cops.'

Hannah told the warden that the man in number five was a dangerous British criminal. She couldn't go into details. She simply wanted the police to pick him up. She would explain to them.

The warden's comprehension of English suddenly appeared to desert him. 'You want I should call police? There is problem?' He looked nonplussed but picked up the telephone and spoke briefly in Kannada before turning back to Hannah.

'Madam, police are tied up with *bandh*. Now is not possible. Tomorrow.'

Frustrated, the two women walked back to their bungalow. 'Where the hell's Ashok?' Hannah muttered. 'He'll get the cops to take us seriously.'

'Unlikely to arrive till morning now.'

Hannah nodded. 'Let's lock up and get some sleep.' She had half a mind to suggest that Willi should sleep in her room, but decided it would be more sensible if they were not in the same place. That way if anything happened to one of them the other one would be free to fetch help.

They were about to retire to their rooms when they heard a knock.

Hannah rushed over to the door. 'Ashok?'

'Message.' Siraj's voice. Hannah swallowed her disappointment and opened the door. Siraj handed her a slip of card. 'Mr Gower say to bring to you.'

'Mr Gower? You mean the man in number five?'

'Yes, Madam. But now he has gone.'

'Gone? What do you mean?'

'Just now I myself watched car drive away.'

Of course. He must have brought the car with him from Bangalore. Hannah cursed silently. Why the hell hadn't they had the sense to retain their driver instead of sending him back to Mysore?

Hannah locked up quickly and took the note to the dining table. A chill spread through her when she saw that it was written on the inside of an opened up Charminar cigarette packet. She recognised the scrawl that she had first encountered in Hyderabad on the note that had purportedly come from Willi.

Apprehensively she read.

You disappoint me, Hannah Petersen, I didn't think you'd be so stupid as to call the cops. You won't find me. I'm too good for you. So don't try again. We'll meet, you can be sure of that. When I'm ready. Tell that fucking Dutch whore to watch her back.

Squashed at the bottom of the card in very small print she read: *If you want to know any more ask your boyfriend.*

CHAPTER 12

As soon as Ashok saw the package that had been delivered from the Chamundi lying on his bed, he knew. It could only be one thing. His hands shook as he opened the Asian Books' bag.

For some moments he remained standing, staring blindly at the book in his hand. Slowly, he opened it and flicked through several pages of photographs near the centre. Most of them were too painful to look at for long; Maighréad in happier days, before evil had overtaken her; the house in Belfast where she had lived with Salers; then close-ups of some of the wounds that Salers had inflicted upon her, propelling Ashok back to the first time he had set eyes on her, lying in the hospital bed covered with bandages.

With increasing impatience, he leafed through the photographs several times more. Where were the pictures of Salers? He checked the list of illustrations at the front of the book. Page three: Mark and Maighréad on their wedding day. Page nineteen: Mark visiting Maighréad in hospital in Belfast after a 'fall'. Page twenty-seven: Mark Salers shortly after his conviction. He turned to where each page should have been. Gone. Carefully cut away so that you could only tell on close inspection. So what? Ashok told himself. Who but Salers could have sent him this book? Now he had no doubt about the stalker's identity.

As Ashok digested this certainty, reality dawned in another guise. Salers knew where he lived. He had placed his family in the firing line. No way forward, no way back. He was caught in a whirlpool, sucked down, slowly drowning. He struggled back to the surface, only to be dragged away by a wave of utter despondency and remorse. Guilt overwhelmed him, as the impact of the day hit him. Everything that had happened was his fault. It was he who had planned the trip to Bandipur. Instead of protecting Hannah, he may have placed her in greater danger. He had asked Hannah to marry him, and she had agreed. How quickly his joy had turned to confusion when he had met Janaki again. How ashamed he was now of his fickleness. Why, oh why had he allowed that lovely young girl's sweet charm and graciousness to get to him? What a weakling he had been. How could he have behaved so despicably towards her too, giving her a glimmer of hope where none existed, leaving the door fractionally open by agreeing to write to her? And now he had brought danger to his own door.

He forced himself back into a rational state of mind. There was no point in panicking. After all, Hannah had been adamant that Salers wasn't at Bandipur. He willed himself to believe she was right. What alternative did he have, while he was stuck in Bangalore? But as soon as the road was passable, Salers would make for the park. His priority tomorrow, when the Fiat was repaired, was to get Hannah back safely. After that, what? Well, firstly he would insist on Willi leaving. That would be one less person to worry about. The next step was to lure Salers out into the open, as they had hoped to do in Bandipur.

He turned his mind to the book. The title *A Small Life* was printed in large letters on the cover. Underneath, in smaller lettering was written *A case history of domestic violence.* Then the author's name. Hannah Petersen. The cover design had been taken from a painting by Munch. Ashok recognised it. *The Scream.* At the foot of the page was a quotation from a daily broadsheet.

'Anyone preferring to exist in the comfortable apathy of ignorance should not read this book.'

Ashok looked at the back cover. A picture of Hannah stared out at him. How young she looked. A little girl. How old was she then? She was born in the same year as Ashok. That would make her twenty-five or twenty-six at the time. He read the short note underneath.

Hannah Petersen read English and Sociology at University College London. Her first book 'Crying Shame,' was received with great critical acclaim. It gained her the 1985 Commonwealth Prize for Non-fiction. She is currently living in Surrey.

Gritting his teeth, Ashok forced himself to open the book. On the front flyleaf was a synopsis of the content. Only it had been tampered with. Certain phrases had been crossed out, but carefully, so that they were still legible. Intrigued but apprehensive, Ashok read:

Hannah Petersen first met Maighréad Salers when the author was in Belfast gathering material for her book 'Crying Shame', a study of the children of the Irish Conflict. ~~Maighréad's parents, prominent members of the Catholic community, had been killed in a Loyalist bomb attack when she was thirteen.~~

At the age of eighteen she married the English journalist Mark Salers.

A close friendship developed between Hannah and the then twenty-year-old Maighréad. Over the next few months Hannah Petersen watched helplessly as she witnessed the results of the terrible physical abuse meted out on Maighréad by her husband, whom Maighréad, fearful of reprisal, was reluctant to report to the authorities.

When she returned to England some months later, Hannah Petersen smuggled Maighréad out of Belfast and took her to live with her in Burfold, where she was able to recover from the wounds ~~inflicted on her by Salers during her two-year ordeal.~~

Her respite was short-lived. Mark Salers traced her ~~and attacked her violently when she was alone in the house~~. After this she moved into a Women's Shelter in Oxford, where Salers once again found her ~~and inflicted wounds of such severity that she spent several weeks in the John Radcliffe Hospital.~~

Mark Salers was arrested and is currently serving a fifteen-year sentence for attempted murder.

Maighréad Salers, unable to come to terms with the traumas of her past, committed suicide exactly one year after Salers' conviction.

As Ashok leafed through the book, he found many more instances of sentences crossed out. It happened on every occasion that Salers was accused of harming Maighréad. If the man was sick enough to believe that someone else had carried out the assaults on Maighréad it explained why he hated Hannah enough to pursue her to India.

Ashok turned with trembling fingers to the end of the book. Hannah had written a postscript.

After the arrest of Mark Salers came a few months when Maighréad was happy in a new relationship with a young doctor who appeared to be healing her psychological wounds with a success that had eluded the rest of us.

In truth, however, wounds of such magnitude were beyond repair. During her first visit back to that city since the fateful day when she had fled with me from its past and present terrors, Maighréad jumped off the third floor of a multi-storey car park. She left a suicide note, addressed to me. It took the form of a biblical quotation.

Come, let us take our fill of love until the morning; let us solace ourselves with loves

For the good man is not at home, he is gone a long journey

Proverbs 7;18-19

Maighréad's message, her last cry of desperation, was so obscure that it has been interpreted in many ways by many people. To me it seems to say that love alone could not sustain her indefinitely.

Ashok closed the book slowly, and with great tenderness, as if in fear of further harming those within. He saw that he was seated on the edge of his bed, and that two hours had elapsed since he first opened the book. He became aware that his father was calling him.

'Just coming, *Bapa.*'

He did not move, but opened the book once more at the postscript. The pain he felt as he reread it was only held from overwhelming him by an underlying sense of incompleteness. Hannah had written her final comment for public consumption. Only they - Ashok and Hannah - could really understand it.

...let us solace ourselves with loves

186

Loves. Plural. A solace that he, Ashok, could not accept, and from which Hannah had also finally withdrawn. Hannah was right. They were both the catalysts that prompted her suicide. The next line puzzled him also.

For the good man is not at home, he is gone a long journey

Did she mean him, Ashok? Was he the good man, who was not at home to her needs? Who had metaphorically gone away from her? He would never know.

'Ashok,' his father called.' Where are you?'

He closed the book once more, and wiped away the tear that had strayed down his cheek. He stood up.

'Coming, *Bapa.*'

* * *

Hannah woke up with a start from restless sleep. Salers' words had been struggling round and round in her brain like a drowning man; *If you want to know any more ask your boyfriend.* What had happened to Ashok? Had Salers got to him after he'd made his phone call to her? How could that be, when Ashok was in Bangalore?

Darkness was absolute. The jungle yielded no light to penetrate through the wire mesh windows. The heat was overwhelming. Hannah realised that she was soaked to the skin. Something had awoken her. Not the heat. Something else. A scream. Had she dreamt it? She fumbled as silently as she could for the torch under the pillow, and turned it on. The claustrophobic veil of the mosquito net surrounded her, like a nebulous, white sea. Slowly she lifted the net a little and shone the torch around the room. Everything was peaceful and orderly. She struggled from under her muslin prison and onto her feet. Her cotton T-shirt, soaked with perspiration, felt suddenly cold in the contrasting air, free of the confines of the net. Her feet on the cool tiles sent a shiver through her body.

The door to her room was still locked. She had to get out. Each small turn of the key sounded to Hannah like gunshot, but finally the lock sprang open. She shone the torch around the little day room. Nothing. The room was as they had left it when they went to bed some four hours earlier. Willi's door was shut. Had she locked it? Knowing Willi, probably not. Hannah crept towards it across the day room. She tried the handle. It was unlocked. With infinite slowness she pushed the door open far enough for her to be able to step into the room. Instantly, she noticed a strong smell of oranges. She shone her torch onto the bed.

Willi was sitting up in bed. She was eating something. Oranges maybe. It was hard to make out behind the mask of the mosquito net. Hannah opened her mouth to say something but stopped herself. Something was wrong, but what?

She shone her torch directly at Willi's face. Willi seemed oblivious. Hannah peered at her. Not even the net could soften the brilliant red complexion of the face that momentarily stopped eating and glowered back at her. Then, in apparent unconcern the monkey continued to munch the Mysore orange that it had stolen from Willi's bedside table.

Hannah shone her torch at the window. It was open, the wire mesh no longer in place. She felt an icy dagger of fear push slowly through her chest. Where was Willi? Had Salers got her? Had he dragged her out through the open window? His words to Willi raced back into her mind. *Tell that fucking Dutch whore to watch her back.*

Why hadn't she struggled? Willi was tough. If she'd put up a fight she could have overcome such a puny adversary. Hannah was coming to an unbearable conclusion. Salers must have disabled her in her sleep. Chloroformed her perhaps, or - Heaven forbid - smothered her with a pillow.

Now Hannah's breath came in short, fast bursts. She was on the verge of panic. Then she reasoned with herself. You're letting the night distort your rationality, girl. Perhaps Willi let the monkey in herself. She might have forgotten to secure the mesh. It's probably nothing to do with Salers. She remembered the scream. Willi's probably scared of the monkey. I bet she's in the bathroom.

She crept somewhat apprehensively around the bed and knocked on the bathroom door.

'Willi. Are you in there?'

She was rewarded with a scarcely audible little moan from within.

'It's me, Hannah. Come on, unlock the door.'

A few seconds passed before Hannah heard Willi shuffle to the door and turn the key.

White as a shroud and totally naked, she was shaking violently.

'Has he gone?'

'It's all right. He won't hurt you.'

'Are you mad? Lock the damn door.'

She pulled Hannah into the bathroom and locked the door once more. Hannah turned the light on.

'What on earth are you talking about? It's only a monkey.'

'A monkey? What d'you mean, a monkey? It's Salers. He tried to rape me.'

Hannah unlocked the door. She grasped Willi by the arm and pushed her into the bedroom. The monkey, seeing Willi's stark, white form emerge from the brightly lit bathroom, let out a shriek and dropped the orange. It made no move to leave the bed.

'I was so sure it was Salers when it attacked me,' said Willi. 'You can't blame me. It was dark, and I was still half asleep.'

'What do you mean, it attacked you?'

Willi shrugged. 'Well, maybe not attacked... I guess I'd been careless about tucking in the mosquito net, and I suddenly felt this thing on top of me.'

'Did it bite you?'

She shook her head. 'It woke me up and I made out this wizened little face inches away from mine. I just shrieked and kicked it away. Then I ran for the bathroom.'

'Why the hell didn't you make sure the window mesh was secure?'

'I did. But I couldn't have, could I? I was so sure I'd checked it.'

'Shoo! Get off!' shouted Hannah, clapping her hands at the animal. It leapt at her, shrieking again and falling back onto the bed when it came in contact with the mosquito net.

'Don't, Hannah,' Willi struggled to salvage a modicum of dignity from her predicament. 'Those things carry diseases like rabies and they have sharp teeth.'

Hannah let her arms drop to her side.

'I guess you're right. You'd better grab your rucksack before he does, and come and sleep in my room.'

At seven o'clock the following morning a knock came on the bungalow door. Hannah wriggled out from under the mosquito net. Willi was already up and dressed. The events of the night had foiled further attempts to sleep.

Siraj had arrived to serve them a breakfast of *parathas* filled with egg and vegetables. He set his tray down on the table.

'We'd better explain about the mess in the bedroom,' said Willi. She signalled to him to follow her. She opened the bedroom door carefully in case her guest was still there, but the room was deserted.

'Pfuh! It's ripe in here,' said Willi.

She pointed to the unguarded window. 'Monkey came. In the night. Sorry.'

The bed was yellowed with dried urine and covered in droppings. The mosquito net hung in tatters.

Siraj shook his head in disbelief and clicked his tongue. For a moment he stood in the doorway staring at the mess. Then he went over to the window.

'Sorry,' said Willi again, as Siraj inspected the window. 'I thought I'd secured the mesh, but I hadn't.'

He called her across. 'Is closed, Madam. Some person was cutting wire.'

'What? Hannah, come and look at this!'

They let the news sink in slowly as they ate their breakfast. So Salers had come back in the night. His threat to Willi had not been a vain one.

'Let's get out of here, Willi. Priority now is to get back to Bangalore and check that Ashok's OK.'

At the reception centre, the duty ranger was pessimistic about their chances of actually encountering a bus to take them back to

Mysore. The look on his face said "unlikely", but nevertheless he pointed them in the right direction and suggested they try their luck.

'Bus stop is outside police station,' he said.

'By the way,' said Hannah, 'did Mr Gower return last night, after he drove away at around ten?'

The ranger shook his head. 'Oh no, Madam. But I am doubting he got very far. All roads were blocked.

*   *   *

As soon as Duncan had booked his airline tickets, he paid a visit to the police. The same constable was on duty. This time he seemed to be falling over himself to please.

'Ah, Mr Forbes, sir, we were just about to phone you to let you know how our enquiry is progressing.'

'Yes? And?' Running scared, Duncan thought. Afraid of what Hannah might do to their reputation if she unleashed her anger over their treatment of her.

'Sir, we've alerted Interpol in New York, and surveillance has been placed on all incoming flights from US to all European and American airports.'

'Why should Salers go to America?'

'Not only Salers, sir. We're following all leads. After all, it's only Miss Petersen's opinion that Salers is involved. We checked on Bannerman. You were right. Seems no one can trace him. We haven't ruled him out yet. Pity we don't know where Miss Petersen is, sir. You sure you've no idea?'

For a moment Duncan wondered whether to tell the police about Felicity. Would it be worth the humiliation? He quickly convinced himself that it would not. Better they spread the net too wide than too narrow. And who's to say that Salers won't flee to the US?

He took a deep breath. 'Yes, yes I do know. Hannah Petersen's in Bangalore, India. And she's convinced she's been followed.'

'Why were you keeping this information back, sir? I have to tell you that it could land you in serious trouble. Hampering our inquiries. Endangering Miss Petersen.'

'I'm sorry. I only just found out myself.' He felt wretched, and stupid. The policeman was right. He should have told them earlier. He'd panicked.

The policeman sighed. 'All right, sir. We'll get onto Delhi right away.'

'Delhi? That's miles away from Bangalore, isn't it?'

'Couldn't say, sir, but we have to go through Delhi. They'll take it from there.'

'Well, let's hope they get a move on then. I've come to tell you that in view of Salers' release, I'm leaving for Bangalore tonight.'

'Oh, very good, sir. Miss Petersen will be most relieved. Please do assure her that we're doing everything possible to catch this man.'

'Here. I've written down an email address, where she can be contacted in Bangalore. Please let her know at once of any further developments.'

* * *

'Did you know,' said Srinivasa between mouthfuls of breakfast *idli*, 'it is Christmas Eve today?'

'I had forgotten.' Ashok said. 'There were other matters on my mind.' Like the Fiat. As soon as it turned up, he was planning to head off to Bandipur. But where the hell was it? It was already nine o'clock and still no sign of it.

'Your friends. You are concerned naturally.'

'Of course. I tried to telephone Hannah again some hours ago, but telephone line is down.'

'That does not surprise me. Situation is apparently deteriorating rapidly. There is talk of curfew. No buses are running. But not to worry. At least they are safe in park.'

'It would appear so.' Let him be right, Ashok prayed.

'Of course, this whole dispute is the fault of British.'

'Oh?' Ashok glanced at his watch.

'You see, it was British rulers who apportioned Cauvery River water between Mysore and Madras.' Srinivasa shook his finger emphatically, 'Divide and rule, Ashok, divide and rule.'

Ashok struggled to show interest, as he willed the Fiat to appear.

'Such policies,' continued his father, 'were uppermost in Britain's dealings with its colonies. Madras received greater share of water.'

'But surely this was reasonable? Madras was bigger.'

'That is as maybe. But even with construction of Mettur Dam in Tamil Nadu, that state was apportioned water from Mysore.'

Ashok was at the window, staring vainly out onto the lane.

'Take, take.' Girija placed another plate of *idlis* on the table before commenting, 'I remember well in fifties when Mysore became what is now Karnataka. Those were exciting times. So progressive. But very nervous, also.'

'Ah, yes,' continued her husband, 'this is point I am making. With this transformation of Mysore, the size of the state expanded - from nine to sixteen districts.'

'And Tamil Nadu on the other hand has very less districts than the original state of Madras,' said Ashok.

'Correct.' said Srinivasa.

'And now?'

'Ah! And now is a question of politics, as always.'

'Only instead of British, they are now blaming Central Government.'

'And why not? Again this year Cauvery Waters Dispute Tribunal has awarded lion's share of Karnataka water to Tamil Nadu. There is widespread feeling in Karnataka press that Central Government is perpetuating British policy of Divide and Rule.'

Ashok looked at his watch again. 'So why has this blown up now?'

'Our Chief Minister called a state *bandh*. There was rioting here even, in Bangalore, some days before you came.'

'And the future?'

Srinivasa shook his head. 'Who knows? In the words of the Mahatma, "Violent means will give violent freedom. That would be a menace to the world and to India herself."'

Ashok got up. If the mountain won't come to Mohammed, he decided.

'I'm just going out for a while,' he said.

At the car repair shop Ashok stared in dismay at his father's Fiat. The steering wheel had been dismantled.

'This repair was supposed to be completed by today morning,' he told the mechanic angrily.

'Very sorry, sir. The part we are needing is coming from Mysore. Delivery has not been able to get through.'

'Well, find one. Make one if you have to. But get that car repaired. I'll come back in an hour.'

* * *

The bus stop at Bandipur was situated some one hundred metres from the park reception centre.

Hannah and Willi set off along the dusty road, fringed by scattered dindalu trees and small shrubs. The morning was hotting up, and even the air smelled dry. They reached the bus stop. Here confusion reigned. They found themselves in the midst of half a dozen excited policemen and a family from Ootacamund who had also been staying at the park. One policeman spoke English.

'No bus today, ladies. There is *bandh*. Public transport is at standstill.'

The family from Ooty, parents and two teenage children, who had been deliberating on what to do, picked up their suitcases and set off on foot for the Tamil Nadu border several miles to the south.

As they disappeared down the road, three blond boys, weighed down with heavy rucksacks, approached from that direction. They nodded at Hannah and Willi.

'*Ja, guten Tag*. Are you also trying to get to Mysore?' said one of them.

'Yes. There seem to be no buses.'

'We know this. We have been given a lift in a jeep to the state border, but the driver would go no further, and fled back into Tamil Nadu as soon as he had dropped us. From there we have walked.'

The police, whose excitement had not abated, were arguing loudly with one another. Although none of the Europeans could understand a word of what was being said, it was clear that the five of them were the subject of the debate.

Hannah addressed the young English-speaking officer.

'Can you help us find a way to get to Mysore?'

'Just wait here, Madam.'

Not very elucidating, thought Hannah, but he seemed quite positive.

Suddenly a large brown and yellow truck came thundering along from the direction of Ootacamund. The young officer waved it down, and spoke to the driver and his mate urgently in a tone that suggested more of an order than a request. Then he turned to Hannah.

'These people are trying to get through to Mysore. They will take you. But you will have to travel on back of truck.'

Hannah, who seemed to have been catapulted into the position of group spokesperson, looked at the three youngsters. They looked at one another and nodded.

One by one they made the ascent onto the back of the truck. To the young men this was evidently no more of a challenge than a pleasant afternoon stroll. With a single, elegantly executed bound they were on the truck. By the time the two women had been ignominiously pummelled and hoisted on board, the boys were already comfortably established on the tarpaulin, alongside several Indians.

The truck roared off at breakneck speed down the hillside. Hannah tried to blot out of her mind the photograph she had once seen of just such trucks lying crippled and crumpled one after another on the Grand Trunk Road.

Thirty minutes later they rolled into Gundlupet, a dusty little town with seemingly little to commend it. An air of tension hung over the place. Several men stood around expectantly, but other than that few people were on the streets. It was as if most of the population were hiding.

'Well, no road blocks there,' said Willi, as they left the town behind.

'No, but somehow I didn't like the atmosphere,' Hannah said, 'and neither did they.' She nodded towards their Indian companions, who had grown rigid and silent.

The wind in their faces softened the ferocity of the midday sun. They hung onto the ropes that held the tarpaulin and started to relax. Hannah learned from one of the Indians that the truck was going on to Bangalore.

'Shall we stay on it, instead of switching to a bus in Mysore? What do you think, Willi?'

'It's a long time to be in full sun.'

'True. It's easy to forget how hot it is while we're moving.' She turned to one of the boys. 'Where are you heading?'

'Not really bothered,' said the second boy.

'Oh!' Hannah was surprised at his perfect English. 'You're not German!'

'They are. I'm from Norwich.'

'I thought you were brothers.'

The English boy shook his head, and lapsed back into the state of disquiet that had seemed to characterise all three young men from the start. Hannah felt sorry for them. They couldn't have been more than nineteen.

'About the truck,' she turned to Willi, 'Let's wait until we get to Mysore before we decide.'

They bounced along in silence for a while before Willi spoke again.

'What are we actually sitting on, do you suppose?'

They pulled back the tarpaulin and stared at their revelation.

'Propane gas cylinders!' gasped Willi.

'Yes.' said Hannah, 'a whole truck-load sizzling in the noonday heat!'

'There is no need to worry,' volunteered one of the German boys. 'It would require a much higher temperature to make them explode.'

The truck sped along the highway, the gas cylinders bouncing with the motion. A car overtook them, then slowed in front of the truck.

'Willi,' said Hannah, frowning. 'I think that's Salers in that car.'

'Are you sure?'

'I saw him when he passed. Weedy, sick looking. Dark glasses.'

The car was now travelling so slowly that the truck, hooting angrily, overtook it.

'Well, the description fits,' said Willi, 'What shall we do?'

'I don't know.'

Strange, Hannah reflected. A few days ago, I'd have been beside myself. Now? He's only a man, and a sick one at that, not some unknown terror in the night. She could deal with him. But how to convince the Indian police? They hadn't had much luck so far. Would the break in at the park bungalow interest them enough to distract them from the *bandh*? There were plenty of them around, patrolling the road. Maybe no need to wait for Ashok. If the opportunity arose.

The car overtook them again and slowed up in front of them. By now they could feel the fury of the truck driver, resonating in the movement of the truck. He overtook once more and put his foot down hard, with the intention of outrunning the car. He had not reckoned with the tenacity of the car driver. Suddenly the car pulled alongside the truck again, and for some heart-stopping moments the two vehicles raced side by side.

Hannah scrambled to the front of the truck and pulled herself round the cab so that she could call into the driver's window.

'That car,' she shouted, pointing. 'Can you force him off the road?'

The driver, intent on keeping his truck *on* the road, was already uttering a long string of incomprehensible abuse at the car. Now he turned his fury onto Hannah, leaning across to try and push her back onto the gas cylinders, which meant controlling the speeding truck with one hand. Undaunted, Hannah clung on, and tried again.

'The man in the back of that car is bad, wicked. We have to stop him,' she shouted. 'Please try!'

But the truck driver spoke no English, and got increasingly enraged until Hannah had to concede that she was doing more harm than good by distracting him. She fought her way back over the load to Willi.

The three boys were sitting bolt upright, wide-eyed in terror.

'*Was stellst du dir vor?*' stammered one of the Germans, '*Du willst uns wohl alle umbringen!*'

'Yea, what the hell d'you think you're playing at?' The English boy found his voice, high-pitched and hysterical.

Hannah didn't answer. She was too intent on watching the car. Suddenly it accelerated and shot ahead. This time it did not slow down, but roared off, disappearing in a cloud of dust and exhaust fumes.

The relief on the truck was palpable. It was not only Willi and Hannah who had been unnerved by the antics of the car. It was only they however who understood its implications. He was letting Hannah know that he was still on her trail. He'd said he'd find her. Now he'd unwrapped another layer of the parcel. He'd let her catch a glimpse of him. How many more layers were there?

The countryside was rich in wheat and paddy, coconut and mulberry groves. In the distance, across the fields, they noticed patches of billowing smoke, which they took at first to be routine stubble burning. They passed a burnt-out lorry. With a jolt Hannah remembered the one she had seen yesterday. Had there been two accidents? Or was something sinister going on? By the time they neared the temple town of Nanjangud, fifteen miles from Mysore, the mood on the truck had grown sombre. An uneasy silence reigned. Is it possible, Hannah wondered, that the distant fires were not as innocent as at first they had seemed?

Shortly outside Nanjangud they once more overtook the car. It was parked by the side of the road, at a stall selling bottled drinks. The driver was negotiating with the stallholder. A police car had also pulled up. Two policemen were sitting on the bonnet with bottles of cola in their hands.

'Stop!' Hannah called out, and in desperation turned to one of their Indian travelling companions. 'Please tell the driver to stop. I've got to get that man arrested.'

The Indian shrugged his shoulders in a gesture that meant, sorry, I don't know what you're talking about, as the truck roared on.

'Are you mad?' said Willi, 'What on earth would you have done if he had stopped?'

'Jetzt fängt die wieder an!'

'Willi, didn't you see the police car? The police are everywhere at the moment.'

'Get real, Hannah. They aren't going to pick the guy up on your say-so. We found that out last night. Not with this strike going on. I vote we steer clear until your guardian angel catches up with us.'

Hannah glared at her. 'You think I can't manage that worm on my own? I could squash him with my little finger.'

'Well, all I can say is I'm glad you weren't given the chance to try.'

'Don't think we've got much choice in the matter at the moment.' Hannah reflected that Willi's brush with the monkey, coupled with Salers' threatening note, had toppled her bravado.

They crossed the bridge in Nanjangud. At this time of year the Kapila river was depleted, but the length of the bridge, and the expanse of dried out riverbed, spoke of a raging, swollen torrent in the time of the monsoon.

At the far side, near a huddle of small dwellings, they drew to a halt. The road in front was completely blocked by an overturned truck, its load of cereal scattered across the highway. The truck had been set alight and was blazing fiercely. Flames leapt several metres into the air. The hot blast from the fire hit the faces of the travellers perched on top of the propane gas. An acrid smell of burning rubber seeped into their nostrils and invaded their lungs. From nowhere, a mass of villagers descended on them and surrounded them. They were shouting, simultaneously, and hysterically at the driver. Hannah, Willi and the boys sat rigidly, unable to understand.

'Are they going to burn our truck too?' whispered Willi.

'Just stay cool,' said Hannah through clenched teeth.

They started to move again, under instructions from the villagers. Slowly they pulled off the road onto a sandy, unmade track to the right. A hundred metres further on, the truck was again ordered to halt. More people, mainly men, surrounded it. Frenzied and animated arguments were taking place. The crowd grew thicker. A jeep pulled up. A man in a khaki uniform got out. He surveyed the frightened bunch on top of the truck and pointed at the boy from Norwich.

'You! Speak English?' The English boy had lost his voice, and shook his head in terror.

'You English?' the uniformed man was pointing to Hannah.

She nodded.

'Come down here please!'

'Don't go, Hannah!' hissed Willi. 'Make one of them do it.' She gestured at the boys, who sat like statues, staring resolutely down at their knees.

'Don't be silly. I've got to.' Hannah jumped down from the truck, slipped as she landed and sat down on her bottom. The crowd roared. Hannah cursed. Not the way she would have chosen to defuse the tension.

The uniformed man took her gently by the arm, as the crowd closed in. More curious than threatening, Hannah surmised.

'Are you all right? I hope you are not hurt.' said the man.

'I'm all right.'

'I am Law Enforcement Officer,' explained the man. 'Please tell your friends that is not possible to get through to Mysore. There are fourteen burning trucks other side of village. Rioting is widespread.'

'And is this truck also in danger?'

'Not from rioters. They are attacking trucks with Tamil Nadu plates only. This one is having Karnataka plates. But there is great danger from heat of burning vehicles. This truck is carrying propane gas.'

'I know that. What shall we do?'

'You must get off road. Even if you were able to get past rioters it would be too dangerous. You do not speak local language and your motives might be misconstrued. Situation is highly volatile. There is old, deserted house some way back. You must wait there until road is clear and it is safe for truck to pass.'

'How long?'

The officer shrugged. 'Maybe hours. Maybe days. Who can say?'

Hannah clambered back on board the truck. This time sheer grit and determination not to look an idiot in front of vast numbers of grinning men paid off. With a superhuman effort she managed to hoist herself back onto the gas cylinders with comparative dignity.

'You were so cool,' breathed Willi. 'I'd have wet myself.'

'I used to live in Belfast,' Hannah said simply, wishing she felt as cool as she appeared. She was remembering that they had overtaken Salers. He was behind them somewhere, stuck, like they were, in Nanjangud.

CHAPTER 13

Apart from the occasional Christmas banners strung across shop windows, and an odd Santa, sweltering inside his red suit, while he drew attention to this shop or that with the aid of his hand-bell, Bangalore made little of Christmas Eve. Throughout the day, reports were coming in about the situation in the Mysore region. Ashok's anxiety grew with each new piece of information. He heard that Tamil homes and farms were being set alight by Kanarese neighbours, with whom they had lived in peace all their lives until now. The reverse was happening across the border. The whole of the area around Nanjangud and Gundlupet was under curfew. Tamils were fleeing from Karnataka to Tamil Nadu, and vice versa. Trains were being halted, and passengers assaulted in both states. Livestock was reported killed in the fires. There was an unsubstantiated report of an old woman burnt in her hut.

Ashok made repeated trips to the car workshop. The mechanic said he was doing his best. Ashok's knowledge of motor mechanics was negligible and he had to accept the man's word. By lunch the car situation was unchanged and he'd still had no word from Hannah. Meanwhile all Ashok's attempts to secure a vehicle from elsewhere had failed. His mind ran amok, and he struggled to curb his worst images of what might have befallen the two women. If they managed to get out of Bandipur before the curfew, they'll have stopped in a hotel along the route, he insisted to himself. The phone lines are certainly down. They couldn't possibly get word through. They'll simply have to sit it out until it's all over. Neither side, he reasoned, would risk harming their cause by attacking Europeans. Or would they?

It was two o'clock in the afternoon when the phone rang.

'Ashok, can you hear me?'

'Hallo, hallo, Hannah? Is it you?'

'Yes. The line is very fuzzy, Ashok. Can you hear me now?'

'I can hear you, Hannah. Where are you? Are you safe?'

'We're in Nanjangud. In a deserted bungalow. Used to be rather grand. We're quite safe. Don't worry.'

'Thank goodness. Hannah? Are you still there?'

'Yes I'm here. I can't hear you very well. Listen. We'll have to stay here till this blows over. We aren't getting much information here. Have you heard anything?'

'Things are a bit hairy, Hannah. It could take some days. Any sign of Salers?'

'Days, did you say?'

The line went dead. Ashok put the phone down with a sense of relief tinged with irritation that they had not been able to complete their call. He had wanted to tell her he was so sorry, that he would come and get her just as soon as he could get through, that he'd been out of his mind with worry. He had wanted to reassure himself that Salers had not materialised.

With nightfall marginal progress had been made on the Fiat. The mechanic triumphantly held up a small pin that he had succeeded in making.

'It was very, very hard to get this to fit,' he told Ashok. 'Now I have to make one more.'

'How long will it take?'

'Come tomorrow morning. Eight o'clock.' No point in arguing.

No further word had come from Hannah, so Ashok decided to go and check Salman's email. Perhaps Duncan had come up with new information. Salman, as always, was at the bench.

'Three emails for Hannah,' he grinned. 'Sorry - couldn't help glancing at them. Looks as if you're in for some competition, isn't it? But one problem has resolved, no?'

Ashok looked at him quizzically. Competition?

He opened the first one.

Have evidence that Salers is Terry Bull - but I guess you'd already worked that one out...

203

He turned to the second email.

Sender: Chief Superintendent Peter Harris, Surrey Police.
Dear Miss Petersen
I am sure you will be relieved to know that acting on new information received from Mr Duncan Forbes, we have today arrested a man at Heathrow Airport.
However the man concerned, who was apprehended on a flight from Bombay, was not, as suggested by Mr Forbes, the released prisoner Mark Salers.
The man's name is Paul Philip Fenton and he is a private investigator, who was hired in England by an American, one Dr Elliott Bannerman. The New York Police Department is, of course, liaising with us to investigate this matter further. However I can tell you that Fenton was found to have in his possession notes pertaining to a Dr Ashok Rao. It would appear that Bannerman was looking for material with which to blackmail you into withdrawing the publication of your latest book. The notes suggest the possibility that this could be achieved by threats to discredit Dr Rao.
We do, of course, need to discuss this with you and would request you to get in touch as a matter of urgency.
On behalf of the Surrey Police Force may I say that I am delighted that this matter has been brought to a satisfactory conclusion. I trust you and Mr Forbes will now be able to enjoy the remainder of your holiday in peace.
Peter Harris

Unable to grasp the meaning of the email, Ashok read it again. It was good news, wasn't it? But it didn't make sense. A Bannerman plot after all? Then what about the altered copy of *A Small Life*? And why wish Hannah and Mr Forbes a happy holiday? Was this email a fake? Someone clearly had their facts wrong. How did they get hold of his email address? Through Forbes? Who else?

'I think you'd better look at last email.' Salman said.

Incomprehension changed to horror and disbelief as Ashok read it.

Sit tight, I'm on my way. Arriving Bangalore Christmas Eve. Try not to worry.

Duncan

P.S. Don't go out at night. And keep your hotel room door locked.

What the hell is going on? First an incomprehensible email purportedly from the British police. And now this idiot. It was a complete nightmare.

Ashok needed to collect his thoughts. He printed out the emails and wandered over to the campus coffee bar. Here he bought a cup of coffee and sat at a table beneath a kapok tree.

He looked again at the second email. Could it be genuine, after all? It certainly made sense that Bannerman could have sent an agent to dig up some dirt on Hannah, or at least find some way to threaten her that would make her withdraw publication. He'd failed to intimidate her by threatening her directly, so he'd get at her through her friends. That also explained the attacks on him and Willi. But what about the book? Could it be that it wasn't sent by Salers at all? That Bannerman's agent sent it and the pearls? And tampered with the photographs? Had Duncan been misled? Of course. And Fenton - hadn't that been the name of the fat guest at the Pandava? Suddenly he understood. It was a false trail to implicate Salers, so that no one would suspect Bannerman. While we were all tying ourselves in knots over Salers, Fenton would slip quietly back to England, to report to Bannerman, who was lying low there. Brilliant. Only…a grin slowly spread over Ashok's face. He'd failed, hadn't he? He's been arrested. Our troubles are over. Ashok sat back, letting it slowly sink in.

Then he remembered Duncan. His euphoria fled. Duncan's appearance on the scene would be about as welcome as a mosquito inside a mosquito net. Hannah had said very little about him, but the fact that he was prepared to come all this way to help her left Ashok uneasy. Hannah had hinted at more than a mere working relationship between them once. This impulsive act implied that

Duncan had hopes of resuscitating it. Well, it's too late to tell him to get lost. He'll be here by now.

* * *

Five minutes after the Law Enforcement Officer had ordered Hannah and her companions back across the Nanjangud bridge, their propane gas truck had turned off the main road onto a track to the left. It made its way down to an ancient, double-fronted bungalow. Despite or, perhaps, because of the tumbledown appearance, Hannah was struck by its beauty. It was set on the banks of the river, in a neglected, tree-studded garden, a silent paradise in the surrounding inferno. The truck was parked under a tree in front of the house, whose shadow protected it from the blaze of the sun. Since the crew spoke no English the Europeans had no way to communicate verbally with them. On impulse Hannah pressed a hundred rupees into the driver's hand, although she knew that the journey was by no means over. Once they were off the truck, the Indians melted into the scenery and disappeared.

The house was deserted except for a retainer, an ancient Methuselah, who had surely been inadvertently left behind when the house was abandoned an indeterminate number of years ago.

'How long do you suppose it's been since anyone lived here?' said Willi.

Hannah shook her head. 'Impossible to tell in this part of the world. Looks like a remnant from the Raj, but who knows. Must have been very grand in its prime though, don't you think?'

They studied the gabled porch, a room in itself, supported by neo-classical twin pillars at each corner, and topped by a pointed roof of red Mangalore tiles. Beneath this imposing edifice, one could just make out a heavy, ornate, wooden door. The porch was flanked on each side by huge, half-octagonal bay windows, over which ran battlemented parapets.

'If I had to hazard a guess, I'd say it's turn of the century,' said Hannah.

'I need to find a loo,' Willi said.

The three boys came across to them. Obviously embarrassed at their previous display of gutlessness, they were intent on appearing chivalrous.

'We are going to look for somewhere to eat,' said one of the Germans. 'Perhaps you would care to join us?'

'Have you tried asking the old boy?' said Willi.

She marched across the grass to where the old man leant against a tree, smoking a cigarette.

'Look here,' she shouted, 'we need toilets, you understand? And lunch.'

The old man studied her for a moment, while he continued to puff at his cigarette, clearly not unmanned by her outburst. Willi looked around at the others. They watched her with interest, but no one moved to help her out of her predicament. They were far too curious to see what would happen next.

'Toilets!' she shouted, this time even louder. 'Lunch! Food! You savvy?'

Slowly the old man lowered his cigarette. 'Come,' he ordered her, and started to walk towards the house.

'I think he understood,' Willi shouted across to the others. 'Come on.'

They followed the old man up the steps to the porch, where he selected one of several large, rusting keys that dangled on a chain from his waist and inserted it with some difficulty into the door lock. The door squealed loudly as it swung ponderously open.

For a few seconds they blinked in the darkness that was such a contrast to the white, heat-saturated day outside. Gradually they could make out a long, dark wood-panelled hallway, into which were set three doors, one to the right, one to the left and the third straight ahead. Fumbling with another key from his set, he opened the door on the left, and gestured to the boys that they should go in. Then he unlocked the right hand door, and pushed it open. It moaned in protest. Hannah and Willi stepped hesitantly into the vast room.

To their surprise, it was furnished. Massive, sun-bleached drapes of once heavy, but now threadbare silk drooped down across the great windows. Under the greying dustsheets, they could make out various shapes approximating chairs, and an enormous dressing table. Near the bay window the outline of a huge, stately bed looked ghostly under its funereal drapery. To Hannah, it all seemed very Victorian.

Stepping past them, the old retainer lumbered through the room to a door at the far end, which he opened. 'Toilet,' he said.

Hannah said, 'Thank you. May we stay here? Until the road is clear?'

The man's head swayed in a gesture that Hannah now understood.

'That's very kind. We will pay for the room, of course. Can we eat here?'

The old man's head wobble was less affirmative this time. 'I don't know, Madam. Maybe. You wait please.'

The bathroom, in keeping with the rest of the house, was very grand, or at least it must have been so in its heyday. The enormous bath was encrusted with mould and other detritus, the gold-coloured taps on the washbasin had long since ceased to function, and the toilet chain hung down, decorative but impotent, from its voluminous water tank.

'This whole place looks as if it's been left over from a Gothic film set,' Willi said.

Hannah laughed. 'After lunch we must go down to the river and fill up that clay pot with water so that we can flush the loo.'

'Good idea,' said Willi. 'Why not do it now, while we're waiting?'

Together they manhandled the pot, which had been standing on the floor in the corner of the bedroom, down to the river behind the house. Although depleted further down, the river was nevertheless quite lake-like here, as if caught behind a floodgate. Snowy white egrets skimmed over the water's smooth surface. There was silence. To the left, the Mysore-Ootacamund road-bridge spanned the river. They could see the smoke from the burning truck at the far side. A wide flight of steps formed a ghat that led down to the water from the end of what was once no doubt a well-tended lawn, but was now dried out and tired-looking. Two women, apparently unconcerned about the chaos in the village, were busy doing the laundry. Clean linen and saris were spread out to dry upon the steps. In the distance other fires were raging, and a feculent veil smudged the sky. Hannah and Willi filled the pot with cloudy river water, and Willi went off to cajole the three lads into helping them carry it back to their room.

The old retainer spotted Hannah sitting on her own by the water, and came to talk to her. 'No lunch here. Sorry,' he said, 'but I take you to hotel.'

Hannah had by now learnt that "hotel" seemed to be the generic Indian term for a small restaurant or cafe. None of them had eaten since eight o'clock that morning. By now it was nearly two o'clock and the prospect of several more hours without food was grim. The suggestion therefore was met with approval from all five. They followed the old man through deserted cattle pens and across the main road.

The "hotel" was set back from the road and amounted to little more than a large hut with a tattered awning. Thankfully they stumbled inside, away from the heat. The place was functional and clean.

After the meal, a simple *thali*, Hannah decided to try and contact Ashok.

'Is there a telephone?' she asked one of the serving men. He stared at Hannah blankly. She took out fifty rupees and repeated her question. The man immediately ushered her into the cooking area, where she spotted a telephone resting in a dark corner on the edge of a stone sink unit. Her call to Ashok was frustrating because they were cut off. She tried vainly to get reconnected but had to content herself with the knowledge that she had spoken to him, and he knew they were safe. His assertion that they might be stuck there for several days left her with a feeling of unease. So far Willi had apparently not registered the fact that Salers must have reached Nanjangud after they did, and had therefore also been turned back. Best not to tell her, she decided. It was not knowing exactly where he was that bothered Hannah. A chameleon poised to spring.

As they got up to leave, several policemen came in to lunch. Willi saw a chance of salvation. She found one who spoke English and explained their predicament to him.

'Position for the moment is hopeless,' he said. 'Very dangerous. No vehicles are able to get through. Only police jeep. You go out onto main road and wait there. Maybe police jeep is coming in Mysore direction.'

This seemed a better alternative than heading straight back to the old house. They knew that, if their attempt failed, there was no danger of the truck going without them for the next few hours.

They sat on the verge in the blazing sun and waited.

*   *   *

Ashok returned home via the Chamundi. Best inform the hotel that Hannah's return has been delayed, he decided. At the same time he could check on Duncan.

'Has a Mr Forbes booked in?' he asked.

The receptionist checked the guest list.

'No, sir. Should have arrived earlier, but there is delay at Delhi airport. Some severe storms. So flight will be arriving very late. I think he will be at hotel by one a.m. only.'

It was impossible to sleep. Ashok kept hearing the telephone, jumping up and realising that the night was playing tricks on his mind. He couldn't wait to tell Hannah the news of the arrest. Thank goodness. She was safe. But there was also the matter of Duncan Forbes. Having resigned himself to the fact of it, he was now impatient to confront Forbes before Hannah did. By four o'clock he decided that there was no point in lying in bed worrying. He got up quietly and dressed.

Even the rickshaw-wallahs were asleep at that time of the morning, so Ashok waited until five o'clock before he went out into the cool dawn air to rouse a sleepy driver into life. He loved the start of a new day. The earth smelled innocent. The trees on the lane, fat with chlorophyll, wafted aromatic perfumes. No rude horns punctured the stillness, and the main road was still free from the airless, fume-laden pall that would strangle the city as the day wore on. Yet activity existed; the first stirring of the ingredients that would bind together into the rich, spicy stew of the daytime metropolis. At this time of the morning, the street traders flocked into the city, wheeling their carts of fruits and vegetables along the main road. Some shops, like little sheds, were opening up their garage-like doors, to reveal the myriad mysteries within. The occasional truck thundered by, pariah dogs began to root in the gutter, a cock crowed.

The Chamundi bustled with early morning arrivals and departures. Taxis and autorickshaws cluttered the long, sweeping driveway to the hotel entrance. Once inside, Ashok had to sidestep ordered lines of waiting suitcases to get to the reception desk.

'Has Mr Duncan Forbes arrived from England yet?'

The receptionist consulted his arrivals list.

'Yes, sir. Arrived in the night. But I think he will now be sleeping, sir.'

Ashok looked at his watch. Six fifteen. Yes, he had rather acted on impulse. After all, there was no rush now the stalker had been caught. But surely Duncan would be awake and impatient to contact Hannah? Then he'd discover that she was not there. Goodness knows what he might do.

'Please connect me to his room.'

The voice that answered was infused with sleep. 'Yes?'

'Hallo, Duncan Forbes?'

A pause, then a hesitant acknowledgement. 'Uhuh.'

'Good morning, Mr Forbes. My name's Ashok Rao. You don't know me. I'm a friend of Hannah Petersen. Could you come down to reception please?'

'What is this? Where's Hannah?'

'Please don't worry. Hannah's away for a couple of days, but she's fine. If you could come down, I'll explain.'

Again a pause. 'Well, OK. But I'm not showered or dressed yet. Can you wait?'

'Take all the time you need. I'll be in the coffee shop.'

Ashok made his way to the hotel's twenty-four hour bistro. It was almost deserted. He sat down at one of the sanitised, white melamine-topped tables and ordered a cup of Mysore coffee and two *idlis*. He spotted the croissants and had a sudden pang of homesickness for Europe. 'And give me a couple of those croissants and some jam,' he said.

He was on to his second croissant, when a couple walked in. The man was athletically built and, Ashok reckoned, touching early middle age. His physical appearance was immaculate. He was some six feet tall; tanned face, handsome by any account; thick, blond hair, greying at the edges, carefully combed into place; crisp, white short-sleeved shirt and impeccably pressed trousers.

Despite his outward appearance, Ashok sensed something awkward about the man, as though he were ill at ease with his surroundings. Not at home in the East, Ashok decided. His companion was a young woman, small, slim, reddish hair, but not natural, like Hannah's. She was fairly creased, and could easily have just been unpacked after spending the past ten hours in an aircraft hold. The man pushed ahead of her, but though he appeared dominant, she had something defiant about her, like a recently captured slave, who has been compelled to suppress a powerful personality. At first, being a couple, Ashok dismissed them from his mind. However the man headed straight for his table.

'Excuse me, are you the person who called my room a little while ago?'

'Forbes? Duncan Forbes?'

'That's right. I'm afraid I didn't catch your name.'

'Ashok Rao,' Ashok pressed his fingers together with mock solemnity, in an Indian greeting. This, as he had anticipated, fazed Duncan, who fumbled clumsily with his hands, not quite knowing how to respond. He diverted attention by turning to the girl.

'Oh - this is Felicity, a friend of mine.'

To Ashok's amazement Felicity immediately pressed her hands together, bowed her head to meet her fingers and said '*Namaskara*.' It was as natural a gesture as a local Indian would make. He acknowledged her with an admiring nod and she smiled, wistfully, but Ashok registered a flash of triumph in her eyes. He started to warm a little towards Duncan too. Maybe he really did have altruistic reasons for his sudden arrival. Since he had a female in tow, Ashok had obviously jumped to the wrong conclusion about the nature of his interest in Hannah.

'Now,' Duncan said, 'perhaps you could explain who you are and what's going on.'

Ashok told him briefly that he was a friend of Hannah's, that he was fully aware of the situation and that it was he who had set up the email contact.

Duncan glanced around. 'This isn't really the place to talk. There are ears everywhere. Felicity, your room's nearest. Let's go there.'

'My room's chaotic,' said the girl. 'It's also very small. I think we'd better go to yours.'

Alarm bells started again in Ashok's mind. Separate rooms? What was going on? Perhaps they weren't an item after all.

'Why the furtiveness?' he said. 'There's no danger now they've caught him.'

'Caught him? You mean they've got Salers?'

'Not Salers. It wasn't him after all. But I forgot, you'd probably left by the time news came through. It was Bannerman's man.' Ashok told Duncan about the email from the police. 'I assume it was you who passed on the email address?'

Duncan muttered, 'So he was after her too. I thought as much.' Turning to Ashok he said, 'Look, I think we'd better fill you in on the rest of this.'

Duncan led them back to his room, which overlooked the garden. Ashok noticed with a pang of disquiet that it was next door to Hannah's room. Had he requested it so?

The room was immaculate. Even the bed had been made. Pyjamas were folded neatly on the pillow, a shirt hung to air on a hanger hooked over the bathroom door. A small travel iron stood on the dressing table. Duncan motioned them to sit on the two chairs while he took the bed.

'Right, Mr...er...er.'

'Doctor,' said Ashok. Somehow it seemed important to make sure Duncan knew this. He repeated his name once more.

'Right. Well, I've got some bad news. They may have caught Bannerman's agent, but Salers is still after her.'

Ashok laughed. 'No, you've got it wrong. That was a set up. It's what Bannerman wanted us to believe. Salers isn't involved.'

Duncan sighed. 'Look. I appreciate the fact that you're trying to be helpful, but since you're not directly involved, you're not aware of the facts.'

Ashok saw red. He fought in vain to control his anger. 'Not directly involved? Tell me this. Why did Bannerman want to use me to get at Hannah?' He pulled the police email out of his shirt pocket and thrust it at Duncan, who read it in silence.

Duncan stared at Ashok as the implication sank in. Ashok could see his mind working. Was it possible that this upstart Indian was muscling in on what he thought was his patch?

He spoke, not taking his eyes off Ashok's face. 'I'm getting a little tired of playing guessing games. Now please tell me how come you know Hannah.'

Ashok was irritated at Duncan's attempt to be officious. 'Hannah and I met on the plane coming over,' he said struggling to hide his hostility. 'I recognised her from her picture on the back of *A Small Life.'* He took a deep breath. 'I am the doctor who was involved with Maighréad Salers in Oxford.'

Duncan's expression was one of incredulity. This was only matched by Felicity, who rose slowly from her chair, and gasped, 'You!'

Ashok looked from one to the other. No one spoke, while the two tried to digest Ashok's information.

Finally Duncan broke the silence. 'Rao. Ashok Rao. Name means nothing to me. You, Felicity?'

'No. Mark never knew the name of the opportunist who helped himself to his wife while he was festering in prison. He only knew the man was Indian.' Felicity had backed away as if proximity to Ashok had become intolerable.

'Perhaps,' Ashok said to Duncan, 'it's time you told me what's going on.'

'Yes, I think it is. While you're sitting back thinking everything's hunky-dory, the maniac's still chasing after Hannah.'

'What? But that can't be. They caught him.'

'Oh yes. They caught Bannerman's man, but he wasn't the only one after her. And he was only watching her. Mark Salers is out to get her.'

'How do you know that?'

Felicity glanced at Duncan, who nodded.

'I'm Felicity Salers,' she said quietly, 'Mark's my brother.'

Now it was Ashok who was lost for words. It was nonsense, of course, that Bannerman wasn't the only person after Hannah. But how on earth had Duncan rustled up Salers' sister? Did he have contacts, or what? 'I don't understand,' he said, 'How do you two come to know each other?'

Felicity opened her mouth to speak, but Duncan quickly cut in. 'Coincidence. Felicity used to work for me.'

A likely story, surmised Ashok. Lies again. The girl had a half-smile on her lips. It was a smile that spoke of embarrassment, Duncan's embarrassment. She seduced him, Ashok concluded. Silly man. You'd think he'd have more sense.

He turned to Felicity. 'Well, I'm sorry you had a wasted journey. I know your brother's been released, but I assure you, he's not involved here, except indirectly, through Bannerman's plot to implicate him.'

'Tell him,' said Duncan quietly, not looking at Felicity.

Briefly, calmly, Felicity told Ashok how Mark Salers had, with her help, been keeping track of Hannah since his release a year ago.

'The last I heard of him,' she said in a flat tone, 'was a month or so back. I told him how to break into Duncan's answerphone messages. So that he could trail her in India.'

Minutes passed. Ashok sat with his head in his hands as the truth filtered through.

'I don't get it,' he said at last to Felicity. 'If what you say is true, why are you telling all this now? What are you hoping to achieve here?'

'I gave her the choice,' Duncan cut in. 'Either help me or I'd get Interpol onto him. Under the circumstances she had no option. She doesn't want to see him banged up again.'

'So Duncan's saying you'll only help if we don't turn him in?'

The girl looked at him with an expression akin to pleading. 'If you have any pity...'

Pity? Ashok's head spun. His world had capsized again. Hannah was out there on her own, stuck in some village. And Salers? Oh, God, it didn't bear thinking about. 'Why should I pity a man,' he shouted, 'who treated Hannah so despicably? And, may I remind you, what he did to Maighréad didn't exactly amount to pity.'

Felicity gave a harsh laugh. Duncan looked down at his shoes. 'I think you'd better let Felicity explain about Maighréad and Mark.'

Ashok felt anger and bitterness well up like bile inside him. 'Explain? You don't have to explain to me. It was I, let me remind you, who had to pick up the pieces, patch together broken bits of body and soul when that brute had finished with her. It was I who listened to her, got her to articulate the horror of what that creature had done to her. And in the end, the damage was too great. You can't explain anything to me. He killed her - young woman, twenty-two years old, and he killed her. You can call it suicide if you like, but Salers killed her just as surely as if he'd pushed her himself. And now, and now, God help us, he's after Hannah. What sort of brute goes to such lengths for revenge?' Ashok shook with anger. 'Don't waste any more of my time. I've got to get to Hannah before he does.'

Felicity's face was smudged with the tears that she was hastily trying to wipe away. 'You've got it wrong,' she said shaking her head. 'Everyone's got it wrong. Please listen to me.'

Duncan turned to Ashok. 'Look, my friend.' His condescension grated. 'Your hang-ups don't interest me. I'm here to find Hannah and take her home. I'm sure Hannah is very grateful for your help here. Hopefully we can resolve this soon and then you can take yourself off the case, so to speak. Meanwhile, if you are interested in Hannah's safety, you have to understand how Salers' mind works. I suggest you listen to what Felicity has to say.'

I hate you, thought Ashok, but nodded at Felicity, tight-lipped.

* * *

Outside the Nanjangud hotel, Hannah and her companions, seated on the roadside, had lapsed into worried silence. Some forty minutes passed with no sign of life at all, apart from a cow that munched its way languidly along the edge of the road. A bus turned up. It was a battered old wreck of a vehicle, crowded to capacity, heading towards Nanjangud. As it drew level with the hotel entrance, a crowd of cyclists and motorcyclists suddenly materialised from the direction of the town and forced it to stop. An animated discourse ensued. From their gestures and shouts it was clear that the bus driver was being told to turn round and go back.

Whether this was simply because there was no way through the block, or whether the bus was in danger of being burnt was not clear, since the Europeans had no idea if it was a Karnataka bus or one from Tamil Nadu. After a great deal of heated argument and discussion, the driver reversed the bus into the hotel drive and headed back towards Gundlupet. The army of cycles dispersed as suddenly as it had come.

For a while all was quiet again. The sun poured down its fire in venomous fury. As they wilted under its power they all lapsed into their personal nightmare worlds of inward speculation. What would happen to them if no help came? Were they enemies or friends to the angry people in the town? They had no idea. Except that the Law Enforcement Officer had warned Hannah to be careful. What chance was there of getting through to Mysore? The incident with the bus had done nothing to increase their optimism. Would they be safe back at the old house? How long would they have to stay there?

'I could kill for some ganja,' murmured Willi.

The English boy fumbled in his pocket and drew out a small metal tin, and some cigarette papers. He offered them to Willi. They watched as she deftly rolled the joint.

'Lighter?' she said. The boy dug into his pocket again and produced a battered box of Swan matches. 'Keep them,' he said, 'I've got more in my bag.'

Hannah watched with increasing disquiet as Willi was about to take a drag. 'You can't do this,' she finally said, putting her hand on Willi's arm. 'This is no time to get muddle-headed. Especially with police swarming around the countryside.'

'Oh, stop being such a misery. Anyway, I don't get muddle-headed. It makes me feel braver, that's all.'

Hannah glared at her friend. 'No, Willi. Please.'

Willi groaned. 'You're right. As usual.'

She gave the joint a regretful look, and passed it to one of the Germans. Hannah watched the youngsters defiantly take it in turns to inhale. It was as if they had something to prove.

She looked at her watch. Five o'clock. It would be dark in just over an hour. They had to make a decision. A police jeep pulled up on the other side of the road. The driver called across to them. It was the policeman who had spoken to Willi earlier in the hotel.

'Situation is getting worse,' he said. 'Best you return to that house at once and stay there. Area is under curfew. No hope at all of getting to Mysore tonight. Police have hands full quelling riots.'

'Well, that would seem to be that,' said Hannah. 'Let's get going before it's dark.' Willi nodded. The boys were huddled together murmuring.

'Look,' said one of them, 'we have decided we will attempt to walk to Mysore. It is not so far.'

'You're crazy. What if you meet trouble?'

'But there can be no trouble. You see, because there is a curfew, no people will be on the streets.'

'You're high on that stuff. You don't know what you're talking about.' Hannah's admonishment was greeted with a dismissive wave.

'Nothing to it,' said the English boy. 'Not for chaps like us. Of course it's different for you girls.'

They watched as the three young men, their blond hair like torches in the fading light, strode off into the distance, towards the town, the bridge and the burning trucks.

'Well, I guess it's just you and me,' said Willi. Hannah nodded. And Salers, she wondered, but kept quiet.

*   *   *

Ashok, seated in Duncan's hotel room, waited to hear what Felicity had to say. The girl sat quietly mustering difficult thoughts into coherent words. Finally she spoke, enunciating each word with slow deliberation.

'Like I said,' she began, 'everyone got it wrong about Mark.' She smiled at a secret memory. 'When my mother first brought us home to England, after our father left us, it was so terrible. I missed India, the freedom, the sun, my friends. I was a little girl - twelve years old. Mark turned my childhood around. Took care of me. He was my confessor, companion, father. But that was Mark. Always put other people first. He had a deep sense of justice. That's why he went into journalism. He'd seen so many bad, destructive journalists - truth-twisters as he called them. He wanted to redress the balance, in some small way.'

She could have been describing Hannah. Ashok dismissed the thought and flapped his hands in a gesture of irritation. 'Is there any point to this?'

Duncan turned to Felicity. 'Cut the sob story and get on with it.'

'The point I'm trying to get across,' Felicity's eyes flashed angrily at Duncan, 'is that he took the job in Belfast with the idea that he could make a difference. He was so full of idealism when he went there. Compromise. Reason. Reconciliation. Tolerance. Love.' She gave a sharp laugh. 'I suppose marrying Maighréad was part of that idealism - she was a Catholic, and we had been brought up by our mother as Protestants. And after all that she'd been through - family wiped out by a Loyalist bomb. He knew she was a mess. Trouble was, he was so wrapped up in Maighréad that he thought

219

he could come along like a knight on a white charger and put everything right. Rather like you.' She looked at Ashok scathingly. 'And Hannah.' Now she fixed Duncan with a defiant stare, before pulling her mind back into her story. 'Maighréad was no sweet, pathetic little victim. She was crazed with hatred and a desire for revenge. So crazed that she was prepared to destroy Mark, and anyone else who got in her way. And Mark did get in her way. As time went on his views became more forceful. Maighréad began to despise her husband. He argued openly in the press against a united Ireland. The extremists hated him. He hunted them down, he exposed them - because of him a number of prominent activists ended up in the Maze.

Eventually Mark woke up to the truth - to what Maighréad was really like. But he always thought she really loved him and that he would eventually banish her ghosts.'

'What the hell are you implying?' Ashok's natural courtesy was lost under a blanket of apprehension. The woman was obviously lying, fabricating a story to defend Salers, so why was he letting her get to him? Duncan was slumped on the bed, clearly discomfited at having to listen again to the story that had so recently been fed to him for the first time. Felicity, on the other hand, was growing in stature as she spoke. She clearly revelled in her vantage point, in seeing the two men squirm.

'I'm not suggesting that Maighréad was ever a member of the IRA. I don't think they'd have touched her - too crazy even for them. She'd have been a liability. But no doubt they were not displeased by her mad fantasies. They would certainly have wanted Mark out of the way. Maighréad was doing their dirty work for them.'

'Your suggestions are abhorrent,' Ashok spoke stiffly and with undisguised disgust. 'But I grant that Salers has indoctrinated you well and I congratulate him on the polished way he prepared your speech for you.'

'Don't patronise me, Dr Rao. I've had to tolerate enough of that from Duncan over the past year. Nobody indoctrinates me.'

'Given,' said Ashok, thinking out aloud, 'that there is an iota of truth in all the fictitious claptrap you're telling, this hardly alters the fact that Salers was abusing his wife. And that he got his just deserts.'

'You think so, Doctor?' Felicity seemed to derive some pleasure from emphasising, in a slightly condescending way, Ashok's medical credentials. 'Well, let me enlighten you. Maighréad, as I've already said, was eaten up with hatred. She hated the Loyalists - naturally enough, I suppose. But she also hated herself. She was consumed with guilt because she'd survived the attack that had killed her family. She talked constantly of suicide, of joining her family in the black abyss and other such emotive terms. Over the years her obsession infiltrated every other facet of her personality. She was like a Kamikaze pilot, fuelled by such violent passions that ultimate self-destruction was a noble goal.'

Ashok had heard enough. He jumped up. 'How dare you,' he shouted, 'come here and perpetuate such filth? You may be able to feed him your little lies,' he gestured contemptuously at Duncan, 'but you forget, I knew her. So did Hannah. Not a word of what you're telling rings true.'

'You and Hannah only saw what you wanted to see, poor fools. She had you in her clutches as surely as I had Duncan.'

'Well, I'll be very interested to hear what excuses you come up with for your beloved brother's systematic abuse of Maighréad.'

'No excuses. Just facts. Mark never abused Maighréad. Never. Not once. She did it to herself.'

The room seemed suddenly oppressively hot. Ashok got up and went to the window. He stared out at the familiar and comforting opulence of tropical vegetation in the garden below. He was crushed. Somehow counterarguments refused to take form in his mind. He should be demolishing this wicked assertion, killing it dead, preserving the sanctity of Maighréad's martyrdom. But he could not. It was just as when Hannah had confessed her true identity to him. As if he had suspected it all along.

Finally he found his voice. 'If that is so, why didn't Salers defend himself in court?'

'He could only do that by condemning Maighréad. He was testing her, if you like, testing the love, which he was sure she had for him, deep down. He was convinced that she'd speak up eventually, that she wouldn't let him go down. But as we all know, she just watched, coldly, when he was sentenced. That woman was devoid of any loyalty, except to her dead family. Everything else was just playacting.'

'None of it makes sense,' muttered Ashok.

'She used you,' said Felicity. 'She used Hannah as a weapon against Mark. She watched Hannah use her contacts to pursue him without remorse after the last so-called attack, until she tracked him down. She let her report him to the police and instigate his arrest.'

'If that's the case, perhaps you'd care to explain to me why she had resisted any earlier attempts to report him.'

'It was the right time,' said Felicity. 'She felt safer in England. In Belfast she no doubt thought she would attract a Loyalist backlash. When she heard Mark was back in England and trying to trace her, she pounced. But be quite certain. Getting Mark put away was always her ultimate aim. In her twisted mind, he represented all the evils that the English had perpetrated in Ireland. He came into her life to be used, as a scapegoat.' Felicity looked at Ashok's distress and softened slightly. 'One thing I will say. You came nearer than anyone else to penetrating the pestilence that had poisoned her mind. If she hadn't gone back to Belfast, with the intention of fulfilling what she always felt was her destiny, I believe you might have got her to confess what she'd done to Mark. As it was, there was just a hint of it in her suicide note.'

Ashok, bewildered, tried to recall the contents of the note. Felicity filled him in.

'*For the good man is not at home, he is gone a long journey* - don't you remember? The good man - that was Mark. The long journey - prison. I believe that to be the glimmer of a confession.'

* * *

Christmas morning dawned in eerie silence and a vague stench of burning rubber. Hannah bullied her stiff limbs into action, and struggled across Willi to lower herself as quietly as she could off the elegant, but rock-hard bed that had provided her with the rudiments of a night's sleep. Willi was lying on her back, open-mouthed, snoring softly. Hannah envied her the knack of blotting out unpleasantness by turning it into an adventure. She was sleeping like a toddler who had worn herself out at yesterday's visit to the fair.

Outside, a peacock announced its presence with an ear-piercing wail. Willi stirred under the dustsheet, opened her eyes and blinked. 'What the hell was that?'

'Happy Christmas to you too,' said Hannah. 'Only a peacock telling you to get up.'

'What time is it?'

'Seven-thirty. In the morning.'

Willi sat up and rubbed her eyes. 'Anything happened?'

'No idea. Only just surfaced. You seemed to sleep well.'

'Out like a light. Not that there was a light. Oh Lord, let's hope we don't have to spend another miserable evening sitting here in the dark.'

'It was pretty miserable in the night too, let me tell you. I kept expecting some horrible spectre to fly in through the open window.'

'Or Salers,' Willi said grimly.

'Well, I know he's all skin and bones, but I don't think even Salers could squeeze in through that small window. There's barely a six inch gap.'

'Hannah, you do realise that we overtook him on the road yesterday? You know what that means.'

Hannah smiled. 'I was hoping you'd forgotten. Should have known you better than that.'

Willi laughed. 'Same here. Anyway, we've made it unscathed through the night, so perhaps he got through the roadblock on the bridge and made it to Mysore after all. Or perhaps the rioters got him.'

'No point in speculating. Though I doubt whether anyone could have got past those burning trucks. I'm going to pay lip service to a wash,' said Hannah. 'There's a bit of that river water left. It's better than nothing.'

'Meanwhile I'll go and get some more,' said Willi, picking up a jug and unlocking the door into the hall with the key that the old man had given them.

Hannah went into the bathroom and inspected the muddy brew at the bottom of the clay pot. She scooped it up beaker-by-beaker and filtered it into the washbasin through her iodine filter, until she had enough to splash her body back into life.

She had no towel, so she waited until her arms and face had dried a little in the air before she replaced her crumpled *kameez* and went back into the bedroom. At once she stood still and looked around. Unaccountably she had a feeling that she was not alone in the room.

'Willi?' No answer. As she glanced across the enshrouded furniture, a whiff of something rotten assailed her nostrils and she saw, standing in the bay of the window, the figure of a man.

CHAPTER 14

At the car repair shop Ashok's heart leapt when he saw the Fiat. The steering wheel was back in place. The mechanic, however, was less than pleased to see him.

'But sir, I am telling to come back at eight. Now is seven-thirty. Car is not ready.'

'Is it driveable?'

'Yes, sir, but still I have to check it over.'

'Never mind that. Just hand me the keys. I need it now.'

At seven forty-five on Christmas morning, Ashok finally drove the Fiat out of the workshop and set off with Felicity to Mysore. He had, with some difficulty, managed to persuade Duncan that it was necessary for him to remain in Bangalore, in case Hannah returned. Felicity however, Ashok decided, might be useful when it came to dealing with Salers.

Some five miles out of the centre of Bangalore, Ashok was pulled over by the police.

'You are heading, sir?'

'Mysore - medical emergency.' The two policemen were young, but for all that determined. They pressed him further, and he spun them a yarn about having come from UK to perform a very delicate operation: technique unknown in India: life in the balance. He showed them his documents, and harangued them with technicalities until there could be no doubt in their minds that he was speaking the truth.

'Very well, sir - but the young lady, no.'

'She's my nurse,' Ashok protested.

'Sorry, sir. Report has come of three young foreign men waylaid by rioters outside Nanjangud late yesterday night. Mistaken for journalists. So you see I can't take responsibility for letting your nurse through, even as far as Mysore. If you care to pull off road and wait until our chief arrives, you can ask.'

'How long?'

'Maybe fifteen minutes, maybe one hour. I really don't know.'

'I can't wait for that.' Ashok turned to Felicity. 'You'll have to go back.'

Felicity nodded, placed a hand on Ashok's arm, and looked at him, resigned. 'You're a good man. If there's any way... treat him with humanity.' Against his will, Ashok touched her hand briefly, and a whisper of sympathy passed across his face. He drove off.

It was less turbulent than he had anticipated on this stretch of the road. All the more maddening that he hadn't been able to persuade anyone to take him to Mysore the previous day. He began to doubt whether public transport as far as Mysore really had been halted. He should have known better than to believe the locals in Bangalore. Too late now. At least he had his own vehicle. He was well aware that the real trouble would start on the road beyond Mysore.

As he drove into the town he heard a sudden clanking sound from somewhere beneath his feet, and the car began to career over the road. Somehow he managed to pull it to a halt before it crashed into a set of market stalls. Within minutes people surrounded him. He spoke to some of them rapidly in Kannada and handed over a wad of notes. With a bit of luck and the promise of an equal sum on completion, they would have the car fixed by the time he got back. But it was a major blow. Now he would have to seek alternative transport.

Mysore was calm, a little too quiet perhaps. Groups of silent men on street corners appeared preoccupied rather than merely whiling away idle hours. But perhaps, reasoned Ashok, if he hadn't been looking for signs of abnormality, he wouldn't have noticed any.

He hurried from one taxi office to the next. Men slouched around like worker ants waiting for the Nippon to finish its deadly job. *Taxi to Nanjangud?* they repeated incredulously. *Where've you been for the past twenty-four hours?*

He ran over to the bus station. Ordered confusion reigned. Buses going nowhere lined up patiently, their prospective customers huddled in groups on the ground, dug in, quietly waiting with their little bundles, tattered suitcases, rope-tied boxes; suckling infants, old men wizened as the trunks of ancient banyan trees, young women like ripples of sunlight on the sea in dusty, dazzling saris. Ashok's enquiries at the ticket office drew a blank. No one seemed to understand his request, or at least take it seriously. Perhaps they thought he was an escaped lunatic. What other explanation was there for his ignorance?

Finally, in desperation, Ashok tackled the dozing autorickshaw drivers near the entrance to the bus station. At first he was greeted with disbelief, then with suppressed laughter, until finally one of them said 'If you really want to go, ask Pandi. He's crazy enough for anything.'

'Pandi?'

The one who had spoken gestured to the far end of the row of autorickshaws where an elderly driver was sleeping in the back seat of his vehicle with his legs slung over the front.

'Eh! Pandi! This fellow is wanting to go to Nanjangud. Just the sort of outing you'd enjoy, isn't it?'

The man opened one eye and scrutinised Ashok. 'One hundred rupees,' he announced nonchalantly, 'and I take you there.'

'Done,' said Ashok, reflecting that he'd have said yes if the man had demanded dollars. He climbed into the back of the rickshaw.

Amid a fanfare of ear splitting Indian pop-music from the rickshaw's radio, they roared off out of the city, leaving the remaining drivers to consider the event with philosophical amusement.

* * *

Hannah stared at the silhouetted figure against the backlit window. She detected nothing intrinsically frightening about it. It was neither large nor looming. On the contrary, the figure seemed diminutive and shrivelled up. In spite of this, Hannah felt the familiar frisson of cold fear pass through her that had, until she met Ashok, dogged her since the whole business began. Although his features were obscured, Hannah knew that this was the man who had bedevilled her life for so long.

For several seconds there was no movement in the room.

Hannah spoke. The sound of her own voice seemed like an echo.

'Where is my friend?'

'Don't worry, my dear. She's quite safe. Just a little held up at the moment.' He gave a laugh, which turned into a cough, a tearing, rasping sound. I could run for the door, Hannah reckoned, as the man's cough turned into an uncontrollable hacking fit; but something held her back, kept her riveted to the spot. The fit passed, and the man straightened up. He had read her mind. 'Don't bother,' he said, 'it's locked.'

'I wasn't going to.'

'Oh?'

'This has gone on long enough. I don't know what you want from me.'

'Game's over now, Hannah Petersen.'

'What is your game, Salers? Why are you persecuting me?'

Hannah was still standing next to the bathroom door, where she had been when she first became aware of the intruder. He had resumed his rigid stance in the bay.

'Tut tut. Such emotive language. I just wanted to get to know you.'

'Why?'

A pause. Had she hit a weak spot? When he spoke, the words seemed blocked, like leaves in a drain. 'But, my dear, to set the record straight. I had to find out what made a twisted mind like yours tick.'

Voices penetrated the room from outside. Two women with wash-loads balanced on their heads chatted unsuspectingly as they walked up the track to the river. The man turned awkwardly and forced the grimy drapes across the window, retching, as he did so, from the dust that was unleashed by his action. As daylight was obscured, the man's features materialised. Hannah gasped as he stepped into the centre of the room. He was thin to the point of emaciation. His skin had the translucence of one who is on the edge of existence. It was stretched greyly across his face, as though pinned back. His mouth looked as if it were part of this operation, the ends permanently pulled towards his ears in a parodied grin. It seemed that only a mummified corpse remained. The eyes were sunk deep into the skull, and ringed with sooty black, limp, two dead jellyfish. Yet stripped of the dark glasses, the face of Mark Salers was unmistakable, despite the ravages of disease and the passage of time.

Twisted mind, Salers had said. What did he mean? It was he, not Hannah, who had the twisted mind. Why was he saying these things to her?

Salers gestured towards the white shape of a sheeted chair some six feet from the bed. 'Sit down,' he said brusquely. He dragged himself over to the bed, and with a supreme effort climbed onto it, sighing with undisguised relief, as propping himself up on the two pillows, he leant back against the headboard.

He's on his way out, Hannah tried to reassure herself. The man's no danger any more. Just a pathetic, stinking wreck. He can't have had the strength to hurt Willi. He must have locked her up again - like at the tombs. The thought should have stilled her fears, but the man's pervasive aura of evil remained undiminished. She willed herself to ignore the part of her brain that was telling her to run for it. No. There has to be an end to this, she decided. She sat down on the chair that Salers had indicated.

'What did you mean, about setting the record straight?' Hannah asked slowly.

'Bitch,' the man replied, the eyes flashing into life for one chilling instant, 'You know exactly what I mean.'

Despite the man's decrepitude, and Hannah's attempts to convince herself that he was harmless, something in his behaviour screamed danger. Perhaps it was the gratuitous pleasure he seemed to be deriving from watching her reaction to his words. Keep him calm, she told herself. Keep him talking. Don't show any emotion.

'Why did you attack me in the tombs,' she said, 'if you were only trying to get to know me? You had a knife.'

He snorted contemptuously. 'Knife? Don't be so silly. I was trying to give you that box.'

So Willi had been right. The weapon at the tombs was nothing more than the pearls.

'Why? Why the pearls?'

'Oh come now. Don't pretend you haven't worked that one out. I thought you'd enjoy my little guessing game - now the book's finished.'

'Book?'

'Unfortunately you won't live to see it on the shelves. So we'll call it your epitaph.'

Bloody hell, thought Hannah. A total fruitcake. But still the need to hear what Salers had to say drove her on despite her inexplicable unease.

'Someone saw you come out of my room at the Pandava. What were you doing there?'

'Looking for your camera, of course. Careless of you to leave your itinerary lying around. That was a bonus.'

'What about the taxi, later that night?'

'I have absolutely no idea what you're talking about.'

Hannah struggled to get her head around what the man was saying. Is he lying? Why? At any rate he's totally out of it. I've got to make my move.

'I'm sorry,' she said carefully, 'but whatever your problems may be, they're not my fault. Now I think you'd better give me that key so that we can get you some help.' She stood up and started towards the bed.

'Come one step nearer,' Salers said calmly, 'and I'll put a bullet through your heart.' He raised his right hand with infinite deliberation, while his eyes bored through her, and the grin on his face turned into a mocking snarl. Hannah saw in the raised hand a silver-coloured pistol.

Slowly she backed away until she felt the chair behind her. She lowered herself onto it. 'You're not going to achieve anything by keeping me here,' she said quietly. 'The old man will come with my bed tea shortly. He'll raise the alarm if there's no answer.'

'Don't worry about the old man. He won't bother us. We'll just sit here and wait quietly, shall we?'

God, what's he done to the old chap? Hannah wondered, but said, 'Wait? What for?'

For some moments there was no response from Salers, who was wheezing heavily. At length he spoke. 'I'm finished. Days, hours maybe. Who can tell? All I know is that you're going before me. Today. In this room. When I'm right and ready.' He paused and fought for breath, wheezing as he clutched at his chest with his left hand, all the while keeping hold of the pistol with the other. 'When you've suffered a little more. Not as much as I'd wanted. I'd hoped I'd be able to eke it out a week or two longer, but these damn riots have done for me.'

He's even crazier than I believed, thought Hannah. 'Listen,' she said, trying to sound calm. 'You need a doctor. Antibiotics. You don't have to give in to this.'

Salers became agitated. 'Shut up, bitch. What do you know? I'm done for, I tell you. You're going to pay for what you did to me.'

'Perhaps you've just been given the wrong treatment. I know someone who can help you...'

'Help me? You ignorant tart. Don't you know anything? Haven't you heard of the Superbug?'

'There are always superbugs, so-called incurable. The next thing we know they've been cured.'

'Oh yes. Like AIDS you mean?'

'You haven't got AIDS. You've got TB.'

'Ah - been doing your homework I see. A damned Russian cellmate with AIDS gave it me in the first place.' Salers was working himself up into a frenzy, sweating profusely, eyes wild with desperation, fear, loathing. 'And it's all down to you and your conniving.'

Salers was suddenly still. He was smiling. A gargoyle's grisly grin. He glanced at Hannah. 'Want to hear something funny?'

Hannah stared silently at her feet. Salers crashed the keys down on the table next to the bed so that Hannah, for all her attempts at coolness, was visibly startled.

'Answer, bitch. Do you?' Salers' voice hovered between a shriek and a snarl.

'Yes. Yes,' said Hannah quickly, 'tell me.'

'Enjoy that kiss in the garden, did you? I did. With a bit of luck you'll have got more than a pair of soggy knickers out of that moment of passion. Not that it matters now.'

Keep cool, Hannah told herself. Don't let him see you panic.

'I've been following you. Waiting. Hoping. Did my little gift to you take root? I wanted to see you suffer. Like I suffered. But where's the fun in hoping that you'll die slowly, agonisingly, horribly just like me, if I'm not around to watch?'

The room, imprisoned behind the closed curtains, was a heat trap, even at the early hour, and even with the one small open window that the curtains had not managed to obscure. Hannah felt sick with terror and disgust at Salers' revelation. Perspiration was soaking through her *kameez* onto the shrouded chair-back. She felt a sudden desperate desire to close her eyes and drown substantiality in sleep. Stay awake, she told herself, for God's sake stay awake and keep him talking. She rallied her thoughts, choosing her words carefully.

'I'm sorry about what has happened to you. If we could just talk about it, maybe we'd both understand each other. Maybe I could still help you. I could get you the very best medical treatment. I have money...'

Salers' eyes glinted with anger from the depths of their black holes. The pointing gun shook in his hand. 'Shut up. D'you think I'd touch your tainted money? The evil fruit that burst from your tree of lies?'

'If I told lies,' Hannah said slowly, keeping her eyes fixed on Salers' face, 'I did so in ignorance. I don't understand what you're saying. Please, you at least were tried in a court of law - you may

232

not have agreed with the verdict, but you were given a chance. Now you're condemning me without giving me the chance to defend myself. Do you want to have that on your conscience?'

'Don't preach to me about conscience.'

Salers was again overcome by a coughing attack. Hannah glimpsed the terror in his eyes as he struggled to control his jerking, retching body. He snatched up a corner of the bedsheet with his left hand and pushed it over his mouth in an attempt to stem the attack, but the effluence of his illness seeped mercilessly through his fingers, staining the cloth crimson. After it was over, he leant his head back against the pillow, overcome with exhaustion, but through it all Hannah saw that the pistol was still grasped in his right hand, and she was under no illusion. One false move on her part would swing Salers back into the full fury of his vendetta. His finger was on the trigger, his reflexes, through all his agony, razor-sharp.

Time crawled. Salers lay back on the bed, his eyes half-closed, but Hannah knew that he was watching. She sat rigidly on the hard chair, aching with the effort to keep a grip on herself. Without moving her head, she managed to glance down at her watch. Nine o'clock. Oh, God, how much longer? Where was Willi? Surely someone would come along soon? And then, what? Would an interruption only increase the danger by making Salers angry? Or would the distraction give her a chance to leap out of the pistol's range?

Through her deliberations, Hannah's eyes started to close again. It was only when her body gave an involuntary jerk that she realised that she had been drifting once more into a comforting netherworld. Her sudden movement jolted Salers back into consciousness and his gun hand shot up, pointing unequivocally at Hannah's chest.

'Going somewhere?' he gurgled.

'No, no. Just getting stiff, that's all.'

'Stiff? Well you can go and get me some water from the bathroom. Leave the door open. I'm watching every move you make.'

'There is no water. Just some damp mud. The taps aren't working.'

'That'll do. Tear off some of that cloth and wet it.' He gestured with the gun at her chair covering. 'No sudden movements.'

With painstaking care, Hannah tore at the dustsheet. It was brittle as old parchment and she soon had a handkerchief-sized piece. She stood up in slow motion and made her way across to the bathroom. No chance of escape, she decided. Between her and the bathroom was clear space. The bathroom door opened outwards, into the bedroom. It was still wide open, as she had left it. She had no reason to touch it. Any attempt to do so would certainly set the pistol into action. Salers had a clear view of the whole bathroom. Every part of it was within pistol range. In any case nothing was to be gained. The bathroom had no window to the exterior, only a narrow ventilation slit.

The pistol traced her every movement. She bent down over the clay pot and dabbed the last remnants of brown water onto the cloth. The task had awakened her senses, and she was once again fully in command of her thoughts, if not her actions.

'Now - very slowly, come over here,' Salers croaked. 'Don't even think about trying anything.'

As she approached the bed, the stench from the dying man intensified. It was like last week's fish in the rubbish bin; as if he were rotting from within. Only with a superhuman effort did she control herself. The sound of Salers' breathing had turned into a rattle, like an old car engine turning over repeatedly with an ever-flatter battery.

'Squeeze the cloth into my mouth,' he rasped. Hannah forced herself to act with detachment from her senses, as she mechanically wrung the filthy brew into the raw, stinking cavity. Salers sighed. In a sudden lightening move he grabbed hold of Hannah's wrist with his left hand, keeping the pistol in his right trained on her.

The strength and speed of his grasp stopped Hannah's breath. She could sense his eyes boring into her face. He shook her wrist. 'Look at me!' he growled. 'Does it revolt you so much to see what you've done to me?'

Hannah fought back panic. She forced her eyes onto his face. He let go. She inched her way slowly backwards to the chair and lowered herself onto it.

Mark Salers' eyes were closed once more. Impasse again. Nine-thirty. A bird with a voice like the tolling of a doomed ship sang outside the window. Ten o'clock. Time hung like the foul air around them. Hannah began to drift off again. She found herself wondering whether or not Salers could really have infected her that night in the garden. There had been only the one contact. Afterwards, so Duncan had told her, though she couldn't remember it herself, she had retched and spat and rinsed her mouth with Dettol. She was fairly sure that not a drop from that man's body could have remained in hers. *Fairly* sure. She wrenched her mind back to her present predicament. What did it matter anyway? What did anything matter if Salers pulled the trigger?

The heat intensified further. The poisonous exhalations from the bed mingled with the stifling humidity and Hannah felt that she was being drowned slowly in stinking decay. At times the man seemed dead, but the slightest movement from Hannah brought the instant response of a sleeping Rottweiler. Hannah's back began to ache, and her limbs were desperate to stretch out, or to change position. This physical discomfort at least now prevented any danger of her drifting off into unconsciousness. She dredged her mind for any hints from her psychotherapy course that would help her to deal with this man, but now nothing seemed to fit the situation. She tried talking to him again.

'Mark,' she began softly. He opened his eyes slowly. At least there was no instant rebuff. 'Can't we talk about what happened to... to Maighréad?'

Salers gave a sharp laugh. 'What happened to *Maighréad*? What happened to me, more like.'

'She must have hurt you a lot, to make you... to make you do what you did to her.'

She felt him burning her, through narrowed eyes.

'She hurt me,' he said slowly. 'You know all about that. Don't try pretending that I did anything to her.'

Hannah measured her words. 'Things were... difficult between the two of you, you know that. You were both hot-headed, and she, being the weaker one was bound to get injured, when things got... well, physical.'

'Cut the crap. Why do you insist on keeping up the lie?' He lay back and groaned, then gasped for breath several times before spitting out the next words. 'Whose idea was it, yours or hers, for her to smash herself up and blame me?'

Hannah stifled a gasp. No, It can't be true, she thought. It's his twisted mind. But if it isn't true, what's this whole bloody business about? Why would he go to such lengths if he really didn't think I'd wronged him? Why would he keep up the lie on his deathbed? She took as deep a breath as she dared without coating her lungs with putrefying air. The taste of it in her throat nauseated her.

'If this is what she did, Mark, my only crime is ignorance. I really believed it was you.'

'Ha!' Salers scorned. He fought to breathe before continuing. 'You must think I was born yesterday. You weren't fooled by her little act.'

'I don't remember it ever being suggested in court that Maighréad's wounds were self-inflicted. So how come you kept it to yourself?'

The man on the bed half-closed his eyes once more. Hannah saw with horror that tears were creeping down his face, like drops from the final pressing of exhausted olives. She felt her stomach curdle with fear of the emerging facts, a fear still greater than that caused by the trembling gun.

Salers' fractured voice was little more than a whisper. 'I loved her,' he croaked, '... believed that she would come through for me... couldn't say anything... would have been like admitting to myself that she hated me, that she wanted me to go down... so sure that my silence would make her tell the truth... had to come from her, not from me, don't you see?' He looked at Hannah, his thickened eyelids lifting slightly to reveal his tortured eyes.

'Maighréad had a terrible past, you knew that, Mark. You couldn't expect her to act rationally. It's no wonder that something snapped after her parents were murdered by the Loyalists.'

'Oh, don't give me that crap.' Salers closed his eyes and seemed to drift off, exhausted by his efforts. Hannah shifted in her chair. He opened his eyes, and his hand tightened on the gun.

'She had no parents,' he muttered, almost imperceptibly. '… grew up in the orphanage.'

Hannah's throat tightened. Keep calm. She glanced down at her watch. Ten-thirty. How much longer? If what the man was saying was true, she'd probably be better off dead anyway, rather than having to face the exposure of her celebrated book as a fraud, based on lies. And despite the man's obvious insanity, his words seemed somehow credible. She thought of Ashok. Had they both been incredibly gullible? If so, it would devastate him. He would need her. They had to get through it together. Somehow she must survive.

She said, 'Is that why Maighréad hated you, Mark? Because you discovered the truth about her?'

His nod was barely perceptible. His eyes, still half open, stared into space. Hannah waited several minutes, then coughed. No response. She spoke again.

'Do you understand now, Mark, that I didn't know the truth until today?'

No response.

'Mark? Can you hear me?'

Thank God. Hannah felt tears of relief. He's dead. She waited a little longer to make sure and slowly rose to her feet.

At first she wasn't aware that she had been hit, only of an explosion searing her eardrums. As the floor came up to meet her, she struggled to fight it off. She tried to get up, but her leg kept giving way. She couldn't see the figure in the bed from there, only the hand that held the still smoking gun.

* * *

'You're a brave man, Pandi,' shouted Ashok over the noise of the autorickshaw. He could see the driver's grizzled face in the side mirror. It had become animated, alive, predacious.

They headed out of the city. The countryside was deserted. Pandi turned off the radio. There was a breathless eeriness, like the air before a thunderstorm. After a few miles they came to a section of the road that was littered with huge boulders, which Pandi tackled like an Olympic slalom skier.

Ashok held his breath as they raced on. Ahead of them now he saw a straight line of even bigger boulders blocking the road completely. Pandi would have to stop. Ashok clung to the hope that his medical papers would save him again. But the driver did not stop, he charged straight at the roadblock. Ashok watched, aghast, certain that his demise was seconds away. As they reached the roadblock the auto swerved violently and shot full speed through a tiny gap that had been left between the two end boulders, a gap so small, that Ashok hadn't even considered that they might get through it.

At last they came to the outskirts of Nanjangud, where fourteen burnt out trucks lay smouldering, blocking the entire road for some hundred metres. Beyond them was the bridge, and shortly beyond that, the bungalow where Ashok hoped to find Hannah.

As they neared the first lorry, half a dozen shouting, gesticulating men jumped out into the road and waved them down. Once again Pandi seemed to regard this as a challenge. Clearly he had no intention of stopping. Instead he veered to the side, onto a soft, narrow shoulder of grass, hardly wider than the vehicle itself, between the road and a drop of several metres into the bordering field. He hurled the autorickshaw along this, vainly pursued by the village men who had tried to stop them.

It was all over. They had left trucks, villagers, and bridge behind them and were turning into the driveway of a derelict bungalow. Pandi had known exactly where to find the place that Ashok had described. Nanjangud was his hometown.

Ashok stopped the auto some distance from the house. As he clambered out he handed the astonished driver fifty dollars. 'And another fifty if you take us back to Mysore later.' Pandi wobbled his head happily, though Ashok had a sneaking feeling that Pandi would have done the trip for the sheer hell of it.

Cautiously Ashok approached the house. He sidled up to the big bay window on the left and peered through. No movement. Dust-sheeted furniture stood around. The bay on the other side of the house was obscured by tattered drapes. They were torn away at the top, and a small fanlight window was open. Too high up to investigate. Silence. Somehow ominous. Parked in front of it was a truck full of propane gas cylinders, which had presumably been backed into the shade of the house to keep it cool.

The heavy front door under the ornate porch was slightly ajar. Ashok pushed it slowly open, stopping each time it threatened to groan and easing it through its crisis. Once inside the long, dark hall he stood and listened. The room on the right was silent. Apprehension stopped him from trying the door. Something rotten lay behind it, he was sure. He knew that he had to get into the room, without alerting the occupants. But how? He turned his attention to the door on his left. He had seen the room through the window. Lifeless but unthreatening. The door swung open easily and silently when he turned the knob. He stepped inside and closed it behind him.

A wintry scene, incongruous in the midday heat. Indefinable white masses rose like icebergs from the dusty, pale stone floor. Only the big bed in the corner was clearly identifiable. Ashok stood still and listened. Nothing. Not even birdsong broke the silence. The bathroom door at the far end stood open. He noticed a large wardrobe. The key was in the lock. Ashok steered a silent course through the white spectres across to the door. He called out, 'Hannah? Willi? Are you there?'

At once scrambling from inside the wardrobe greeted his ears. Someone was trying to move, trying to talk but only managing to make moaning sounds. With trembling hands Ashok unlocked the door and opened it. Two large-eyed faces stared at him from the gloom. Huddled on the floor were Willi and an elderly Indian. Each was bound hand and foot with red nylon cord, and sticky tape covered their mouths. Ashok tore the tape from Willi's mouth. At once words came tumbling out.

'Salers - he's here. Probably got Hannah. He's got a gun. Made the old boy tie me up. Then bashed him over the head with the gun. He came round just before you arrived.' Ashok untied the two prisoners. He checked the old man over and spoke to him in Kannada. The fellow was shocked and woozy. Ashok carried him to the bed, but he struggled up muttering, staggered out of the house and disappeared into the trees.

* * *

'Don't try that again. Could have killed you... not quite time yet. Almost. Now get back onto the chair.'

Unable to stand up, and scarcely able to take in Salers' words, Hannah pulled herself up by the chair and collapsed upon it. Her shin, she could see now, was covered with blood. The pain began. Salers stared at her, open-eyed, the gun once more pointed at her chest.

Another eternity. A painful wound that was becoming unbearable. Still the unblinking stare. Time crept like a silent metronome. Ten minutes. Fifteen. Twenty. Was that the distant sound of a motor engine? It stopped. Was she imagining the crackle of footsteps sneaking around outside? Pain was blurring the crisp outlines of reality. Once more Salers looked dead. This time Hannah knew better.

He made an effort to speak. Words exhumed from flesh already putrefying.

'... the end. Darkness...' A flash of terror crossed his face. Then hatred; intense, evil. 'Say your prayers, bitch. On your knees.'

A blanket of calm enveloped Hannah. Salers' last words drove out the fear. If she was going to die, it would be on her terms, not his. Slowly she lifted her head and faced him.

'No,' she said quietly. 'I won't do that.'

Before Salers had time to react, a knock sounded on the door. Salers flinched. 'Keep silent,' he hissed, as the gun leapt once more into the offensive position, and a bullet whistled past Hannah's ear and lodged itself in the door.

Hannah could hear Willi screaming, 'Oh my God! He's shot her!'

Another voice, a dear, familiar voice, 'Hannah, Hannah, answer! It's me.' She heard him frantically throwing himself at the heavy door. 'Say something!'

'Keep your mouth shut,' snapped Salers.

The silence that followed was so sudden and so deep, it was as if someone had turned off a background radio, hitherto unnoticed.

Ashok was calling again. 'Salers, are you in there? Let me in. I'm a doctor.' He flung himself again at the door.

'Salers, if you're in there, listen to me. Felicity's here. Your sister. She's waiting for you in Bangalore. Don't you want to see her?'

A peacock started up its horrible wail. But no, it wasn't coming from outside. It was Salers. 'Traitor! Jezebel! Keep her away from me.'

None of it made sense to Hannah. The pain in her leg was beginning to dominate her consciousness, and Ashok's voice, the mention of Felicity must be manifestations of her hallucinatory state.

'Salers.' Ashok was clearly struggling to keep the desperation out of his voice. 'I'm the person you sent the book to. I read your comments. Can we talk about it?'

'It's that interfering fool you picked up,' spat Salers.

'Listen to me. Felicity's told me the truth. We know you're innocent.'

Salers muttered hoarsely, 'Does he think that'll give me back my life?'

'Do you know who I am? I'm the doctor who lived with Maighréad after you went to prison. It's me you want, not Hannah.'

A sharp snake-like hiss and Salers' face contorted as if several thousand volts had just passed through his body, then all at once he seemed to rally. He started to laugh hideously, with a sound like a cat vomiting grass balls. 'Poetic justice,' he spluttered. 'Finally... the unknown enemy.'

Wriggling grotesquely, he pulled the door key from somewhere beneath him, and held it out to Hannah. 'Pass it to him under the door.'

Hannah momentarily toyed with the idea of making a lunge for Salers, as she reached for the key, of taking the gun off him. If she failed he would shoot her and kill Ashok anyway. Was it worth a try? But it was no good. As soon as she tried to get up, her leg gave way. Pain and weakness overwhelmed her. She flopped back down onto the chair.

'I can't walk.'

'Try.'

'No,' she said, 'so kill me. Do it now.'

Cursing furiously, Salers, like a dying wasp, found the strength for one last sting. He hurled the heavy key with surprising force and accuracy through the small fanlight that Hannah and Willi had left open.

'The key's outside the window,' he called, his voice like worn-out chewing gum.

'Ashok, don't,' Hannah called in desperation. 'He's got a gun. Don't give him the satisfaction of killing you.'

Silence. Agonising stillness. Had he gone away? Oh God, let him have gone away. Were those whispering voices, or was it only the rustling of leaves outside the window?

She heard the key in the lock, the door opening behind her. Through the fog of her pain, she heard Ashok's voice from across the room. 'Let her go, Salers. She's done nothing. I'm the one who took Maighréad away from you. Let Hannah go.'

She watched the sneering grin spread slowly across the dying man's face. 'You first. Then her. Your lady friend will have the pleasure of watching you die.'

Hannah saw Salers point the gun at Ashok. Something finally snapped inside her head. 'No!' she screamed, 'No! No! No!' Sobbing and screaming uncontrollably now, she felt herself trying to get up. Somehow she had to protect Ashok. But why wouldn't her body move from the chair?

Her outburst unnerved Salers. 'Shut up!' he croaked weakly. 'Shut up or I'll shut you up.'

'Please,' she sobbed, 'please leave him alone. He's innocent.'

The voice from the grave spoke again. 'Enough. You're dead, bitch. Say your prayers.'

She saw the gun swivel away from Ashok. Now for the third time it pointed at her. At once her fear seemed to leave her. She gazed calmly into the barrel. Behind her she sensed Ashok creeping closer. She willed him to go back. What good would it do? He couldn't protect her. They were both doomed. She saw the twisted look on Salers' face; the weapon shaking in his hand; get on with it, bastard. Why was it taking so long? Why was she still alive?

A noise like a siren blasted through the bungalow. Startled, Salers momentarily dropped his guard. It was enough. In an instant Ashok threw himself across the room and grabbed the gun that was still tightly clasped in Salers' hand. For an endless minute they struggled, Salers somehow finding the strength to hold on. Now the barrel was pressed into Ashok's chest. Salers' finger groped for the trigger. Ashok rolled out of the way just as the gun went off.

It was all over. Salers fell back limply as Ashok tore the weapon from his hand.

* * *

'What the hell took you so long?'

Ashok was standing next to the bed, feeling for Salers' pulse. He scowled at Willi, who was peering nervously around the door. It was a reaction of shock rather than of anger. 'Give me two minutes then create a diversion,' he had said. Willi had waited almost five minutes before sounding the horn of the truck.

'Sorry,' she said, coming into the room. 'Only I thought if I could light one of the cylinders, I could blow out the window. I had the box of Swans from when I rolled that joint. But the damned gas wouldn't light. So I had to think of something else.'

'Well, I'm glad you did,' said Ashok, calming down. 'It was well done.' He let Salers' arm drop. 'Dead,' he said. 'That last effort finished him.'

CHAPTER 15

Voices, breaking like waves in the swirling mist; rhythmic, rushing to pierce the space between them. 'Hannah, Hannah can you hear me?' 'Hannah, wake up.' 'Hannah, open your eyes.' 'Hannah, it's me, it's Ashok.'

Her eyelids struggled to resist the commands of her brain. Sealed, overgrown with the slimy cancer of intolerable exhaustion. 'Sleep, let me sleep...'

'Hannah, open your eyes. Hannah, it's me, it's Ashok.'

Someone or something was exhorting her. Exhorting her back to life, tugging the cork out of the bottle that held her trapped. Suddenly she perceived that her eyes were open. The mist was still around her, but she could make out the faces poised above her. Familiar faces - Ashok, Willi, and... *what? Duncan?* Oh God, the nightmare's not over after all.

'Where am I?' Events flashed back like an odd, rapidly presented slideshow. 'Where's Salers? And what's *he* doing here?' She lifted a heavy hand and waved it anxiously in the direction of Duncan. 'God, I must be off my trolley. I keep seeing Duncan.'

Now she was fully conscious, suddenly alert and struggling to sit up. 'Wait,' said Ashok. 'Put your arms round my neck.' She felt herself being manoeuvred into a sitting position, and started to take in her stark surroundings. A small, cell-like room. White, clinical, minimalist.

'Where the... ?'

'Now, don't worry.'

'Don't worry? I don't know if I'm dead or alive, I keep hallucinating, and you say don't worry!'

'You're safely back in Bangalore. In hospital. And you're not hallucinating. It is Duncan.'

A few moments passed while Hannah digested this news. She closed her eyes in resigned confusion, then opened them to take in the reality of her publisher's presence.

'Duncan? You here? But why? You, of all people. You can't stand the tropics.'

'Duncan had some important information about Salers, Hannah.'

'Why didn't he email it? Oh, Duncan, sorry, sorry. I really don't know what the hell's going on.'

Duncan, crestfallen at the damp enthusiasm of Hannah's reception, seemed to cheer up a little.

'What happened?' she asked wearily. She took Ashok's hand in hers. It was warm, alive, loving. Tears welled in her eyes as she relived the horror of the last few moments with Salers. 'I remember the door opening. And the gun pointing at me. I remember screaming at you not to come in. After that it's all a red blur. I remember the pain stopped. The pain in my leg, that is... My leg! What... ?'

'It's OK. The bullet's been removed. Luckily there's not too much damage. It'll be painful for a while though - and you won't be running the marathon just yet.'

'I can live with that.' She smiled with her eyes at her lover. 'Thank God. Thank God you're safe. But how? It's just incredible. And Willi.' For the first time Hannah really registered the presence of the Dutch girl. She squeezed Willi's outstretched hand, unable to articulate the feelings that suddenly overwhelmed her.

Briefly, Ashok went over everything that had happened. Hannah listened with a mixture of horror and amazement. Duncan sat pale and shocked, eyes downcast, hands folded in his lap. Willi chipped in now and then, helping Ashok to piece together an accurate account.

At the end of the telling, Willi stood up and took hold of Hannah's hands. 'Hannah, I've got to go now. My train leaves in half an hour. I'm off to Cochin. I didn't spend Christmas in Kerala, so I'm determined to spend New Year there instead. Then home to Holland. Now I know you're OK, I can go with an easy mind. In spite of everything I wouldn't have missed a moment of it. I'll write.'

They hugged and both fought back tears. Hannah's eyes spoke the words that she was unable to form. I'm so sorry for what you were put through, just because of knowing me. Thank you is inadequate.

With a final cheery wave, Willi was gone, leaving a small but poignant emptiness behind her.

'Duncan,' said Ashok. 'Go and get us something to drink, will you? There's a shop on the corner.'

A vexed expression crossed Duncan's face. 'If you need to talk to Hannah in private, I'd oblige you to say so, instead of treating me like a fool.'

He walked out of the room, closing the door heavily.

'He'll be a while,' said Ashok 'At least he had the good grace not to argue.'

'He's not a fool, you know. Except when it comes to women. He's not used to being talked down to.'

'Neither am I, Hannah. It's tit for tat with him and me.'

Hannah sighed and shook her head. 'What is it, Ashok? You obviously didn't send him away so that we could make love on the hospital bed.'

Ashok laughed briefly. 'I wish,' he said, meeting Hannah's eyes, and taking her hands in his. It was all they needed, to reaffirm their feelings.

'Ashok...'

He stopped her, and looked at her gravely.

'I know what you're going say, Ashok.'

'Yes? What?'

'It's about the TB, isn't it? I might be infected.'

His hand tightened on hers. 'How did you know?'

'I can read your mind. In any case, it's been on my mind too. Tell me, if Salers did have a new, resistant strain, does that mean it's resistant in everyone?'

Ashok's face suddenly looked old, weary. 'It's the bug that's resistant Hannah, not the person, so I'm afraid the answer's yes.'

'So if I've got it, I'll die.'

'*If*. That's the important word. It's very unlikely that bastard infected you. You're young and strong.'

'But,' insisted Hannah, 'if he did, nothing can be done.'

'Let's not jump the gun. While you were still unconscious, they did a skin sensitisation test. Then an X-ray. At the moment you're negative.'

'At the moment? How long does it take for symptoms to appear after exposure?'

'Good question. No easy answer, I'm afraid. Depends on a lot of factors. Chances that you've caught it are fairly remote. You're vaccinated, of course?'

Hannah nodded.

'However,' continued Ashok, 'to be on the safe side, I've arranged for a six-month course of antibiotic drugs.'

'I thought you said the new strain was drug-resistant.'

'We have to attack it on all fronts. Try not to worry. I'm pretty sure you're in the clear.'

'I'm not worrying,' said Hannah.

Duncan returned, bearing bottles of Thums Up.

'You will make sure that Pandi's set up for life now, won't you?' Hannah said. 'Anything he needs - it's OK. I'll take care of it.'

Ashok laughed. 'Don't worry, I've tried. I even offered to buy him a taxi. He just wasn't interested. He could hardly take in the hundred dollars I'd given. I suppose if I'd suggested a hot-rod racer he might have pricked up his ears. In the end though I managed to squeeze out of him that he was worried about a dowry for his daughter. Well, that's one problem less for him now.'

'Mm.' Hannah looked thoughtfully at the two men. What a contrast they made. Ashok, a little haggard and dishevelled in blue jeans and sloppy chappals, the sleeves of his collarless grey shirt turned up to his elbows, and yet in spite of this exuding healthy ease and confidence. And Duncan. Perfectly turned out in crisp, casual LaCoste and smart white trousers, with matching immaculate white trainers. He could have been captain of the England cricket team. And yet somehow he looked awkward, crumpled in spirit if not in dress. He's just lost the Test Match, Hannah thought. She felt a pang of pity. Duncan, like Hannah, was used to being in control.

'Just explain to me, will you,' she said to both of them, '... *Felicity*? Salers' *sister*? What the hell's going on?'

'Over to you, Duncan.' Ashok folded his arms and sat back. Was that a smirk of *Schadenfreude* on his face? With excruciating embarrassment, Duncan laid bare the saga of his entrapment by Felicity, and its repercussions. Hannah avoided Ashok's eyes. Laughter or tears? She teetered on the brink of both. A black comedy. Poor, gullible Duncan. She recalled Salers' bitter words as he lay dying. Truth was a slippery prize. Had Maighréad duped them all? In the end Duncan may not have been any more gullible than they had been, and his uncoerced flight to rescue her was humbling.

'I don't know what to say, Dunc. We've all been fools. Perhaps I've been the biggest of all. But you and Ashok aren't far behind, you know.'

'Thanks,' said Ashok.

'So,' ventured Duncan, 'there's going to be one hell of a storm when Salers' book gets out. What's to be done?'

Hannah was grim-faced, but fired with new determination. 'Nothing. Not until the book's out anyway. Then I'm going to write a biography of Mark Salers. I'm going to get to the truth one way or another. Put the record straight as far as he's concerned. And help to explain my own actions.'

'Sounds good to me.' Duncan was clearly impressed. 'I'll get onto it as soon as I get back. Try and trace Salers' publisher. May give us a headstart.'

*   *   *

After two days in hospital, Hannah had endured enough. She scribbled a note to Ashok.

Much better. Have checked out. Gone back to Chamundi. See you there, Hannah.

Much better? Was she hell? Her head was an inflated balloon and her leg scrunched and screamed when she put weight on it, but she knew she had to get out of the hospital before Ashok arrived, because he'd veto it. The nurses too were horrified and at first forbade her to leave, but finally compromised by lending her a pair of crutches and calling a taxi.

At the Chamundi she showered and slipped into clean clothes. She lay down on the bed and felt reborn.

A knock on the door.

'Hallo?'

'Me.'

'It's open.'

The next moment she was in his arms. No smiles. No tears. Simply an outpouring of relief. Ashok was muttering. 'Damn you, woman. Damn you. Will you never learn? What the hell are you doing?' He broke away and held her at arm's length. 'Look at you. It's obvious you should be in hospital. What were you thinking of?'

Hannah laughed feebly. 'I'm fine. Really. I just wanted freedom, a change of clothes, a proper shower instead of a bedwash, privacy, you...'

A pause. Both minds working overtime. Awkward thoughts unspoken. Each entangled in a recurring shockwave to twist and stab at the comfortable certainties of their lives.

'Look,' he said at length. 'I know what you're thinking. We've both got to come to terms with what's happened. With the past.'

She nodded. 'That's it, isn't it? It's an enormous chunk out of both our pasts. Are we up to it? Is it something we can face together? Or do we have to do this alone?'

Ashok paced the small room for a few nervous seconds. Then he swung round to Hannah. 'I can't speak for you. We all have own way of dealing with trauma. All I know is that I'd rather tackle this with you than without you.'

'Are you sure? You seem...'

'What?'

'You seemed to be wrestling with your conscience just now.'

He placed his hands on her shoulders and looked steadily into her eyes. 'Hannah. You remember what I told about reaching a crossroad? How life had been too easy for me?'

She nodded. 'I remember. You said Maighréad took the final decision out of your hands.'

'Yes. But this time no-one's going to take the decision away from me. No crossroad this time. Only one way to go. I'm doing this because I love you. Not because I need to prove anything to myself.'

She spoke slowly. 'We have to promise each other though - no deceit, no lies. Cards on the table. Honesty. Always. We've both had our lives shattered by someone we trusted. I will find it very hard to trust anyone ever again.'

'That's why we're so right for each other. We understand each other in a way nobody else can.' He sat down and took her hand. 'I promise you, you will never have cause to doubt me.'

*   *   *

Willi's flimsy postcard arrived at the hotel on New Year's Day. It was postmarked Cochin and showed a poor reproduction of rural Kerala - tranquil waters against a backcloth of waving palms. In the foreground an ancient Chinese fishing net, slung across the sea like gauze across a stage to separate reality from dreams. On the back a scribbled note, squashed to fit into the small space.

Brilliant here. Staying at cool palace on island in bay. Coconut palms, paddy fields, and blue, blue sea. What more can a girl want? (Don't answer that!).

I've signed up as a deck hand on a three-master sailing to Amsterdam on 4th January. Why don't you come down for a few days before then? You'll love it!

Hugs,
Willi.

'Why not?' said Ashok. 'Let it be our honeymoon.'

'A honeymoon before the wedding,' she replied. 'All right then. Let's go. I think I can hobble well enough to get around now.'

* * *

Ashok braced himself. The atmosphere at home was fat with the unresolved matter of his marriage plans, his mad dash to Nanjangud and his continual absence from the family fold. The subject of Hannah hung like a poised avalanche over them. There had been no more talk of inviting her to the house. Now he had to tell them that he was off to Kerala. They would all know. He wouldn't even have to mention Hannah.

As it happened, it was his sister, Priya, who forged an opening to the discussion. Ashok had left Hannah to rest at the Chamundi until the evening, and gone home for lunch. For once the whole family was together. Not because it was New Year's Day. That meant very little to them. Priya had just returned from a field trip in the Western Ghats, where she had spent the past week studying the movement of elephants as part of her Forestry degree course. Incensed at first that the trip coincided with Ashok's visit home, she had been unable to change it. Now she was bursting to catch up with the news.

'So tell, Ashok! I can't wait to hear what you have been up to. Have you found girl of your dreams?' Her eyes sparkled with anticipation, and her enthusiasm and innocence numbed her to the tension around her. Ashok cursed inwardly. He was under no illusions. His own plans could have a devastating effect on Priya's future. Some months previously she had agreed to marry Harsha, a young dentist living in Canada. It was this arrangement that had opened the way for Ashok's own marriage. In keeping with tradition, his parents would have preferred Priya to marry before him. However she insisted on first completing her studies. Like Janaki, reflected Ashok bitterly. Why did Priya have to be so stubborn? If only the marriage had already taken place. But now how would Harsha's family feel when Ashok's news broke? Would they still accept Harsha's commitment to Priya? It was one hell of a mess. He knew that he could no longer expect any support from his father. At first Srinivasa had taken a philosophical line and had apparently convinced himself that Ashok's infatuation with the English girl was a temporary aberration that would not, in the long run, affect his relationship with Janaki. Lately however, Srinivasa's patience had worn thin. His mood of appeasement had hardened in line with Ashok's inexplicable behaviour of the preceding days. Now Srinivasa wanted the matter settled. Ah well. Nothing for it, Ashok decided. Time to smash open the termites' nest and break the news.

But Srinivasa cut in before he had a chance to open his mouth. 'He has a very nice girl in mind. Janaki. Is it not so, Ashok?'

Another lost moment. Like so many recently. Ashok struggled to let his father down gently. '*Bapa*, Janaki is a very nice girl. But she is not wanting to marry for many years yet. She is intending to complete PhD studies first. This could take four, five years...'

'A clever student can complete in three. And even if it is taking longer, Janaki is young, twenty only. As long as matter is settled, no rush.'

Girija, hovering with a plate of *chapatis* in her hand, had been regarding Ashok through anxious, motherly eyes. As ever, he reflected, in her quiet, undemonstrative fashion she had a way of knowing his thoughts. However, she kept silent, eyes now downcast, resigned.

'I have spoken to Janaki's father,' continued Srinivasa, 'It would seem that the girl will not be persuaded to consent to marriage before studies are finished. It would appear, Ashok, that already you and she have come to some arrangement.'

Ashok looked up sharply. 'Arrangement? What arrangement? We were telling only we would write.'

'There, you see.' Srinivasa sat back. 'As good as settled. A few loose ends only. And this match will be approved by Harsha's family also. Now we can put our minds to Priya's wedding.'

'*Bapa*...' Ashok began to protest. His father was blinding himself. Refusing to accept the obvious. Then he saw his sister's animated face. Not the moment to explode the myth. Better to tackle *Bapa* in private. Or talk to *Amma* or *Ajji* first. He caught his grandmother's eye. Shrewd. Conspiratorial even. She was no fool. Like *Amma* she knew. But somehow he felt she would understand, if not condone. *Amma*, no. It was tearing her apart.

'I have to go away for a few days,' he announced coldly.

'Again? Is it too much that you should spend at least small part of your holiday with your family?'

'It's just for two nights, *Bapa*. After that I'll be here for another two weeks.'

'So where is it to be this time?'

'Kerala. My Dutch friend is in Cochin. I should like to say goodbye to her before she sails for Amsterdam on fourth.'

Questions left unspoken. Ashok knew their thoughts. *Alone? With the English friend?* Answers that would be unbearable for them to hear. Protest was useless. Instead, a faint nod from Srinivasa, clearly searching in brave desperation for a reason to justify his son's action, and thus make the pill less bitter.

'After all,' he said to the women, 'it will be at least three years before the wedding. Ashok is a healthy young man. He cannot be expected to shun company of women until Janaki is finished with studying.' Lakshmi Devi said nothing. Priya and Girija scuttled back into the kitchen to disguise their disappointment in a flurry of culinary activity.

Later that afternoon Ashok paid his grandmother a visit in her rooms downstairs.

Here it was cool under the fan, away from the oppressive heat. The room smelled of sandalwood and frangipani. Lakshmi Devi had been burning incense in her little shrine room behind the ornately carved teak doors. She was seated in the corner of the couch, as insubstantial as a wisp of curling incense smoke. Carefully and with slow deliberation she rearranged the silk of her fine cream sari around herself.

'So.' she said at length. 'You have come to tell me something.'

Ashok took her small, bony hand in his. '*Ajji*...' But she placed a trembling finger over his lips.

'Ashok, think, my child, before you are telling me secrets of your heart. Is it really that you are wanting to place this burden on me? After all, I cannot help you. It is for you to weigh up consequences of your decision and act according to your conscience.'

'*Ajji*. I have already decided. I am going to...'

'... then is no further discussion necessary, isn't it? Ashok, whatever you are deciding, you must be telling your parents first, no? And the girl, Janaki. She has a right to know your decision also.'

'I have tried to tell *Bapa*. He refuses to listen. I have to find right moment. Tomorrow I am going away. But I will tell them, *Ajji*, I promise, before I return to England. And now I must go. I have some parcels to deliver.'

He stood up and quietly opened the door.

'Ashok,' He stopped and turned. 'Know that whatever you will be deciding, you have my blessing.'

Ajji: wise and fragile like an ancient, lovingly-carved Saraswathi.

By the time Ashok had torn himself away from the effusive hospitality of Dr Patel's mother-in-law, it was early evening. He caught an autorickshaw to the Chamundi. There was no answer when he knocked on Hannah's hotel room door.

Worried, he went back down to the reception desk. 'Is there a message for Dr Rao from Miss Petersen?'

The receptionist leafed through a pile of papers. 'No, sir. No message. But she was checking out not half hour ago. I myself procured a car to take her to airport.'

*   *   *

Hannah's departure was inexplicable to Ashok. He had rushed to the airport after her. At Bangalore airport there was chaos. The usual crowds were thicker than ever, and airport officials were turning back non-ticket-holders. The Chief Minister of Karnataka was expected from Delhi. Only passengers were allowed inside the building. Goodbyes had to be said outside. Ashok was stopped at the terminal doors. Still he scrutinised the scrum of travellers for hours. He checked the timetable of departing aircraft. Delhi;

Mumbai; Chennai. She could have been on any of them. As night fell, he tore himself away and went back to the Chamundi. Perhaps there had been a mistake. But no. No mistake. No message. Nothing.

Next day Ashok flew down to Cochin as they had planned, in the hope that Hannah had gone there. Willi was waiting for him at the airport. Alone. She could offer no explanation for Hannah's disappearance. She was as baffled as he was.

For the next two days they toured the churches and synagogues, palaces and temples in and around Cochin. They scoured the backwaters, the restaurants, the hotels, but the search was fruitless. By the evening of the third of January Ashok was drained, bewildered and bereft of all hope of finding Hannah. The emptiness inside him mauled his senses.

Willi's ganja was comforting. Her bed was warm and inviting. He needed to be held.

When he awoke with a headache next morning, she was lying next to him, grinning. 'Thanks,' she said, 'You don't know how much I wanted that.'

Ashok stared at the ceiling, 'What the hell were we thinking of?'

'Well, you certainly know how to make a girl feel good.'

'Sorry,' he said sharply, 'but you know what I mean. Damn. What a mess.'

'Chill out, Ashok. It's not a major crime. Hannah would understand.'

'I doubt that. It won't happen again.'

She laughed it off. 'I'll live off the memory,' she said. 'How about you? Feel any better?'

He softened. 'If I don't, it's not your fault. Thanks for trying.'

'The pleasure was all mine.'

'Not all.'

'You're a star, Ashok. Come on. I don't want them to sail without me.'

That afternoon, Ashok saw Willi onto the three-masted schooner, *Helena*. He stood on the dockside and waved as the ship slowly pulled out to sea. He felt empty, lonely as he realised that he

256

would probably never see Willi again. They had, in their confusion, forgotten to exchange addresses.

Back at his parents' house, discretion reigned. It didn't take the women long to realise that the Englishwoman had slipped from the scene. Srinivasa though appeared not to notice the change in Ashok's demeanour; how he was distracted, downbeat, morose even. His father did not comment on the constant telephone calls to hotels - the Chamundi, the Pandava in Chennai, even the Krishna in Hyderabad, asking whether a red-haired Englishwoman was staying there. When Ashok took a car to Mysore, Srinivasa convinced himself that his son was paying a secret visit to Janaki, despite overhearing his arrangement with the driver, to drive on from Mysore via Nanjangud to Bandipur.

Srinivasa chose to block out of his mind the call to the police in Mamallapuram, and overseas calls to directory enquiries in England, where Miss Hannah Petersen's telephone number appeared to be unlisted. There were also the calls to some publishing company in London, where a Mr Duncan Forbes was never available, and never rang back despite being entreated to do so. Srinivasa managed to sail through Ashok's troubled seas as nimbly as a seal in an Arctic storm, refusing to be distracted from steering a sure course to an eventual liaison between Ashok and Janaki.

'I myself will be travelling to Mysore weekend next to visit family,' he announced cheerfully.

Girija and Priya exchanged anxious glances. They were perfectly aware, as was Srinivasa, that all was not well with Ashok, but, unlike him, they were not able to hide behind the electric fence of obstinate determination. Ashok himself appeared oblivious to, or did not care about, his father's machinations.

The day before he was due to return to England, Girija found him walking in the garden, amidst her potted jungle foliage, absently clipping the new shoots off an ancient coffee bush with his thumb nail.

'That is not a good idea. It will stop tree from growing, Ashok.'

Ashok shrugged.

'What is it, my son? I know all has not been well since your English friend has departed. But we must clear up this matter before you are returning to UK. Your father has all but agreed to a marriage with Janaki. Does this arrangement suit, or no?'

Ashok turned to his mother with glazed, uninterested eyes. 'Does it suit you?'

'Me? Well, yes. Although I am wishing it could be happening sooner. But it is the girl's will, and you, I believe, are agreeable to wait.'

'It is soon enough for me, *Amma*. Do as you wish. I respect your decision.'

Despite Girija's evident relief, the look on his face must have told her that the fight had gone out of him. Thus he knew, though he was helpless to alter the fact, that her happiness was tempered by great unease.

Just before the taxi arrived to take him to the airport, Ashok paid a last lone visit to his grandmother.

'I've come to say goodbye, *Ajji*.'

Lakshmi Devi nodded and clasped his hands between hers.

'Try to be happy, Ashok.'

'I'll try, *Ajji*.'

The old lady looked at him tenderly but unflinchingly.

'She has left you?'

Ashok nodded, avoiding her frank gaze.

'Then perhaps she is wiser than you understood.'

He looked at her uncomprehending.

'All is for the best, my boy. You will see. All is for the best.'

CHAPTER 16

The rain hit Ashok like an icy slap around the face when he stepped out of the taxi in Richmond and struggled with his suitcase up the slippery steps to his flat. He opened the door with frozen, shivering hands and pushed his way inside, against the resistance of four weeks' accumulated mail.

'Damn!' he cursed. 'What the hell has happened to Mrs Maxwell?' It was instantly clear that his twice-weekly cleaner had not been doing her job. The place was freezing, despite her promise to 'have the flat all warm and snug for you when you get back, Doctor.' It even smelled damp and neglected.

Ashok put down his suitcase in the hall, and gathered up the mail. Frantically he searched through it, letting each unopened envelope fall out of his hand, when he had checked that it was not from Hannah. When the last envelope had fluttered to the floor, and with it the hope that he had carried with him from Bangalore, he went into the living room. At least his armchair was still waiting for him, welcoming if not warm. He flopped down on it and let the anguish of his dashed hope sink in. Ganesh, purveyor of good fortune, gazed down at him from the poster in the corner. Ashok avoided his glance. He could do without being patronised by the elephant god. The two whisky glasses were still on the sticky coffee table where he had left them, after Dr Patel had called round with the packages. One month ago. The absurd thought struck him that perhaps Mrs Maxwell had walked out in disgust at his slovenliness. Rubbish. She knew him too well for that.

For some moments he stared at the answerphone, afraid to push the play button. There was just a slim chance... It hadn't even occurred to him that Hannah did not have his ex-directory number.

With a supreme effort of will, he pushed the button and played through the pile-up of messages that had been left. At least half of the callers were answerphone-phobics and telephone sales people who slammed the receiver down without leaving a message. Normally Ashok would have been irritated. Now he was glad. He was in no mood to return social calls. Most of the messages that had been left were non-urgent calls from friends, wondering if he was back. One was from an awkwardly embarrassed Mrs Maxwell saying that she was sorry she couldn't go on working for him as she was starting a fulltime job in the New Year. Ashok wondered how long she'd known. The final call was from Dr Patel, who had left his message that morning.

'Welcome back, my dear boy, and felicitations on your forthcoming marriage. That family is well known to my mother-in-law, and I understand you have indeed made an excellent choice. You will please dine with us tomorrow, that is Friday evening. We look forward to hearing your news.'

Insult to injury. Salt into the wound. He sat, sunk in despair until his bones ached with cold and he started to shiver. His discomfort jolted him into decision. No. He would make his excuses and not go to the Patels. He was due to start back at the hospital on Monday. There he would be unable to avoid Dr Patel, though opportunity to discuss private matters was, thank goodness, limited. At any rate he would cross that bridge later. At least he would have an unmolested weekend. He glanced at his watch. Three-thirty. Dr Patel would be at the hospital. His wife would be doing her ante-natal clinic. He picked up the receiver and dialled their number. The housekeeper answered.

'Ashok Rao here. Please thank Dr Patel for inviting me to dinner. Unfortunately I have picked up a severe cold and must therefore decline the invitation.'

If he sat there in the damp chill long enough, he reflected, it would be a self-fulfilling prophecy. He forced himself up and switched on the central heating. Slowly, he and the flat began to thaw out. Jet lag caught up with him, and he lay down on his still unmade bed, where finally, he fell into a deep but troubled sleep, filled with fears for Hannah.

It was not simply that his feelings for her were still strong - indeed they seemed to grow in strength with each passing day. It was also the helplessness, the fear that something had happened to her; after all, her departure was less than a week after the Salers affair had come to its grotesque conclusion. Perhaps it had all been too much. Perhaps she had snapped. Perhaps she was wondering around India in blank incomprehension. Perhaps she'd fallen foul of the innumerable dangers lurking there. Perhaps...

The next day he swallowed his pride and telephoned Duncan at Hamilton and Forbes, giving a false name to the secretary who put him through.

'Duncan. Ashok here. How are you?'

A split second then an over-effusive reply.

'Ashok. Good to hear from you, old man. I'm well. And you?'

'Yes. Listen. I just got back. Is Hannah back yet? I don't suppose you've heard from her?'

Ashok could almost hear Duncan's mind ticking over.

'Er...'fraid not, old man. Don't know where she is.'

'But she told me you'd always know - because of the impending US publication of her book.'

'Yes, well the book's out now. You missed the storm. But I'll send you a copy if you want.'

Ashok swallowed hard. Keep your temper, he said to himself. Don't make even more of an enemy of him.

'Don't you have any idea where she is? Look, I'm really worried. She just disappeared...'

'Well, that's Hannah for you. I'm sorry, I can't help you.'

'At least you can let me have her UK address.'

'Sorry, old man. Haven't got it on me. Anyway it won't do you any good. She's not there.'

'I thought you didn't know where she is.'

'I don't. But I know where she isn't.'

That's it, Ashok decided. Enough of this idiot's cover-up.

'OK, Duncan. I'm not stupid, you know. So you don't want me to trace her. I don't know if that's her doing or yours. At least tell me if she's safe.'

Mind ticking again. A telephone time bomb.

'I think we should terminate this conversation, Ashok. It was nice talking to you.'

The phone went dead. Fuck you, thought Ashok. He slammed down the receiver. Bracing himself against the unaccustomed winter cold, and hoping that his car would start after its long sleep, he decided to take himself off to Burfold. Hannah had told him she had a cottage there. He knew it was somewhere near the village green. The drive took him an hour. Speeding down the A3 in his ageing Saab 900 channelled his anger and anxiety, and it wasn't until he heard the police siren that he realised he'd been doing eighty-five. Damn. Better not try the medical emergency line with this lot, he decided, or they'll offer to escort me. So he admitted guilt, meekly, only wishing they'd get on with it and let him continue his journey. By the time he reached Burfold, he was in a foul temper, in keeping with the weather, which had turned to sleet. It was lunchtime and he parked in the car park of the Red Fox Inn, recalling with a pang that it was from here that Salers had first followed Hannah home. He asked around the bar for the whereabouts of the cottage of the writer Hannah Petersen. Nobody seemed to know, or at least they weren't prepared to divulge the information. He couldn't blame them. At least it meant they were not telling all and sundry where she lived.

A cheese ploughman's and a beer later he set off on foot around the green, eyeing-up each cottage as nonchalantly as possible in order not to arouse suspicion. Although the sleet had stopped, it was bitterly cold and sludgy underfoot. He remembered that she had mentioned that the cottage was down a dirt track, and that it was not therefore situated directly on the green itself. This narrowed down his search. He continued to explore, inspecting every path, drive or dirt track that was anywhere near the green.

After a good hour's investigating, he spotted a fairly wide, hedge-bordered lane. A wooden sign nailed to a tree had the words

"Drake Lane" carved into it. A road sign at the beginning indicated that it was a dead end. Not a dirt track, thought Ashok, but worth a try. He headed down the lane. There was a large house some fifty metres along it, beyond which the lane narrowed and the tarmac petered out, and became a sandy track. After another fifty metres the track ended. On the left, behind an unruly assortment of hawthorn and elder, nestled a small, but attractive half-timbered cottage. Ashok knew, without a doubt, that it belonged to Hannah.

He turned onto the gravel drive leading to the front door. The lawn on either side of the drive was soggy with winter neglect. Most of the garden, he noticed, was at the front of the house, with only a small, fenced-in strip at the back separating Hannah's property from the field behind it. The shed, whose slamming door had brought Hannah out of bed that November night when Salers had rushed her, was half-concealed behind shrubs at the far right of the front garden. The scene that had taken place that night forced itself into Ashok's imagination. He saw the shed door banging, Salers' sinister presence, Hannah lying on the wet grass in front of the shrubs, the sound of Duncan's car turning onto the drive and the glare of its headlights. He shuddered at the thought of her vulnerability, holed-up there alone in the middle of nowhere. Damned plucky, he thought. Or foolhardy. Not sure which.

He made his way round to the back of the cottage, and peered first through the kitchen window. Modern but rustic. All neat and tidy. No sign of life. Next to the kitchen were French windows, which led onto a small patio. Through these he saw Hannah's neat living room. In his mind he could see her working at the computer on the desk in the corner. Careless, he thought, to leave it in such full view while she was away. Uncharacteristic. A sign of how distracted she had been at the time. He could see through the open door into the hall, and noticed that some of Hannah's post was neatly stacked on a hall table next to a black telephone. Someone's been in.

'Can I help you?'

Ashok wheeled round to see an elderly man in tweeds and Wellington boots, standing behind him, leaning on a stick. Beside him, a senescent spaniel stood panting, more from the effects of overweight than over-exertion, Ashok reckoned.

'I'm looking for Miss Petersen. Do you know if she's back?'

'And who, might I ask, are you?'

'An old friend.' The man looked wary. 'I'm - from Oxford.' Ashok added hastily, as if this were some sort of pedigree that would place him beyond suspicion.

'Oh. I see. Well, I'm afraid you're out of luck. Miss Petersen's away for some time I believe. She went off quite suddenly before Christmas. Some secret assignment I suppose, knowing her line of work. She didn't know when she'd be back, but I said I'd keep an eye on the place. I live at the house back down the lane. I saw you walk past and thought I'd better check.'

'Oh, so it's you who's been picking up her post.'

'No, not me. I haven't got a key. It's that publisher fellow - what's his name? Ford?'

'Forbes. When was he last here?'

'About a week ago.'

A spark of hope flickered.

'Did he say if he'd heard from her?'

'Mm... yes, I think he did. Bit vague though. Said she was well, but in no rush to get back, it seems.'

'Did he say where she is?'

'Oh no. He wouldn't tell me that. As I said, she's always involved in some cloak and dagger stuff.'

'Yes. Well thanks, anyway. I'd better be going before it starts snowing again.'

'Nice lady, Miss Petersen. Always ready for a chat and a cup of tea, y'know. Never put on airs and graces. I felt so sorry for her last year. Some maniac was giving her a hard time, but the police - well you know what they're like.'

'Did you ever see him, this maniac?'

'Well. I thought I did, once. I was taking Bert for a walk up the lane - late one evening round about August it must have been - when this man suddenly appeared - thin, and very white. Real shifty. I don't know if he'd been hiding in the hedge or what. He saw me and shot off towards the green.'

'Did you report it?'

The man laughed. 'I tried. Just made me look a fool.'

'Poor Hannah.' Ashok said, half to himself.

'Why don't you leave her a note?'

'Would you hand it to her?'

'Why not post it through the letter box?'

'No,' Ashok said, a little too quickly. 'I'd rather you made sure it gets to her.'

'Any reason why it shouldn't?'

'Um…well Mr Forbes and I … it's rather personal.'

Hannah's neighbour frowned. 'Look. I've a feeling this is something I'd rather not get involved in. Ford's looking after things for her. I wouldn't like to deceive him. Sorry.'

The expression on the man's face was set. No point in pursuing the matter. It was closed.

Ashok nodded. 'I understand. I'll call again.'

This inauspicious start to Ashok's return to Britain was to set the pattern for the coming weeks. Bouts of depression and withdrawal from social contact punctuated his private life. He made no attempt to find a new cleaner, unable to bear the idea of another Mrs Maxwell intruding on his privacy. Once a week he cleared the papers off the floor and added them to the pile on the desk, which gradually built up in front of the Ganesh poster until it was almost entirely obscured. If he had time, he half-heartedly passed the vacuum cleaner over those parts of the floor that he could reach without having to move the furniture. Since he ate at the hospital, his kitchen remained mostly untouched, with the exception of the occasional coffee cup or whisky glass when the going got really tough. Some evenings, music provided him with escape. Others would be spent in silence, searching. He would travel in his mind over every moment that he had spent with Hannah, from their first meeting to their final, ecstatic hours together at the Chamundi, in the desperate search for anything that could provide a clue to her disappearance.

The US publication of *Fair Game* had fuelled a controversy that even lingered on in Britain for some weeks. Hannah had exposed a network of corruption that shocked America. Ashok followed up every press report, but her whereabouts remained a mystery. Rumours abounded in the press: she was investigating the Russian Mafia; she'd been kidnapped in Burma; she was probing into the activities of a major oil company in Africa. She'd adopted a new identity to protect her from Bannerman's wrath. Rumours which Ashok read in despondency and fear. Darkest of all were moments spent imagining her dying alone in some Oriental gutter, coughing up blood and gasping vainly for breath though sponge-choked lungs.

Once a month he made a pilgrimage to Burfold. It was always the same. The cottage, untouched except for the pile of mail getting higher on the hall table. As winter faded into spring, the cottage took on a new persona, seemed less austere and isolated as new buds broke out on the trees and the lawn began to sprout new shoots. This gave Ashok an idea. He had seen through the shed window that Hannah kept her gardening tools, including a lawn mower there. When, and if she returned, the lawn would need attending to as a matter of urgency. The door was locked, but the window, though rusted solid, was slightly open. He rummaged in his pocket for a scrap of paper, finally tearing the last paying-in slip from his chequebook, and wrote.

Dear Hannah,
I'm so worried. I'm sorry if I did something wrong. I need to know that you're OK. Please ring or write. At least do this for me.
Fondly
Ashok

Underneath he added his home and hospital address, his telephone number and the date. He folded the paper and slipped it through the window. He watched it as it floated down and came to rest facedown on the lawn mower. Good, he thought. As long as Forbes doesn't decide to mow the lawn. After that he always checked to see if the note was still there. It was, and the grass grew higher.

In June he received a letter from Janaki.

Dear Ashok,

I hope this letter finds you in good health and mind. I myself am well. My parents also.

This morning I have learnt of my success in entrance examination for MSc degree programme at University of Agricultural Sciences in Bangalore. This, God willing, will be leading to eventual PhD at BTU.

Now I will be living in Bangalore I will have opportunity to visit your family often, and to help your sister Priya with marriage arrangements. To this I am looking forward very much, and to your return in December next year for her wedding.

I hope you will soon write to me and tell me about UK.

May this year continue to bring you the brightest of joys, the warmest of friendships, the nicest of memories.

With deep regards,

Yours sincerely,

Janaki

He scribbled a short reply.

Dear Janaki,

Nice to hear from you. I am very happy for you and wish you success in your studies. Perhaps you will write and tell me exactly what you will be doing. Most of it I should be able to understand - to some extent at least. What would you like to know about England? It is very different from India. Very less people.

He racked his brain for something else to say to her. Words came painfully and slowly. It was a duty, but one that came without pleasure.

There are many cars here. London is getting very noisy and polluted.

Stop being mean, he said to himself. Stop putting her off.

The gardens are beautiful at this time of year. Everything is breaking into flower after the winter. There is a lovely village that I know. It has an old

white inn with low, oak roof-beams. And a village green with a duck pond,
where people play cricket. And a little half-timbered cottage with a lawn,
and sweet-scented elder and hawthorn hedges covered with pink and white
blossoms.
Please convey my best wishes to your respected parents,
Yours sincerely,
Ashok

As much as Ashok withdrew into himself at home, his professional life blossomed. He developed the capacity to shut out all private preoccupation and switch entirely and unshakeably into work-mode as soon as he entered the hospital. He was highly regarded, widely praised, and sought after by patients unwilling to place the care of their eyesight into less sure hands. Dr Rao's reputation grew with each considerately handled consultation, each successful cataract operation, each reattached retina, each comforting bedside reassurance, each kindly pat or smile.

Time spread like a film of hydrocortisone across the past, dimmed pain and calmed inflamed passions. By the end of the first year of his return to England, Ashok was able to look beyond the still festering wounds of his time with Hannah.

He began to take more interest in Janaki's letters, and his replies gradually became less stilted, more sincere. Hannah, yearned for and undiminished, became in his mind an ethereal, untouchable dream; a warm and loving memory; a mythical, vanished goddess. Janaki was reality. They could make a life together. It would be OK. Genial if not fervid.

The following year, Priya graduated from university and was free to marry her Canadian fiancé, Harsha. The wedding was arranged for December.

As the time for Priya's wedding approached, Ashok began to look forward with growing anticipation to his visit home. One Friday evening in September he sat in Dr Patel's living room cradling an after-dinner cognac. He felt warmer and more at ease than ever in the Patels' company of late, as though being in their home were satisfying some need in him.

'Well now, my boy. We will have to start thinking about your future, isn't it? You have reached the dizzying heights at Queen Anne's. What is next step to be, do you think? You can't stay there forever.'

'Strange. I've been mulling that over in my mind also. I think you're right. It's time for a change.'

'Listen - there's a consultancy going at the John Radcliffe. As soon as I heard about it I was thinking - that's made for Ashok. It's your job, Ashok. It's sitting there waiting for you.'

Ashok let the prospect wash over him briefly.

'You know, Dr Patel, a few years ago I would have jumped at this chance. It's everything I would have wanted. But now... I'm not so sure. When I was in India last time, I realised that sooner or later I would have to return for good. I'm not the same as you, Dr Patel. I can't stay here forever. And well... during the last year or so things have happened to make me even less inclined to get too comfortable here. I feel I've repaid England for all it's given me over the years. Now perhaps it's time for me to make the break, and give something back to India.'

Dr Patel smiled.

'How did I know that would be your answer? You will be a great loss here, but perhaps you can do even more good back home. I will not try to dissuade you.'

In October, Ashok secured a consultancy at Shanti Sagar Hospital in Bangalore and handed in his resignation at Queen Anne's. In November he sold his Richmond flat and moved in with Dr and Mrs Patel.

On the first day of December, Ashok drove down to Hannah's cottage. The grounds were slippery and rotten with two years' accumulated autumn and winter debris. Paint was beginning to peel off the once-white exterior walls. Tree branches hung limp and bare. The pile of correspondence on the hall table had stopped growing. People no longer wrote to Hannah, it seemed.

Ashok slipped and slid across the muddy remains of lawn to the shed. The note that he had posted so long ago was still untouched, if a little mouldy. He stood for a moment, looking back at the cottage, as if he were trying to seal into his memory forever this final association with Hannah. He drew from his pocket a folded sheet of paper. Slowly, carefully he unfolded it and gazed for the last time on the gaudy poster of Ganesh that had hung above his desk in Richmond. Briefly he touched his fingers to his lips and passed them over the face of the elephant-god. 'May good fortune always go with you, my Hannah,' he whispered. He refolded the poster and slipped it through the window-gap into the shed, where it came to rest next to his note. He turned and walked away. The cold wind stung his tear-filled eyes.

Three weeks later, almost exactly two years after he had stepped off the aeroplane in Delhi, Ashok returned to India.

CHAPTER 17

The island shimmered below the aircraft like a delicate, green mayfly hovering over the sapphire sea. Here Hannah would abandon herself to timelessness. Here she would forget. The first day of 1992 would bring with it a new beginning.

By the time she reached her half-brother George's house Hannah was feverish, bordering on delirium. The wound on her leg had burst open during the flight from Bangalore to Chennai and, despite antibiotics, was septic by the time she boarded the aircraft to Colombo some hours later.

From the moment that she collapsed on their doorstep they had welcomed her as one of their own. George's wife Ranee and the other women of the household were solicitous in their care of her. Slowly, week-by-week they nursed her back to health, taking it in turns to sit with her, feed her, mop her brow, read to her. George, the consummate diplomat, asked no questions, made no demands, came and went like a benevolent spirit, smiled and patted her hand. He was simply overwhelmed to meet his sister at last, and to be able to welcome her into his world. Lounging around in a batik sarong on his days off, instructing the servants, studying one of his beloved Buddhist commentaries, he was the epitome of a well-heeled local businessman. But although he had never known his father, there was no mistaking him, thought Hannah. He was a toffee-apple clone of the old man. Odd, she reflected, that Dad had so completely broken ties. Was it for Mum's sake? Surely Mum would have understood? Hannah knew that he had never ceased to love the island: he spoke of it often, but he had never come back to it. Perhaps the pain was too great. A son, who could never be his, never share his life.

George lived with his wife's family in the well-to-do Colombo suburb of Wellawatte. They lived in a narrow lane off the Galle Road, leading down to the sea. The house was large, accommodating not only George, his wife and their three children, but also his wife's parents and two younger sisters. When George's first child was born, his parents-in-law converted the top of the house into a large flat, and moved into it with the two younger daughters, thus freeing the rest of the house for the new family. The rooms were dark and sparsely furnished. Stone floors, swept by a stunted servant girl, were cool in the fierce heat. But when the electricity cut out and the fans stopped, which happened almost daily, the house became a sauna.

During that first year on the island, Hannah set all thoughts of work, of writing, of returning to England aside. It was a time of healing, and hand in hand with her lingering sorrow, a joy, hitherto undreamt of.

At the end of twelve months came the promise of reprieve. Although she had taken the advice of her brother's doctor, to discontinue the antibiotic drugs, Hannah had not developed tuberculosis. Now, the doctor assured her, the danger was to all intents and purposes past. She gave a prayer of thanks to her universal God, and laid an offering of frangipani blossom at the foot of the Buddha statue in the nearby temple. It was the turning point. From then on she took renewed interest in the world around her. She turned her mind to the enigma of the island that she had made her home. She studied the plants, the animals, the architecture, the religious and ethnic diversity that was both its blessing and its curse. And she began to write again.

Sri Lanka - teardrop of India. Life has been returned to me here. Over the past year I have learnt to live, and to love again, unconditionally. Here I have found greater happiness and peace than I could have imagined during those first, terrible days in this tainted paradise. For paradise it is, a voluptuous island, a lush garden of swaying coconut groves lapped by the Indian ocean; of mountain peaks and savage jungle; of ancient temples and elephants; of gentle people and enigmatic faiths. But this paradise has been violated; for it is also a place of brutal conflict and intolerance; of civil war and repression.

It is easy to forget the dark secret of this sensuous land. It is easy to be seduced by it, when we idle along the Galle Road to the market where they sell ladies-fingers as fat and as long as broad-beans; ten different kinds of banana, pineapples so succulent that they seem to have no core; snake gourds and bitter gourds straight out of a sci-fi movie; hard little green amberella fruits for making chutney; paw-paw and guava, mangosteen and mango. It is easy to be lulled into complacency when together we take a three-wheeler (as they call the auto-rickshaws here) to Mount Lavinia and spend a happy afternoon in the pool overlooking the ocean. It is easy to surrender to the island's charms, to close your mind to the bombing and the shooting, the roadblocks and the routine handbag searches in the big stores. Oh yes, it is all so easy.

Sometimes, when George has a day off, he takes me to a forest hermitage. He's trying to 'heal' me by showing me the Buddhist way - the middle way. We drive for hours, first along the coast and then inland, through paddy, coconut and tea. The road turns into a pot-holed dirt track. Virgin forest and the encroaching hills are punctuated by teak and betel nut plantations. We leave the car and climb for an hour through dripping, steamy rain forest, past spring-fed ponds of little jewel-like fish. We wade through leech-infested rivulets, the air thick with the heady scent of verdure. Fiery temple trees and darting butterflies and dragonflies form luminescent highlights on the green canvas. We trudge upward through tangled undergrowth until we reach the monastery. Near the top there are many small grottos for quiet contemplation dotted among the trees. The hermitage itself is a place of tranquil beauty, timeless. Here George sometimes comes to spend an hour, or a day or longer searching for serenity, for the middle way.

Maybe one day, she thought, she would turn these little sketches into a book, a book not centred, as all her other books had been, around some worthy cause, some social injustice, but around herself. She would write about the island in terms of what it meant to her, all that had happened to her here, all that she had learnt from its people. She would write about its dark side too, and the resulting dichotomies which her mind found hard to reconcile. Perhaps by writing she would complete the healing process.

The conflict between the Tamils and the Singhalese was ongoing. The undercurrent of risk was ever present. However the trouble now seemed to be mainly confined to the north and the east of the country, where the Tamil rebels were trying to establish a separate independent state. There had been relatively few disturbances in Colombo while Hannah had been in the country. She had no qualms about her safety. She'd felt less secure in Belfast.

During the 1993 May Day parade, the nation's President was assassinated by a suicide bomber, an alleged member of the rebel Liberation Tigers of Tamil Eelam, commonly known as the Tamil Tigers. Still Hannah dug in her heels.

'Don't be too protective of me,' she said to George when he warned her against travelling into the city centre for while. 'You forget, this kind of thing is my bread and butter.'

'Don't underestimate the danger,' George said, frowning. 'Until now it has been relatively calm in the city. But, as you see, trouble is never far beneath the surface. And news is censored, you know. We don't hear what the government doesn't want us to hear. Partly to stop feelings getting out of hand and more trouble escalating. What we don't want is a repetition of eighty-nine.'

'What happened in eighty-nine?'

'A reign of terror because of military and political bungling. Many innocent people got caught up in it. Families wiped out, some fifty people getting killed daily. They used to burn the bodies with tyres on the roads leading to Colombo. They even closed the universities and schools for four months. You regularly saw corpses floating in lakes and rivers. Not a pleasant time to be here.'

'But you stayed, none the less.'

'It's my home, Hannah.'

'Yes. I do understand, George.' And now it's my home too, she told herself.

But her earlier comment to George had triggered a certain unrest in her. It's my bread and butter - why did I say that? It was my bread and butter, certainly. But now? Have I opted out? Have I perhaps unwittingly slipped into the middle way?

Slowly she began to contemplate, to reassess her life...

Middle way? Yes, for you maybe, George, but I think not for me. Avoiding the destructive forces of extreme passions, of love and hate, of sorrow and joy. I could have saved myself a lot of heartache in the past if I had been a follower of the middle way. But I wouldn't have missed a moment of those highs in order to avoid the lows. Isn't that what's in danger of happening to me now though? Aren't I steering a middle course, choosing the blindness of serenity by lingering so pleasantly here? Eyes closed to the violence around me, eyes closed also to the need to purge myself of the shadow of Mark Salers? And the shadow of Maighréad? And the shadow of...? I don't know. Perhaps I'll never come to terms with what's happened until I finish what I began...

Almost a year previously, Duncan Forbes had sent her a copy of Salers' book.

Hannah hadn't read it. It lay in the back of her wardrobe unopened. Duncan's world had seemed so far away. What did Salers matter? What did anything matter, except the here and now? The ghost of those dark days had dissipated in the light of the miracle that had taken place here.

Now finally, as the last of the southwest monsoon rains darkened the summer sky, Hannah opened the book.

By October she had made her decision to return to England in the New Year.

Once she had made the booking, her final days on the island were hard to bear. It was one thing to talk about going. It was quite another to face the reality of it. To face the reality of the final break with the sub-continent and its memories, so bitter and so sweet.

For almost two years Hannah had appeared impassive. No inkling of a broken love affair had leaked into the image that she outwardly portrayed. Only at night, solitary, private under the mosquito net, did she allow silent tears to flow. Tears for her lost love, for the face that forced itself, unwished for, into her dreams. Tears for her incomprehension. *Ashok betrothed.* It was all so clear now. His reluctance to talk about his home, or to take her to meet his family. It all made sense.

And suddenly it was January and the day of departure was upon her. In the morning Hannah walked along the beach for one last time, committing to memory the sound of the breakers, the distant tower blocks of Colombo to the north, the rocky outcrop of Mount Lavinia to the south. A train chugged past on the beachside railway line. A couple of foolhardy men, clinging like caterpillars to the exterior of the train, released one hand to wave in greeting. Hannah smiled and waved back.

Two old coconut palms on the shore seemed to signal to her, old friends bidding farewell. Hannah would never again see the sun go down behind the palm fronds.

As she walked along the beach, listening to the sea, and watching the child at the water's edge as she once did in Mamallapuram, she found that she could think of that happy time without bitterness. It was as if an earlier Ashok walked beside her, unsullied, incorrupt.

'Siddarth,' she said to the little boy, 'time to go. Our aeroplane is waiting.'

She held out her arms and the child toddled into them; a plump, charming child with pouting lips and deep, dark, laughing eyes; eyes with which, unknowingly, he struck his mother a hammer blow each time they met her own.

CHAPTER 18

Of all the things that Ashok missed about England, his daily *Guardian* stood near the top of the list. Thus he had decided, after his first *Guardian*-deprived month in Bangalore, to order the *Weekly Guardian* for himself, as well as for his sister, who had been carted off by her new husband to what Ashok was convinced would be a life of cultural deprivation, in Winnipeg, Manitoba.

Early one October Sunday morning, nearly two years after his return to India, during a precious few moments' relaxation before he set off to the hospital, Ashok, recumbent in the garden hammock, was flicking through his flimsy fix of weekly world events, when a book review caught his eye.

Seeker after Truth?

As a Matter of Fact: Hannah Petersen, (Hamilton and Forbes).

Whatever one thinks of Hannah Petersen's frequently-demonstrated inability to remove herself to a safe aesthetic distance from her subject matter, one has to admire the chutzpah of the woman who does not take a beating lying down, even if the beating so defeats its purpose that it amounts to more of a pat on the back.

Whether Petersen's latest book As a Matter of Fact is seen as an attempt to justify the actions documented in her book A Small Life, (published by Hamilton and Forbes, 1986) which was famously discredited by its antihero in his posthumously published and grotesquely farcical booklet In the Name of Love, or whether it is a genuine attempt to seek out the truth is a matter of conjecture. Nevertheless it makes compelling reading.

When Petersen wrote A Small Life there was no doubt in her mind that the journalist and broadcaster, Mark Salers, was alone responsible for the terrible physical abuse of his young wife, Maighréad. A Small Life told the story of Maighréad's miserable existence and eventual suicide, and of Mark Salers' arrest and conviction in April 1985 for grievous bodily harm. Salers was subsequently given a fifteen-year prison sentence of which he served five years. Upon his release, Salers began a relentless persecution of Hannah Petersen, which took the form of persistent stalking. Salers' obsession was such that when Petersen left England for India a year later Salers followed her there and continued to pursue her. In India Salers finally succumbed to the tuberculosis with which he had been infected during his time in prison, but before he died, he made certain statements to Petersen, in which among other things, he asserted that he had never abused Maighréad Salers. The book, which he completed shortly before his death, was a vulgar and abhorrent attempt to expose his conviction as a miscarriage of justice.

Hannah Petersen spent the next two years in Sri Lanka, then returned to England in order to begin research on A Matter of Fact. One would question the wisdom of this venture. Surely Salers' ravings would have been better off ignored? The first part of the somewhat curiously set out document is devoted to the events that took place between the time of Salers' release and Petersen's departure for India. The eloquent style of her writing takes the reader graphically into the nightmare world of her persecution at Salers' hands, filled with shadows and terrifying events that were at the time inexplicable, and brushed aside by a cynical police force. Matters were further complicated by the unrelated arrest of a private investigator recruited to spy on Petersen by American psychiatrist Elliot Bannerman, whose fraudulent activities were exposed in Petersen's book Fair Game. The account ends with Salers' gruesome demise in India, which he compelled the unfortunate Petersen to witness.

The second half of the book is an attempt to establish the truth about Mark and the mysterious Maighréad Salers. Whether it succeeds in doing so is for the reader to determine but, if nothing else, it demonstrates that truth, like a gob-stopper, is multi-layered, and may be swallowed by mistake before its core is reached.

Ashok, now bolt upright, let the paper drop onto the ground. No, he thought. Two years in Sri Lanka and then back to England?

How could God have allowed this? He must have practically brushed past her, as they swapped continents.

'Ashok,' his mother called, 'Come, you will be late.'

Shit! Shit, shit, shit! Ashok picked up the paper and screwed it up into a tiny, hard ball, before flinging it into the rubbish bin. Two years late. She's probably married and I'm practically married. Ah well, no use brooding on what might have been. At least I know she's safe. Better come to terms with it and get on with life.

Life, in fact, had not been so bad since Ashok's return home. He had quickly established an enviable reputation at Shanti Sagar hospital. His capacity for hard work was undiminished, and despite working long hours at the hospital, he had found time, with the help of the charity Third World Action, to establish a monthly mobile eye-camp, where the city's poor could be treated free of charge. As well as sight tests, the provision of free spectacles and treatment for infections and other minor ailments, routine operations such as cataract-removal were carried out at the camp. The fame of Dr Rao's eye-camp quickly spread, and soon his name was known throughout Bangalore. Ashok threw himself wholeheartedly into this venture. Through his persuasive charm, he managed to enlist the help of an army of doctors and nurses, so that the camp's working hours could be gradually extended, and it became weekly.

'You know, we are very proud of your work at eye-camp.' Lakshmi Devi said to Ashok, one evening when he was visiting her in her rooms.

Ashok looked at the floor, slightly embarrassed. 'That's not why I do it, *Ajji*. But it makes me happy that you approve of my work. Believe me, there are many who are looking down their noses at me. It seems it is not fashionable these days to occupy so much of one's time in helping the helpless, instead of setting one's mind on making more money than one could ever use.'

The old lady bobbed her head approvingly. 'After all, you are earning enough at hospital to ensure a comfortable life for us all - and for you and Janaki when you are married.'

Ashok avoided her glance. The conversation was heading in the wrong direction.

'Remember when I was a child, *Ajji*? The ancient tales you used to tell? They made me realise that things that are supposed to happen will happen, however impossible they seem. So it is thanks to you that this dream came true.'

For an instant he thought he saw tears in the old lady's eyes.

'But tell me, Ashok,' she said. 'Where did that dream come from? Why *did* you decide to open camp?'

'Mm. Why? You know, *Ajji*, some foolish things I have done in my life. Things that I would do differently if God gave me a second chance. But in life we rarely get second chances, no? So, perhaps this is my penance.' He laughed. 'I am lucky that something that set out to be a penance has turned out to be so rewarding.'

'And what were these foolish things? Will you humour a curious old woman, by telling?'

'Well.' He paused for a moment. It was so difficult not having a soul mate, no one to whom he could open his heart. He and *Ajji* had always been close. But would she understand? He decided to tread carefully. 'There was a girl once. Long ago, in Oxford. Perhaps I misunderstood her. And because of that, it could be that others were suffering terrible consequences. If only I had not been so blind, so much evil might have been avoided.'

'As an eye specialist, my boy, I am surprised that you do not understand that blindness cannot always be avoided.'

'Some people are blind, *Ajji*, because they do not want to see, they refuse to open their eyes. Maybe I was like that.'

Lakshmi Devi looked at him gravely. Carefully she continued. 'And the Englishwoman who came here, to Bangalore? Are you serving your penance because of her, too?'

'I don't know. Maybe.' He left it at that and Lakshmi Devi had the sense not to push it further. Later, swinging in the hammock under the stars, Ashok thought about it, as he had so many times before.

As far as Maighréad goes, Hannah and I are quits, I think. If we were blind, we were equally so, *ergo* equally responsible for subsequent events. But is it my fault that Hannah left me? I know I was weak in those days. I couldn't see my way clearly. I was a person of two worlds - and they were tearing me in opposite directions. Perhaps Hannah could detect my confusion and was afraid that I'd let her down in the end. Who could blame her?

In line with Ashok's success in his career, his relationship with Janaki was gently prodded into something that was acceptable. She was due to complete her PhD at the Biotechnology University in January. Both sets of parents started talking about a possible wedding the following March. Ashok and Janaki let them talk. Neither of them displayed any positive or negative feelings towards the idea. Once a week, Janaki came to Ashok's parents' house to eat with them, though Ashok noticed that she spent more time in the kitchen with his mother preparing the food, than she did sitting with him, eating it. Perhaps I'm still too used to English ways, he told himself. Occasionally he would call in on her at the University. She worked incredibly hard, and could be found at the bench at all hours of the day and night. Dedicated, thought Ashok, and smiled at the thought that she was more dedicated to science than to him. It didn't worry him. At least she'll never turn into a grovelling little *Hausfrau*, he decided, despite his mother's best efforts. Luckily they would be able to afford a cook.

When he called in on her at the lab, he caused a flurry of excitement among the other female students. By now everyone had heard of the saintly (and gorgeous) Dr Ashok. Janaki had acquired a certain status because of her association with him. She shrugged this off. 'Don't admire me because of him. I want to be admired for my own achievements - and I will one day, you'll see.'

No one doubted her words. Janaki was becoming a formidably brilliant scientist. On the occasions when he called, Ashok would drag her away from the bench down to the campus coffee bar where she would grant him ten minutes audience over a hot, milky coffee before excusing herself and rushing back to her work. If he had time Ashok would amble over to the bedraggled old garden. The bench, where he and Hannah had sat, was gone, reabsorbed into the moist, pungent earth. He would wander among the bougainvillaea, remembering the bittersweet moments they had spent together in this place. It was an effort then to refocus on the present, and head back to the hospital or the eye-camp.

It irked him that Janaki refused to visit the eye-camp.

'Ah no,' she laughed. 'You can get your hands dirty, Ashok, not me. I couldn't be doing with all that sickness and misery.'

Three weeks after Ashok had read the review of Hannah's book, Janaki telephoned him at the hospital and asked to see him urgently.

They met at the coffee bar, under the kapok tree.

'What is it that is so important that it cannot wait?'

Janaki contemplated her steel beaker silently for a moment, then looked him straight in the eye.

'I have been offered a very good three-year post-doc, Ashok.'

'Oh? Where?'

Another slightly awkward pause.

'It is at UCLA. In America.'

'I know where UCLA is, Jan. So, I take it you intend to accept?'

'That is why I needed to talk urgently with you. It will mean removing to US. Is this acceptable to you?'

'You must do as you see fit.'

'I am thinking of you, Ashok. You will have fantastic opportunities in LA, I am told.'

'Jan,' Ashok looked at her seriously. 'I don't want fantastic opportunities in LA. I have all I want here. You will have to choose. Is it to be marriage, or is it to be research in US? We have waited long enough. Another three years would be absurd, no?'

She nodded slowly. 'Yes. Especially for you. I am still young. It would be unfair to be expecting you to wait yet longer for me. I'm so sorry, Ashok, but I must accept that post-doc.'

'I understand. Really, I do.' Why am I not more upset, he asked himself.

'I think you do,' Janaki replied, and continued carefully, 'I think this is best for both of us, isn't it?'

'Perhaps you are right. But I am wondering - how on earth do we tell our parents?'

They broke into laughter, and Ashok suddenly felt a slight twinge of regret.

Ashok's premonitions were correct. The breaking of their commitment caused a storm. His parents were vitriolic towards Janaki, blaming her unfeminine aspirations for the whole thing. It took a great deal of persuasion on Ashok's part to calm them, and to convince them that the decision had been mutual. Lakshmi Devi alone understood, without being told, that Ashok had been a little too ready to agree to break off the relationship. It took several diplomatic missions to Janaki's parents too, to lift them from the mortification and shame that they felt at what they perceived as their daughter's outrageous behaviour.

In November Ashok received a letter from his sister Priya in Winnipeg.

My dear brother,

I hope you are keeping well. I am thinking very frequently these days of the lovely sunshine and warm weather back home, when here it is already becoming so cold now that breath freezes, and we are all obliged to wrap up in layers of fur.

The reason for my writing to you this day is not easy. Amma has informed me of breaking with Janaki and I want to tell how much it grieves me. It was my understanding and fervent hope that you two were most happy with one another, that this was match made in heaven, as astrologers had told. However it was not to be. Amma was telling that both Janaki and you had come to that decision, and that you were not agreeable to removing to US, in spite of good career opportunities.

Since I have received Amma's letter, I am asking myself all the time, WHY? What was going wrong?

Now I am coming to most difficult part. You see, I am wondering what would have happened if that English lady, Hannah, had not left you so suddenly in Bangalore. Would you have married her and been happy?

I hope you will forgive me for what I am writing now. Please believe that I was acting for best intentions. That is what I was thinking at least, when I paid visit to your English friend on that afternoon when you were taking parcels to mother-in-law of your friend, Dr Patel.

I was absolutely certain from what Bapa was telling, that your forthcoming marriage was all but settled. He and Amma were so happy about it, Ashok. Then you are coming along and telling about going to Kerala. Our parents were terribly worried, thinking that you will be going with that English lady, and how to explain to Janaki's parents and all. And you were so strange in behaviour, Ashok. As though family was not important. These were the reasons why I went to Chamundi Hotel and asked for room number of an English lady called Hannah, friend of Dr Ashok Rao. This they were finding quickly. I was very nervous and nearly went home again, but then I thought of Bapa and Amma and of what would be best for you, and I went up to her room. She was most surprised when I was telling who I was, but - this is what was bad - I liked her very much. I am sorry but I think I made her very sad when I was telling that marriage was already arranged for you with local girl. She is a proud lady though, Ashok, and was strong to hide her feelings. I did not stay long as she was in no mood for conversation with me, except that she could not help herself but to say 'I knew he was hiding something. This is why he did not want that I should meet his family.'

My dearest brother, now I am thinking that what I did was very, very wrong. I did not realise you were not committed to Janaki at that time, that it was Bapa's wishful thinking. However, I was sure it had all worked out for best when you two did decide to go ahead with marriage. Now I know we were all deluding ourselves.

This secret was a great burden to me and although I fear it is too late for you and Hannah, I hope you will find it in your heart to forgive the actions of your foolish and misapprehending little sister. Harsha and I are so happy that it is very painful for me to think that I myself may have prevented my darling brother from same chance of happiness in marriage. Please write, forgiving me, for the sake of your little nephew Rahul. I have been telling him so much about his famous uncle Ashok.

Your sister,

Priya.

P.S. Some weeks past I have read in Weekly Guardian about a writer, Hannah Petersen, who was in India at that time when all this happened. Could it be possible this was same Hannah you knew?

When Ashok had read the letter, he folded it neatly, put it in the drawer of his desk, and went out of the house. He headed out along Eighteenth Cross Road and turned onto Margosa Road, not bothering, in his daze to sidestep the rotten hand-cart debris littering the pavement. When he reached Mariamma Circle, he walked, stumbling occasionally on the uneven surface past the science institutions and research parks until he came to the entrance gate to the BT University, and here he turned in. He made his way, still stupefied, to the old campus garden. For the next hour he ambled slowly along its overgrown paths, oblivious to burning sunrays, buzzing insects and even to the sudden lightning plunge into the undergrowth of a terrified green snake that had been basking on the stones until his presence disturbed it.

When he finally returned home, he sat down at his desk, the same fine desk that had been in his flat in Richmond, one of the few items of furniture that he had bothered to ship out to India after he had sold the flat. He pulled out a pen and an airmail letter and started to write.

Dear Priya, he began. And then he stopped. He'd had it all worked out in his mind, as he walked through the campus garden; but now, now that he actually had to write it down, words would not come. He forced himself to try again.

Dear Priya,

When I read your letter I found it most hurtful and shocking, and I was, at first, very angry with you for meddling in my affairs and interfering in things about which you know nothing. But then I realised that the fault is not only yours, but equally mine. I was to blame, because I had not been honest with you or with Hannah. She was correct in suspecting that I did not want her to be meeting you all. I wanted first to remove the obstacle of the suggested marriage to Janaki and to tell our parents of my intention to marry Hannah. But because I could not find the words I kept delaying until finally she had gone.

You say it is too late for Hannah and me, and this doubtless is true. But she also deserves to know the truth about what happened. You were quite right about the book review that you read in the Guardian - it was indeed the same Hannah. So now perhaps you will understand why I was preoccupied. It was not because of lack of love for you all, but because of the terrible ordeal that she was going through. I now know also why for two years I was unable to trace her, since she was in Sri Lanka, and that she is now back in England.

With this in mind I will be travelling to England as soon as possible so that she can learn the truth from me with the help of your letter.

As for forgiving you, well, you have hurt me greatly, but I have hurt myself more, I think. Let us put this behind us for the sake of the family. Please convey my best wishes to Harsha, and give little Rahul a great big hug from his uncle.

Yours,

Ashok

CHAPTER 19

Ashok booked into the Cumberland in the late afternoon. The pretentiousness of the place irked him but he'd had little choice. London in late December was choc-a-bloc. Only the luxury hotels were, at hugely inflated prices over the festive season, able to offer any accommodation at all. Or so the travel agent in Bangalore had told him.

It was bitterly cold, and the darkening sky was crystalline. He made arrangements with the hotel reception to take delivery of a hire car the following morning, and then went for a walk. London was humming with life, even in winter. The shops were still full of Christmas hype, and in addition the city was gearing itself up for New Year's Eve, a few days hence. No doubt Oxford Street would be impassable at night, when the lights were switched on. He made a mental note to stay in. He was far too nervous about his mission to be able to appreciate the razzmatazz.

Back in his hotel room, he lay down on his bed and opened the book that he had managed, after much searching, to track down at a fringe bookshop round the corner. It was more of a booklet really, hyped up in a glossy red hardback cover. Its title: *In the Name of Love*. The author: Mark Salers.

He wondered why he'd never seen it for sale in Bangalore. It had never occurred to him to order it from UK. He hadn't wanted to know - then. After all, what could it tell him? Merely a pack of lies. Nothing to throw light on Hannah's disappearance. Now? Now, it was different. Now he had a sudden urge to get into the lunatic's mind, to confront Hannah with understanding, and not with ignorance.

The style was sensationalist. Designed to appeal to the lowest common denominator of humanity, Ashok mused. Full of exaggerations and untruths. Salers maintained that, as he had told Hannah, Maighréad had been born in Belfast to an unmarried Dublin girl of fifteen. She was raised in a Belfast orphanage. When she was eighteen she met and married Mark Salers, twelve years her senior, having convinced him that her parents had been killed by a Loyalist bomb when she was fifteen. Only Salers didn't let it rest. He wanted to get to the truth. So he investigated. He maintained that when she found out what he was doing, she started abusing her own body, and telling others that he, Mark had done it to her.

At this time also, I discovered that my wife was involved in a relationship with the lesbian writer Hannah Petersen. Petersen was not only encouraging Maighréad in her self-mutilation, but helping her to achieve it. It became clear to me that not all of Maighréad's wounds could have been self-inflicted. No, of course not. Because they were inflicted by Hannah Petersen. It was all part of a plot to discredit me, to have me arrested and put away, as I was an obstacle that got in the way of their plans.

Ashok had to stop reading. Filled with disgust at the monster's raving, he got up and helped himself to a whisky from the minibar. For a few moments he let the fiery liquid revitalise his pounded mind.

Reluctantly he picked the book up again and leafed through the next few pages. He came to the section that concerned the trial.

In prison I was often asked why I did not speak out at the time. There is no mystery about this. I loved Maighréad, so I kept silent while she was alive. I was convinced that she would come through for me in the end. Perhaps it was necessary for her to witness my suffering in order to come to terms with her own guilt. In the end, she could no longer live with what she had done to me.

Ashok put down the book and poured himself a second whisky. Absurdly, he suddenly craved a cigarette. He hadn't smoked since he had held the obligatory Havana between his fingers at May Ball in Oxford. He shook off the idea.

He took up the book again and turned to the section headed Hannah Petersen.

Hannah Petersen was born in London in 1960, the daughter of Miryam Rosen and Christian Petersen, a Danish archeaologist.

A much older brother converted to Buddhism and retreated to a hermitage in Sri Lanka.

Older brother? Hannah never mentioned that. What rot.

He skimmed through the rest of the book to make sure he hadn't missed anything important. Something near the end caught his eye.

... escaped from the clutches of Hannah Petersen simply to fall into equally treacherous hands, those of an Indian doctor, who took advantage of her once I was out of the way, and whose treatment of her resulted in depression and self-doubt. To get away from this man she fled back to the place where she and I had been happy. It was in Belfast that she finally confronted her guilt. However, instead of confessing and thereby securing my release, she was so disturbed as a consequence of her treatment by her two lovers that she took her own life.

Her suicide note, with its biblical quotation was intended to prove my innocence and acknowledge the guilt of her actions.

'Come let us take our fill of love until the morning: let us solace ourselves with loves... For the good man is not at home, he is gone a long journey;' Proverbs Chapter 7.

Chapter 7 of the Book of Proverbs is a warning against the adulteress, which ends with the following words:-

For she hath cast down many wounded: yes, many strong men have been slain by her. Her house is the way to hell, going down to the chambers of death.

Ashok threw the book down in disgust. The hateful thing seemed to stab at his eyes whenever he looked at it. The fact was the man had obviously been completely psychotic when he wrote it. How could any decent publishing company have considered it?

He looked at the publisher's insignia. Ah, Shining Light. That explains it. A sensationalist, unscrupulous, fringe publisher. Fighting revulsion he picked it up again and spent the next twenty minutes systematically tearing it into tiny shreds, which he flushed bit by bit down the toilet.

*　　*　　*

The falling snow and the unaccustomed Ford Escort made Ashok drive cautiously, despite his impatience. Due to the bad weather, the car had been delivered late to the hotel. It was almost eleven before he had managed to get away. Now it took nearly two hours to reach Burfold. By the time he got there his nerves were on edge. He parked in the car park of the Red Fox. He was reminded of his first bitter visit to the village in similar weather. Would today bring a happier conclusion? He walked through the driving snow past the frozen duck pond, along the green and turned up Drake Lane. As he passed the tweedy man's house, Bert the obese spaniel staggered down to the gate, his ears stiff as stalactites and greeted him with a furiously wagging tail. Ashok stopped to pat him. 'Glad to see you're still around, old chap.' Somehow, seeing the dog seemed a good sign. Ashok felt at home.

And suddenly, there was the cottage. He stopped at the gate and stared. It was just the same - and yet different somehow. Then he realised that Hannah must have had a clean up. The peeling paint had been replaced. The trees had been pruned, and the drive re-laid in tarmac. Cautiously Ashok opened the newly painted gate. He felt his heart beating with such force that it was likely to push him over. He reached the front door, hesitated for an instant, pulled himself together and knocked. The wait seemed interminable. He knocked again. A woman's voice. 'Yes, yes. Just coming.' The door opened.

For several seconds they stood like statues just staring at each other. Ashok broke the silence.

'You,' he breathed.

'*Namaste*, Ashok.' A pause, then, 'you'd better come on in.'

Stumbling in his confusion, Ashok followed Felicity into the hall.

'You're wet. Give me your jacket.' Blindly he obeyed. 'Come on,' she continued, 'let's go into the living room.'

'Sit down,' she said, but he shook his head.

'Where's Hannah?'

'She's not here, Ashok - as you can see.'

'What the hell's going on? What are you doing here?'

'I work for Hannah. I've been helping her with her book - about Mark. And I'm looking after the cottage while she's away.'

Ashok couldn't take it in. Felicity in Hannah's house? There was no mistaking her. She had filled out a little, and her hair had reverted to its natural blonde colour, but for a moment he saw again the young woman who had walked with Duncan Forbes into the twenty-four hour bistro at the Chamundi, and impressed him with her composure.

Ashok said, 'Where is she?'

The telephone in the hall rang. Felicity went out to answer it.

Ashok looked anxiously around the room. He didn't know what he was looking for. A sign that would link Hannah to him; something perhaps that would give him hope, would tell him that India still had a place in her heart. He'd been standing facing the French window, with his back to Hannah's desk in the far corner. Now as he turned, he saw the desk. He stared at it, spellbound. For there, expensively framed and hanging above it, just as it had hung above his own, was his old poster of Ganesh. And as if that were not enough, he then spotted, sitting on the desk, the blue-grey soapstone Ganesh that he had bought her that day long ago at Mamallapuram. He could still picture it so clearly. *It's yours. So that you'll remember Mamallapuram.'* And her reply. *'I'll treasure it. But do you really think I could forget today?'*

He felt his eyes brimming over, but then, just as Felicity came back into the room carrying two bottles and glasses, he saw on the desk something else that completely engulfed him.

'Who,' he said slowly, 'is that child in the picture with Hannah?'

Felicity placed the glasses on the coffee table.

'Cognac or would you prefer whisky?'

'Felicity...'

Undaunted, she poured out two cognacs and offered one to Ashok. 'You'd better drink this.'

Angrily he shook his head. Felicity put the glass back on the table and sat down, cradling her own glass in her hand.

'That's Siddarth. Hannah's son.'

Bewilderment. Incomprehension. Disbelief. 'Son? Siddarth? When...?'

Once again Felicity calmly handed Ashok the brandy glass. This time he took it, with shaking hands.

'Siddarth was born in Sri Lanka, Ashok.'

'He's... he's Sri Lankan?'

'I think you'll have to ask her that. It's not really for me to say.' But she was smiling at him, quite tenderly. Silently Ashok drained his glass and Felicity poured them both another.

'I can't ask her anything if you don't tell me where she is.'

'Why, after all this time do you think she'll want to see you?'

Ashok's mind was still cauterised by the news he'd just received. He struggled to explain to Felicity, as coherently as possible about Priya's letter.

'Look,' he added, 'I know she'd want to see me if she knew. Look at this room.' He waved his hand in the direction of the desk. 'It's obvious she must still care for me.'

'OK, Ashok, I think you deserve a chance to put your case. You realise she'll probably kill me for this? Ah well. So be it. Hannah's taken Siddarth to India.'

No, thought Ashok. This can't be happening. 'Where in India?'

'Well she didn't exactly say where she'd be at any particular time. You know what she's like when she takes off. Secretive. She likes to get away from it all.'

Ashok nodded.

'She did say though something about the honeymoon she never had. She wanted to take Siddarth there over New Year.'

'Kerala. She's going to Cochin. Thanks, Felicity. I owe you.' He stood up, with the unsteady pitch of a recently KO'd boxer.

292

'What are you going to do?'

'Back to my hotel, pick up my bag, airport.'

'Now steady on, old man. You're all hopped up. You shouldn't be driving anywhere. In any case by the time you get back, it'll be too late for a flight today.'

She was right. He shouldn't be driving.

'I'll drive you to the airport early tomorrow morning. Today you're going nowhere. You can stay here tonight.'

By now he was ready to agree to anything.

'OK,' he heard himself saying through lips unwilling to be mustered into speech, 'tomorrow it is.'

Felicity nodded. He watched her as she poured him a whisky.

'That was Duncan on the phone, earlier. I didn't tell him you were here. I thought you'd prefer him not to know. In any case,' she grinned, 'I thought he might get jealous if he knew you were here with me.'

He grimaced. 'Duncan? Ugh! Felicity, really. Not again! Not that bozo.'

'Hey! Watch it, you. He's all right really. It's a good thing he's in New York till the weekend though, isn't it?'

'Tell me, why did you help Hannah? I thought you were so devoted to Mark?'

'Why?' She gave a harsh laugh. 'It's all in Hannah's book, Ashok. If you can bear to read it.'

*　*　*

Once on board the aircraft, Ashok stretched out in First Class comfort and tried to sleep. But the headache was too insistent, like a warning signal in his brain. His euphoria of the previous day had fled with the remaining traces of alcohol, leaving a sense of let down and uncertainty. All this way and she wasn't even there. And a son. Whose? A dark child, yes, but could just as easily be Sri Lankan as Indian. That the child might be his was a possibility too charged to risk consideration. Then - what if Kerala was a bad guess? Maybe she had another honeymoon in mind. Who knows what happened during the last four years.

To distract himself from his discomfort he opened the copy of *As a Matter of Fact* that Felicity had thrust into his hand as a parting shot. He opened it with some misgiving. Wasn't it futile to dredge up the past? According to the *Guardian* review the book had revealed no definitive answers. Nevertheless he started to leaf through it, and gradually became so absorbed that the headache backed off grudgingly like a discarded lover. The first part of the book yielded no surprises. Ashok knew every word of Hannah's story up to the time she had arrived in Bangalore. After that it continued, selectively, until Salers' death. The facts were reproduced with chilling objectivity. Some details, too personal for public airing, were left out or disguised. Several names had been changed or omitted, *to ensure the privacy of those concerned*, as Hannah explained in her preface. Willi and Ashok had mutated to become one person, a woman whom Hannah had called Beattie, and the sequence of some events, and some minor details, had been changed to make this plausible. The feeling of discomfort briefly returned. Why a woman? Why couldn't they have been combined into masculine form? Surely he was more masculine than Willi was feminine? Was there a message in this? Ashok swallowed hard and read on, struggling to overcome his aversion. He found no mention of Duncan, other than as Hannah's publisher, or of Felicity. They were irrelevant to the events that had directly involved Hannah. Thus she had included her encounters at Golconda, Beattie's incarceration, the snake in Beattie's bag and Beattie's sighting of Salers on the train, the falling rock, the stolen film, and all that had occurred between their arrival in Bandipur and Salers' demise at Nanjangud. It was Beattie alone who was involved in the final moments of Salers' life, which were handled with cold detachment. This section concluded with some information about the gun.

It was an early 9 mm Beretta automatic circa 1935 that appeared to have started life as a sidearm in the Italian Militia. Where Salers obtained it is uncertain, but it is clear that he had many contacts in Hyderabad and Chennai. Due to its poor condition its trigger mechanism was unreliable. This accounted for the few seconds' delay that gave Beattie the opportunity to disarm Salers.

The rest of the book was an attempt to disentangle the facts of Salers' life from the fiction. It was now that Ashok straightened up his posture-contoured, ultra-snug-pile backrest and dug deeply into the cocktail of disclosures, hypotheses and conclusions that Hannah presented. Felicity's input had been vital. Facts, hitherto unreported, emerged about Salers' youth in India. Facts, which Felicity, in her blind devotion to Mark, had suppressed for all of her adult life. A drunken, depressed father, who was frequently and, at the time inexplicably, absent. A weak, dominated mother, who disliked her son, and lavished all her love and attention on her daughter. And something else that Felicity had blocked out, but that Hannah half-coaxed into the open. A faint memory of Mark taking comfort in Felicity's bed, when she was too young to understand. It stopped when she was six, and the exact truth remained locked in Felicity's mind. Hannah was convinced that that this went some way to explaining Mark's hold over Felicity. She also postulated that his early days contained ingredients that could, arguably, given the catalyst of imprisonment have bonded together into a psychosis.

Ashok closed the book. Enough, he told himself. He knew that if he read on, he might discover more about Maighréad. Where was she born? Who were her parents? Were they killed by a Loyalist bomb? Ashok though had no stomach for further revelations, further enigmas, further doubts. So what? He said to himself, so fucking what?

He closed his eyes, but sleep evaded him. An image of Janaki started to urge itself into his mind. He tried to shut it out, but it persisted. 'What would have happened,' she was asking, in that forceful, direct manner of hers, 'if I hadn't gone to LA? Would you still be on this mission to find Hannah?'

Ashok opened his eyes with a start, and tried to push Janaki out of his thoughts. Some questions are best left unanswered. But her question kept tugging at his mind until the answer came to him: this whole sequence of events was meant to be. If Janaki hadn't left him, Priya wouldn't have made her confession. He would never have known about her visit to Hannah. He felt a surge of excitement. Now he knew beyond a doubt that he would find her.

'Your book fell down, sir' said the steward handing *As a Matter of Fact* to him. 'You'd left it balanced on the armrest.'

'Thanks.' Ashok took the book back and started, almost mechanically, to thumb through it again.

Maighréad always maintained that Loyalists killed her parents, he read, and nodded to himself, remembering that she had told him the same.

According to Mark Salers, on the other hand, she grew up in an orphanage in Belfast. Neither version tells the true story.

Through my enquiries I was able to ascertain that Maighréad was indeed placed in an orphanage for the first five years of her life. At the age of five she was adopted by a Belfast couple. Her adoptive parents were killed in a bomb attack in Belfast city centre when she was fifteen. Maighréad was there, but unhurt. Mark Salers was one of the first reporters on the scene. He married her three years later.

Bingo. So she was telling the truth. I'm not that bad a judge of character. But hang on - what did Hannah mean - Neither version tells the true story?

Further investigation, however, revealed that it was not a Loyalist bomb that killed her parents. The bomb had been planted by the IRA. Why did Maighréad lie to me? I can only conclude that the truth was too painful for her, a Catholic girl, to acknowledge.

Ashok nodded to himself. In spite of this latest snippet, it was all beginning to make sense now. Maighréad gets dumped at the orphanage, is then adopted, her parents are killed in a bomb attack, and Salers comes to the rescue. After he marries her he starts roughing her up. This sort of behaviour, remembered Ashok, coaxing his mind back into the contents of his undergrad psychiatry course, can often be completely detached from a person's genuine feelings for their partner. It would appear that Salers was really obsessed with Maighréad, and flipped when Hannah rescued her from his clutches. Up until his conviction he remained sure that Maighréad would retract her accusations. When she didn't and he was hauled off to the Scrubs, it was the final straw. After that all he wanted was revenge against Hannah. Meanwhile Maighréad's traumas caught up with her, despite his (Ashok's) best efforts. When she died, Salers was freed from the need to keep silent, and was able to fabricate the lies about her and spice these up with lies about Hannah. By this time the man was psychotic and probably believed them. Ashok felt a surge of relief. They'd been right all along, he and Hannah. They hadn't lived a lie.

He flicked through the book again and came to a chapter entitled *Did Mark Salers abuse Maighréad?* It was based on interviews Hannah had conducted with some of Maighréad's friends from her teenage years. One of them quoted an occasion when Maighréad had come in with a black eye and said she'd run into a door.

Could this be taken as evidence of self-abuse? Well, if you dig deeply enough you can read anything into anything to prove a point. However, weigh that against Salers' character: his record of cruelty, his instability, his obsessive behaviour. Weigh that one incident against the lack of any other incidents that could be construed as self-induced injury. I can only conclude that in my opinion, based on all these facts, and my own first-hand observations, Mark Salers was guilty of inflicting abuse of the most horrific nature on his innocent, and vulnerable young wife.

Ashok suddenly felt drained. For the first time in years an image of Maighréad standing in the hospital corridor seared into his mind. She'd called in to see him at the John Radcliffe, and was holding a bloodied handkerchief to her nose. 'Damn,'she was saying. 'Someone just swung the door into my face.' Then the image faded.

This, thought Ashok, is one secret that I'll keep from Hannah. Forever.

CHAPTER 20

It seemed as if the train journey to Cochin would never end. Ashok arrived in Ernakulam, Cochin's grimy, modern Doppelgänger, hot and exhausted in the pitch-blackness of a late, tropical night. A silver sliver of moon lent no light. He made his way down to the harbour, and realised that the huge, black shapes looming out of the darkness to the right meant that he had somehow ended up to the left of what appeared to be an impenetrable storage depot. He should have been on the other side, from where the boats to the island ferried guests across the bay. When he reached the water's edge he could make out a quay in the distance, dimly illuminated by the glowing neon insignia of the nearby Seagull Hotel, but he could see no way of traversing the massive industrial area, packed with cranes, containers, and warehouses. In any case, there were no lights around the quay itself. Ashok guessed that the boats had stopped for the night.

He stood for a moment, wondering what to do. He could go back to the road, get an auto to the Seagull Hotel, spend the night there, and make the journey to the island tomorrow morning. There seemed no alternative. He was desperately disappointed. If only there were some way.

Suddenly the silent night was shattered by an unearthly clamour, like an army of deranged *roti* beaters. A primitive sound perfectly suited to the decrepit little wreck that now loomed out of the night and made fast at a small jetty that Ashok hadn't previously noticed. The boat stank of creosote, oil and rotting garbage. A figure emerged from the shack that masqueraded as a cabin, and called across to Ashok.

Ashok shrugged and shook his head. Sorry, don't speak Malayalam. Still the character persisted, shouting urgently at Ashok across the din of the ancient engine.

Is he offering me a lift, I wonder? 'Residency Island?' he called back.

The man wobbled his head affirmatively, and held up ten fingers.

'Ten rupees?' called Ashok. Another wobble. The man held out a calloused hand to help Ashok on board, guiding him down a couple of steps into the cabin. Without further ado, they cast off.

Ashok surveyed his saviour warily as the boat pulled away into the blackness. A real cutthroat. Was he really only after ten rupees? It seemed unlikely. He felt around with his feet and located a loose piece of planking. If it came to an attack he would have to make a lunge for it. At least he stood a fighting chance. But the man was thickset despite being a foot shorter than Ashok. A life at sea had turned his muscles to steel. Ashok imagined the headlines. 'Body of Eminent Ophthalmologist washed up on beach in Kerala.' It was with some relief that Ashok saw that the boat was indeed heading out towards Residency Island.

They couldn't dock directly at the island. A pontoon of ferries was moored between them and quay. Ashok had to negotiate these in the blackness, struggling across each one to step over into the next. Was that the fourth or fifth? He lost count. Finally he hauled his exhausted body onto the shore.

He could see the lights of the Resident's Palace shining through the treetops in the distance. He felt a twinge of guilt-ridden familiarity. It was here that Willi's eager body had consoled him when he had lost Hannah four years and a lifetime ago. Another secret to be kept from her.

The palace, a run-down affair largely composed of timber, had once belonged to an English Resident, and now provided rooms for unfussy, adventurous travellers who were not pushed for time.

He stood, looking at the warm glow from the windows and wondering. Is Hannah in one of those rooms? Is there less than half a mile between us? His heart was beating fast now, and he felt weak with anticipation. He forced his legs to take him down the path through the trees to his destination, to his destiny.

Inside the palace, the lights were dimmer than they appeared from outside. The reception desk was manned by a sleepy night watchman, whom Ashok startled into life, and who viewed him with the terror of one who has just seen a ghost materialise at the foot of his bed. Ashok glanced at the clock over the reception desk. *Ten past eleven!* He had no idea that it was so late.

'From where you are coming at this hour?' demanded the night watch.

'From UK,' replied Ashok, watching the man's mouth drop open in shock. 'I'm looking for Miss Hannah Petersen. Is she staying here?'

The man consulted the guest register, all the time casting nervous glances at Ashok.

'Mr and Mrs Petersen were here. They left today.'

Ashok's heart nearly stopped. 'Mr and Mrs Petersen? Let me see that?' He snatched the register off the man and whirled it round to face him. The entry showed that Hannah and Siddarth Petersen had arrived on the twenty-ninth, yesterday. Ashok's sigh of relief was audible. 'Not Mr and Mrs, you fool! Hannah Petersen and Siddarth Petersen. Siddarth is a small child. Hardly a Mr.'

The man looked offended and bristled with hostility. Damn, thought Ashok, cursing himself for his rudeness. 'Look,' he said, 'I'm sorry. I'm very tired. Could you tell me where they've gone?'

The man looked dubious. 'She was only saying, sir, she would spent some nights in Ernakulum.'

Ashok could scarcely credit it. All this way and she'd gone. He forced himself to fight back his frustration. After all, she hadn't gone far. Tomorrow, he would find her. Right now, disappointment and jet lag had got the better of him. He turned to the smug-faced night watchman.

'Well, could you fix me up with a room for the night? I can't get back to Ernakulam now.'

'So sorry, sir, all rooms taken.' Ashok detected the triumphant tone of one who has the upper hand.

'Then tell me. What am I to do? I can't stay here, it seems. And I can't get away.'

Night watch shrugged. 'Nothing to be done, sir. So sorry.'

Confound the fellow. Exhaustion and disappointment overwhelmed Ashok.

'Look,' he said, 'all I need is a bed for the night. You can put me in the boathouse for all I care. Just get me a bed.' He plunged his hand into his pocket and brought out a well-stuffed wallet, which he placed nonchalantly on the counter.

'Well, there is one room unoccupied, sir. But bed is not yet made. Room is not yet cleaned.'

As soon as Ashok entered the room, he felt Hannah's presence stamped upon it. The lingering scent of her perfume hung in the heavy, still air. *Fleurs de Provence* thought Ashok. Still the same. He stood for a moment and glanced around him. Other than the perfume he detected no tangible evidence left of Hannah.

As he pulled back the blanket and fell wearily onto the bed, his shoulder caught on something hard. A book. He picked it up. It was R.K.Narayan's *Gods, Demons and Others*. Ashok remembered recommending the book to Hannah. He opened it. Hannah had written something inside the front cover.

The murderous cut of time
the guarded hand of love
such mysteries of the inner self
of which the heart alone can tell.
All these and so much more
within the moon's complexion dwell.

He fought back tears.

As he leafed through the pages something fell out of it. He felt his heart quicken. It was a photograph. Ashok remembered Willi taking it with Hannah's camera. He and Hannah together outside their room at the Pandava Hotel in Chennai.

*   *   *

There were over fifty elephants on the Maharaja's College Ground: temple elephants, gathered together for a monumental celebration, a fair for locals and tourists. The line of elephants fanned outwards in a huge semicircle, according to size, the largest in the centre. Each was festively attired in gold livery and coloured parasols. In front of them was a pandimelam band, which looked to Hannah to be composed of an array of strange wind instruments. The sound they made briefly took her back to another band and a wedding in Madras.

'Sounds more like pandemonium to me,' she shouted to her delighted son. 'What a raucous din! But I suppose that's only because we're not used to it.'

As they made their way across to a large grandstand at the far end of the field, Hannah was aware that their progress was being watched by a group of white-clothed officials at the entrance to the grandstand. Not surprising, she thought. Hers was the only European face in a sea of several thousand Indians.

'Hallo, Madam!' A well padded, carefully coiffed woman stepped out from the group. 'We would like the little boy to open fair, please.'

'What? Open the fair? How?'

'He will please make an offering of sugar cane to lead elephant. It will be very nice. Then Chief Minister of Kerala will speak. You both sit here, Madam. I will call you.' It was clearly an order. Bemused but obedient, Hannah sat with the child on her knee, and waited.

'What's happening, Mummy?'

'Who knows, darling? This is India. Anything's possible.'

The official lady was back. 'You will come, please.' She led them across the grass to where the elephants were swaying in patient grandeur. Ramdas, the lead elephant, was huge. Hannah picked up her son so that he could reach its mouth with his piece of cane, which was bigger than he was. Siddarth clapped and shouted. Press cameras flashed. The band, which had stopped for the ceremony, struck up again. A young reporter singled out Hannah, as the official was whisking them back to their seats.

'You are coming from?'

'England.'

'Oh, UK. And your name, please?'

Hannah told him.

'This is your first visit to our country?'

'No. My second.'

'Ah, Madam, I see you like India! And what is your profession?'

'I'm a writer.'

The young man looked impressed. 'Of course,' he said, 'Hannah Petersen. I have heard of you. You are very famous writer. I have read your books.'

A likely story, thought Hannah. Wonder what he'd do if I asked him to name any?

'Yes,' he continued, '*Fair Game, As a Matter of Fact...* I have read them all, you see.'

'Well, I'm flattered!' said Hannah, in genuine amazement.

'And you are currently working on?'

'A book on Sri Lanka.'

He scribbled on his notepad.

'And what else do you intend to see in Kochi?'

'Want to see sindog!' chipped in Siddarth.

Hannah smiled. 'He means the synagogue. We're going there tomorrow.'

Later that evening Hannah and Siddarth made their way through the darkness to the Seagull Hotel.

Hannah sat on the bed next to her tireless child and smiled. What a day it had been. Siddarth's eyes were still bright with excitement.

'Mummy...' The child took her hand.

'What is it, darling?'

'Will you read to me? About the gods?'

Hannah rummaged in her shoulder bag. *Gods, Demons and Others* was missing. It must have dropped out of her bag at the elephant fair. But it wasn't the loss of the book that stabbed at her heart.

The child was looking at her, smiling. 'Never mind, Mummy,' he said. 'Can buy anuver.' And his eyes closed and he was fast asleep.

Hannah stayed by her sleeping son, stroking his hair, and chiding herself for letting the shadow of her lost photograph cloud a perfect day. After all, she had others at home. *How can I be sad when I have you to share my life? What fun we had today at the* Gaja Mela *watching all those fabulous elephants. And that reporter! Well! He tried his best, poor man, to find out how I'd acquired my cute little Indian baby, but I'm afraid he drew a blank there. That's my secret. One day it will become yours too, though that's a day I dread.*

Once again her joy was obscured. Unbearable thoughts surfaced as she watched the child. *One day he'll ask about his father. What shall I tell him? That he would have given his life for me, that day in Nanjangud? That we had such a short time together? That we shared a past tragedy? That I thought we were so much in love. That I couldn't imagine a future without him? That the thought of him still burns a hole in my heart?*

She gave an involuntary sob and bit her lip for fear of waking Siddarth. But still the unwelcome thoughts forced themselves into her mind. One day she would have to face them head on.

And he'll ask me why we parted. How shall I answer him? Shall I say that he deceived me? Or that perhaps Kipling was right when he said East is East and West is West? *Perhaps indeed* never the twain shall meet. *Perhaps we never really understood each other at all. Perhaps the whole affair was merely an illusion triggered by the circumstances that brought us together.*

She stood up, and started quietly pacing the room, caught now in a web of eventualities and heart-searching.

And yet, and yet I keep asking myself, why was I so ready to believe that he'd deceived me? What if it were not true? Was I so fickle, to change from one moment to the next? Why was I so ready to believe the worst of him? Was this the legacy of Mark Salers? Was it that in some way Ashok still represented the past, whose horrific conclusion had so nearly engulfed me? In fact, was it really he who betrayed me? Maybe it was in the end I who betrayed him.

By now she was obsessed by the train of her thoughts, struck down again by the despair that she dreaded so much, but that always seemed to catch her out when she should have been at her happiest.

There are so many questions I can't answer. Like the Asian who used to come to the cottage while we lived in Sri Lanka. He used to stop and talk to Bert when he passed Colonel Henry's gate. It must have been Ashok, though I have no proof. But who else could it be? Who else would have left a poster of Ganesh in the shed for me? Who else would have understood the memories that Ganesh would evoke? Memories of the day we met in Bangalore, and the day in Mamallapuram, when he said he loved me. The god of good fortune. I am quite certain that this is what he was wishing for me. And did he try to leave me a more tangible message? That torn off scrap of paper on the shed floor? But I'll never know, will I? All the writing had been smudged and faded to oblivion by time and lawnmower oil.

She lay down on the bed and turned to look at her son, as she fought back insistent tears.

Perhaps you will want to find him, your father. What shall I say to you then? You must not look for him? He doesn't know that you exist, and he must never know? It would destroy his own family, his wife, his children, his parents, his in-laws? How can I tell you that you have no right to meet your father, and he has no right to know about his son? And yet, my darling, that's the way it has to be.

We were planning to come to Kerala together, your father and I. That's why I brought you here. It was to be our promise of a life together. Now you are the fulfilment of that promise, because through you, your father will always be a part of my life.

*   *   *

A misty sail of *Fleurs de Provence* had blown Ashok soothingly through the night. In his dreams the huge bed had become a ship, steering him steadily onwards to a safe anchorage.

He had been the first passenger on the first morning ferry back to Ernakulum from Residency Island. Waiting at the jetty, Ashok had tried to usher his fragmented ideas into some sort of logic. The night watchman had said that Hannah was in Ernakulam. He would wait at the main jetty. Wherever she was headed, she would almost certainly have to take a ferry.

At the main jetty, chaos reigned. An ordinary workday with the work force piling up to squeeze a fraction of space on the overcrowded ferries to Willingdon Island or Fort Cochin. Other workers pouring off arriving boats. Ashok was again hit by despondency. The Residency Island ferry was mainly for tourists, therefore may have come to life later than the other ferries from Ernakulam, which very likely had been plying the waters since the early hours. If Hannah had made an early start, she could be anywhere by now. He was faced with a dilemma; to wait a while in case she showed up, or to chase off after her to God knows where. He decided to wait for an hour and then move on. He stood near the ticket office, where he could watch the departing passengers, and started to make contingency plans.

Where would she spend the day? 'Remind me to take you to see the Jews of Kerala one day,' he had said to her that day in the train to Chennai. This then, might be her first priority. In that case she would certainly head for the synagogue in the Mattancherry quarter of Cochin. But Hannah had a day's head start on him. Surely she would have been there yesterday? In which case, what would be her destination today? The Dutch Palace perhaps, with its magnificent frescoes of the Hindu pantheon? Or the ancient Chinese fishing nets, unchanged since the time of Marco Polo? Or would she opt to take a boat along the backwaters? He could see her stretched out on the cabin roof, pointing out the emerald paddy fields and fringing coconut palms to the child. They would speak in hushed tones, in order not to disturb the cormorant drying its wings on a passing driftwood perch, or the girl, waist deep among the water hyacinths, washing the baby in her arms. Oh please, please, not the backwaters. Finding her on that vast expanse of water would be impossible.

Ashok watched the motley crowd of dock labourers, smart secretaries in silk saris, travellers, chickens, goats and bicycles scrambling onto the departing boats. No sign of Hannah. An hour had passed and Ashok was still searching for inspiration. Where to now? On the floor by the ticket window an English-language newspaper had been dropped by one of the embarking labourers. Something about it caught Ashok's attention. A headline on the front page proclaimed 'An Elephantine Feast for Foreigners'. A subheading in smaller lettering read 'Famous Author opens Gaja Mela.' Beneath it was a large picture of an elephant. A woman was lifting a child to the elephant's mouth. The child was feeding it with sugar cane. Ashok peered at it, momentarily stunned. No. It couldn't be. Could it? He rescued the paper before it was trampled underfoot by the next hoard of ticket purchasers. The woman in the picture had her back to the camera, but the arm holding up the dark-skinned child was white. The hair, the figure, the familiar shalwar kameez. It was Hannah, he was sure of it. He glanced down at the accompanying article.

Tourists and Kochites alike thronged the stadium at the Maharaja's College ground in Kochi yesterday for the Tourist Fair... Ashok skimmed impatiently on through the article. *... was opened by a mass feast to the elephants in which the chief guest and foreigners took part... Little Siddarth Petersen aged three from England was thrilled to be chosen to feed Ramdas, the giant tusker who was carrying the fair's emblem. The picture shows Siddarth with his mother, Hannah Petersen, the well-known author. The pair are planning to continue their tour of Kochi tomorrow with a visit to Mattancherry synagogue...*

'Yes!' said Ashok out loud. 'Thank you, God.'

The ferry to Mattancherry headed out across the bay, where Lake Vembanad blends imperceptibly with the Arabian Sea. The water was dotted with islands and headlands, sequins on a shot-silk gown of turquoise-blue. Two pilot whales steam-rolled through a tanker's bow waves towards the open ocean. Ashok relaxed and felt a surge of excitement and optimism.

At Mattancherry he scrambled off the boat and wove through a throng of predatory cycle rickshaws, ignoring their insistent offers to take him here or there for outrageous sums. He made his way up through Jewtown, aptly named judging by a name plaque that caught his eye: 'J. Cohen, advocate and tax consultant', displayed above a series of Stars of David along the whitewashed house wall. The street was shady and narrow, the white and ochre houses with wrought iron balconies, fancy window bars and shutters as redolent of their Dutch and Portuguese ancestry as of their Keralan heritage. Little curio shops huddled beneath some of the window shutters.

The seventeenth century synagogue, nestling against a Krishna temple at the end of the street, looked unprepossessing. Blink and you'll miss it, thought Ashok, thankful now, that his search for Hannah four years earlier had led him there once before. He had come to the right place. He remembered the little clock tower. But the synagogue had been closed by the time he and Willi had got there. Now he stood outside for the second time, willing his heart to beat more soberly. He took a few deep breaths and talked his nerves into relaxing. A few heavy drops of rain struck his face, and quickly gathered momentum. In seconds the sky was a vertical torrent, great cupfuls exploding on the earth like breaking chandeliers. On the street black umbrellas started up, like a flock of startled crows. Ashok pressed against the synagogue wall, unsettled still further by the unexpected deluge. An old man, skin the colour of ochre houses and wearing a moneybag round his waist, appeared in the synagogue doorway. 'One rupee, sir - if you wish to go inside.' Wordlessly Ashok handed him the money. The old man moved aside to let him enter.

Ashok stood for a minute in the doorway brushing the rain off his face and his hair. Then he stepped inside. He was dazzled by the crowded opulence of the interior. Red and gold predominated. A firmament of chandeliers swung low from the ceiling, reaching down to touch the golden rails of the *bimah*, the raised dais in the centre of the floor. Gilded lamps reached upwards to the chandeliers. Red silky curtains framed the red and gold carved doors of the Holy Ark. Only the blue and white floor tiles broke the pattern of red and gold.

At first Ashok didn't see Hannah. The *bimah* obscured his view of the far end. As he began to circle the room, his eye caught a movement through the *bimah's* golden balustrade. And then he saw her. She was crouched down by the steps leading up to the Ark and was talking quietly to the boy. Ashok caught his breath at the sound of her voice. Silently he moved closer. She had her back to him and was pointing to the floor tiles.

'Brought here all the way from China,' she was saying, 'and do you know, Siddarth, every single one is different? Look. See that one? And that? Isn't it lovely?'

'Uvly,' agreed the child. For a moment they continued to study the tiles in silence, each engrossed in the separate world that a particular tile evoked. Ashok stood still, unable to move. Then the boy, becoming bored with the game, turned round and found himself gazing straight into Ashok's eyes. They stared at each other in shocked silence. The child's enormous, dark eyes were unafraid, curious, profoundly perceptive. Ashok tried to smile at him, but every muscle seemed frozen. The child, still staring, reached out to his mother, and gently tugged at her *kameez*. Ashok saw Hannah stiffen, as if she had received a hidden message from her son. She got to her feet unhurriedly, still with her back to Ashok. For a moment she paused rigidly, as if afflicted by the same paralysis that had stopped Ashok in his tracks. Then she slowly turned to face him.

And so they stood, unable to overcome the shock of their reunion, or the chasm of time and space that divided them, until finally Ashok, mustering his inner strength, walked slowly up to her. No greeting. No show of any emotion. With outward calm Ashok pulled two letters from his pocket, as if he were about to serve a writ. The letter from Priya. And a copy of his reply to her.

'I've come a long way, Hannah,' he said, still staring at her, 'just to show you these.'

Hannah looked at the letters, then back at Ashok. Bewilderment and disbelief still registered on her face.

He pushed the letters at her hand. 'Read them.'

When she still did not move he said again, 'Read them, Hannah, read them.' This he repeated until finally stunned beyond protest, she took the letters from him.

As she read, Ashok saw her face change from disbelief to shock; from shock to remorse; from remorse to sorrow.

Just as she finished reading the second letter, the little boy tugged at her *kameez* again. Shyly he glanced at Ashok. 'Is that my daddy?' he said.

A flicker of discomposure. Then Hannah's face changed again; from sorrow to hope. 'Yes, darling,' she said. 'This is your daddy.'

Silently, gently, Ashok took Hannah by the arm, closing his other hand around the eager fingers of the child. Together they walked out into the rain.

Also available from Goldenford

Esmé Ashford - *On the Edge*

Tramps with bad feet, a sheep rustler, a busker invited to dinner; a weird monster who devours a nasty husband and a child who learns from a visit to the fun fair; limericks and blank verse; it is all here.

Jacquelynn Luben - *A Bottle of Plonk*

It's 1989 – a time when Liebfraumilch, Black Forest gateau and avocado bathrooms are all the rage, and nobody uses mobile phones.

When Julie Stanton moves in with Richard Webb one Saturday night in May, everything is looking rosy. She certainly doesn't expect their romantic evening together to end with her walking out of the flat clutching the bottle of wine with which they were to toast their new relationship.

But then Julie and the wine part company, and the bottle takes the reader on a journey through a series of events revealing love, laughter and conflict.

'Luben proves herself to be a sensitive and pithy new novelist.'

Sophia Furber, editor, London Student Newspaper

Anne Brooke – *Pink Champagne and Apple Juice*

Angie Soames is determined to leave her home in the idyllic Essex countryside and set up her own café in London, but before she can achieve her goal she has to overcome potential disasters in the shape of a glamorous French waiter, a grouchy German chef and her transvestite uncle.

And, if she manages to keep the lid on all that, what will she do about the other hidden secrets of her family?

'an amusing, fast-paced novel, full of action and comedy'
Marsha Rowe, co-founder of Spare Rib

Jay Margrave – *The Gawain Quest*

Priedeux – a character who changes the course of history ...
In the first of a trilogy Priedeux sets out for the wilds of Wirral on a quest to discover the writer of *Gawain and the Green Knight*, a seditious poem with a hidden agenda - a call to rebellion against Richard II. Can Priedeux find the writer in time to stop the rebellion and save his own life?

GOLDENFORD

info@goldenford.co.uk
www.goldenford.co.uk

314